IN THE FOOTSTEPS OF GIANTS

Gawain unsheathed his sword and jammed it through the heavy ring of the tower door. Grabbing the haft and the blade, he twisted. The latch moved with a groan and the hinges creaked. He put his shoulder to the weathered wood and pushed. Wintry light knifed into the darkness revealing a vast chamber. A massive granite staircase spiraled around the wall disappearing up into maw of the tower. As he walked to the bottom step, two startled bats flew out of a cobwebbed brazier and he stood watching until the sounds of their leathery wings faded.

The step came up to his knees. He tapped the huge stone with his boot. *Who in the name of God built this place?* Bracing himself, he placed a hand on the rough edge, gave a grunt and began climbing towards the waiting silence ...

Yesterday's Falcon

by Tim Newman

To Dave, Enjoy the read, my friend.

Tim

BRIGHID'S FIRE BOOKS
SIDNEY, NEW YORK

Brighid's Fire Books
a division of Wahmpreneur Publishing, Inc.
P.O. Box 41
Sidney, NY 13838
USA

Yesterday's Falcon

ISBN 0-9713278-3-1

To strive, to seek, to find and not to yield.
Ulysses Alfred Lord Tennyson

Sir Gawain, have a care
to keep your courage for the test,
and do what you've dared.
You've begun: now brave the rest.

Sir Gawain and the Green Knight

Negative Capability, that is when man is capable of being in uncertainties, Mysteries, doubts, without any irritable reaching after fact & reason —
John Keats

Chapter One

He stumbled through the blizzard onto the drawbridge leading to the towering battlements of Bercilack's castle. A deep dry cough racked his chest, making his eyes water and forcing him to reach for the chain drooping the length of the drawbridge.

A few more unsteady steps and he swayed to a halt. Wheezing painfully, he raised a hand to his iron visor and peered through the veil of flakes to where an arched door loomed across the moat. The wind gusted and he staggered sideways. He grabbed for the heavy chain but this time it swung away from his frozen fingers and he fell slamming to his knees. His chin dropped to his breastplate and he stayed there for a moment, like someone praying. Then his battered armor gave an eerie squeal and he toppled forward into the drifting snow.

On the other side of the moat, bolts shot back and yellow torch light spilled into the wintry morning. A slender figure in a dark cloak ran out of the castle and hurried across the bridge. Even from within, her keen Druid senses had flared when she felt the touch of death on the wanderer.

He lay crumpled near the center of the drawbridge. She ran clutching her cloak at the neck and waist. When she reached him, she knelt. Deep snow pooled around her thighs as she lifted his head onto her lap and pushed back the visor. "By the Great Cauldron," she whispered, flinching at the sight of his gaunt face and the bruised pouches under his eyes.

She loosened a rusty clasp at his throat and ran her fingers down the worn chain mail to where the tattered remains of Arthur's golden lions lay emblazoned. Channeling the elemental power within her, she traced a Rune a few inches above the royal crest. The intricate pattern she drew burned a silvery white, causing the snowflakes to eddy and swirl away as it formed and shimmered above him like a halo. She gazed at its heartbreaking beauty for a moment then she held his hand and whispered the binding words.

The Castan Rune she'd drawn instantly coalesced, fusing into a spell that blasted through his consciousness. The effect was startling. His eyes snapped open and he looked around in wild surprise.

"You only have a few minutes of this strength, knight. My abilities are not what they used to be. Here, up now." She stood and helped him to his feet.

Still feverish, breathing in ragged gasps, he slumped against her and they swayed precariously for a moment. When she regained her balance, she cupped an arm around his waist and they stumbled across the rest of the drawbridge.

Heads bowed against the storm like wayward pilgrims, they neared the castle door. She felt his strength begin to ebb and shifted his weight, almost buckling under the added pressure. Her heart raced. *Be strong, Rhiannon,* she told herself, *he's not like Bercilack, not this one.*

She shouldered the door open and struggled with him down a passage lit by torches angled on the walls. After a dozen steps, the hallway forked. They took the left branch and passed under an arch where a carved face leered down from crumbling masonry high above. A few more steps and he broke into a fit of coughing, sending echoes flocking through the columns of the empty castle. And if he could, he would have asked a question as she urged him on: "Where are all the people, the retainers, the bondsmen . . . your husband?"

Another left and they came to a stout door. Summoning all her strength, she shifted his weight, nudged the door open with her hip and stumbled with him into the Great Hall.

At the far end, wintry light from two stained glass windows bled over bare flagstones. She lugged him towards a fire crackling in a wide hearth. Somewhere deep within the castle a dog barked.

"Almost there knight . . . ," she panted.

The aroma of peat and pine, mixed with a faint scent of lavender, hung in the air as she struggled the last few yards to a couch near the fire.

"There!"

She rolled him onto cushions she had embroidered in her efforts to make the castle more bearable and stood back rubbing her numb arm. When the feeling returned, she eased his legs up and took off his battered helmet and torn mail shirt. Next, she tugged off his frayed leggings and boots and threw a warm fleece blanket over him. Once his breathing had fallen into a steady rhythm, she set about piling up logs for the fire she knew she would have to keep burning throughout the long night.

When she finished, she went through the Shield Hall to the kitchens to prepare a bowl of rabbit stew. From the sparse pantry, she took the last of the seasoned herbs and a handful of beechnuts. She ground them into a paste adding them to the stew for extra nourishment. Then she stacked two thick slices of cocket bread along with the stew and a jug of mulled wine on a wooden trencher and made her way back through the hushed passage.

He hadn't stirred. She set the food down and walked over to a tall window recessed in an alcove. Outside, the snow fell in thick flakes, blanketing the hedges and fences, burying the wide lonely valley. *The first sign of spring, the first and I'll risk the journey home*, she resolved. *Let the Christ worshippers have this place, hang their wooden crosses on my walls, fill these halls with their sins. I'll not weep for what I've lost. I'm past that – past all of it.* She stood by the casement, fists clenched, watching the world whiten. *Where is the laughter of my children?*

With a last look at the wintry world, she tugged the drapes closed and went over to her two wolfhounds, Fennris and Brighid. Crouching between them, she ruffled their coarse fur and when she bent her head to theirs, they nuzzled her with cold noses. "I'll tell you a secret, little ones, I'm not strong enough anymore, not for this silence," she confided.

Later, as evening came stealing across the stark Northumbrian hills, she tucked an extra blanket around the knight and sat with him on the edge of the couch. She gazed down, absently pushing back the graying hair from his eyes with her fingertips.

His face held a past like hers. There was pain there – pain of something lost. The sorrow of it spoke to her in keen Druid whispers. She glanced at the untouched food on the hearth and at the flames glimmering across the empty room, and of their own free will, memories came tumbling from the halls of her mind.

The Baron Bercilack had thundered into her village five years ago, when she was only nineteen. She swallowed dryly, recalling the first day she'd seen him – the huge warhorse he rode, his coal-black armor studded with hammered rivets. *By the Sacred Cauldron, how the people had scattered - like leaves in a wild March wind.*

He had taken her then – simply packed her up along with the weapons he purchased on his journey from the North. And when all was ready, he had slammed the grill of his visor shut, and with the help of his retainer, mounted his warhorse. They left the village then, galloping away over rutted fields without so much as a goodbye to friends or family.

She discovered in less than a day's ride what he truly desired. Even now, every detail rang with clarity. Inside his tent, he snapped back the inlaid hasps of his breastplate and dropped it clattering to the ground. Next, he stripped off his padded undershirt and tossed it over a footstool. Then he turned to her, naked to the waist, rivers of sweat running down his great barrel chest, the thick cords in his neck glistening in the warmth of the late afternoon. She had no God but she prayed all the same and began unbuttoning her simple blouse.

"NO!"

Even after all these years, ice clawed at her spine as she recalled that voice. The sheer power of it had terrified her and she had stopped undressing for him, her hand frozen on an amber broach her sister had given her.

"Come here."

The words brooked no question. She stepped forward, head bowed, expecting to feel a blow at any time, but what happened next truly surprised her. He drew a gleaming broadsword from a stack of weapons piled by the entrance and holding the burnished point to her chin, tilted her head up.

"Charm it, Druid. Make it kill my enemies," he hissed through clenched teeth.

Dear Bran, the eyes – dark smoldering embers, the coils of wild hair and great mitten hands clutching the hilt. Before she'd known it, she slashed a *Falk* Rune.

"What ... what was that?" he said, stunned by how fast she'd moved.

"A blood Rune, my lord."

He stared at the blade. Then came the change she had seen so often, the look of ferret cunning creeping across his face. He reached out and pulled her close.

Narrow eyes bore down a nose swollen with broken blood vessels. "What does it do, woman?"

His breath, sour and full of belly warmth from the previous night's wine, had sickened her. Instinctively, she held the knight's hand, squeezing tightly at what came next. Bercilack had belched – a loud, gut belch. She had started to tell him the blood Rune would stop any wound the sword made from ever closing but she rocked back, gagging in the wake of his stale breath. He laughed at her reaction, bellowing loud enough to bring his retainer scrambling to the tent flap. Then he yanked her close again, fist buried in her blouse, and in that hoarse voice she had come to hate so much, he rasped, "If you ever use your magic against me, young Druid, it had better work well, devil or no, because if it doesn't, I'll rip the living skin off every person you've ever known."

She shuddered, closing her eyes. So much had happened since then: the countless times he'd forced her to his bed, hit her if she didn't satisfy him, or worse, cursed her if the Rune spells failed or lost their potency. But she had gained courage in the darkness of those long nights. *Yes, I did. I did, you bastard.*

One Beltane eve, as crackling bonfires stitched the northern lands, he had beaten her and thrown her out of his chamber in a drunken rage. On this most sacred of Druid nights, she had limped down the winding stairs and out into the castle gardens. Under a blaze of stars, she slowly made her way to a grove of willow trees near the moat. Wincing, she lay down beneath drooping bows and closed her eyes.

The moon had risen high above the water by the time she had managed to center her energy. Then the healing began and with it came a distant revelation – the essence here didn't just flow gently, it pounded in waves.

Just then the knight awoke snapping her back to the present with a start. She couldn't help but stare. His eyes were the gray of Welsh slate, deep and wide and spoke to her so clearly of his loneliness. He struggled to sit up, his thick hair falling to his shoulders.

"Merlin, is he here? I ... ." A fit of ragged coughing took him and he clutched at his chest, bringing up his knees with the pain.

"Rest," she said drawing a *Por Fell* Rune of sleep above him.

She spoke the binding words, fusing the Rune in a haze of light. She supported his weight as he slumped, then she eased him back onto the couch. *So much pain. So much sadness. Who is he? And just how in the name of Bran, does he know the great Merlin*, she wondered. She tucked the fleece blanket around him, searching for the secrets of his past with her Druid senses but there were no answers, only ghosting memories.

When his breathing returned to a steady rhythm, she went outside and made her way through the thick snow to the sacred willow grove. Standing beneath the bare branches, breath pluming into the cold air, she replenished her spent essence and silently vowed to use her magic to keep him safe because he bore the gift of light, and because – she knew deep down it was more – because of her own aching loneliness.

The storm eased and days passed in the quiet of whispering snow. But his condition worsened despite her nursing and once, on the third day, he coughed so hard he sprayed bright red blood across the white sleeve of her dress.

She became desperate then, knowing if she didn't do something more, he would surely die. Pacing the gloomy halls with Fennris and Brighid at her heels, she lit upon a plan. She would imbue him with enough energy to get him to the Terran Stone. If she timed it right and if she could hold enough elemental power, she could channel the energy into a spell that would sustain him for the long journey. *If I can just get him to the island, I can use the Stone.*

She prepared; first, she gathered warm clothing and food. Next, she retrieved two ancient *Tarn* necklaces from a chest hidden beneath the pantry floor. Finally, she went out to the willow trees again. Pulling up the hood of her dark cloak and plunging her hands into the deep pockets, she closed her eyes.

Later, shivering from the winds howling across the valley but fully imbued, she entered the Great Hall through a side door. The wolfhounds padded close behind, happy to get back to the warmth of the fire. Their amber eyes followed her in the flame light as she crossed to the couch. Brushing dry snow from her shoulders, she knelt beside the dying knight and drew the *Castan* Rune above his chest. When it writhed into view, she whispered the binding words.

This time the knight did not awaken with a start, but as if he were coming out of a long and restful sleep. He stretched and yawned, gazing around the vast hall with its crumbling arches and vaulted ceilings. Bewildered, he turned to Rhiannon. "Pray tell me . . . where am I, my lady?" His voice, though raspy, still held the clear edge of nobility.

"You're in my castle, knight, but there is precious little time for me to explain," she said pulling back the hood of her cloak and tossing her dark hair free. "We must travel to a place far from here. It's a long and difficult journey but if you are to recover, we have no choice. Stand, careful now."

16

She helped him to his feet and thrust the warm clothing into his arms. "Here, change into these," she said.

He tried to thank her but she raised her hand. "Please believe me when I say this – each time you speak, you put more strain on your body and it weakens you. How much time we have and how long my magic will hold, I have no idea. All I know is, if we don't complete the journey, and soon, you'll die as surely as darkness falls. Now hurry, I'll explain as we go."

She waited, turning her back while he tugged on the clothes. When he finished dressing, she handed him his longsword and chain mail and led him from the Great Hall down a dark passage to the west wing. Near the siege turret, they passed a guest room where rays of early sun from a broken window highlighted chairs and a solitary table. When they entered the armory, Rhiannon pulled up a trap door and they made their way down a steep flight of wooden steps.

At the bottom, they turned left passing through dank smells and dripping water, the torchlight fanning rats back into the shadows. Neither spoke until they reached the dungeons and the spot where she had first discovered the way to Natal Lake.

She stopped a pace short of a stone wall at the end of the last section of iron bars and set the torch in a rusty sconce. "Don't be alarmed at what you see," she said, motioning him back.

She raised a slender hand to draw the Rune that would reveal the wall's secret, then hesitated. "What do they call you, knight so far from home?"

"Gawain," he said. "And you?"

"Rhiannon," she answered, oak brown eyes reflecting splinters of torchlight.

"A beautiful name."

The compliment took her by surprise and she reddened. "Speak no more or you'll bring on the coughing." She turned back to the wall. "Look closely, knight Gawain and behold the power of Druid magic."

She slashed a Rune in the air and watched it swirl away from her fingers and snake toward the wall in a smoky blue twist. When it encountered the glyph there, it hissed as magic met magic. Suddenly the Rune flashed, like a mirror catching the morning sun. A moment later, an archway shimmered out of the dimness. She turned and smiled – a wide, easy smile this time, full of girlish joy. "Come," she said, the lightness in her voice so at odds with the dreary world around them.

She took the torch from the sconce and ducked through the arch. "There are many more mysteries in store for you yet, brave knight. This way lies a Terran Stone, the very heart of our faith."

And before he could say that Merlin had told him all about these mystical Stones long ago, in the days when they plotted to kill the murderous Uther, she had disappeared down a narrow stairway into a well of darkness.

Chapter Two

Gawain followed Rhiannon down the crumbling stairs, the blackness receding before the flickering torch in her hand. As they descended, her boots splashed up water from the hollows of the worn steps.

At the bottom, a tunnel gleamed in the torchlight. Muffled sounds echoed from the other end and a faint breeze blew in, carrying with it a cloying smell of decay. When Rhiannon reached the entrance, she turned to him. "What you hear is an underground river, Natal Brack. Its source lies deep in the wastelands. From there, it travels through the hills and fens and ends here, where it forms an underground lake."

She held up the torch and a wavering flag of gold lit her face. "The Stone lies in the middle of the lake, on a small island. Once we get to it, I'll be able to use its healing powers. I know no other way to cure your sickness." She gave him a reassuring smile. "Come, careful now."

She guided him through the tunnel to the opening at the far end. There they halted next to a damp rock face and she reached into the pocket of her cloak. "Here."

She held out the *Tarn* necklace – a thin chain woven from twisted silver and embedded with tiny glowing gems. "They get their power from Natal Brack. Whenever they're close to the source that shaped them, they shine like this. Go ahead, put it on. See what happens," she said extinguishing the torch and shrouding him in darkness.

He slipped the chain around his neck and gasped as the night receded into murky twilight. From where he stood, he could see the outline of an immense body of water far below. In the distance, perhaps two or three miles away, spires and peaks of an underground mountain range circled the brooding lake. Directly ahead, a jutting ledge led to a flight of steps disappearing down a cliff. As his eyes continued to adjust, shapes of outcroppings and giant fungi topped with drooping mushroom caps loomed into view.

Rhiannon slipped on her own necklace smiling at his slackened jaw. "I told you there were more mysteries in store. Stay close now. When you feel the need to rest, let me know. We do this little by little. We mix haste with caution."

The long cloak swirled around her feet as she threaded her way between the spidery plants. Gawain followed, finding it difficult to keep up with her lithe, easy pace. When he reached the top of the stairs, he cast a last look over his shoulder at the gaping mouth of the tunnel then he descended after her.

Halfway down the perilous cliff, near a place where the steps narrowed, a fit of coughing forced him to halt. He leaned against a jagged rock hacking and beating at his chest until a bout of dizziness brought him to his knees.

From somewhere distant, he heard sounds like faint wind chimes and a breeze as light as a summer wind washed over him. When it passed, his coughing stopped and the bright sparks pulsing behind his eyes disappeared. A new strength coursed through his body and he looked up to see Rhiannon, her hand out, two long fingers gracefully curved from the Rune she had drawn.

"What did you . . . ?"

"No." Her voice cracked with the fatigue of casting the Rune. "Please, don't talk. We have less time than I thought. I don't know how long this magic will hold. It's not like it used to be, not anymore. Are you ready?"

He nodded and they set off again, moving like two insects down the towering cliff face. She led and he trailed behind, willing himself with each shaking step to reach this Stone and heal, to finish the quest for Athlan and Merlin.

After an hour, the stairs widened, flattening out onto the sandy shore of the lake he'd viewed from the ledge. The unearthly stillness and heavy air there started him coughing again. Rhiannon waited at his side, heart racing, hoping she wouldn't have to use more of the precious essence. Finally, his breathing eased and he looked up, eyes red and brimming with water.

"Can you go on?"

He nodded.

"Are you sure?"

He managed a weak smile.

She waited a moment longer searching his face and then pointed across the ribbed sand toward a crop of rocks near the cliff. "There's a small boat over there. Wait here. You'll need all your strength for the journey ahead."

When she left, he turned to the desolate lake. It stretched across the horizon like a sinister stain. A chill ran through him as he stared over its surface and his mind wandered to thoughts of Tintagel, Uther's stronghold and to Merlin. He touched the silver ring the wizard had given him, twisting it around his finger but its entwined dragons remained strangely silent, strangely cold. *Where are you now with all your wonders, my wise friend?*

At the sound of shuffling feet, he turned. Rhiannon was emerging from behind the rocks tugging a battered boat across the sand in a series of little jerks.

"From here on . . . we must be wary," she called to him over her shoulder. "The lake is poison. It can take from us . . . all that we are."

When she reached him, she straightened up. Brushing away loose strands of hair from her cheek with the back of her hand, she nodded toward the lake. "Anyone falling into that water will lose their willpower, their desire to live, all thoughts, everything. The words Natal Brack in the Druid tongue mean *Soul Shadow*.

"Long ago, in the time of the Far Druids, the river feeding this lake once ran pure. Then something terrible happened. We don't know what, but when the Far Druids disappeared, a blight swept across the lands north of the Cumbrian Ridge, destroying everything. Up to this day, the trees, the grass, even the earth itself lies sick and dying. Natal Brack brought that fever with it, poisoning everything as it ran south from the wastelands." She hesitated, wanting to tell him about Bercilack, to say that maybe it had affected him too as it flowed deep beneath the castle, the vapors leaching his soul, leaving him bitter and twisted but she couldn't bring herself to say his name -- not here, not now.

"Our priests used to journey to the Stone to celebrate Samhain," she continued instead. "But they gave up the pilgrimage long ago. This is all that's left." She tapped the boat's wooden trim, her wide brown eyes shining like deep pools in the strange half-light. "If I am to heal you, then we must brave the lake. As long as we don't touch the water, we'll be safe," she added resuming her tugging.

Walking by Rhiannon's side, Gawain wondered if she would be so quick to help if she knew what lay buried in his past. Then, from somewhere deep within, a feeling of regret began to grow. The intensity of the losses and failures in his life became more acute as he neared the shoreline. Unbidden thoughts of Athlan and Arthur stole their way from the dark corners of his mind. And, no matter how hard he tried, he couldn't stop the aching loneliness that came with them, or the sorrow welling at their sad, siren song.

Rhiannon glanced at him and stopped in her efforts. "It's the lake, the poison," she said straightening up. "From now until we reach the Stone, the feeling of despair won't let go. But you can fight it, just don't dwell on the past – think only of the future. That way Natal Brack won't be able to feed on the sadness within you."

"How do you . . .?"

She held up a hand, her eyes intent upon his. "No, don't talk. If you bring on the coughing, I may not be able to stop it again. I've crossed the lake many times and each time the sensation of despair lessens. It's as if Natal Brack has had its fill of all the pain in my life."

She paused, gazing at the far mountains. "One night, almost a year ago, I felt the Terran power in the castle gardens above. I swore then I would find its source. It took me months to discover the glyphed wall, but nothing could have stopped me reaching the Stone – nothing.

"Once I got to lake, I thought the hard part was behind me. So much for my keen Druid senses." She turned to him her voice hardening. "I had no idea what lay ahead. By the time I got to the shore, nothing seemed important to me anymore. I just wanted to walk into it. I wanted to forget my life, forget everything."

She bent and resumed jerking the boat across the coarse sand. "But time and again ... I found myself thinking about the Stone ... what I'd do when I got there ... what it would be like ... and the feelings grew weaker ... . That's when I realized the lake was losing its power over me ... when I thought about the future ... not the past ... . There!"

She halted at the shoreline and leaned on the bow, her high cheekbones and smooth skin accented by the glowing *Tarn* necklace. "Can you do it; can you face the very worst in your life again?"

Gawain hesitated and nodded slowly.

She patted his arm and gave him a bright smile. "Then we will succeed, brave knight."

He stepped back giving her room to go around to the stern. Small waves, more like oil than water rippled thickly from the hull as she pushed the boat into the lake. When it steadied, he climbed over the side and sank down thankfully on the little wooden seat. Careful not to touch the viscous surface, Rhiannon gave a final push and hopped in.

Once the craft cleared the shore, Rhiannon took up the oars and nodded over her shoulder at the distant silhouettes. "If we keep the bow headed between those two peaks, we should make the Terran Island in an hour, maybe less. I'll row; you take the tiller and remember, don't give Natal Brack a grip – keep your thoughts on the future."

Dipping into the unnaturally thick water, the oars created the only sound in the underground world. The soft, heavy plop they made when they broke the surface sent high ripples rolling away into the gloom.

The craft moved ahead ponderously. Sitting at the stern, Gawain kept a lookout for signs of land. The feelings of sadness sloughed away as he watched Rhiannon pulling on the oars. He took in the long curve of her neck and the lean strong muscles standing out along her arms, her dark hair with its wild curls and her eyes the brown of late autumn. She glanced at him catching his gaze and a flush ran up her cheeks.

A little over halfway to the island, she pulled the oars out of the water and cocking her head slowly to one side, she motioned him to sit still. "I hear something."

He listened, searching the lake.

"There!"

Before he had time to turn, a bird the size of an albatross swept past him on dark sinewy wings. It cut through the air with a swoosh then circled up high above the boat.

Instinctively, Gawain drew his sword. The hissing ring sent a shower of sparks dancing down the blade as it cleared the scabbard. Blinking away the brightness, he held the weapon in practiced hands.

"Be careful. Don't tip the boat," Rhiannon warned.

"What is it?" he whispered, targeting the creature.

"I don't know. A giant bat? I'm not sure; I've never seen anything like it before."

They waited, frozen, watching the dark shape circle in the twilight above.

"Rhiannon . . . ."

"Don't speak, please. It will only bring on the coughing."

Her mind whirled with Runes. *Jard, no, Karnn, no. Wards, yes! Ward the boa ... .* A piercing cry cut off her thoughts. She spun around. To her right a second bird drifted out of the gloom. It joined the first and they glided together. After a few passes, they descended in a series of wide, easy spirals. When they neared the boat, they crossed flight paths then soared up and away from each other.

"They're preparing to attack," she whispered, still searching for the right Rune. "I know it. I feel it."

"I'll guard us . . . . Row on . . . ," said Gawain hoarsely.

She had barely taken up the oars when one of the birds dropped out of the twilight and sheered toward them. The air thrummed with the sound of heavy wings and Gawain reared back, narrowly avoiding the outstretched talons. The bird circled back over the water. Gawain waited until it came within range again then he swung the sword. The blade thunked into a leathery wing sending the creature spiraling away into the darkness.

An angry cry from above shattered the silence and Gawain shifted to the center of the boat.

"Be careful," said Rhiannon, her voice full of panic as the little craft rocked violently.

"Hold the oars wide. Try to give us ... more stability."

He braced himself against the sides with his knees and held the sword ahead of him.

The thing cried again, this time more plaintively.

"We must kill it ... before it's joined by another," he said, coughing. "We'll not survive ... if they both attack."

"Don't talk, Gawain. Please, just don't talk," Rhiannon pleaded, desperate now, pulling on the oars with all her strength, frightened of falling into the terrible waters, frightened of losing him -- of returning to the castle and facing the awful silence again.

Another chilling cry broke over the lake and with it came a flash of Druid insight.

"It wants your eyes," she called from her backbreaking work. "It's going for the necklace."

High above, the bird shrieked as if it somehow knew she had disclosed its plan. Before the echo faded, it plummeted.

When the ribbed wings snapped out to check the creature's flight, Gawain dropped the sword clattering to the bottom of the boat and grabbed it by the neck and legs.

"What in God's name are you?" he breathed, tightening his grasp and pulling back from the talons raking at his chest and the wings beating around his shoulders. He held his grip steady until the struggling ceased, then he cautiously lifted his hand from the damp neck. The creature sat hunched over his knuckles like a sullen gargoyle. Two malevolent eyes set deep in hooded sockets glared at him.

As Gawain stared at those stony eyes, he felt the body beneath his hands grow colder. The creature drew its head back and Gawain watched, puzzled as the leathery mouth slowly widened in a parody of a human grin.

The perverse smile thinned into a sneer. At the same time, Gawain felt a jittering shudder run down the length of the creature's body. Its dark features tightened as if it had tasted something bitter, and without warning, it catapulted its head forward and vomited a thick stream of bile into Gawain's face.

Crying out, his skin on fire, Gawain leapt up. He flung the creature's still shuddering body away and drove his knuckles into his eyes, grinding them against the caustic pain. Behind him, the bird he had wounded earlier swept out of the darkness. Even Rhiannon with her heightened senses didn't hear it glide silently past. It hit Gawain in the center of the back with the force of a mace, sending him tumbling out of the boat and into the black lake.

Rhiannon's cry of warning faded like an echo in a tunnel as the water closed over him and Natal Brack's dreadful effects took hold. First, the boat, and then everything else around him, fragmented into a spinning void.

The world closed.

Pain subsided.

He sank beneath the deadly lake. A montage of images and faces he knew reeled out of the darkness: knights and kings, a dying father, a wizard and a hissing serpent and then a moment of stunning clarity when a young boy with haunting eyes ran down a hill of late summer grass. As the poisoned water leached each memory from his mind, the patterns began to fade, each face pressing desperately upon him, seeking their whos and whys.

So much sorrow.

He sank deeper, knowing somehow as each image passed, it did so irrevocably, never to return. In his thoughts, he tried to say *stop, don't leave me in this empty world* -- but each memory fled out, away, disappearing one after the other, the spaces between them blooming into inky roses.

High above, on the surface of the lake, Rhiannon gripped the edge of the rocking boat and peered down into the water where he'd vanished. He wouldn't be able to swim. Within minutes, he'd lose the memory of that learned skill along with all his other memories.

Leaning over the stern, her face close enough to smell the rankness of the water, she was calmer than she would have thought possible. The time she spent calling on her inner strength with Bercilack had paid off. She didn't panic. Instead, she summoned all her remaining elemental power and drew two *Angeald* Runes – a Rune of summoning and a Rune of knowledge. The crackling magic arced from her fingers and snaked like blue lightning across the water. The forks hissed and sizzled above the sluggish ripples awaiting her command. With knuckles whitening on the wooden trim, she called out the Druid words. The ancient sounds harmonized and the elemental power flowed from her, leaving behind a wave of weakness. Ahead, the Runes flared with wild brightness illuminating hundreds of yards of the lake.

Angeald. As a child, she'd made animals come to her with that Rune: cats, dogs, horses, field mice. Even without a Rune Staff to help, she had been able to hold its shape and the words to bind it.

She waited, fingers gripping the boat so hard they were cramping. "Don't let him die. By all I hold sacred, don't let this knight die," she breathed.

Moments later, Gawain's body broke the surface with a thick plop. Her heart leaped. She sought his mind.

Yes.

He was there – cold, empty, like an unborn child, but he was there. She concentrated on the motions of swimming and commanded his body to move. Sluggishly, the bones and muscles of the Gawain hulk stirred. His bulging eyes glinted stony white and his hair clung to his shoulders like kelp. Calling softly, chanting the harmonic words over and over, she urged him to the boat. And he swam, his arms windmilling listlessly in the cursed water.

When he reached the little craft, she helped him grasp the stern then she used the last of her energy to bind his grip to the tiller.

As she chanted, her head pounding from expending so much magic, she considered their plight. Out here on this dead lake, it would be hours, days, before she could recover enough essence to cast another Rune-she had to get to the Terran Stone before the spell weakened. She didn't have the strength to lift him out of the water and get him into the boat. She would have to row with him clinging to the stern. It would make the journey twice as long, twice as tiring.

Scanning the distant peaks to get her bearings, she took up the oars and began pulling with long deep strokes. Under her breath, she continued reciting the binding words, fearful he might let go and disappear into the depths of the lake again.

Her back cracked with the effort of rowing but she never slowed. Blisters rose and popped and the water below them ran down her palms in long bloody streaks but she never loosened her grip on the oars.

Weak from the loss of essence, her mind wandered as the boat made its ponderous voyage across the lake. *All those nights. Great gloomy castle with wolfhounds whose amber eyes followed the awful loneliness everywhere. Turrets soaring up into thin winter skies. Sheering winds. And everyone leaving after Bercilack had died, frightened when the Christians came with their whispers and pointing fingers.* For a while, time and memory blurred with the pain and the endless rowing. The distant cliffs distorted into darkness and the lake seemed to stretch on forever. Then, suddenly, the vessel ground up onto the beach of the Terran Island.

Rhiannon sat dazed for a moment, trying to clear her head. When the dizziness passed, she dropped the oars and rose on stiff legs. She clambered over the side and stood shakily on the shore. Near the far end of the island, the top of the Terran Stone shone above a shadowy hill like a star in the night sky. The concentration of essence there sang to her in the voice of ancient rituals and she bowed to it as a Christian would to a cross.

Holding onto the boat's wooden trim, she made her way to the stern. The spell had been strong; Gawain still clung to the tiller. Returning to the bow, she tugged the craft clear of the lake, leaving two long furrows where Gawain's boots ploughed through the sand. When they were at a safe distance from the water, she pried his fingers loose and he dropped to the beach with a dull thud. She leaned over the stern, staring down at him from between aching arms. "Just what is it I see in you, knight?" she muttered.

When her strength had returned, she knelt by his side and brushed away small clots of sand from his cheeks and the corners of his slack mouth. "I have no magic left. Rest, wherever you are. I'm going to the Stone. I'll use its power to restore my energy. I'll return as soon as I can." She pulled up her dark hood and went to rise, then hesitated. She turned and traced a Rune above the hair plastered on his face, wishing she could cast it, make him get up and walk with her, talk to her. "Be brave," she whispered.

The island was roughly a mile long. The first time she journeyed here, it had reminded her of a footprint. Where the boat came ashore was the tip of the sole, while ahead of her lay the narrow part of the foot. Further, where the Stone towered behind a small, steep hill, the beach flattened out to make the heel.

This would be her fourth crossing but she was still in awe of what she was about to see: one of the great Terran Stones set in place by the Far Druids before they disappeared. Sweet Bran, the power it held, the strength it gave. She thought of the first time she had made this journey, ironically for the same reason – for a man – then to kill, now to save.

She hurried along the beach, the hem of her long cloak brushing up sand as she reeled off Runes in her mind, searching for the one that would work the best to heal him. Far across the lake, the jagged mountains rimmed the horizon. Something in their deep silence unsettled her and she combed the twilight for signs of the birds. *Where do they come from? Why is it so different this time?*

When she neared the hill cutting off the heel of the island, she stopped to catch her breath. *How long will he last?* She glanced back and a question arose in her mind that she didn't want to face: *will the Terran power be strong enough?* She loosened the hasp at the neck of her cloak and was about to continue when she caught a sudden movement to her left. She squinted through the gloom.

"What in the name of the great Henge?" she muttered. A hundred yards away, something shimmered near the shoreline. As her eyes adjusted, she drew in a long slow breath. A column of crabs was filing out of the lake and marching to the rocky outcropping at the base of the hill. Oddly, they didn't move sideways but crawled forward like ungainly spiders.

She cut across the beach, halting when she came to within a few feet of the column. The crabs, each the size of a battle helmet and pale to the point of transparency, took no notice of her. Although the large watery eyes on the stalks passing below her seemed almost sightless, they were fixed on one thing – the place beyond the hill where the Terran Stone lay.

To the side of the procession, she noticed small humps of sand shaped like molehills. As she bent for a closer look, a fresh mound broke open and a pair of tiny claws poked out of the black soil. Slowly, purposely, a bloated beetle struggled out of the hole. Gaining the beach, it shook the earth from its glistening back and joined the crabs scuttling toward the Stone.

She frowned, the last time she had been here and the times before, she'd never seen a living soul. The journey was always solitary. *First the birds, now these. What's so different?* "Why now? Why are you so driven on getting to the Stone?" she murmured.

A thick splash sounded to her right and she turned. A shimmering jellyfish ringed by a luminous green fringe heaved itself out of the water and flopped onto the shore. It lay there inert for a moment, then, to Rhiannon's astonishment, it too began undulating toward the Stone.

Another splash and a second jellyfish emerged, this one bigger, skirted by a red fringe. Druid foreboding swept through her. What else lay hidden in the depths of Natal Lake? Casting an anxious look back at the boat listing in the graying distance, she pulled her cloak tight and hurried on toward the outcropping. Once she made contact with the Stone, she could replenish her elemental power and her ability to use Runes would improve dramatically before it evened out to a level steady enough for her to maintain.

She thought back to her first time here. She had stayed by the Stone for wondrous hours, casting spells charged with a power that had amazed her: summoning spells erupting from her Rune tracings like forked lightning, charm spells that made the island smell like an alpine meadow. Only later, when her shame returned, did she use the Stone's essence to cast a disrupting spell, sending it thrumming angrily across the lake to where Bercilack lay asleep, the heart she'd aimed it at beating with a sound she could almost hear.

And by the Sacred Cauldron, it had worked. From accounts told to her later, she learned he'd exploded awake, clutching his chest and crying out in terror. He'd suffered for months after, fearing death and fighting for breath whenever he climbed the winding castle stairs. But it wasn't enough. He still took her when he wanted.

Finally, one night after he'd beaten her and thrown her out of his bedchamber in a drunken rage, she'd returned to the lake and the shadowy fingers that searched for her sadness. As she rowed across the water in search of the answer that would free her from his iron grip, she'd cried child's tears. *Yes, I did. I did you bastard. But no more. No more, damn Bercilack.*

Bercilack. The *Karnn* Rune had given her the idea -- the Rune mothers used to dispel hunger pains in children when food was short. She had bound the spell with the *Angeald* knowledge Rune. Steeling herself against the knot of revulsion rising in her throat, she'd conjured up an image of him naked and sweating and then she sent that neat little package humming, sizzling with vengeance over the Natal Lake to resolve in his filthy bedroom.

She must have absorbed more power from the Stone than she'd ever thought possible because when she returned to the castle, he didn't send for her that night, or the next, or any night that followed. Indeed, so profound was the effect of the spell, he not only lost his sexual appetite but his physical appetite as well – from the moment she cast the spell, Bercilack never ate or drank again. Within a week, he lay dead in his bedchamber.

But now was not the time for bitter remembrances. Ahead, large rocks ringed the hill shielding the Terran Stone. Vegetation sprouted around and between them in wild profusion. These were not the fungi of the distant shoreline though, but plants and bushes, many as tall as trees, all dense with dark aromatic leaves. Rhiannon parted the first fleshy stalks and ploughed through the heavy undergrowth to a path winding up the hill.

After a steady climb, she could see the tip of the Terran Stone breaking out above the giant fronds. "Bran's sweet song," she muttered, savoring the pounding waves of energy.

When she gained the summit, she crossed to the far side and peered over the edge. She caught her breath. At the base of the Stone, a seething mass of pale bodies jostled for space: jellyfish, beetles, and innumerable gangling crabs waving and clicking their claws high in the air. Between the last of the rampant plant life and the Stone, the creatures formed a living moat.

Rhiannon tugged back her hood and wiped the sweat from her brow. When the crabs in front touched the Stone, their raised claws turned blue. A moment later, the color raced down to their shells and dissipated in a swirling haze that left them shuddering in ecstasy. Climbing onto a fallen trunk, she followed one battling its way back through the ranks toward a fissured trail running under the rocks to the left of the hill. Light in all their terrible darkness. The unbidden words sprang to her mind.

The tidal flow of creatures maintained a constant balance, keeping the moat full at all times. She eyed the snapping pincers apprehensively. *How will they see me – friend or foe? Either way, he'll be lost forever if I don't hurry.*

She scrambled down the hill, ignoring the scrapes and bruises and hurried to the rim of the moat. The sounds there were deafening. *You can do this, Rhiannon.* She hesitated, sweat trickling down the back of her neck. The thought of them brushing against her legs, or how it might feel to have a crab crack beneath her feet made her stomach knot. Clenching her fists, she slid her foot down into the moat, shoveling it under the cold shells and bristling claws.

With the next step, her cloak floated up around her knees as if she were wading into water. The noise grew louder. Some of the taller crabs snapped at the air, pale eyes wobbling as they turned to look at her. But they didn't attack.

She focused on the Stone, forcing her mind away from the creatures seething between her legs and took the next sliding step.

Yes.

The next.

Yes.

Then, with the third step, one of the bloated beetles forced its way up from the churning broth and scrambled onto the carapace of a lumbering crab. It teetered there for a moment before falling wetly against her thigh as the crab beneath it twisted away. She wanted to scream, to rub the smear into oblivion, but she waded on, choking back her loathing.

The Stone.

As she entered its pulsing aura, the clamoring in the moat faded to a background murmur, then to a calm.

Dear Bran.

The Far Druid gift of life.

She reached out.

Contact.

The frantic world around her dissolved. The Stone spoke to the very center of her Druid being. Her heart and soul fed on its manna like a babe on mother's milk; she drank deep and long, and during those moments the world around her blazed in bright new colors.

Somewhere, from the depths of her blissful state, she heard a faint click clacking and felt cold claws and shells brushing against her legs. She came back reluctantly from her reverie to find the creatures milling around her, jostling for their chance to touch the Stone. They no longer repulsed her; instead she felt a kinship with them – a link forged by mutual understanding. They paid her no heed as she waded back toward the rock fissure. She was imbued. Now it was their turn.

She had little difficulty returning and stepped out of the living moat as if it were a shallow pool. Climbing back up the hill, the Terran essence pulsed within her like a heartbeat, the new awareness filling her with confidence and a beatific sense of self.

She hurried down the path and when she broke out of the thick foliage onto the beach, she ran along the shoreline to where Gawain lay huddled near the curved rib of the boat's stern.

Nothing had changed; he lay motionless, eyes wide, staring up vacantly into the thin twilight. His chest rose and fell, but slower now than when she'd left. She dropped on her knees beside him.

"I'm here, knight."

With trembling hands, she rolled up his chain mail and the thick woolen shirt beneath. She drew a *Castan* Rune – above his cold skin and watched the magic crackle from her fingers and float over him in a roiling pattern. Gently, she placed her palms flat on his chest. She hesitated, looking down into his empty gray eyes, her hands swimming under the blue fire of the Rune. *What if this doesn't work . . . if the essence is not strong enough . . . No!*

Pushing aside thoughts of failure, she bent and whispered the sacred words. When their sounds harmonized, she released the brimming power and the Rune instantly fused.

From the darkness, Gawain saw a face. He knew not whose. He felt hands like the warmth of afternoon sun on his chest, and from somewhere distant, he heard fading chimes. He tried to speak, but knew no words; he tried to think, but had no thoughts.

Rhiannon whispered desperately, her lips feathering his ear, "Help me now. We have to get to the Stone. Come on, on your feet, knight."

The strange sounds held no meaning for him. Only when Rhiannon slipped her arm under his neck and urged him to his feet did he comprehend.

"Good, after me, that's right."

She took his hand and pulled him gently after her. He followed stiffly, like a child learning to walk. As they made their way along the beach, she scanned the twilight and the dark lake-no thrumming, no plaintive cries. *Safe.* Atop the hill, the tip of the Stone blazed like a star.

When they reached the outcropping and the start of the towering plants, she pushed aside chest high ferns and guided him into the dense vegetation. The path she followed earlier lay up ahead beyond a thick tangle of briar. *Will the magic hold, stay stable until we get there?*

Once they gained the narrow trail, Gawain let her hand go. He wandered ahead a little then turned into the undergrowth on his right. Behind the dark shapes, a beam from the Terran Stone speared into a clearing. Rhiannon followed him and watched as he stood mutely before the gleaming shaft. What happened next took her by surprise. He leaned forward, cupped his hands and gazed into the beam as if he were looking through a parlor window.

"What do you see? What's in your mind?" she murmured, heart racing.

But before she could say any more he dropped his hands to his sides and stepped into the center of the beam. She moved to his left, watching. He closed his eyes and tilted his head up letting the glow bathe his face and shoulders. Long minutes passed, then, the brightness in the light began to fade and he stepped away. Sighing with relief, she took him by the elbow and gently guided him through the undergrowth back to the path.

"Soon now. We're so close," she said, pointing toward the crest of the hill.

But his eyes stared through her and she led him away without looking into them again because the emptiness there terrified her.

After that, he wandered to every shaft of light that pierced the towering vegetation. Each time he stood in one of the beams, Rhiannon waited patiently, not understanding what was happening, only hoping somehow the power there was giving him strength, starting the healing.

Finally, when they reached the summit, she guided him to the edge she had gone to earlier. "Look to your courage, Knight Gawain," she said nodding toward the base of the Stone, her face highlighted by the Terran glow. "There lies the source of your healing. Come, follow me." She gave him a wan smile and then began picking her way down the slope.

At the bottom, she hurried to the rim of the moat looking back for any sign he understood what lay ahead, but his face remained expressionless.

Tensing, she inched her foot into the chittering swell and waded forward. She heard him enter behind her. The noise around them grew louder as they forded to the center of the moat.

Rhiannon could feel a growing eagerness in the crabs now. They seemed more desperate to get to the Stone. Claws waved and snapped. Some of the beetles had pushed up from the bottom and were racing over the humps of shells lying between them and the Stone. The tension in the air was palpable.

Rhiannon glanced over her shoulder apprehensively. Creatures boiled around Gawain's legs. Then she saw his eyes. They were no longer empty. They blazed with purpose. As she stood knee deep in the swell of crabs, he ploughed past her leaving a trail of upended bodies in his wake.

When he neared the Stone, he reached out as a child would to a mother. Then a startling thing happened, all the creatures turned to face him and a preternatural calm fell over the moat. Nothing stirred. And in that moment of breathless tranquility, a thousand eyes on sinewy stalks watched him take the final step and touch the Stone.

A blinding flash ripped away the veil hiding him from the world. An instant later muted thunder tore through the air. There was a brief moment of ear-ringing silence, then the sound of a faint crack. From the base of the Stone hissing fissures began running upward like plant tendrils. Gawain spun to Rhiannon. The fissures were already widening into dark veins when he took her hand and ploughed through the crabs to the rocky ledge. They had barely scrambled up the bank when the Stone gave a sheering groan and collapsed into the moat, burying the crabs in a hail of rocks.

In the following stillness, Gawain turned to Rhiannon. Terran dust flashed and shimmered around her head and shoulders like a meteor storm. She held her hands out to him but the complete and utter loss of essence had drained her of all energy, and before he could catch her, she collapsed.

He dropped to his knees and took her in his arms. "Hold on, we'll get through this," he whispered, "Stay with me, Rhiannon. I don't know the way back and I have to reach Lancelot before it's too late."

Cradling her to his chest, he made his way to the base of the hill. As he began the climb, he noticed for the first time the nightmarish scene around him. Each crab had halted in its pilgrimage. Claws once held high in worship, now shone in the gloom like wet sickles, and eyes that had so eagerly sought the Terran light stared ahead dull and milky white. He skirted the frozen lines of worshippers and headed up the hill to where the path tunneled through the foliage. Arms tight around Rhiannon, he ducked under the arching fronds and weaved his way down the trail to the beach.

Shouldering aside the last of the giant ferns, he glimpsed the boat along the shoreline. It lay where they had left it, listing on its side, oar locks glistening. He scanned the beach. Except for the strangely silent columns of crabs, there were no other signs of life.

When he reached the boat, he laid Rhiannon on the sand and pushed the little craft into the water. Steadying the tiller, he lifted her gently and climbed in. He set her down, back against the wooden seat and took up the oars. Balancing them across his knees for a moment, he looked at her pale face. "Bless your Druid heart," he whispered. "I owe you my life." Then, bending forward, he plunged the oars into the water and began rowing.

Once the boat had cleared the beach, he turned and scoured the mountains behind him. In the twilight, it was difficult to make out any familiar landmarks. It seemed to him Rhiannon had taken a direct route from where they'd beached but she may have changed her approach after the bird attack – he had no way of knowing. The shoreline to the north was the closest, perhaps two or three hours away. Once he got to the castle, he could contact Merlin.

Turning back, he pulled on the oars. He had barely made a dozen strokes when he caught a movement on the shore. He peered through the half-light. With effort, he was able make out what it was: the crabs had recovered from the shock of the Stone's destruction and were scurrying to the water's edge – but they weren't going in. They were lining up along the shoreline. He watched mystified as the columns grew three, four rows thick. Then he saw a sight that would haunt him forever: each creature raised its right claw and began snapping the pincer. At first, it looked as if they were saluting him. Then he realized what it really was; they were click-clacking their anger, waving claws at him like children shaking angry fists.

A shudder rippled through him and he lowered the oars. When he pulled further away, the crabs began marching down the shoreline. After he gained another twenty yards, they dropped their claws and slowly filed back into the dark lake. What intelligence guided them, he couldn't guess but the feeling he was a long way from safety never left him as the little craft journeyed deeper into Natal Brack.

An hour later, he rested his burning arms and looked up at the hump in the distance where one of the twelve great Terran Stones had once stood and now only dust and rubble remained.

The Stone ...

YESTERDAY'S FALCON

CHAPTER THREE

When he first saw the light from the Terran Stone, it shone like a star. From the well of darkness where his world had shrunk after he had fallen out of the boat, the sliver of light shone impossibly bright, impossibly distant. And after Rhiannon had revived him on the beach, it had somehow called to him and he had somehow answered.

The Terran Stone.

The Far Druid gift.

He didn't know then the journey to the Stone would be a forever journey in his empty mind – for he had no way of reasoning, no understanding of self, no measure of time. Natal Brack had leeched him clean.

The search to find himself began with his first step when Rhiannon had taken his hand to guide him along the beach.

He'd trailed behind her in darkness, for even the *Tarn* necklace would not work anymore. As the shadowy figure led him toward the path beyond the rocks and wild plants, he drifted in a void.

He could not have pinpointed when or why it happened but somewhere along the way, a face shaped itself from the great pillow of night surrounding him. It was a boy's face, young, with quizzical features fringed by raven black hair. It pressed in upon him with an urgency that racked his soul. It floated above him, looking down through wide grey eyes. Then, without warning, the striking face broke into an impish grin and Gawain shook with dread. He had seen himself. It had started; his memories were returning.

He turned instinctively to the distant light. It seemed brighter. Hope flowed within him as the Terran magic bathed his terrible wound.

Another fragment from his past. This time his mother loomed out of the darkness. She sat weaving a tapestry in the castle keep, blue thread looping from her hand, graying hair swept back and tied in a bun. He reached out for her like the child he'd become, wanting her warmth, the familiar smell of her but as quickly as it appeared, the image vanished into the dreadful night.

He went on, because somehow he knew that's what he always did. Faces from his childhood materialized, shifting in and out of the dark like wandering ghosts. He tried to call to them but his words were dusty and unformed.

Further, passed where Rhiannon had encountered the crabs, the images grew in number and intensity, flitting like bats, smiling, pulsing, fading, each one leaving hope to pool where the loneliness had gathered.

When they arrived at the base of the hill, the shadowy figure pushed the lower fronds of an enormous plant aside. A little way beyond, a path burrowed through the thick vegetation and wound up the hill to the Stone on the far side.

Once Gawain entered the undergrowth, the light disappeared and all the images vanished. Fear raced through him at their sudden loss and he froze. A gentle hand took his elbow. He could see nothing, but trusting in the touch, he groped his way forward.

Sweat ran down the cords of his neck as he took one blind step after the next. When he stumbled out of the thick vegetation onto the path, the hand steadied him then slid down into his.

"Hold true, knight."

The words meant nothing to him.

She had barely led him a dozen paces along the twisting trail when a beam of light from the Terran Stone sliced through the towering shapes to his right like a shaft of morning sunlight piercing an ancient forest.

Drawn by its magic, Gawain left the path. Fighting off vines and squeezing through willowy stalks, he broke into a clearing. He stood at its edge staring. Long sheaths of mist were curling away from the bright light and spiraling up into the night. He started. Something dark flickered within the beam. Cupping his hands, he went closer and peered into the hazy glow. He gasped and stepped back, the blood draining from his face. Swimming in and out of view was a scene trapped in the center of the light: a banquet hall full of people – and they were talking!

He reached out to the cloudy surface with childlike curiosity. The mist dissipated at his touch. He was thunderstruck. Before him stood a table full of steaming dishes, candles burning brightly and people – blessed people carving pheasant, ladling gravy, piling their plates high with mutton and boiled potatoes. He stared open mouthed as they jostled and chatted and poured from flagons brimming with wine.

It was like looking into a wizard's glass. At the far the edge of the scene, a gangly, dark haired lad wearing a red and white surcoat entered the banquet hall and walked awkwardly toward the end of the table. At best he was sixteen. Gawain watched as he took his seat and cast a furtive glance toward the fireplace where a young girl his own age approached with her hand cupped around the flame of a tallow candle.

45

And suddenly he *knew*. The memories came flooding back. He was looking at *himself*!

He stood before the shaft of Terran light staring as his image eyed this graceful girl setting down the candle next to her father. Shy young Gawain peeking over the rim of his wooden bowl, taking in the roundness of her body, the swell of her breasts, the falling curve of her hips.

Athlan!

Gawain swallowed thickly and closed his eyes, weak from seeing her again after all this time. Dark shapes flocked across his vision and he bent, pressing his fingers against his throbbing temples.

When the pounding eased, he looked up. The light before him was blazing brighter now. Then he felt it, felt himself being drawn towards the beam. It was as if the younger Gawain there were reaching out to him, calling to him. He knew what he had to do. Taking a measured breath, he clenched his fists and stepped into the light.

He passed through arcing bands of colors. When they cleared, he was in the scene, part of it. He turned to the younger Gawain. The world blurred. And that's all he knew, because his mind was no longer his own, it had joined with his younger self.

The sounds were overwhelming: the clanking of stock-pots, the clattering of plates, coughs of people clearing their throats, logs crackling and spitting. All blasted their way through the silence he had endured since Natal Brack.

He watched through new eyes.

He was Gawain – so young, so healthy.

Dolmar, Athlan's father, stood to bless the food. He closed his eyes and steepled his fingers. The small Christian gathering bowed in response. Silence again but now without the aching loneliness of the void.

"Dominus vobiscum. Et cum spiritu tuo. Benedicamus Domino ... "

The litany droned on and Gawain watched the baron, head bent, struggling with the Latinate structure of the Grace. One side of his face shone unmarked in the firelight; the other showed a raw flap of scalp and a missing ear. The king, Uther, had done that to him. *Yes.* Before they arrived, his mother had warned him not to stare or comment on the wound. *My little curiosity cat,* she had dubbed him. The memories came from everywhere. When Uther learned that Dolmar, his own liege lord, had attended a Christian gathering, he had ripped his sword from its scabbard and swung at him, narrowly missing his neck.

Uther. Gawain shivered.

The Latin praises droned on. A draft swept under the door and gusted across the room making shadows cast by the long curtains ripple along the walls. A simple wooden cross hung above a votive candle. So many secrets. And his father's hands one night, cupping his shoulders, as strong as the words he'd whispered. "The true way is the Christian way, my son. Uther's a Godless king whose time has long since passed."

Memories.

Nights of family prayer held deep in the castle and the joys shared in their newfound faith. Others coming on Sundays to worship the new God the Romans had brought across the wild seas. Images crisp and clear. A quiet mother kneeling on a stone floor, head bowed before an altar, a string of amber beads running like muddy raindrops through her fingers. Tallow candles burning and the smell – the scent of pine and breath sweetened by communion wine – and always the hushed secrecy.

Conflict, then and now: Druid blood flowing in a Christian body, two faiths, two worlds opposed and somewhere there, buried amidst all the passion was a truth the quiet little boy sought but could never find.

And here, a day after his fifteenth birthday, he sat watching Athlan whisper something to her father. Elegance in her every gesture: slender hands taking up a flagon, long fingers holding the bottom of the swan-white jug as she poured the wine for him. Her short hair shone the color of tilled earth and her eyes swam with the blue of Welsh skies. Then, a moment later, he froze because she caught him looking and smiled. *Dear God above, that smile.* And amid all the noise and laughter and clattering bowls, the world began to shimmer.

Emotions careened through him and he felt himself losing control, leaving the younger Gawain like a soul parting from a corpse. He had no way of containing the growing sensations or of controlling them. In his rising panic, he strove to hold on, to stay in the bright, living world but an immutable force wrenched him away and he traveled back with his early memories as the magic in the Terran light faded.

Silence.

His temples drummed. *Athlan.* The name so strong. He felt weak knowing what it could mean because he had found lost love. But there was something else, something waiting, lurking in the folds and clefts of darkness ... .

When he turned, the guide was waiting. A gentle hand touched his arm then cupped his elbow urging him away from the dimming light. *Come,* it seemed to say, *follow on to other worlds.* Gawain stole himself against a growing sense of dread as they left the beam and fought their way back through the undergrowth to the winding path.

Rhiannon had taken him no more than a dozen paces up the trail when another beam of Terran light broke between the overhead fronds to her right. She turned to see the knight's reaction, but he was already crashing through the chest high foliage.

When Gawain saw the next shaft of light, he turned from the shadow, pushed aside a cluster of heavy leaves and burrowed into the undergrowth. A thicket of tall fleshy stalks barred his way but he shouldered through them. His arm caught on something, twisting him around. He tugged free and stumbled into a small clearing edged with mossy rocks.

In the center, mist snaked around a towering column of bright light. Gawain neared it tentatively. Throat dry, palms clammy, he reached out. The mist cleared.

This time the scene trapped in the Terran light revealed his younger self walking toward a flight of stairs winding up into the gloom of a high turret. As the solitary figure passed beneath an oil lamp, Gawain bent forward, his face almost touching the beam. A red griffin emblazoned on the chest of the young lord's tunic caught the light as he stepped into the stairwell. *The family crest!*

The image turned, peering up the stairs, dark hair falling to strong broad shoulders. Gawain tried to guess his age but found it impossible, seventeen, eighteen at most. A hand reached for the iron rail bolted to the stonework and the figure began to ascend. *The ring. He doesn't have the ring!*

Heart pounding, Gawain stepped into the beam and into the chilling air of Dolmar's castle. The young Gawain staggered and grabbed the wall for balance. Then *he* felt the wall – the rough, uneven stone digging into his hand – and *he* caught the heady scent of tallow and smell of stale straw strewn on the floor.

The steep steps wound around a tight column. A series of lamps set in banded cages lit the well but he barely noticed his surroundings. He was on his way up to the Siege Armory to meet with Athlan. His father had taken him to Dolmar's castle to observe another Christian day – this time an Easter celebration. He had slipped out of the old library before vespers. While his father and the others were talking, discussing Bede and Saint Augustine in huddled groups, he had made his way to a lancet window overlooking the disused garden. From there he slowly edged to the door and slipped out into the hallway leading to the dark stairwell before anyone noticed. Now, climbing up to the armory, he could hear the voices below fading and the muffled sounds of movement.

Athlan had passed him a note earlier when they filed into her parents' new chapel – a room once used for storing sacks of grain against the harsh winters. She had slipped it into his palm as she went by. After a few paces, she turned, short hair framing ruddy cheeks, eyes the piercing blue of robin's eggs. He stood there shuffling his feet and she broke into a smile. At that moment, he thought his heart would burst. Then she was gone, leaving behind a lingering fragrance of lavender.

While he sat through the service, the paper smoldered in his pocket like a hot ember. It was only during the Creed, when all heads were bowed, that he had been able to take it out and secretly read by the light of the votive candles.

You must not stare at me so in public, my Lord.
In private, it would be a different matter.
If you like, we could meet in the Siege Armory
when the service is over.
Athlan.

After an eternity of litany, the service mercifully ended and when everyone had crowded into Dolmar's library, he'd managed to slip out and find his way to the west turret.

Thoughts chased each other in passion-crazed circles as he climbed the last few stairs. During past visits, he'd seen her only briefly and when he had, she'd never shown any interest in him. But now, now!

At the top, he took his bearings. The Armory door loomed to his left. He pulled out the wooden peg and eased the door open. A full moon shone through a high window at the far end shredding the darkness into ribbons of pale light. He crossed the room, skirting racks of spiked war maces and broadswords and halted near a row of bow staves. Behind them, a series of alcoves held clay vats and covered caldrons of oil. He found a stash of lamps on a nearby shelf, took one down and lit the wick with a flint. The flame flickered and jumped, casting goblin shadows on the walls and beams. Protecting the flame with his hand, he made his way carefully back across the room. He was near the war maces when the door opened and Athlan slipped inside. She called in a hushed voice, "Gawain, is that you?"

"Yes, my lady."

"I'm not quite that yet," she said, relief flooding her voice.

She ran to him shivering.

"You really are quite handsome in this light, you know," she said, taking the lamp and holding it up to his face. He could see her breath as she spoke and he had to fight an impulse to reach out and touch her long smooth neck. She threaded her fingers through his. "Come, I have something to show you."

They walked past the looming hulks of war machines to a small postern leading out onto the castle ramparts. She set the lamp down, pulled up the bobbin and pushed the door open. They ducked through into bright moonlight. Beyond the ancient battlements, the countryside lay in silvery silence.

51

Gawain crossed to the parapet and peered down. Under the clear, star bright sky, he could make out hedges and groves dotting the fields and in the distance, small pockets of mist hovering over streams and lakes.

"It's like God's breath," he said quietly.

He felt a movement from behind. Then a sudden arc of heat raced through him as Athlan slid her arms around his waist.

"Not everyone can see that beauty, only those with poetry in their soul," she said resting her cheek against his shoulder. "I feel that in you, you know, and more – a greatness, something, unlike anything else. Maybe it's your will; it's stronger than my father's, Lord Ork's, even Uther's."

"How do you ... "

"I just feel it."

She fell silent as a stray cloud drifted across the moon's face and plunged the castle into shadows. After a moment, she added, "Somehow I just know these things. And I know this as well, you'll fight your whole life and you'll suffer so much, God knows you will, but one day, a long time from now, you'll find the peace and love you deserve."

They watched moonlight sweep across the fields and dales as the cloud passed. "Come, there's something else I want you to see," she said.

She led him by the hand along the parapet to the western battlements. High above them, Dolmar's blue and white flag snapped and fluttered in the night breeze blowing from the hills. When they reached the rampart, she slipped in front of him and leaned back into his chest. "I could never own this, not like you," she said, gazing at the haunting scene below.

She pointed to one of the misty patches. "See that lake out there? The small one. It's mine, truly mine, no matter what anyone says. When I was a little girl, I used to ride there all the time – I've cried there and laughed there, I've whispered my secrets to it on sad days and yelled at it when I was mad, but soon it will be taken from me – like everything else. You see, all this will be given to my brother when he's old enough. I found out when I got back from Glamorgan, my mother is with child. I should be happy, I suppose, but I'm not, I can't find it in myself."

"I . . . "

"No." She touched a finger to his lips her earnest eyes upon his. "You don't have to say anything. I didn't mean for you to listen to my woes. I didn't bring you up here for that."

They both fell silent then, neither one moving, each so close their breath rose and twisted together.

After awhile Gawain spoke. "How do you know she carries a boy?"

She brushed his thick hair back from his face with her fingertips. "The same as I know about you, I suppose, it's the Druid in me. It's strong in my blood, even if I can't hold the Runes."

"Hold the Runes?"

She shrugged. "There was a time when I could remember them easily. Not anymore though. Most disappear before I have a chance to cast them – slippery like eels." She tickled his ribs, smiling. "Seems like even the wisest Druids have difficulties holding them now though. I think one day all the magic will vanish, just dry up." A note of resignation crept into her voice and she looked up at him. "But it wouldn't make any difference because I couldn't stop what's going to happen no matter what Runes I cast."

"Your brother may make you assurance of the land when he's old enough."

"It's not just that. This year I'm nineteen. I'm nearly past marrying age. If I'm not spoken for soon, it will go hard for me." She hesitated. "Last month my father met with Lord Llewellyn, a Christian baron from Harlech."

"But that's in northern Wales!"

She turned back to the fields. "If things go according to my father plans, I'll be gone long before our families have the chance to meet again. A dowry's already being discussed."

The silence between them deepened. Thoughts of a world without her filled him: days with their autumn shortness, evenings of twilight skies with their bleeding sunsets, hollow halls and hours of endless study poring over the worn pages of the vulgate Bible his father kept hidden beneath the castle flagstones.

"Such a sad face for a night so full of promise," she said.

"I'm sorry."

"Those eyes," she whispered, taking his hand. "Sure to God, Gawain, they're the most beautiful eyes I've ever seen. They're grayer than a goose's down, grayer than anything."

Sounds of a hymn, one of the psalms, filtered up from an open window below. He could hear Dolmar's voice deep and gritty and somehow sadly out of key.

"Do you truly find me so attractive?"

"Yes, my lady."

"Some say I look like a boy because I wear my hair so short."

"It only serves to make you more beautiful."

A smile dimpled her cheeks. "What am I to do with you, my clever poet?"

Moving in front of him, she gently eased her hands underneath his tunic. "Perhaps something for us to remember. Something to last," she said, sighing when she found the warmth of his skin. "Do you remember vespers at Monmouth?"

"Christmas?"

"Yes. That night I dreamed about you, how you kept looking at me."

She searched his solemn face. "Listen. I'll tell you a secret. When I was that mad young girl who ran to her lake, I swore the first night I spent as a woman, I'd spend with someone I could keep in my heart forever, for me – after that, I told myself, dowries, marriage, it wouldn't matter."

She tugged his shirt free and ran her hands over his flat, muscled stomach. "This loving isn't so difficult, my lord," she added coyly.

His throat tightened. The nearness of her and the scent of lavender he caught when she bent forward left him dizzy.

She nuzzled his neck, her lips blazing trails where she whispered into his skin. Without thinking, he sought her hips, running his hands over their rising curves.

"Here." She pulled away, slipping off her cloak and spreading it on the hard stone.

They knelt together like penitents in a wayward church, Gawain shaking as he explored the roundness of her.

"Wait." She reached up with gentle hands, slipping them over his, calming their urgency. Then she bent and helped him take off her velvet dress. And in one of the truly profound moments in life, he saw the beauty of a woman's body for the first time – every dip and swell and curve of her.

She let him look. Then she moved to him with ageless grace. Reaching out with her slim, young arms, she pushed her impossibly soft, impossibly firm breasts against him, taking from him all his will. And under the blaze of stars he lost himself in her as he found there a time of slow silence where the world went its way and the moon shone on in a forever sky.

The emotions that followed were so strong, Gawain discovered himself for an instant in two places. He felt the perspiration beading on his brow where he lay on the high ramparts at Dolmar's castle and where he stood now on the Terran Island. And even though he closed his eyes, he couldn't stop the tears burning at the loss of those rare moments.

He stood there helpless, fearing the eternity separating him from her, never wanting to let go – but slowly, inexorably, the magic in the Terran light waned and the scene faded.

Silence.

A hand touched him and he flinched at the unexpected contact. The shadow pulled back, beckoning toward the path. Leaving the dimming beam, he followed, wanting to ask, *Who are you? Where are we? What happened to my Athlan?* But no words came, because try as he might, he had no voice to speak.

When they reached the path, the ghost led and Gawain trailed behind pondering the mystery of the magic and of the light shining into his past. Near the first bend, his mind suddenly darkened and his steps faltered. *Uther. What was it about that name? And Harlech? There's a castle there. No, more ... a place, a cave ...*

The ghost took his arm, cutting off his jumbled thoughts. A hand gleamed white for a moment as it slid down to his and guided him safely around the curve.

At a place where the path straightened, another dazzling beam of light speared between the dark shapes. This time as he fought his way through the undergrowth, a cold dread closed around his heart because a picture clearer than any other flashed through his mind: thick blood pooling across a stone floor.

Brushing away sticky buds and tugging a knot of prickly vines from his legs, he crossed the clearing to where the beam sheered down. He hesitated before it, contemplating what it might hold, then steeling against the moment, he reached out to the cloudy surface.

When the mist dissipated, the scene held captive in the light revealed his father, Owyn, sitting in a winged back chair by a roaring fire. The Scriptorium was a small but cozy room he kept for the maps and books he collected. Dolmar and his mild wife Glenned sat huddled forward on stools, hands outstretched to catch the warmth of the bright flames after their hard journey from Crickhowell. Another figure, young Gawain, stood by a bookcase pouring red wine into beaten silver goblets.

Casting a lingering glance at the darkness behind him, Gawain tensed and then stepped into the beam . . . and into his father's study. His stomach churned as if his horse had leaped a fence.

" ... before. He's not worthy of licking the dirt off Miramar's boots," Dolmar was saying, the words breaking the exiled silence like a whip cracking. "I tell you, Owyn, Uther'll be the death of us all. We've got to do something. Look at this place, it's falling down around my ears, for God's sake. He's been taxing me to death because I gave shelter to a priest. One month, that's all. One month. How could you not help someone like that-dying right there on your door step?"

Dolmar stood, face flushed. "He's the Devil's own. I'm telling you, he'll wipe out every living Christian in the kingdom at the rate he's going. None of us are safe-especially you. God alone knows, Owyn, you've been a pillar of strength. We can't afford to lose you, not now." He suddenly became fidgety glancing around as if he expected the Battle Lord himself to stride from out of the shadowy corners of the room.

"You know he told Powes he trusts you? Imagine what he'd do if he found out you had a chapel in your castle, that you were a practicing Christian! My God, he'd string you up by that long neck of yours and hang young Gawain there alongside you." He dug the toe of his boot under a smoldering log sticking out of the fire and kicked it back. "It's only a matter of time," he added amid the dancing sparks.

Owyn rose, crossing his hands behind him. He wore a deep blue tunic patterned with a silver griffin on the breast. He presented a picture of elegance: hair thick and curling, patrician nose, slate gray eyes like Gawain's, clear and penetrating. The silver handle of his sword slung from a leather belt gleamed in the firelight as he spoke.

"There may be a way we can stop him, for good, my friend." He hesitated, reluctant to add the next words. "But it involves Merlin."

"You know how we feel about him," said Glenned, rising to her feet, suddenly looking so much older than her years.

"I understand, believe me. We've been through this many times, but now we've no choice," said Owyn gently.

Dolmar cut in, sweeping up a goblet of wine from the small table. "There has to be another way. I don't trust him, not a wit. The Druid's too strong in him, you know that. Ever since the business with Arthur. I think he's behind all the persecution. He's worse than any damn Saxon that ever set foot on this precious soil. Mark me, he'll not be satisfied until each and every one of us is moulding in our graves."

"You're wrong there. He's offered to help because he wants Arthur on the throne," said Owyn.

"Aye, so he can do his bidding."

"No, my old friend, I grant he wouldn't say much about the future, but what he did say made perfect sense. He believes Uther will destroy more and more of what we all hold dear. There'll be no chance of Christianity gaining a foothold in this country as long as he rules."

"And Merlin agrees to that!"

"He's not so opposed to the True Faith as you think. He may be a High Druid but he knows the benefits Christianity brings. Uther's the stumbling block here. We can tolerate his excesses if they're confined to Tintagel, but when he brings them outside those walls, we have to take a stand. On that,

Merlin's in full agreement. He told me outright, if Uther abdicates in favor of Arthur, he'll do everything in his power to see the young king is taught tolerance and rules wisely."

Owyn's articulate plea rang with conviction and he looked from one to the other. "Merlin's with us in this. He desires peace as much as we do. Besides, it may well be our last chance. Things aren't what they used to be, you know. Even he's finding the Runes difficult to hold these days."

"Aye, so he says," growled Dolmar, tossing the dregs of his wine into the fire. "But if you think Uther'll ever give up the reins of power, you're mad. He'd as soon go to mass."

"Maybe not voluntarily," said Owyn lowering his voice, "But what he proposes is this: when Uther calls for the year-end tithes, he'll invite Gawain and myself, along with his other so-called trusted lords, to the banquet at Tintagel. He'll travel with us, disguised as Gawain's tutor. Once we're there, he plans to use a spell he's prepared." He stopped, waiting to see Dolmar's reaction at the mention of magic. He looked surprised when his friend skipped over the usual lecture. Instead, in a flat, even voice, Dolmar asked, "Exactly what Rune casting does your wizard propose?"

"He wasn't specific, but this much he did say. There's an extract, called *Hebbona*, if administered under certain conditions, would allow him to enter Uther's mind and control him for a brief period. For all intents and purposes Merlin would actually become Uther during that time." He paused again.

"So what happens if he decides he likes the taste of power? Then we have ourselves a dangerous animal indeed," said Dolmar in the same flat voice.

"No, Merlin told me once he enters Uther's mind, he loses all of his powers."

"So how does he plan to return to himself?"

"That, he didn't say."

"I don't trust him, not one damn bit," grumbled Dolmar turning back to the fire. He gripped the edges of the hearth and leaned over the burning logs, the side of his face with the missing ear shining waxy in the firelight. When he spoke again, his words were measured, despite the passion behind them.

"In the name of our Lord, I ask you to rethink this, Owyn. With Merlin in control of Uther, anything could happen. Can you guarantee he wouldn't turn around and have us all killed? He knows just about every Christian in the land. He's a High Druid, for God's sake, you said so yourself. He has no love of Christians."

"You forget I was brought up in that faith," Owyn added quietly.

"Aye, I know that well enough."

"This hasn't been easy for me, but what choice do we have? Uther's too powerful. Not even the combined forces of the Saxons threaten him. Alone we don't stand a chance. But, if what Merlin says is true and he's able to enter his mind, he'll make him announce his abdication in favor of Arthur that very night. No matter what happens after, Uther won't be able to rescind his proclamation. Once it's signed, it's irreversible, irrevocable, he'll be finished."

He looked from Dolmar to his wife, trying to read their reactions, but all he saw were faces full of winter hardship, years of hidden belief. He took the jug and refilled the goblets. "Merlin's preparing the documents as we speak."

Another deep silence, then the talk continued, forceful at first, but easing when Dolmar's objections weakened. Finally, as the night drew on, they began to plan for the time the young king would take the throne and rule from Cornwall.

By the dying fire Gawain only half listened, his mind on Athlan, catching the passion of her voice in Dolmar's words, her movements in Glenned's gestures. His memories were still needle sharp. The passing years since she wed Llewellyn had done nothing to ease the pain that came every time the moon shone in a clear sky, or he caught the scent of lavender.

Sitting in the warmth of the room, he had looked for the opportunity to ask how Athlan was. All the time his father had been speaking, he had waited – serving, helping, standing back in the shadows. Before she left so long ago, she'd written a second letter. He'd read the tender words so often he knew them by heart.

My love,
Today I am married and am to journey to the far north. Our lives are richer for having touched. I believe in you and having your love will sustain me through all the long nights that are to come. The man I'm married to is my Lord and husband but he is NOT nor ever will be my true love. That person is here, locked in my heart forever. Be brave, my Gawain, be true to all the things you spoke to me about that night on the ramparts. Hold to your faith. May God keep you safe always. Remember me, for soon we will both grow old and weary of our time.
My love forever,
Athlan

Two long years had passed, each one full of days to share and no one to share them with. Knowing that once there had been someone to talk to, who knew you, and who listened when you tried to say all the impossible things your heart held – two years of empty fields and distant hills, of snaking rivers and frosts and wheat bowing in stormy winds.

When the fire died down and talk of Arthur and Merlin ended, Gawain finally summoned up the courage and asked Glenned about Athlan. The tired eyes in the drawn face before him turned to gaze into the struggling flames.

"Dolmar and I were planning on telling your father later," Glenned said pulling out a small wooden cross from under her shawl and clutching it in her palm. "Athlan hasn't been seen since she was riding by the Radnor Forest last month. Lord Llewellyn is still searching for her, but so far, there's been no word. I fear the worst, I do, I really do." She rubbed the crucifix nervously with the ball of her thumb. "It's the Dark Druids there. The place is full of them. Nobody dares go near anymore." She kissed the cross and tucked it back under her shawl.

She took his hand and gently squeezed, her knuckles white and swollen with the harshness of Welsh winters. "I know this must be hard for you, Gawain, Athlan was never very good at hiding her feelings from me."

And even if he'd wanted to, Gawain couldn't have said anything to comfort her or ease the pain, because his breath had gone and his throat had filled with the dryness of ash.

The emotions built and despite his efforts to hold on, the room began to waver. The voices fell away and he felt his mind shift – *his* mind.

NO!

The scene around him flickered as he absorbed the last of the magic in the light. Then all became still and silent. He struggled with the shift, trying to adjust to the sudden emptiness of the Terran world. He took an unsteady step away from the dimming light and turned to the darkness, the experience already beginning to fade into scrapes of memory. At his elbow, he felt a gentle but insistent tug.

He stumbled after the shadow back to the path. With a heavy heart, he made his way along a trail now knotted with roots and rocks. Once, he tripped but the ghostly figure caught him by the elbow and steadied him before he fell. Where the path evened out, he brushed by a clump of bushes that moved like a slow wave. Further ahead, they started up a narrow incline and he trudged behind again, shoulders slumped, head bowed.

How much time passed this way, he didn't know but suddenly, from out of the depths of his despair, words blared in his mind: *you will show the strength of your father and the courage your mother bears. You will do this and you will accept fate with the grace God gave you.* He looked up from under damp locks of hair. To his right a beam of Terran light shone between the dark shapes like the blade of a newly forged broadsword.

Clenching his fists, nails digging into his palms, Gawain turned from the shadow. *I will know the things bound in your magic. I will find my answers.*

As he groped his way between stalks and leathery fronds, he felt the soft earth give under his feet. A heady smell of ferns and compost rose from the soil and he realized something: each time he recovered another part of his memory this world became more real.

Breaking through a sheath of tall bulrushes, he found himself facing the beam. A thin mist swirled lazily around its surface. Behind him, the night lay poised, waiting to take him back into its dark folds. *Life and death and somewhere between, the mystery of all my lost years.* He reached out.

At his touch, the vapor dissipated, revealing a scene so vivid, he stumbled back. The sheer size and majesty of what he beheld amazed him: his younger self in a massive, baronial hall. It was Michealemas day and an early September sun sheered through high windows, slicing the floor into squares and triangles of golden sunlight. Holding his breath, he leaned closer watching the silent scene unfold. At the far end of the hall, his younger self scooped up an armload of parchments and toted them to his father who sat writing at a long oak table beneath the Bainbridge tapestry.

Dear God above, Llansteffan, our castle. With tears of joy burning at the back of his eyes, he stepped into the light. The familiar dizziness swept over him as he left the husk of who he was and the vitality of his new world burst around him. Then, simply, he was Gawain and he found himself walking the last few paces across the flagstones to his father.

His stomach growled as he neared the table and his father looked up as he set down the bundle of parchments.

"You're wasting away, son," he said tapping his belt with the long spine of the goose quill he was using.

"I'll go down and get some of Bronwyn's shepherd pie from the pantry, father. Would you like some wine while I'm there?"

"No, I need a clear head for this," Owyn said turning back to the scroll lying on the table and melting a stick of red wax over a candle to affix his seal.

Gawain crossed to the side door, but before he had chance to raise the latch, a wave of faintness washed over him. His knees buckled and he grabbed for the wall to steady himself. At that moment, the light dimmed and an angular figure strode into the room from the Shield Hall. He wore a dark robe dusted with stars and hemmed with Druid lettering. The sleeves swung wide at the wrists. In his hand, he held a thick yew staff. The Rune symbols carved in the wood glowed, causing the very air around them to shimmer and dance like summer heat rising from cobblestones. When he reached Owyn, he threw back a braided hood and ran his fingers through the tangle of graying hair that sprang free.

He scanned the room, eyes the green of lichen taking in everything before settling on the young lad staring open-mouthed by the wall.

"What have we here?" he said. His face was etched with deep, finely cut lines reminding Gawain of a hawk's, inquisitive, alert, but above all indefinably hungry.

"This is Gawain. I've asked him to join us, as you requested, Lord Merlin."

Merlin! The room ballooned and Gawain suddenly felt the shift . . . felt himself moving back outside the boy's mind.

No!

He fought desperately against the rising emotions, concentrating on the walls, the fireplace, anything to hold on.

Dizziness.

Then the shift again and out of nowhere the distant sounds of the castle returned and he found himself looking across the hall at Corvan's tapestry of the Carmarthen siege.

The dark robed figure was still appraising him, his piercing eyes taking in his height and build, but seeming to search for something more. Gawain could feel furnace power radiating from him. *How could anyone ever hide secrets from this man?*

"He's grown. He's bigger than I expected, broader in the shoulder." His voice had an unusual hesitancy to it, almost as if he had been educated to learn the language thought Gawain.

Merlin leaned over his Rune staff, his wild beard nestling over his hands. He spoke thoughtfully while light eddied around the carvings on the smooth yew wood.

"So, son of Owyn. You have your father's build, strong and true, I see. Your eyes tell me of your honesty and ... perhaps of some sadness in you," he added in milder tones. "But the bravery of your parents you've yet to find, I think."

He straightened up, unfolding his hands and blinking with hawk-like speed. "However, you may well have that chance, when you learn why I've traveled so far, young lord."

"Come, let's go up to my study," said Owyn slipping his arm around his son's shoulders.

They walked through the long baronial hall and out into a passage lined with racks of spears and polished suits of armor. At the far end, Owyn opened a door leading to a steep flight of steps. A high stained glass window at the top bled reds and greens over their shoulders as they passed beneath and turned down a short hall to the study.

They opened the study door and entered. Merlin swept his robe to one side and settled back in a sheepskin-covered chair with a sigh. Owyn stood before the hawk eyes not showing a shred of the nervousness Gawain felt. "I've procured the invitation for Uther's tithing banquet as you requested. I've arranged for you to travel with us in the guise of Vortigan, a descendent of a Roman legate. I thought it safer if you go as Gawain's tutor – this should give you at worst limited access once we're in the castle."

Merlin nodded. "Good, I have the *Hebbona* prepared. It should have aged sufficiently by the time the king's celebrations begin. Will the boy be able to administer the compound? The timing is critical."

"Of course."

Merlin arched an eyebrow and reached for the white jug on the side table. "Remember, once in the castle my abilities will be limited. I cannot expend any essence before I enter Uther. I'll need all my power if I'm to control this madman and survive. I can allow nothing, absolutely nothing, to distract me." He filled a goblet with wine, raised it to his lips then hesitated. He peered over the rim. "I must be able to walk into his bed chamber, without hindrance. I must find him asleep under the influence of the *Hebbona* compound, completely free of willpower – completely free."

Owyn placed his hand on Gawain's shoulder. "My son is my life. In him I have absolute faith."

"Then it shall be done," Merlin concluded draining the wine.

The three of them talked through the rest of the afternoon, testing Merlin's plan by throwing every conceivable obstacle in its path. And when they'd exhausted each possibility, they went back over the details and refined them. In the dying light of the afternoon, a tousle-haired servant Owyn had taken in after his parents died, brought fresh wine and they agreed the risk of entering Uther's mind was as small as they could possibly make it.

Merlin left before vespers and later, after the final prayers, Gawain climbed the winding stairs to his room high in the north wing. He undressed, pulled back the thick down quilt on his bed and sank thankfully beneath the covers.

He lay on his back and laced his hands behind his head, fingers buried beneath locks of thick hair. Outside, a field of stars blazed in the dark sky beyond the window. From the branches of an ash tree in the courtyard a tawny owl hooted. High above, a bone-white cloud drifted across the moon.

Gawain tossed and turned. He felt sleepy but thoughts of Tintagel and of what awaited him there kept him wide-awake. Finally, when he could stand it no longer, he turned back to the window and the stars.

Orion had wheeled into view and when he gazed into the core of the churning firmament, he found unaccountable peace. Its hazy light seemed to bathe him, filling him with wonder and from its heart, Merlin's last words came back with haunting clarity. "You're Druid, Gawain. It's deep in you. Don't let the Christian faith rob you of your heritage."

They had been standing at the portcullis, Merlin's hand on his shoulder as the iron spokes clanked over the ratchet. "Only a few of us can cast the Rune spells, my boy. The secret lies in the elements. Those who have been blessed are able to draw from them: the earth, the water, the trees. Your strength is unusual because it comes from the stars. Without discipline though, you hardly notice it – but it's there, I can feel it. That's why I asked for your help. One day, after we rid ourselves of this troublesome king, I will teach you how to draw on that power and we shall see if you can hold the Runes."

A chill wind gusted across the road winding down to the village, sweeping aside late autumn leaves. This time Merlin's words seemed to lose their strange hesitancy and flowed with natural ease. He looked beyond the castle walls and out toward the estuary where the grey sea sent cold fingers burrowing through the earthy shores.

"I'll share a secret with you before I go – one I cannot tell your father for fear his newfound religion will hamper his judgment. Once I've entered Uther's mind, I will not be able to leave until one of us dies." He continued gazing into the distance, then he turned back to the ashen face at his side. "Not quite the Christian way, hmm?" He patted Gawain's shoulder. "Chin up, lad; I don't intend it to be me," he added, the hawkish expression suddenly loosing its sternness as a shrewd smile swept away all the fierce intensity.

When Orion and its misty cluster of stars sank from view, Gawain finally fell to sleep and for the fist time since his strange journey began, he left his younger self without the roiling emotions. One minute he was lying curled up in the warmth of his bed at Llansteffan, the next, he found himself facing the dimming shaft of Terran light.

He turned to the hill, ready to go on. But before the shadow led him away, he glanced over his shoulder at the mist. He frowned, struck by how much the lazy swirls reminded him of the distant nebula of Orion. *All pieces of a puzzle to solve before I know who I am*, he thought starting up the path.

Walking in silence through the looming vegetation, he thought about Merlin, about what was about to happen in the great castle of Uther Pendragon and how it would shape their world. Then he stopped, taken by the sudden fear of his father being caught; a man so gentle, who had found in the Christian faith all that was missing in his life: hope and purpose in a foundering land. "There is more to existence," he had said on the night Merlin came, "than Runes and spells, my son. It is the purity of the soul and splendor of the human spirit that will be our salvation, not the fleeting solutions Druid magic affords." His face shone then with a strength that could rule a kingdom.

And when Gawain saw the next shaft of Terran light sheering through of the darkness ahead, he knew, as certainly as he had known love, that when he touched the mist playing on its surface, he'd once more see his father's unwavering eyes and the glowing Runes of Merlin's staff in the heart of its beam.

CHAPTER FOUR

This time when the mists cleared, he found himself looking at a scene in which his younger self stood alone before the wizard in his father's study. He watched silently from outside the beam as Merlin dug his hand into a pocket buried deep in his robe.

The Bauble! I know, I know this! His heart leapt at the fragment of knowledge that had somehow managed to escape the beam and then he felt the familiar pull. Images whirled around him like fireflies as he stepped into the light . . . . Then *he* could smell the forest pine about Merlin who was drawing a smooth glass orb the size of a quail's egg from his pocket and holding it out. "A Sithean Bauble. A lost relic some claim the Far Druids, left behind," he was saying in his strange, halting voice. "But that's a story for another time, for now you must learn a little of our own magic."

He pressed the milky white orb into Gawain's palm and closed his fingers around it. "Do you feel anything, my boy?" he said, patting the back of his hand.

"No, nothing."

Merlin harrumphed. "Nothing? No strange experiences, no headache, no queasiness in the tummy perhaps?" he added with a playful poke at Gawain's midsection.

"No, I feel fine," said Gawain, smiling.

"Hummmm." Merlin tugged his beard, twisting strands around his finger then he suddenly thrust his head forward. "Look into my eyes. Deep now. What do you see?"

"Green eyes."

"That's all?"

"Yes."

"By the Sacred Cauldron, it seems you may have more of the Druid in you than I thought. Listen hard, now." Merlin said something that sounded to Gawain like a fragment of some long forgotten song. "What did you hear?"

"I'm not sure, words."

"Just words?"

"Yes, words I don't understand. Two, I think. Are they Rune words?"

"You didn't feel anything strange – emotions, desires, needs – when you heard them?"

"No, nothing, just the words."

"Then it's as it should be," declared Merlin, sweeping the Bauble from Gawain's hand and polishing it on his sleeve. "It doesn't exert any power over you, my boy. It obeys you. It's yours to invoke. Maybe things are going to get a little easier for a change."

"I don't understand."

"All in good time," Merlin said.

He held the sphere up to a nearby candle and squinted at its surface. "Hmm, not so much as a blemish," he muttered. "Now, I want you to put this in your pocket. Then I want you to repeat the invocation I tell you, and as you do, I want you to turn the Bauble over in your hand. I'll use the easiest phrases I can. You'll need to feel comfortable doing this when the time comes, so practice is in order."

"What does it do?" asked Gawain fingering the smooth globe and gazing at its mirrored sheen.

"Don't trouble that lax brain of yours with esoteric concerns." said Merlin tapping him on the head with his finger.

"Merely repeat the words as you turn the Bauble. Repeat them until they feel natural – until they become a part of you, then you'll see the power, my boy."

"Will I be using it on Uther?"

"Questions, questions. You'll have me in an early grave. Just say the words, carefully mind, exactly as I do," said Merlin huffing before he began the incantation.

"Hreran mid hondum."

Gawain listened and repeated the strange chant, trying to inflect the words the way Merlin did.

"Turn the Bauble, lad. Turn the Bauble."

Gawain did as he was asked, repeating the invocation while he slowly turned the orb.

He could not have pinpointed the exact moment it happened, nor could he have described the subtle shift in the perception he experienced, but at some time during the ritual, the light in the room dimmed and Merlin's voice became softer, somehow more distant, almost as if he were speaking from outside the room. Feeling unsettled, Gawain ceased intoning. A wave of dizziness swept over him and the new perception shifted back to the old.

"Good," he heard Merlin say clearly. "Now we know the Bauble will work for you. Take it out."

Gawain pulled the orb from his pocket. Instead of the pale milky color he'd first seen, it now glowed a clearer, cleaner white.

"Look closely, young Druid," said Merlin putting a gentle hand on his shoulder and nodding at the Bauble.

Gawain started. Spider black lines were crawling over the sphere in random patterns, fish netting the surface.

"The Sithean webbing," breathed Merlin reverently. He moved back and took up his Rune staff. "With time and a lot of practice, you'll learn to manipulate its strands. When you've perfected the invocation, you'll create a life-pattern. That pattern will be absorbed into the Sithean web. It'll be unique to you and you alone. Once it's complete, you'll just need to release enough energy into the Bauble for the web to grow until it envelops you. Then you'll be all but invisible, even to those near you. At best they'll see a faint shadow, and if you're moving, likely nothing at all. No matter what angle they look from, the webbing will bend the light away. You'd be surprised at the fun I had when I first learned to use it."

Gawain looked at the Bauble with newfound respect; he took it to the light of the fire and turned it over thoughtfully. "What happened to me? I mean, what did I feel when I was chanting?"

"Merely a pattern shift in the web. After much discipline, and I might add, a great deal of effort, it's possible to change that pattern to, let's say, protect yourself from a sword blow or ward against a controlling spell. When you've become adept at manipulating it, you can even give the illusion of being somewhere else – quite useful in one as young as you, I should imagine," he added, green eyes flashing beneath arched eyebrows.

"Now, let's try again, this time push away all other thoughts and focus on the invocation. Practice makes perfect, my boy."

And he did. And in that room where his father had taught him so much and had shown him truth through God on long cold nights, Merlin rejoiced in his arts as he busied himself pointing out arcane lore and explaining Druid earth spells. Merlin at his finest, a light in a darkening night. A tree cut from ancient forests. He spoke of nature, of the power stored in the elements surrounding them and how, with time and training, Gawain could find his roots. And all the while he spoke, his hawk eyes blazed and the Rune staff crawled with shifting gules of light.

The moon was high before Gawain finally built up enough courage to ask the question weighing so heavily on him.

"Merlin, who are the Dark Druids?"

Merlin looked up from the small pan of red powder he was weighing, a shadow passing over his face. "They're deviates, every last one of them."

The sudden brooding look and the sharpness in his voice took Gawain by surprise.

"A long time ago, they aligned themselves with evil. Just as I've sought my power from the light: the trees, water, even your stars, they sought theirs from the dark: the suffering, the pain and fear that rule us in time of defeat."

He pushed the bronze scales back sending them rocking and squeaking and stormed over to a desk stacked high with rolled parchments. He grunted and cleared a space. Then he pulled down a leather tome from a shelf behind him, propped it open and promptly began reading.

Gawain waited. The light from the candle flickered and the wax hissed. Merlin looked up, surprised to see him still there. "Practice boy, patience will win the day."

Gawain nodded, turning to go. He wanted so much to ask more, to find out why they took Athlan and what they planned to do with her. But he remained quiet instead, because Merlin's last words had said clearly enough – no more, not now.

Frustration and love surged within him when he opened the door. Outside, fine flakes of an early snow tumbled from the night sky and without warning, the roiling emotions began to build.

No, no ...

Silence, then the gentle sense of his leaving as he absorbed the last of the magic in the Terran light.

Once again, he found himself staring at a dimming beam. He closed his eyes trying to recall the things Merlin had said before the images faded into memories. *Did we rid ourselves of him, Merlin, armed with your magic and the Bauble in which you had so much faith? Somehow, I survived, but what happened to you, to my father, to Athlan?*

Still trying to make sense of the last fragments and puzzling over what lay ahead, he left the beam and followed the ghostly figure back to the winding path.

They had traveled only a short distance when he felt a gentle hand slip into his and guide him over a fallen trunk. A dozen more paces brushing passed columns of fleshy stems and he stopped dead. A shaft of Terran light gleamed from behind tall shapes further up the trail. His throat tightened because with it, a name sprang unbidden to his mind: *Uther Pendragon.*

Is this king so powerful he can escape the confines of the beam? Tentatively, Gawain pushed ahead. When he reached the spot where the light cut into the clearing, he stood before it, heart hammering.

What?

It was as if he could sense the hidden vagaries of his destiny waiting for him there. He glanced over his shoulder at the outline of drooping fronds and the harrowing darkness beyond. Then he reached out and the mist vanished.

In the scene held captive in the center of the beam, grassy hills rolled into the distance and under an open blue sky, the Cornish peninsula of Barras Point flashed like a polished shield on a field of battle. At the edge of the scene, he caught sight of three figures riding along a high ridge.

A sudden desire to smell the salt sea air and feel the keen winds blowing off the Celtic sea again overwhelmed him. He took a slow breath and like a swimmer anxious to return to familiar waters after a long absence, he plunged into the light.

Then he was *there*, on horseback, riding alongside his father and Merlin, wind lashing his face and whipping back his heavy cloak. Ahead, perched high atop craggy cliffs stood Tintagel, the iron stronghold of Uther Pendragon. Even over the dull clomping of the horses' hooves and the howling wind, he could hear the sea roar and crash along the rocky shoreline below its great fortress walls.

He peered up at white clouds hunched across the clean blue horizon and then down to where the winds swirled through the gorse and thin grass of a late December, and he knew on this day, the world would change forever.

Tithing, the year-end celebration in honor of Uther's rule. The time when all the barons and lords showed their largess – to buy the king's favor, his father had told him bitterly. And when they'd set out that morning he had smiled to reassure him. "Like the others, we too will pay our debt this day – but not to a king, my son, to a kingdom."

They rode along the beach gazing up at the towering ramparts and hunched battlements where the royal flags snapped in the squalling wind. Gawain turned to his father, struggling to steady his horse. He shouted into the gale, "It's so big. It covers the whole headland. Can we do this, Father?"

Owyn nudged his black warhorse closer to Gawain. With his pennant whipping back and forth, he cupped his hands and bent forward. "Yes, we can, because it's what we do best. In this, in all things, we fight and we go on. We will find triumph in adversity tonight. Put your faith in the good Lord, my son."

Up ahead, Merlin, dressed in dark tutor's robes, rode on calmly unaffected by the sheering gusts. His cloak flapped open only occasionally as if the winds were afraid to anger such a great wizard, thought Gawain.

With his back to them Merlin spoke, his words cutting through the gale with ease. "As your father says, young one, we will indeed prevail but first we must play our parts and play them well. Keep in mind all is for naught if you cannot get the *Hebbona* into Uther's drink on time. Remember, empty the contents of the pouch into his mug or into his pitcher after he's eaten. I've no need to remind you whatever he eats after he takes the *Hebbona*, he'll surely vomit back. Then all will be lost – the effects of the potion will be gone for good."

Gawain balled the leather reins in his fist. The wizard had been at his father's castle night and day going over the details of Tintagel from the battlements to the dungeons. He'd shown him how to mix the *Hebbona* with the dissolvent so that it was undetectable in posited ale. He'd let him taste the resin he distilled from the sap and then he'd mixed it with the dissolvent again so he could see there was no difference.

Gawain dug his heels into the horse's flank. *I could do it in my sleep, Merlin. You know I could.*

The wind howled endlessly as they wound their way up the narrow path to the mainland courtyard and the outer walls. At the top, the immense portcullis guarding the castle entrance began a jerky ascent. The deafening roar of sea and wind muted even the ratcheted winch.

Two tall guards stepped out from sheltered sentry posts, long cloaks whipping around their backs, pikes at the ready. The older of the two, a man with shoulders as wide as an armory door, spoke in a rumbling voice as they approached. "In the name of Uther the High Pendragon, state thy business."

Merlin stood dutifully behind Owyn who stepped forward and tendered the king's invitation. Gawain watched, taking courage from the way his father carried himself. How could he speak so easily, act so calmly, knowing what Uther would do if he had even the vaguest idea of what they planned? Although Gawain could make little of their conversation, he could plainly see how at ease the guards were as they moved aside to let the small party enter the inner grounds.

They rode through an archway and out onto a narrow bridge spanning the crashing waves securing Uther's island fortress. Once across, they made their way through a bare courtyard where two guards wearing breastplates embossed with golden lions stood posted at the final gateway. Gawain glanced at the hardened faces as he passed and his fingers sought the Bauble deep in his pocket. They handed over their horses to waiting retainers at the bottom of a flight of wide steps leading to the castle stronghold and ascended in silence.

Inside, Tintagel teemed with life. Guests from distant baronies milled through the vaulted hallways. Gawain and his father squeezed by servants toting chests and hold-alls and shouldered their way toward their quarters in the west wing.

At a wide foyer joining the two central stairways, a steady stream of dukes and barons funneled in from a smaller wind-blasted courtyard. Loud and demanding, they yelled orders to retainers, hailed old friends and filled the halls with great guffaws of laughter as they flowed east to the Shield Hall.

From somewhere deeper in the castle, strains of music and sounds of early drinking floated through the air. Gawain looked around, peering through the throng. Merlin had vanished. With sudden understanding, he realized how irrevocable events had become since they'd entered the great portico gates.

The evening began with surprisingly little fanfare. The royal banquet table, a huge oak burl seating twenty guests, stood on a raised floor at the far end of the hall. One step down, twelve long tables faced the king's place, each seating parties of ten. Busy servants in laced white shirts and blue baldrics directed Gawain to the last table on the right –

the first stroke of luck – or artful work by Merlin. His seat, near the stairwell, would afford him the chance to slip away unnoticed when the time came.

He took his place with lords from the southern baronies and settled down to wait out the long evening. Around him, heavily accented voices complained about poor weaponry and the endless taxes imposed by the king. Curses flew and jokes were cracked. He glanced ahead to his father's table where the First Lords sat dressed in surcoats bearing the sigils of their houses: crested stags, crossed swords, golden oak leaves, lions with paws upraised. Gawain could see his father hunched over, deep in conversation with Glastonbury, a lord of similar tastes but, more importantly, a practicing Christian.

After another round of drinking, Uther arrived. Conversations in the hall petered out as the archway darkened. Uther's massive bulk cast a long shadow into the room. The wind moaned in the high rafters above him, stirring the royal bunting and rows of gilded banners. Someone coughed. Then Uther entered, his boots striking tiny sparks out of the cold stones as he strode across the floor.

From where he sat, Gawain could see him clearly, a man taller by a head than anyone in the room. The sheer physical size of him was daunting. His huge body, made thick and misshapen by time and crippling battle injuries, sent rivers of dread racing down Gawain's spine.

He was every inch the ogre of childhood nightmares. His great craggy head sprouted clumps of wild red hair. On the left side of his face, a lightning bolt scar ran from his chin, across his cheek and plowed through his scalp leaving behind a swath of mottled skin.

When the Battle Lord reached his place at the royal table, he leaned his weight over two massive fists and studied his subjects like a cat pondering the fate of cornered mice. The dark eyes sweeping the room told clearly of the scheming that had made him king. He smiled grimly – a smile that left the young Gawain uncertain, empty of the faith Merlin had so carefully nurtured. After a long pause, Uther straightened, nodded to a row of councilors flanking him and sat down with a grunt in a high backed chair. Gawain let out his breath. At the same time, the company around him roared back into life.

Dear God above. Gawain tore his eyes away from the Battle Lord. He picked up his goblet and stared at the red wine rippling in tiny waves below its rim. He steadied his hand. *Merlin, are you ready for this? Can you cross into this man's mind and control him as you say? If so, surely your magic is even greater than the Far Druid's.*

The king would not be ready for the potion for hours yet. Gawain took a long slow drink and forced himself to settle down. For the first time in years, he would miss vespers. *In nómine Patris, et Fílii, et Spíritus Sancti.* The words were a balm for the panic threatening to engulf him. Then a brooding thought followed: *And do I kill in His name also?*

He looked around at the battle-hardened lords and barons, recalling his father's warning when they set out from Collamoor earlier that day. "You must never trust these men; they'll take from you anything they can profit by. We are and must always remain alone in this venture."

It would take a great deal more than Uther's death to change this world into the one Merlin envisioned, thought Gawain, watching them swill back mead from their beaten silver goblets. "All the lords you'll meet there are Uther's men," his father said when he brought round the horses that chilly morning, "chosen by him, appointed by him, ruled by him. They live in perpetual fear of his every whim not knowing one day to the next whether they'll be lord or peasant. He selects them for their subservience, not their abilities. As long as he rules and they're loosed upon our kingdom to leech the land, there will be no light, no faith in what is right-there will, and only can be, a lust for what is bestial."

The three of them had ridden out from the holdfast then, hooves grinding on the rough path and for the first time Gawain could remember, Merlin looked tired and somehow older.

At the far end of the hall, near windows overlooking the raging sea, a small group of musicians clad in red and white tunics, opened events with a piece Gawain recognized as Provencal. He was just beginning to tap his fingers on his thighs in time with the light chords when he heard a growl. He turned in time to see Uther hammer his fist down on the table.

The players froze. Plates and goblets jangled. The hall fell silent. Nodding nervously to each other, the ensemble quickly struck up a Welsh victory song and the dark scowl disappeared from Uther's face like a passing storm cloud. He turned and opened his arms expansively, a smile revealing stubs of brown teeth. Then he set to stamping his feet and clapping his huge calloused hands. Below him, the hall roared approval.

Gawain felt for the Sithean Bauble. He glanced across the room and caught his father disappearing through one of the archways. *On his way to Rafe Castle, to prepare Arthur and Igraine. All as you planned, Merlin.*

Time crawled after that and the hall grew more boisterous. Dice clattered. Lord Monmouth, whose leather doublet was unlaced to the chest, tossed a handful of struck-coins across his table. A knight dressed in wide ringed mail, stopped to look, a flagon in one hand, a haunch of venison in the other. At the high table the Battle Lord gorged on, flames from a burning oil embrasure bathing him in a mixture of black and deep demonic red.

Finally, after a long drawn out ballad, the music stopped. Uther shoved his plate aside. He grabbed his chalice and drained the wine, sending a crimson river flooding down his royal tunic. Servants appeared, heads bowing furiously as they set to clearing away the food. The eating was over.

Time.

Sweet Jesus. Gawain rose. Palming the Bauble in his pocket, he excused himself and made his way to the stairwell. He slipped into the deepest recess, closed his eyes and cleared his mind. After a pause, he breathed the invocation.

"Hreran mid hondum."

The ancient words wove their magic instantly. Webbing spidered across the smooth face of the Bauble.

"Hreran mid hondum."

Fuzzy gray lines took shape, lifting from its surface like smoke rising from embers. Twisting and writhing, they coiled around him. Then, vibrating soundlessly, they found the harmony they sought and knitted into an airy thinness that shielded him from the visible world. He released his energy into the Sithean web the way Merlin taught him and he felt a tremor as the weave strengthened and then locked. He'd be safe now – at least until the energy dissipated.

Although the room appeared gloomy from behind the webbing, Gawain could still make out Uther's image in the distance. He stepped out from the shadows of the stairwell and into the unnatural silence of the hall. It had become a ghostly parody of the living world, everyone and everything in it drained of color – no orange flames fanned up from the open hearth, there were no gold crested helms or blue in the tapestry skies; all were simple, eerie shades of gray.

No matter how many times he'd experienced the web's effects, he still felt the nausea of disassociation. It was like being in the place dreams began, he'd told Merlin after one of his long lessons.

As he moved, the world before him shimmered. According to his speed, objects shifted in light intensity from gray to silver and finally to white, where they became indistinguishable from each other. He knew he must be vigilant in this ghostly realm or all would be lost. The dilemma – walk too quickly and you'd end up bumping into things you couldn't see, walk too slowly and you would become a shadow that might catch a keen eye. He readied himself, judged his pace and crossed to the wall.

Safe.

Taking a deep breath, he stole forward hand trailing along the rough-cut stone as he watched the images to his right mouthing laughter and clanking soundless tankards. Nearing the last group of lords, he saw a silvery white dish slide off a servant's tray, hit the ground and spin in circles. He didn't stop. He kept tight to the wall – the faintest of shadows in the dim candlelight.

He crept ahead until he reached the fireplace and the raised floor where Uther's table stood under the yellow pall of the oil embrasures. It was less than ten paces from the corner of the hearth to where the king sat with his councilors. He must be quick, but steady – if he waited too long by the fire, his shadow would become visible. Also, once in the open, he wouldn't be able to hear anyone behind him. It had to be done in a single movement.

He slipped the pouch containing the *Hebbona* powder from his pocket and left the wall. Suddenly Uther grabbed for a wine flagon. He grunted, shook it, then turned it over and peered stupidly up the neck. Gawain halted, wary. He watched Uther yell mutely and then thump the empty vessel on the table. The king's glare swept past the fireplace in search of a retainer. For one heart-stopping moment, Gawain thought he'd been seen and he shrank back against the wall, seeking cover of the gray stone.

What happened next caught him totally by surprise. He doubted even Merlin could have predicted it. Uther drew back the empty flagon and hurled it at the fireplace. His aim was poor and the vessel smashed silently against the edge of the chimney.

Pain erupted in Gawain's head as sharp fragments of earthenware bounced off the stone and tore through the webbing. He gasped as each piece ripped the mesh holding his life force together. The shock was wholly unexpected. He felt as if a volley of arrows had struck him. His head swam with the pain of the raw intrusion. Then he heard muffled sounds. The Sithean web was collapsing!

Knowing he would be seen within seconds, Gawain closed his eyes and concentrated on the invocation. He focused his mind, pushing away the pain and growing fear as he searched for his life force. Castle sounds were breaking through the silence all around him. He turned in panic. Firelight flickered behind him. He gasped. Three holes gaped over his right shoulder where the Sithean web should have been.

"Hreran mid hondum." He fought the rising fear.

"Hreran mid hondum." He chanted the words desperately, forcing his mind to bond the weave.

"Hreran mid hondum." The invocation was holding the web together, but no matter how hard he tried, he couldn't close the breach at his shoulder. He looked up. Now he could hear the Battle Lord's fist hammering on the table, hear him yelling for the new flagon, face red, spit flying from his purpling lips.

Gawain turned sideways in an effort to hide the tears in the web and shield himself from keen eyes. Desperately, he started for the shelter of the stairwell. But, just as the room began to blur, he caught sight of something that stopped him in his tracks-a servant hurrying from the kitchen to the king's table. On top of the tray he carried sat a white jug embossed with Uther's royal crest.

Take a chance – find a way.

Surrounded by a jumble of muffled voices and clanking echoes, Gawain moved. Praying the inexplicable sight
of a floating shoulder and part of an arm would go unnoticed, he cut between tables as the servant neared. Keeping
his eye on the wine, he closed alongside. He drew out the
pouch and matching the man's steps, slipped the contents
into the jug. The nervous servant whose attention was riveted on the Battle Lord never noticed the faint splash, or felt
the bump as the tray caught Gawain's hand after he drew
back the empty pouch and stepped clear.

Done.

Gawain let out a sigh and stole back to the wall. He
waited until the servant delivered the jug, then turned to the
stairwell ... and froze. Less than three feet away, two inquisitive eyes were staring at him – right though him. Brynmor,
a warlord from the Rhondda Valley, black wine streaks glistening in his beard, appeared to be trying very hard to
understand what was causing the distortion between him
and the wall. Instinctively, Gawain backed up shielding his
shoulder. Brynmor blinked, squinted and took a curious step
forward. Gawain knew the breech showed a small circle of
stone behind him, but what did it look like with a shadow
sliding across its surface?

He backed up further.

Brynmor reached out slowly, sweeping his hand in
front of him like a blind man. To Gawain's left, two benches angled toward the center of the hall. The lords either side
sat hunched over the tables deep in conversation. Keeping
his shoulder low, Gawain slipped between the benches and
stood perfectly still. Brynmor grunted when he caught the
momentary change in light.

Gawain held his breath and waited. Brynmor swiveled
his head from side to side, eyes narrowing as they searched.

Murmuring the invocation, Gawain backed along the
hall. At the flicker of movement, Brynmor slid a bright

edged dagger from his belt. Gawain checked over his shoulder. A dash to the hall and he'd make the stairwell in less than twenty paces.

He was about to chance the run when one of the lords to his left unexpectedly blurred. The hazy figure rose and stepped out from behind the bench. When he shimmered back into focus, he was standing between Gawain and the hall.

Brynmor closed. The lord, who stopped to reach back for his chalice, caught the puzzled expression on Brynmor's face. Then his eyes dropped to the dagger in his hand.

Gawain seized the opportunity. He tapped the broad shoulder blocking his way. The lord spun to his left. Gawain deftly slipped to his right. A brief scan showed a clear path down the hall to the safety of the stairwell. Hunching, he ran and the benches, tables and barons writhed into dangerous smoky shadows as he flew by.

Several yards before the pillars at the base of the stairs, Gawain slowed, erring on the side of caution. The images in the hall swam back into view. He shot a quick look over his shoulder. Brynmor was talking to the lord now, one hand scratching his beard, the other sheathing the dagger.

Gawain ducked into the stairwell breathing a sigh of relief. When his nerves steadied, he ended the invocation. The Sithean web dissolved and he felt the stomach-churning shift in perception. The colors of the hall and the clear sounds of laughter burst around him as if he'd surfaced from deep water and he held onto a pillar to fight the rising nausea.

Uther!

He edged around the stone curve. The king was hunched forward talking to one of the white haired councilors. The old man suddenly threw his head back and cackled. Uther nodded, swept up his tankard and drained the last of the wine.

Final thing – secure safe access to the bedchamber.

When his heart had stopped pounding and the nausea had worn off, Gawain returned to his table. Monmouth's dicing had drawn the others away from the two adjacent benches. *Now, the next move.* The world so violent within and without. *Merlin, we're so close.*

Taking his seat, he reached for a rib of venison stacked on a platter. Lord Powes turned away from the gambling. Gripping the edge of Gawain's table, he leaned back, one eye from an old sword wound glazed over, the other glinting in the low light. "Money'd say there'd be a lot of people who'd like to know where ye got that nick, young lord."

Gawain followed the flinty glance. A bloodstain had blossomed like a rose on his shoulder. His mind whirled. *That's why the tears in the web were irreparable. The wound's the source of the breach in the life force – as long as the blood flowed, the web couldn't close.*

"I . . . . It happened this morning, my lord, when I . . . I was practicing in the armory. It must have opened when . . ."

Powes' raspy voice cut him off. "Aye, lad, that's as maybe. But ye be mindful. This is Uther's lair yer in, not some Christian gathering hall." His single eye drifted toward the king, then, without another word, he turned back as dice clattered down the length of the table.

Silently thanking God for the warning, Gawain slipped his cloak off the back of the chair and pulled it tight around his shoulders.

Time seemed to crawl after that. The barons got drunker and Uther grew louder. He bellowed and grunted and cursed and drank, but he never seemed to tire. By mid-night Gawain began to despair.

After a final Welsh lament from the musicians, the Battle Lord pushed himself away from the table, threw up his massive fists and stretched. Grease and honey glistened on his knuckles. His beard gleamed with threads of wine. He yawned loud enough to turn heads at the back of the hall then he roared for his retainers. As they closed in, he held out his arms like the wings of a giant bat and draped them over the proffered shoulders. Half awake, half asleep, he staggered through the door under the growing influence of Merlin's drug.

Gawain forced himself to wait until the musicians played out their last few songs, then he slipped away from the banquet hall and headed up the wide staircase. By now the Hebbona would be taking hold. At the top, the steps flattened out to a wide foyer lit by torches angled from iron cones bolted high on the walls. Merlin had taught him well. This part of the castle seemed almost familiar after the exacting lessons.

Down the unlit passage to his left lay Uther's war room. At the rear stood a heavy door banded with iron. If Merlin had done his job, it should appear locked but a simple pull of the latch would open it. Beyond the door, a small set of stone steps wound up to a hallway that in turn led to the king's bedchamber. Close by, he'd find guards posted but again Merlin had prepared. He'd written a hidden glyph on the wall opposite where they stood. The Runes he'd chosen would create a faint image on the stonework. When the guards looked at it – and they would, because the essence would attract them as nectar attracts bees, said Merlin – they'd begin to feel a deep sense of longing. At first, they'd see in the glyph something they desired – something to drink or eat perhaps. Then they'd see more – gold maybe, or a woman. The glyph would fuel their growing desires, fleshing out every detail of their fantasy. As their dreams grew, so would their belief in attaining them. After an hour, you'd be able to lay siege to the castle with a hoard of Saxons and they'd no more than blink, Merlin had added with one of his rueful smiles.

Gawain set off down the darkened passage to the war room. Nearing the entrance, he heard voices behind the door. He stopped. Servants. He'd be hard pressed to explain what he was doing here at this time of night. He palmed the Bauble and began the invocation. When the webbing had cocooned him, he checked for gaps – nothing. The breach had closed now the wound had stopped bleeding.

Gawain inched open the door. Directly ahead stood a long table covered with maps of Uther's kingdom. Candles dripping wax burned in heavy brass holders on the wall. Two servants were clearing away chairs and removing royal seals. At the far end of the room, he could just make out the banded door guarding the final staircase. He edged through the entrance and ducked into shadows cast by racks of spears.

Gawain judged the distance from where he stood to the door at the far end to be roughly fifty yards. He picked a clear route and the world blurred as he ran. Thirty paces and he stopped. The room swam back into black and white focus. One of the servants, a balding, pot-bellied man in a stained tunic, had glanced up as he'd passed but that was all. At most, he would have appeared as a fleeting shadow thrown by the candles.

Just ahead stood the final door leading to Uther's chamber. Two marble gargoyles flanked the upper lintel, their curved claws glinting with reflected light. Gawain's stomach tightened.

An iron latch, shot through with a padlock, secured door. Trusting in Merlin, Gawain grasped the handle and slid the bolt to the side. The image of the padlock remained undisturbed. The door swung open. He slipped through closing it quietly behind him. He ceased the invocation and the perception shifted. As the web collapsed, a wave of tiredness washed over him. Breathing heavily now, he started up the steep staircase, the ache in his wounded shoulder growing into a nagging pain.

The stone steps wound around the central column in a tight spiral. Gawain felt for the wall as he ascended and the sounds below faded. A short while later he saw light from a passage beyond a small postern spilling across the top step. This door too was unlocked. He eased it open.

As Merlin had predicted, two sentries were guarding Uther's sleeping quarters but from the angle Gawain looked, he couldn't tell if they were under the influence of the glyph or not. They stood feet apart, hands resting on the ringed hilts of their broadswords. At least it meant Uther was in his bedchamber.

For the last time Gawain palmed the Bauble. He began the invocation, stepped through the small door and when the webbing knitted, stole silently down the passage.

He could always blur into invisibility if necessary. But there was no need; the two were lost somewhere in the dreamy depths of desire and he slipped by easily, maintaining the Sithean web only as a precaution.

A little further, past a windowed alcove where drafts from the howling winds blew across the hall, lay Uther's chamber. A heavy door appeared out of the thick walls as Gawain approached. Wrought iron bands crossed diagonally. Above the lintel, another gargoyle leered down, this time with its mouth open and blunt teeth gleaming.

Time.

Gawain slid the latch to the side, eased the heavy door open and slipped inside. Moonlight streamed through arched windows, cutting the room into swaths of silver light. At the far end, he could see a massive four-poster bed and the vague shapes of three high-backed chairs. To one side stood a low table and a yawning fireplace, to the other a high chest of drawers. *Be cautious. Maintain the web. Check on Uther.*

Whispering the invocation under his breath, he crossed the cold flagstones. Although shadows hid most of the bed, he could clearly see the polished gargoyles perched on top of each post. If Uther were sleeping with his eyes open, it would mean he was under the influence of the *Hebbona*. All he'd have to do then would be to leave the chamber door ajar as a signal to Merlin all was well and then wait for the wizard to do his part.

"Hreran mid hondum."

He stole closer, the webbing safely cloaking him. An odd thought occurred to him as he passed through the streaming moonlight. *Do I leave a shadow?* His foot bumped over the edge of the lush carpet. On then quietly to Uther, shades shifting, mottling the room as a cloud passed before the moon. He caught a glimpse of a copper ewer atop a table. On the wall above the bed crossed longswords shone in the pale light.

"Hreran mid hondum."

Somewhere deep in the castle he heard muffled sounds of shouting and laughter. Then silence. Two more steps and he felt the braided tassels hanging from the bedspread brush against his knee.

Gawain looked down at the hump under the quilt – the sleeping king. He grasped a corner of the coverlet. *Will your eyes be open, Uther of these wild lands?* He gently pulled. And the answer to his question he would never know, because at that moment the impossible happened.

The drawn coverlet did not reveal the king but a woman curled up, sleeping next to him. When the sheets moved, her eyes flew open and she snarled into action. Even from behind the Sithean webbing, he heard that growl. The blood drained from his face. He fought back the faintness threatening to drown him and sought for something, anything to tell him this was not happening. *Sweet Lord. Dear Jesus and the Saints above.* But try as he might, he couldn't change who he was looking at – Athlan! His hands went out to her but she was already grabbing for the knife on the headboard.

She was Athlan yet not Athlan. Gawain gaped at her stupidly as she scrambled off the bed and passed through one of the moonbeams. The light revealed a face writhing with knots and humps of muscle; loose folds of skin distorted her left eye, making it droop into a milky white teardrop. Her lips were little more than bloodless lines slashed below a collapsed nose. She looked like a walking corpse.

He must have stayed still too long because her one good eye suddenly widened, filling with panic and she jerked straight. She had seen him! Switching the knife into her right hand, she lunged. He stumbled backwards, barely escaping the gleaming blade.

Athlan.

She exploded after him, one hand sweeping out in front, the other hacking the air wildly.

"Athlan!"

This time he called her name but the web muted his voice. He backed up, seizing her wrist. She screamed at his touch and tore free. He sidestepped almost tripping over the edge of the carpet and she swung at him again, scarecrow hair wiry straight, face twisting beyond recognition.

He managed to evade the next chopping swing and grabbed for her again but she was cat quick. She cut inside reefing the knife up. He wheeled left crashing into the bed table and sending a ewer smashing to the floor. She slashed as he stumbled and the deadly blade found its mark. Slicing through the webbing, it sank handle-deep into his stomach.

His hand went to the wound and he staggered back, knees buckling. Her lips writhed over her mottled gums as she drew out the knife. He tried to call her name again, but the desperate words would not come.

Slowly, the webbing began to disintegrate and somewhere in the darkening part of his mind, he thought of all her beauty and he held his bloody hands out to her like the lover he once was.

When disembodied hands materialized in the air before her, Athlan wailed in terror. She drew back the blade and slashed again. But this time her aim arced wide and Gawain, falling to his knees, threw himself forward. The web dissolved and with it came a rush of light and sound. He heard her cry out as he crashed into her legs and sent her tumbling backwards. And he heard too, a sickening crack as her head struck the stone wall behind Uther's bed.

Silence then – so absolute, he thought for a moment he was back inside the webbing.

With the yawning edges of the world darkening around him, he dragged himself to the wall where Athlan lay. He sat, back against the stone and looked down stupidly at the blood pulsing from his wound. Trembling, he tried to staunch the flow but his hands simply slid down into his lap, palms up, twitching like the wings of a dying bird.

Athlan's head lolled back, blood seeping through a gash in her scalp and matting her wild spiky hair. Tears welled as the awful truth set in and Gawain wept for what he had become on that fateful night – a killer at twenty-one, of the only woman he had ever loved.

Time stretched and the moon shone on, its silver light rippling over the pitted floor like a thin wave on a pebbled beach. He had no voice to call or strength to ask what had happened to change his Athlan into the creature that had stabbed him. He simply sat there, legs apart, the blood running from his wound, down the inside of his arms and pearling from his fingertips. In the awful stillness, he felt his life leaving him. He looked up at the leering gargoyle with its pitiless eyes and blunt teeth and in his mind, the words were ridiculously strong:

It is done, Merlin, as you asked – unimpeded access.

CHAPTER FIVE

The light falling on him then was not silver, but gold. From a place far away, Gawain struggled to lift his head and when he did, he saw a misty shape drifting toward him. It wavered and flickered like a candle flame. A voice whispered from the center of the eerie radiance and its loving tones eased his pain.

"Stay still, young one. You've done well. Uther will be ours yet."

The wizard drew a Rune above him and then laid his hands on his wound stemming the flow of blood. Gawain felt the power of life splutter through his veins and the golden haze around the wizard slowly faded.

"Merlin. What ... what have I done?" he groaned.

"What was necessary, young one."

"I've killed her."

"No, he did, with the help of the Dark Druids." The wizard looked toward the body on the bed. His voice was deep and penetrating. "This is their handiwork, the way of their kind."

He turned to Athlan and ran the crook of his finger tenderly down her cheek. "We will return you to the earth in peace, as you were born, little one."

He slipped the royal quilt off the bed and gently covered her. Then he drew a Rune on the flagstones at her feet. When he'd finished, he whispered the sacred words and the Rune snaked around her ankles in wisps of gauzy light. Sighing, he placed his hands on his knees and pushed himself up.

"He has a special talent for killing, does this king," he said. "We must move soon. The opportunity won't present itself again. If he wakes as himself in the morning, he won't rest until he finds out who got so close to him."

"I ... "

Merlin held up his palm. "Perhaps when I enter him, I can find out the things you wish to know. But for now, if her death is to mean anything, we must concentrate on finishing our task. First, I must restore the essence I channeled into you." He paced to the window hands clasped behind his back. "Unfortunately, I won't have the luxury of taking his mind while the *Hebbona* is at its strongest. Controlling him now will be a lot more difficult."

He turned and Gawain saw doubt clouding his eyes. "While I rest, so should you. The wound is sealed but there is still much inside to heal. Is there pain?"

"A little. Not much."

"Good."

He gazed out of the window for a long moment, then he pulled the chord of his tutor's robes tight around his waist and crossed to the bed. "Now it starts," he breathed quietly, looking down at the battle-scarred face. "The *Hebbona* should hold him until dawn. Pray with great devotion to your Christian God that I'll be able to control him after that. Wake me the moment the sky lightens," he added settling down next to the king and closing his eyes.

Gawain struggled to his feet and crossed to the window seat. He sat on the cold stone with his back to the death and stared into the night. Alone in the room with the body of

Athlan, he tried to fight back the hopelessness of going on without ever seeing her again. Outside, the great waves of the Celtic Sea roared and boomed against the sheer cliffs sending plumes of spray funneling up the castle walls. Moonlight shone between horsetails of white clouds in the dark sky and he shivered when a draft blew through the cracks in the casement.

His loneliness soon became too much to bear and he left the window and went to where she lay. He sat on the cruel floor beside her and pulled her to him. In the growing chill, he kissed her neck, her brow, her pale lips. Then he laid his cheek against her blood soaked hair and rocked himself to sleep.

A pearl gray light spilled over the far eastern hills heralding another short December day. Subtle changes stole slowly across the frosty headland and from somewhere in the castle grounds, a cock crowed and Gawain stirred.

His hand went to his stiff neck as he awoke to the horrors of the previous night. Wincing, he slipped his numb arm from around Athlan and laid her tenderly back on the floor.

His stomach ached when he stood but the sleep had helped the healing and now he felt stronger. He went to the bed and gently shook Merlin. The wizard blinked.

"I want to give her a Christian burial – away from this place."

Merlin sat up, rubbing the cold from his arms.

"I'd like the priest from Caer Dunnod."

"Of course, my boy, of course. First, though, we must hide her. She cannot be found here. When our work's done, we'll come back and then I promise you'll have the priest and the burial you want."

"And we'll find out what happened?"

"That we will," said Merlin gripping Gawain's shoulder as he struggled off the bed. "How is the wound?"

"Much better," said Gawain rolling up his tunic and showing Merlin the pink flesh where the knife had entered. "It's almost healed."

"True," said Merlin tracing the outline of the wound with his finger and inspecting the surrounding area with soft prods. "Any pains?"

"No, nothing."

"Good."

They carried Athlan's body between them to a small room behind the east wall and laid her carefully amid spare sheets and blankets. When they returned to the Royal Chamber, Merlin went to the window and glanced up at the gray belly of clouds.

"How does Uther see you, I wonder?" he muttered.

Turning back to Gawain, he said, "I have one more task for you, my boy. As you know, when I make the crossing, my body will remain here. At that time, I'll be conscious only in Uther. Although the power is strong within me, it's far from complete. Indeed, it may not be enough to suppress his will, so you must be close at hand in case I need you. Here, take this." He dug into the pocket of his robe and pulled out a small ring – a tarnished silver band wreathed with dragons linked tongue to spiny tail.

"It's my connection to you. By wearing it, we'll be bonded through an essence glyph. It will provide us with limited communication. Be prepared though, when I contact you, it will be a strange experience. And it'll have to be brief. I won't be able to direct much energy away from Uther or he'll soon gain a foothold."

"Is it Far Druid?" said Gawain taking the ring and inspecting the snaking dragons.

"Nothing so special, I'm afraid. Go on, put it on. It was a gift from a woman I knew long ago in Penwrith."

"A woman?"

Merlin huffed. "You don't think these veins ran with fire once?"

Gawain slipped the ring over his finger, trying to picture Merlin courting, wondering if he had to use magic to capture hearts.

The wizard glanced at the gathering dawn. Then he gripped Gawain's shoulders, hawk eyes lightening to the green of spring lichen. "You've proven yourself brave beyond your years, my boy. In you lies the seed of new dreams, a way to a better future." He nodded at the bed, his voice losing its strange hesitancy. "Let's take this animal and use him to open the door to a newer, kinder world."

Merlin leaned over the body of the sleeping king studying it. "Remember, stay close or the ring won't work," he said, flashing a look at Gawain.

"I will."

"Then it begins."

He lay down next to the king and held his hand as a child would hold a father's and without another word, he closed his eyes, released the essence and began the crossing.

At the same time Merlin's body relaxed, the vacant eyes of Uther fluttered and Gawain felt a fleeting warmth ripple through the ring. All he could do now was to wait.

Outside, the flat gray light sharpened into beams of early sun; the haunting cries of herring gulls and a voice of someone calling out a greeting below broke the morning stillness. Uther remained motionless. The cock crowed again and in the courtyard, a horse whinnied. Gawain started. Uther's eyes suddenly blinked open, wide, like a hawk's.

The king grunted and heaved himself into a sitting position. Gawain backed away as a huge hand groped for the bedpost and Uther struggled to his feet. The scarred face turned to him, jaw working up and down with audible clicks, thick lips oddly slack. "I don't know how long ... I

100

can hold him, my boy. He's ... much stronger than I thought," the voice rumbled. "We must convene the lords immediately. Ready the war room. I'll ... give ... orders ... ."

Uther swayed dangerously for a moment, then he straightened up, let go of the bedpost and lurched across the room.

Gawain glanced back apprehensively at the figure of Merlin lying in the early dawn light and with a prayer on his lips, he hurried into the hallway after the hulking Battle Lord.

The guards remained transfixed before the glyph. Uther stumbled by them without a glance. When he reached the end of the passage, he paused. Making a stiff-legged turn to the left, he grasped the iron handrail and lumbered down the steps leading to the retainers' quarters.

At the bottom, he turned to Gawain, sweat running in thin lines from his temples down his cheeks and disappearing into his great ragged beard. "We must get ready ... get the papers signed." His breath rattled reminding Gawain of the last sounds the dying make on a battlefield.

A few more clumsy steps and Uther reached the first of three arched doors. Raising his massive fist, he pounded on the oak panels. "Bron, Ludens, up, up, you lazy bastards ... I want everybody in the War Room, now," Merlin thundered in Uther's voice.

Gawain could see the battle raging as Merlin strove to maintain control: the dewlap lips trembling, the jaw working, temples pulsing behind drum-tight skin.

"Gawain, I must rest ... I need darkness. Ready the war room. Tell the lords I have an important ... announcement. Send Aritrades to me before I ... I ... rest."

He paused, his breath coming in jerky rasps. "Whatever ... happens, do all in your power to bend their will ... to Arthur." He'd barely finished when the door flew open and a red-faced retainer emerged, tugging a leather belt tight around his ample waist.

"Lord," he said bowing with a grunt.

"Ludens, you lazy oaf ... follow Lord Gawain's every word ... or I'll have your sorry hide, I will," Uther growled lumbering off as Ludens straightened up.

Gawain tapped the retainer on the shoulder, directing his attention away from the Battle Lord's awkward stride. "Ludens, Uther has asked me to have you ready the war room for a meeting of the lords."

"But sir, they've had no warning, they're still sleeping," Ludens protested, glancing after the king. "They'll be furious if they're woken at this hour."

"Would their fury match Uther's?" said Gawain stepping in front of him.

"I beg you, sir, speak to the king. Have him call the meeting later, after the lords have rested."

"Ludens, I don't think you understand. The meeting is to take place immediately. There's no room for negotiation, here. Uther's ill. Did you not see him? Whatever he's preparing is of vital importance to us all. He needs to be helped, not questioned. He needs you, *I* need you, Ludens." Gawain spoke as his father had spoken to the sentries at the gate – quietly, purposefully. Ludens took a deep breath and nodded.

"As you will, sire."

"Good, and tell them of Uther's illness. Warn them he may act strangely, that he's likely to become easily angered if he's questioned or crossed. He's already sent for remedies but it's unlikely they'll arrive before nightfall. After the meeting, he'll need to rest until they get here."

"Yes, sire."

Gawain turned as a young servant with carrot red hair and a round freckled face, hurried toward them from the adjoining chamber. Ludens beckoned him. "Bron can prepare the war room, my Lord."

And with that, Ludens gave another awkward bow and hurried off to the Castle's west wing where the barons were quartered.

Gawain turned to the nervous youth. "Perhaps it would be best if you ordered food for our guests first – something hot to take the chill out of the bones. I'll meet you in the war room when you've finished."

"Of course, my Lord." Bron crushed a basinet helm over his unruly hair, snapped the strap shut and fled down the passage to the kitchens.

Gawain needed time alone in the war room to arrange the seating so he could ensure easy access to the gargoyle door. Hurrying down the turret stairs, he subconsciously rubbed the Dragon Ring. A warming glow spread around his finger and he stopped under an oil lamp to look at the entwined dragons. Is this how you see us, Merlin, chasing in circles? Or is this your vision of a new future where Druid and Christian unite?

He flexed his hand and continued down the steep steps, stemming the urge to touch the crucifix that seemed to burn beneath his tunic.

The war room was clean but deathly cold. Gawain crossed the stone floor and opened a lancet window. Terns and petrels dipped and glided far out over swelling seas. A raw west wind battered the tower walls and far below, the waves rolled and broke over great jagged rocks in hissing arcs.

He leaned over the ledge, watching the clouds shoulder their way across the bruised morning sky. "Will we prevail, Athlan? Will Arthur bring peace to our world as Merlin claims?" he muttered. Then drawing in a long breath, he added. "As long as I live, I'll not rest until I find those responsible for what happened to you."

103

"My lord?"

He turned to see carrot-red hair sprouting from beneath a polished helm.

"It's all right, Bron, I was thinking out loud, that's all."

"Oh, sorry sire."

"Have the cooks been notified?"

"They're on their way as we speak, my lord."

"Good. A fire would perhaps make things more comfortable, don't you think?"

"I'll get right to it." The lad bowed and rushed off to gather wood.

After he'd gone, Gawain began arranging the seats. He was pulling up the last of the high backed chairs when Ludens entered, face pale, eyes downcast. The Lords Bannack and Salisbury swept in close behind. Bannack, who was almost as big as Uther, kicked out at a chair as he passed.

"A plague on him. This had better be bloody well worthwhile. Damn, damn, that bastard's done this on purpose. It's just like him to get us up like this without so much as a by your leave. I'm telling you, Renly, he's playing us for fools."

Salisbury, who looked more like a harried shopkeeper than a lord, followed at Bannack's heels, pulling his cloak around him.

"Ulrich, you don't suppose he's going to bring up the Brittany thing again, do you?"

Bannack stopped in his tracks and glared at his disheveled friend. "If that stupid arse so much as looks toward France, I swear I'll take a blade to him myself."

He turned as Lords Monmouth, Glastonbury, Glamorgan and Somerset entered though a far archway.

"By Sauron's teeth, he'll pay for this," Glamorgan was saying.

"I treat my damn hounds better," said Glastonbury, a bright silver helm tucked under his arm, neat tunic of white and blue squares uncharacteristically gaping at the throat. "Perhaps someone should teach him a lesson in civility."

"And just who among you would be willing to give our Battle Lord such a lesson, I wonder?" cut in Monmouth knotting the laces of his leather doublet.

The comment brought a moment of sober reflection.

"Here come the others," announced Somerset.

The room began to fill. Soon all the seats were taken and the last few lords stood in groups around the fire grumbling as they huddled for warmth.

The cooks arrived and placed wooden trenchers of venison, lamb and mint sauce on the war table. Before long, the room began to take on the aroma of steaming meat. The cooks and potboys returned with flagons of wine and beaten goblets. Gawain mingled with the few guests he knew while he kept a wary eye out for Uther.

The lords complained bitterly as they ate and swilled back the hot wine. Despite the roaring fire, the room remained chilly, matching their mood. Finally, the gargoyle door burst open and Uther rumbled in. The strain still showed on his face as the battle for control raged within him, but Gawain was relieved to see he looked stronger, more in command – more like Uther.

The barons ceased their grumbling and bowed as one.

"Be seated, my lords. It's good of you to come on such short notice. What ... what I have to say won't take long. Please, sit." Despite his stiff walk, he no longer lurched.

He was dressed in a padded surcoat of royal velvet. Over the top, he wore ringed mail that ended in a skirt below his knees. He leaned gloved fists on the table while he waited for the lords to settle. Gawain slipped quietly to the gargoyle door and watched.

Uther cleared his throat. "I'm ill ... I need rest until my purgatives arrive, so I'll be brief. I've called you all together to witness a royal proclamation."

Uther turned to his counselor, Aritrades, an old man whose white hair hung in wisps over the shoulders of a wine red cassock. With a nod, Aritrades deftly unrolled a parchment he carried. Gawain could see small muscles twitching under the surface of the king's face as the old man flattened out the document on the table. He could imagine the effort Merlin must be exerting to suppress Uther's will at this point. The very nature of the impending abdication was anathema to him – a betrayal of everything he had schemed and fought for over the long, bitter years.

Aritrades took two brass candleholders and placed them on the edges of the parchment. Then he stepped back and stood unobtrusively to the king's right, heating up a stick of crimson wax over a candle flame.

Uther clutched the edges of the table as he spoke. "I've decided to abdicate as your king so my son ... Arthur ... may take the throne ... in my stead."

He almost spat the final words, his voice breaking with the effort it took. In the shocked silence, his heavy breathing rattled around the hall. The lords stood transfixed, numbed by the sheer impossibility of what they'd just heard. No one moved.

"Aritrades," Uther rasped, the power draining from his voice as he clumsily tugged off a glove.

The old councilor stepped forward, held out the quill and readied the royal seal. Uther took the pen with a shaking hand, sweat beginning to run down his scarred neck. As he began to sign, his arm shuddered violently. His hand shot out straight, flinging the quill away as if it had bitten him.

The lords glanced at one another, all signs of anger wiped out by this latest, incredible spectacle. In the midst of the stony silence, a voice came out of nowhere, literally consuming Gawain.

"Help me, he's getting stronger. I don't know how much longer I can control him."

Gawain didn't hear the voice – he felt it. The words blasted their way through his mind with an urgency that made him cringe.

At that moment, Uther's head began twitching and his body shook as if it were trying to rid itself of the skin. Gawain moved swiftly. He scooped up the goose quill from where it lay by the wall. "Your majesty, allow me."

He took the quill, placed it in Uther's great paw of a hand, and guided it stiffly to the parchment. The lords gaped at the breach of protocol. They stared in disbelief as Gawain steered the hand through the motions of signing. When it was done, Aritrades quickly dusted the signature with fine chalk and blew it dry. He removed the document, folded it, then stamped the hot wax seal of Pendragon over the edges.

Uther looked up, shivers contorting the skin around his clenched jaws, "I am ... sick ... I'll rest ... Gawain," he managed. The voice had lost all its strength now and quavered in an unnaturally high tone. Holding out an unsteady arm, he gestured to Gawain.

Stunned by the shock of what they had just witnessed, the lords sat riveted in their seats. In his long and cruel life, Uther had never once asked for help. What he wanted, he plotted and schemed for, what he couldn't have, he took by force.

Gawain cupped his arm around the king's waist taking as much of his weight as he could. Together they swayed toward the door leading up to Uther's bedchamber. As they neared the archway, Uther began convulsing. His head snapped back and without warning, a long, primal growl escaped his lips and he lashed out. His massive fist caught

Gawain in the side of his face and sent him reeling into Aritrades.

Gawain crashed to the ground and lay there dazed for a moment. Blinking away the pain, he peered up through the haze at Uther and further to the gargoyle leering above the door, thinking for a moment how oddly like his dark, satanic twin it looked.

Somehow, Merlin managed to regain control and Uther's growl faded to an animal whimper.

The lords shifted uneasily in their seats. Marmsbury and Gloucester rose, hands on sword hilts. Others glanced around warily, some openly crossing themselves before they drew their weapons. Gawain struggled to his feet, head ringing.

"My lords, it's just the king's distemper, his illness. In a few hours Theodicus will arrive with the purgatives." He blinked again, the fuzziness hampering his vision. He had to stay sharp or all would be lost. "Please, my lords, peace and rest are all he needs."

They moved forward, scabbards clattering against greaves and chain mail skirts.

"How do you know all this?" demanded Marmsbury pushing in front, his keen-edged sword pointing at Gawain's chest.

"I had an audience with the king before the fit came upon him, my lord."

Marmsbury frowned. Gawain pressed. "He felt his distemper getting worse and thought it best he name Arthur in his place, in case he succumbed to the illness. He asked that each of you swear an oath of fealty to his son. He named everyone here his trusted lords and said you would all prosper under Arthur's reign."

"Arthur's a bastard, born of Merlin's trickery," said Monmouth simply, without rancor.

"That may well be, my lord, but Uther recognizes him as his son and heir," replied Gawain, searching the blur of faces for support. "He said he's made provisions for you all through Arthur."

"What provisions?" said Marmsbury slowly lowering his blade.

"He didn't confide in me, my lord. He only said those who are loyal to Arthur will reap the rewards of fealty," Gawain continued, seeking the words Uther might have used.

"Ye speak as though the king's dead a' ready, young pup," broke in a gruff voice. Gawain didn't know the man but he recognized the heavy cuirass and ancient broadsword. He was a lord from Pembroke-not a man to mince words.

"Forgive me, sire. I'm merely repeating what the king said. I, like you, pray for his health and full recovery."

The burly figure grunted. Gawain took advantage of the moment and asked for his indulgence. Then he bowed and returned to Uther's side.

Whatever Merlin had done to the king had wrought profound changes. The Battle Lord stood still now, head bent like a spent bull. Drool gathered at the corners of his mouth and crawled down his chin in pale strings. He stared ahead vacantly, arms loose at his sides. Gawain took his weight again and helped him through the iron-banded door to the stairs leading up to his royal chambers.

Uther stumbled from one step to the next. They climbed slowly, the rumble of angry voices growing in the War Room below. When they reached the postern, Gawain turned to Aritrades. His head still rang but the fuzziness had cleared. "We must ensure the safety of the parchment, Aritrades. Pick two of Uther's closest guards and take it to Igraine's castle. I don't know if the king will live to see the end of this day."

Aritrades shifted uneasily from one foot to the other. "You realize of course, young sir, this puts me in a very difficult position. Our Lord King may not look favorably upon this action. If he recovers his wits, he may wish to rescind his interdiction and if he finds out I have taken the document, he would most assuredly have me hunted down and brought before him – possibly in pieces."

Gawain studied Aritrades carefully, taking in the long white hair and darting eyes. He needed his support to lend credibility to the king's actions. Without him, the death of Uther and his own involvement would surely be called into question. Yet, he couldn't reveal any details of the plot. He decided to gamble on the old councilor's cowardice.

"Consider the consequences, Aritrades. If you don't get the document to Arthur, he may never become king. While Uther lives and Arthur remains without the official proclamation, we are inter-regnum. The illustrious lords below will soon discover this and when they do – God help us. There's only one way we can avoid a wholesale slaughter and that's to ensure Arthur's safe passage to the throne. Look at your king, Aritrades. He'll not recover, no matter what Theodicus conjures up. I have some knowledge in this area. Take my word for it when I say Uther will not see the sun set on another day."

Aritrades considered. He shot a worried glance at the drooling king then down the darkened stairwell. "Perhaps you're right young lord, but be it upon your own head."

"Good, I'll get Uther to his room and wait for Theodicus. When you get to Igraine's castle tell my father I'm safe and all's well with Vortigan and me. God speed you, Aritrades."

The old councilor opened the door and stood aside to let Gawain and Uther through. He followed and hurried off down the left branch, red cassock billowing around his gaunt frame as he disappeared.

Gawain helped Uther passed the guards transfixed by the glyph. He shouldered open the door to the royal bed-chamber and lumbered in under the growing weight of the king. Ahead, a shaft of bright December sunlight bathed the unearthly form of Merlin lying on the bed.

Gawain stumbled the last few yards, just managing to pull his arm from under the Battle Lord as he tumbled him onto the quilt.

The same time the massive body hit the bed, the Dragon Ring warmed and words boomed in Gawain's head. *No time ... . Use the potion ... I'll control him. I'm drawing on my own life force. Now! Quick! We ... hurrrrry!*

Hands still shaking from the strain of shouldering the king, Gawain fumbled in his pocket for the potion. His numb fingers stubbed the vial. They groped helplessly for a moment until found the base. He pulled out the small glass tube and after two tries, managed to work out the stopper. A strong smell of loam wafted up and he held the trembling liquid over Uther's slack mouth.

Gawain was on the verge of pouring the contents between Uther's lips when the teeth snapped shut with a jaw-breaking crunch. He snatched his hand back. The War Lord's eyes suddenly blinked open, showing a ferocity that froze Gawain's blood. An instant later, they blinked closed, another moment passed and they sprang wide again. This time they were different; they showed the opiate dullness of Merlin's failing control. They blinked again, showing hatred. Open, closed, open, closed-dullness, hatred, dull-ness, hatred. The blinking sped up, eyes blurring with speed. Then the mouth began to open and close in time with the eyes.

Gawain watched, helpless to do anything as the jaws pounded together, chipping and splintering teeth. The ring warmed again but this time no words followed. He glanced at Merlin. The gaunt body was beginning to spasm.

Then the words came, words thundering with a power that made Gawain flinch.

FOR YOUR GOD'S SAKE, NOW!

Gawain hesitated no longer. He jammed the vial between the slamming teeth. Uther spluttered and coughed as pulverized glass and loamy fluid filled his mouth and began frothing down his chin. Gawain leaned over him, jamming the lower jaw up with the heel of one hand and pinching the flaring nostrils with the other.

Uther swallowed. He bucked and jerked like a fish out of water, but he swallowed, and when he did, Gawain drew back and watched the second person he had killed that day take a last shuddering breath.

The same time Uther's body went limp, Merlin's eyes fluttered open.

"He's dead," Gawain whispered weakly unable to tear his gaze away from the bloody king.

Merlin took a few moments to find his voice and when he did, it sounded somehow older, thinner. "That he is, my boy. That he is. Never in my long life have I encountered such a barbaric will."

He sat up, holding onto the post with a shaking hand. "I had to use my own life force to control him in the War Room. If I hadn't he would have broken free and killed us all."

"My jaw will testify to that," said Gawain, pulling the royal blue and gold covers over the dead king.

"I'm sorry, my boy. I should be able to heal you in a few hours."

Merlin walked unsteadily to the casement, put a palm on the wall and throwing the window wide, took a deep clean breath. After a long pause, he spoke absently, his words private, for the elements only. "He did not see you as I see you: the poetry in your dark skies and churning waters, in your gray clouds and the soft shoulders of your earthy

112

beaches. He saw only lands to conquer and towns to take. I'm truly blessed and richer by far than ever was that indifferent beast."

He fell silent then and the mournful sounds of the sea-wind buffeting the turret filled the chamber. Finally, he turned to Gawain. "We've done the right thing, my boy. Arthur has all of his strength and indomitable will but none of his evil nature. He'll be the one to lead us now – hopefully to a time where Christian and Druid can live together in harmony. Uther's own lust brought about his death. We were merely the instruments."

He nodded toward the window. "It's all like this. We need the storms to clear the skies and then, for a while at least, the sun will show us the paths we must take and the dangers that lie in wait."

He cleared his throat and pulled the braided cord of his tutor's robe tight around his waist. "Arthur is our sun – he'll make each of our journeys a little easier, a little safer. This storm has been long in passing, my falcon."

The wind dropped and a hush fell over the room. In the distance, herring gulls cried as they circled high above the heaving sea. Gawain struggled to hold on, but try as he might, he could not help glancing at the chamber where Athlan lay.

Merlin shivered and pulled the window closed. "She was no longer the person you knew," he said softly. The wind rose again, almost drowning his next words. "She is at peace now."

He reached for the iron hasp and locked the window tight. "While I was in Uther's mind, I learned something of her fate. The Dark Druids took her a little over a month ago. Somehow they charmed her, changing her into what you saw. Afterwards they gave her to Uther. Morganna, their high priestess, arranged it all. Unfortunately, despite probing every corner of his mind, I was unable to discover her purpose or what she had planned."

A gust blew in through the cracked masonry ruffling his hair. "Morganna's magic is much stronger than I imagined. While our Runes get more difficult to hold, hers become more powerful it seems. Why, I cannot explain. I fear I've neglected my duties. I've been too busy pursuing my personal goals, I'm afraid. After we ... " He stopped when he saw Gawain was no longer listening.

He went over and sat down next to him on the edge of the bed. "Athlan never knew what happened after she was taken – there was no pain, no sorrow, nothing. She died while she was out riding that morning – her memories, her life, ended there. You need to believe that."

At his words, Gawain felt something give inside. He looked up, tears burning at the back of his eyes. In committing a mortal sin, he feared they would never meet in heaven; never know eternal joy or the grace that comes with absolution. His shoulders folded and the tears rolled down his cheeks like the sad gray waves that came to lay themselves bare on the shores of that ageless land.

Merlin slipped an arm around him, pulling him in and holding him tight. Heart breaking, temples throbbing, Gawain turned his face into the rough spun wool of the tutor's robe and gave in to his grief. As the emotions built and the last memory of that dreadful night fell into place, the bedroom began to fade. He left the lonely figure to Merlin and the distant scene dissolved.

He turned to the night. The shadow stood waiting.

CHAPTER 6

He obeyed the tender touch; Gawain, Druid, Christian, hero, regicide. Gawain, Merlin's friend, king maker – king destroyer. Gawain, who had stepped away from death's grasp with a sin forever staining his soul.

He trailed behind the shadow up the steepening path, tears still drying on his cheeks. Near the next curve, where tips of strange rubbery leaves seemed to reach out for him, he stopped. Ahead, another Terran beam shimmered between the tall shifting shapes. And for the first time on this journey, he paused, not wanting to go on. Then, from somewhere deep within, Welsh strength flowed. *I will see this end. I will find my answers.*

This light differed from the others. It shone gray and watery thin. He left the path and went to where it filtered between the deep shadows. Jaws clenched, he stood before it, watching the swirling patterns for a moment, then, slowly, he reached out.

The mist cleared. He swallowed thickly. The scene trapped in the beam showed a grave in a clearing fringed by towering elms. A fresh squall had swept across the land earlier and the high grass still drooped under the weight of clinging raindrops. There were no mourners – the funeral had ended long ago.

He stood on the edge of the path, hands cupped, staring into the beam like some wayward spy. *Dear God above.* He swallowed again. The younger Gawain was bending before a simple cross and running his fingers over an engraving on the headstone. Even from outside the beam he could feel the roughness of that granite as his image found the name and traced the chiseled letters there:

A-T-H-L-A-N.

A GIFT GIVEN. A LIFE LIVED.

Fresh violets lay beside the grave. His younger self picked them up, weaved them in a Celtic knot then looped them around the headstone. Eyes filling, Gawain watched his image kneel in the fresh mud. A rainbow suddenly arced from the sunlit clouds behind him, tingeing the treetops orange and red as he bowed his head in prayer.

He knew how much this was going to hurt. He stepped into the waiting Terran light and as he did, a name, dark and fleeting, raced through his mind: Morganna.

Life, the smell of rain-washed earth, wet wind, a distant feeling of spring. He breathed in the clean air and tasted the living world. Then the grief of the Gawain he'd entered took hold and his heart seemed to falter.

No one had known his part in her death while he stood in the quiet ceremony that morning. The old priest from Caer Dunnod had spoken the Latin words her father had written, hand extended as he intoned the dolorous phrases and made a palsied sign of a cross above the coffin. All eyes had turned heavenward then to where the swollen skies sent rain sheeting across the empty fields.

Gawain had watched while Glenned wept. Behind the coffin, hooded figures hunched together and somewhere in the high branches of a dripping elm, a magpie cawed as they lowered the body into the yawning grave and shoveled on dark clods of earth. An inviolable love to take through life. A world forever changed.

Alone now, knees sunk in the heavy mud, he recited the *Agnus Dei*. And somewhere in the safety and sanctity of those words a new truth suddenly came to him – Athlan was not the only one abducted by the Dark Druids that bitter day – there were others captured and taken to the Radnor forest – three. He concentrated and their faces flashed before him, stony-eyed, mouths slack and drooling, hair bramble wild. Then, as quickly as they appeared, the images vanished.

He blinked and found himself looking at the dripping elms again. His mind reeled. Why had he had a Druid vision in the midst of Christian prayer? But before he could pursue the conundrum, the Terran light began to dim and he felt the familiar sensation of leaving. This time he didn't fight to stay; he closed his eyes and welcomed the gathering darkness.

More pieces of the growing puzzle fell into place as the guide led him away. He walked behind, glad of the reprieve, thankful to be back on the winding path again. *The earth of her grave soft like her lips. Take these rare moments. Keep them locked away forever. Stop the loneliness from rising up like the seas of my childhood dreams. Go on. And Merlin, tell me, why is your magic failing? And your eyes, did you know they're never the same green? Always changing, you, this world, my life.*

Further on, where the path angled sharply to the left, another beam of Terran light speared through the high canopy. This beam was so bright it glittered. Shielding his eyes, Gawain left the path and groped his way through the bushes.

Where the beam lit the ground, a tangle of roots bunched up as if it were trying grasp the precious light. Vapors snaked and crawled up the column in long sheaves. Gawain could see something moving in the center. He peered closer, but the ghostly image appeared little more than a faint smudge behind the thick mist. He reached out. At his touch, the vapor cleared. His jaw dropped. Unexpected joy raced through him. The startling beauty, rather than the surprise of the captive scene, held him spellbound: rolling hills, deep furrows of a distant valley dotted with trees. From behind a line of bowing poplars a rider approached – himself, galloping west. *Yes. Oh, dear God and all the blessed saints, yes.* He stepped into the light and the healing magic, eyes misty, throat so dry it would take a river to slake.

He was returning to Caerleon, Arthur's castle, after staying with a friend in Caerphilly. The memories of his morning spent helping Dylan raise a roof over his barn greeted him as he entered the younger Gawain. Sun fired the fields with burnished gold. Ahead the shining towers of Arthur's royal city scored a wide blue sky. He breathed in the scented air and sighed as he thundered through the soft spring grass.

Camelot.

Everything Merlin promised had come true. Arthur had ascended the throne with little opposition. At first, the lords were leery of the young king, but they soon warmed to his affable nature and quick wit. The darkness of Uther had never touched him. His ambitions were noble, his dreams inspiring, but most of all, his efforts were unflagging. From the onset, he had championed the weak and looked to God for comfort and guidance.

It was Gawain's crowning glory to be numbered among his knights, and a day never passed when he had not given thanks to the Lord for blessing him with a place at the king's side. He loved Arthur like a brother. And this summer day, seeing Camelot, his joy knew no bounds.

He spurred Gringolet and galloped recklessly down the hillside. The bay charger and he were one as they splashed

118

through the Usk ford. On then, pounding up the dark earthen banks to the winding path leading to Caerleon.

In the nine years since Arthur had become king, he'd indulged himself in only one thing – the building of this magnificent castle. It stood apart from all the other structures in Camelot. The four turrets marking its design towered high above the main keep. The ramparts, built of pure white stone, joined them in massive, square abutments. The castle gleamed and on this day, it seemed to take on a life of its own.

Gawain glowed with pride as Gringolet thundered across the drawbridge. Home. The two great pennants flying high above the battlements dipped and seemed to wave to him as he cantered through the portcullis.

He slowed Gringolet to a walk when he entered the castle gardens. In the courtyard, he saw Guinevere, Arthur's new wife, talking to Sir Pelles. She was striking, even from afar. At seventeen, her thick red hair fell in tangled curls half way down her slender back, and Gawain knew when she turned, he'd see the mischievous flash in her blue eyes and he'd delight in the wide smile lighting up her freckled face.

"Your Majesty."

She spun around at the sound of his voice. Her beauty this day was dazzling, irresistible.

"Gawain!"

She ran to him, almost tripping over her long blue dress. "Arthur's most handsome knight, I do swear by all that's holy," she said, hooking her arm through his and beaming up at him. "Where have you been? No, don't tell me," she said, holding a finger to his lips, trying to look serious. "I'll be overcome with jealousy. I know you've been out rescuing young maidens from the jaws of Basilisk Dragons and consoling them when they wept for fear of the terrible death they faced. Oh, to be a maiden in peril!" She held the back of her hand to her brow feigning woe. Then she straightened and beamed at him again, her playful smile more radiant than the spring sun.

"Why so serious, brave knight?" she said stepping back, hands dropping to her hips. "I command you smile. I will not have my champion looking so grave." She waited a moment then when he gave in and smiled, she broke out into an infectious laugh and tugged his arm. "Come," she said, "Arthur's waiting at the Round Table. Do you realize, you and Pelles are the last to arrive."

"I received the message by way of the King's carrier pigeon, my lady. There was no explanation, just a command to attend the Round Table," he said as they walked through the palace gardens past rows of herbs that Guinevere had ordered grown.

When they reached the large unicorn fountain marking the entrance to the barbican, she stopped. She took his hand between hers and looked at the steps sweeping up to the castle doors.

"I shouldn't tell you this," she said in a low voice, "but I'll risk the king's displeasure if what I say will take away that stern look."

Unable to conceal her excitement, she took both of his hands and pulled him to her. Pushing up on her toes, she whispered in his ear, "The last knight has been found. He's with Arthur now. The Table's complete. Gawain, Arthur's so happy, he's beside himself." Her eyes danced with pleasure.

Gawain couldn't help but smile. "Who is he?"

She dropped back on her heels. "I didn't get too much of a look at him, but from what I saw, he seemed awfully serious and devilishly handsome. He comes all the way from France they say – his name is Lancelot du Lac."

Her last words hit him like ice water. The shock was so strong and the erupting emotion so unexpected, he felt himself slip feebly from his younger self and begin drifting toward the yawning darkness. The gardens and castle fell silent. Before him a scene of Guinevere, hands out steadying the knight who had fallen to one knee, shimmered and began to fade.

Then, out of nowhere, the pictures came. And for the first time since he'd started on his journey, he had a glimpse of the future – of things he'd lived but was yet to see. From somewhere in his mind, a door opened and a tangled mass of faces and sounds rushed forward. The images smothered him with their overwhelming urgency. He fought them back in panic, pushing them away, trying to make sense of them, to make order out of their wild chaos. Then, as quickly as they came, they vanished. The door slammed shut and he found himself alone.

Slowly, still disoriented from the terrifying experience, he turned back to the light and saw his younger self walking with Guinevere up the long wide steps toward the fated meeting. He wanted to cry out – to say no, don't go, don't see this man again, but mist swept around them as they entered the castle.

Inside, he knew where they would go – down a long wide hall to see a king and meet the knight who would start the world dying.

The weight of the future fell on him then as the magic Terran light burned mercilessly and he returned to his younger image, and to the last few moments of true happiness he would ever know.

They walked down the long wide hall under high windows stained with amber and cinnabar. The strong sunlight bathed them with shifting rays of light as they talked of the mysterious knight from distant France. At the end of the passage, Guinevere stopped and gripped Gawain's arm. "You must promise me you won't say anything to Arthur about Lancelot. I'd rather he didn't know I told you." She smiled her beguiling smile again, unaware that this was the first time first time she had ever deceived her husband.

Gawain nodded and turned to the great double doors leading to the Chamber of the Round Table. Royal escutcheons embossed each door covering more than half their towering height. He pushed one of the golden lion paws and entered. Before him, dominating the circular room sat the great table itself, hewn from an ancient oak Merlin had found at Llangollen. Cut with a charmed blade years before Arthur was born, its strange pattern of whorls and knots seemed to float magically under the soft light of the burning candles.

Each knight sat in his designated place in a high-backed chair cut from the same oak as the table. They were all dressed similarly, in black tunics and silver chain mail shirts crested with Arthur's triple lions. Emblazoned on the right shoulder was each knight's personal insignia: Bors a hammer, Percival a thistle, Gawain a griffin, Lionel a fawn - each as unique as its bearer.

Gawain had scarcely closed the doors when Arthur entered from the small chapel at the far side of the room. Despite his slight build, his presence was imposing. Unlike the silver mail shirts of the other knights, his was wrought from fine gold – a color matching his short blond hair and finely groomed beard. He was every inch a king in presence and bearing. He smiled an open greeting to Gawain as his knights bowed.

"Sir Gawain, we were fearful some maiden had way-laid you."

"You need not have worried, my lord, Pelles came ahead of me and frightened them all away."

Pelles stepped forward. "I object, sire, Gawain has it all wrong. The women were running to fetch their friends so they could look upon a true Knight of the Round Table, but alas, I dared not tarry, for I carried the king's word," he said, hanging his head.

Gawain joined in the laughter, staying his reply and letting Pelles win the small exchange – a rare feat for the powerful knight better known for his fierce loyalty than his sharp wit.

Arthur settled the room and, as was customary, said a prayer asking that each of his knights live a long and noble life. When he'd finished, he opened the meeting with issues of state. He followed with accounts of local jurisprudence and asked for a report from each knight. Finally, he begged indulgence for one last item.

"I have some good news to share," he began. "But first I have a story to tell. Last week I was out riding with Sir Lionel and Sir Turquine. We were on our way to Llanbrach when we came to the Wyvern Bridge. We saw the strangest thing as we approached – a great warrior had set up camp at the base of the footbridge. When we made to pass, he stepped forward and challenged us saying no one could cross unless they bested him in battle. Well, you know Sir Turquine, at the mere mention of a challenge, he had his sword out at the ready." Arthur looked at Turquine and smiled.

"I'll spare you all the details. Suffice it to say we settled on a joust – unfortunately, our champion fell at the first charge. The warrior who held the bridge remained unscathed. He sat atop his black horse and leveled his lance at Sir Lionel and without missing a beat, asked if he cared for some of the same." All eyes turned to Lionel who sat with lips pursed.

"Well, I'm sorry to say," continued Arthur, "he fared little better than Turquine, although I must admit it did take two passes before he was unseated." The room broke into chatter and Arthur raised a hand.

"I was next." The room fell silent; everyone knew he was no Battle Lord like his father. "I held my lance and set my pace as Ulwyn taught me. I must have been a fair sight," he said. "I galloped on, and though the bridge itself began to sway, the warrior at the other end moved not a whit. He simply sat there astride a mare as black as any midnight. Only at the last minute did he move. I swear he was quicker than a Druid's spell. He reined his horse aside and I sped right on passed. By the time I'd managed to turn my charge he was facing me, lance at the ready. I wasted no time in spurring my horse back into action. We met where the trestles began. There was an almighty clash of armor and steel and I was unseated in the fray – toppled from my mount. I was down, my lords, but not quite out." He shook his head sadly, though he seemed happy to tell the tale.

"We continued the fight with chain and mace. As God is my witness, he was as deft in movement as he was powerful in action. We fought toe to toe but with the wind knocked out of me after my fall, I was no match for him and I was soon forced to surrender.

"He took my oath with great courtesy and upon discovering who I was, offered up his weapon. Then he knelt before me: he the victor, me the vanquished!"

Visible relief showed in the faces of the knights around the table as Arthur finished his tale. "My lords," he added, scanning each one, "there can be no doubt about this warrior's prowess in combat or honor in the victory he earned. In short, I have invited him to Camelot to meet with you." Arthur's final words had lost their initial excitement and had taken on the keen edge of authority. "Lancelot du Lac, who held the Wyvern Bridge and bested your king, will join us presently and I ask that you all celebrate his triumph and witness his knighthood."

The world was so ready to welcome this proud warrior who would become the final link in Arthur's vision to forge the chain that would hold secure the most distant, dreamy peaks and valleys of his realm.

A herald dressed in a blue and white surcoat brought news of Lancelot's arrival and the curious knights flanked the throne. Moments later an old retainer bent low with the weight of years quietly opened the doors. Lancelot was standing in the shadowed entrance. The knights bowed; and he walked into their midst with a slow, deliberate stride. Halting before the king, the daunting figure bent to one knee.

"Greetings, Lancelot," Arthur said, beaming down at him.

"Mon Roi."

The French accent hung in the air as the swarthy warrior arose. He stood a full head taller than Arthur and opposite to him in almost every way. His coal black hair hung shoulder length, his face was a deep and even brown and his dark eyes, thought Gawain, were the most intense he had ever seen.

Lancelot looked directly at Arthur. "You sent for me, Mon Roi." He bowed again, this time less formally.

Arthur rose from his throne. "Yes, we have been deliberating upon your investiture." He smiled. "You made a noble conquest at Wyvern. In recognition of this victory, we wish to welcome you into our brotherhood."

Lancelot looked at the knights then at Arthur, the severity vanishing from his face, his eyes lighting with joy. "It is a great 'onor, Mon Roi."

Arthur beamed. He turned and took up a sword and scabbard from a scarlet cushion atop a footstool. "I command thee kneel, Lancelot du Lac," he pronounced in deep, solemn tones.

Lancelot did, and in the dying light of that late summer afternoon, Arthur drew Excalibur. It rang as it cleared the scabbard and when he brought it to his lips, it flashed with a shimmering brilliance that sent rays of light spearing through the gloom of the dusky chamber.

The proud warrior remained on one knee, head bent, and Arthur brought up the magical sword with measured grace until its tip was poised above the knight's left shoulder.

"For the strength given by God. For the honor of our fellowship. Do you give the word?"

"Oui."

"For the lives of those in peril. For those stained in sin. Do you give the pledge?"

"Oui."

"Deus per omnia."

"Saecula saeculorum."

Arthur lowered the coruscating blade.

"Arise Sir Lancelot."

A cheer broke out from the knights and they closed in to congratulate Lancelot. Clapping him on the back, they spilled out into the hallway leading to the courtyard. The cheering blasted into the warm afternoon as they tumbled through the wide doors and ran clamoring down the steps.

The knights crossed the inner courtyard to where Guinevere sat painting by the unicorn fountain. Arthur hailed her. She set aside her palette and ran to meet him. Every knight stopped to watch her in the late light. Her simple flowered dress swayed, blowing in the breeze as she neared. Her fiery red hair caught the last rays of the sun, and when she smiled, her face radiated a health and happiness that could only belong to someone so young and so in love. She lowered her head and curtsied.

"Guinevere," Arthur said, eyes glowing with pride, "I would like you to meet Sir Lancelot, the newest member of our Round Table."

The French knight stepped forward. He swept low with practiced grace and took her hand. He kissed it gently and dropped to one knee.

"Please, arise, Sir Knight," she said, face flushing from the touch of his lips.

Guinevere turned to Arthur. "The last knight, I'm so happy for you, my Lord."

They left the cool of the late spring garden and the gurgling fountain and made their way toward the high vaulted halls and the sacred chamber. At the top of the wide stone steps leading into the castle, Gawain turned. When Guinevere took up the palette and dipped her brush into the paint, an ineffable sadness stole its way into his heart.

At Round Table, the knights sat late into the night, telling of adventure, but Lancelot seemed removed, his words measured, his mind far away.

Darkness swept over the face of the moon from a passing cloud. In the castle, servants battened windows to ward off the approaching cold. And while Gawain stood next to a pillar, Arthur walked and talked and filled the room with his joy. And slowly, confusion building, Gawain felt the lightness of his leaving.

CHAPTER 7

Outside the Terran light, the sorrow weighed on him as the restorative magic faded. The shadow took his arm and led him back to the path. He thought of Arthur and Guinevere and of the proud French knight seated at the Table, helpless to stop the love and jealousy eating away at his heart.

Gawain trailed up the hill sorting through the many new events. Despite cautious steps, he stumbled over a twisted root and fell to his knees. He rose slowly, brushing away damp twigs and cods of earth. When he looked up, he caught a flash — another shaft of Terran light to the side and a little ahead. Hands sweeping a passage, heart thumping at the thought of the news it might bring, he ploughed through the undergrowth.

Behind the mist of this beam, the shape of a small bed wavered as if it were under deep water. Puzzling over the significance of what he was seeing, Gawain tried to recall the object from his past, but it meant nothing. Steeling himself against the changes he knew would follow when he entered the light, he reached out.

The mist cleared and in the bright scene held captive in the center of the beam, three images sprang into view. He saw himself and Merlin standing, looking down at a frail figure lying deathly still on the simple bed.

Dear God above. His stomach churned. Now he knew. The memory reached him even before he stepped forward. His father was dying.

No longer shielded, Gawain felt a wave of grief wash over him when he entered the light. He suddenly missed the hands cupping his little shoulders as a child, hands that gave strength and took away the shame of failure. All those years his father was a light as bright as any star. Gawain stood in the gloomy chamber staring down at the unconscious figure, heart breaking as he felt for Merlin's hand.

He turned to the wizard, noticing the toll the passing years had taken. His hair, once rich and thick had now thinned and lost much of its wild curl. His body had become gaunt, little more than a clothes rack for his drooping wizard's robe, and the eyes that once held the power to command kings, were now the tired green of winter seas.

Merlin leaned over the Rune staff, long braided sleeves ending at swollen knuckles. After a moment, he spoke in his halting voice. "He'll soon be at peace, my falcon. Then, if your priests have it right, the angels will speed him to his resting place."

He bent with effort and gently kissed Owyn's forehead. "He was far braver than many knew," he said straightening up. "It was his courage alone that made Camelot a reality."

He rested his staff against the edge of the bed. "This morning, when your father fell from his horse, I felt his pain sharper than any keening wind. I knew it was mortal. I reached out for him and found his aura dark and fading. But his thoughts were still lucid; they were of you."

He crossed the room, pushed the heavy door closed and snapped home the top and bottom bolts. "Without a Hebbona potion, I was unable to communicate for very long but while I was with him, he asked to see you one last time," he said returning to the bedside. "I don't know if you understand how remarkable this is. He wanted me to use my magic to help. Since that day at Tintagel, he's struggled for redemption with his Christian God — he's never forgiven himself for involving you in the killing, or calling on my blasphemous magic." He paused straightening Owyn's dark blue tunic. "But now he's asked me to help you make the crossing — if you're willing."

"Of course."

"You must travel both with me and through me. I'll be your guide. It won't be dangerous, but because we lack the *Hebbona* you won't be able to join fully with his mind. You'll only be able to listen to what he has to say and perhaps get a fleeting chance to leave a message."

"He'll be able to hear?"

"Perhaps not hear. But he'll know what you think."

"Then, I'm ready."

"As you always are, as you always are, my boy," muttered Merlin, taking out a small leather pouch from his robe and extracting a pinch of black and white powder. He ground it between his thumb and finger, then sprinkled it over Owyn's body. Next, he sifted through more folds in his long robe and pulled out two small crystal globes.

"The Currian seed will help guide us, keep us safe on our journey as you'll see. They work much like the Sithean Bauble."

Gawain took one of the shining spheres and Merlin nodded as he held it up to the light sifting in through the bedroom window. "You've ever made me proud, lad. There's so much of your father in you." He turned and looking down at Owyn, let out a long sigh. "Come, let's say farewell to an old friend."

He drew a glyph over the prostrate form then gestured for Gawain to lie on one side while he lay on the other. They joined hands across the body, and in the stony stillness, he spoke the ancient words.

At first, all Gawain experienced was a faint warmth. Moments passed and a hazy glow crept in from the edge of his vision, slowly obscuring each object in the room. Then he felt an indefinable lightness. From out of the white haze enveloping him, he saw a something moving. When it neared it took form — Merlin, and he was beaming, his perfect features made up of countless drops of clear water. He shone, refracting and reflecting all the light around him.

As Gawain watched, he found himself becoming lighter. He had the sensation of transforming into the same, vaporous image. The two forms floated toward each other and slowly began to merge. Then the world expanded. Around the single crystalline entity, a vast ring of fine white and black granules spun like lazy planets. It was a moment frozen in time, and out of that moment a thought came — a single, piercing word-thought.

I have helped kill a king and change the fate of a nation. I am a sinner but the world is better off for my sins.

Another word-thought followed.

Of all of my work, you have given me the greatest pride and satisfaction, my son. Through you, I shall live on. But now it is time to help Arthur — in my nearness to death, I've glimpsed the future and I've seen long days of darkness in its passing.

Gawain tried to speak, but there was no way to voice his question. More word-thoughts followed in simple, clear waves.

Beware Morganna and her unholy sisters. If our land is to be saved, you must find a way to stop her before it's too late. I'll not be there to guide or help you. For that, you must look to Merlin. He is true — trust him, my son.

Silence, and then the last words came in a single flash.

I love thee, Gawain. Dominus vobiscum.

And finally Gawain found voice to his own thought.

I love thee too, Father. Et cum spiritu tuo.

132

He watched the fine water drops materializing from the edges of the slowly spinning circle. They formed a trail that moved outwards, gathering speed as more and more drops ripped away from the edges and joined the growing comet. They reached an impossible brightness then finally disappeared in an arcing spiral.

When the blinding whiteness subsided, Gawain felt a slow sense of detachment and Merlin began to separate from him. After the images split, Merlin faded into a single crystal drop.

Gawain blinked.

He had returned.

They rose from the bed and stood looking at each other. Between them, the cold body of Owyn lay in peace.

"Wizardry is never achieved without a price," Merlin said at last. "What your father foretold is true. There are indeed dark days ahead. I've felt this for a long time – even before Morganna showed her talent for magic. From now on, we tread lightly, my boy – even in the court of Arthur."

Merlin went to the window, gray hair almost white in the pale light. "Although we disagreed in our faith and spent many years apart because of it, your father's passing is very hard for me. There are few his equal in this world." His thin shoulders barely filled a quarter of the window frame as he leaned over the ledge and stared out at a distant river snaking through the woodlands.

A breeze blew in, stirring the fringes of the bedspread. The room took on a deep stillness and Gawain felt the familiar experience of dissociation.

This time he didn't struggle to stay. He simply watched the scene dissolve around him as the Terran magic faded. But when it winked out, it left behind a glowing kernel – a clear memory fragment gleaned from Merlin when they'd merged. Turning to the shadow, it thrummed within him: Athlan had been in Uther's thoughts when Merlin had controlled him. She was more than a means of pleasure; she was meant to have his child.

Gawain looked around. Tall trunks with branches thick with spiky leaves loomed to his left and right, their tops mushrooming into a canopy of darkness. For the first time since he'd started on this extraordinary journey, he could see. It was like looking through thick smoke after a battle but he could see. Absently, his fingers went to the *Tarn* necklace running over the smooth gems embedded in the woven chain. The strength there was growing. He frowned, knowing it was important but unable to fathom its meaning. It didn't matter. Not yet. All that mattered was the next beam. He turned at the touch of the shadow's hand. The slender figure moved, sweeping ahead of him, but not before he caught a glimpse of dark hair framing a strikingly beautiful face.

Where the path narrowed, he stopped. Something new again, this time sounds. They came from a little way in front. He peered into the heavy gloom, concentrating. The shadow had spoken! The words were muffled and oddly distant, but he knew they were for him, and he knew also that somewhere, not far distant, this long journey had an end.

The next Terran beam differed from the others. When Gawain approached it, he found the cloudy surface denser. He puzzled over it for a moment then bracing himself for what might come next, reached out.

The mist cleared instantly and he saw his younger self on horseback riding through a fog-filled vale. *Early morning? Traveling west?* He watched the figure trek up a gentle slope then disappear into a wooded area. *Where to?* He waited, but this time there were no sensations. Tensing, he stepped into the light. His stomach churned.

The smell of turf and clover assailed him in the chill morning air, and guiding Gringolet around the sturdy oaks, he shivered. A thin sun shone down, sending beams spearing through high branches into a soupy fog that swilled around the horse's legs. Ahead, the shifting shape of Arthur's white warhorse flicked in and out of view between the trees.

The hollow echo of the king's voice called back to him. "Not long now. We're almost there."

They'd left Camelot two hours earlier and had ridden north toward the Mountains. Arthur had not said where they were going, or his reason for the early departure.

From the drawbridge of Caerleon through the silent streets of Camelot, they'd ridden side by side, the king as quiet as a cloistered monk. Gawain had tried to read his face as they passed by the shuttered windows and red clay houses of the narrow streets, but all he saw there was the look of someone far away.

The silence of the ride was welcome after the last few weeks at the castle. Talk of Guinevere and Lancelot had grown. They had been seen together too many times and in too many places: while she painted, he stood nearby in the palace gardens, when she rode to the guilds, he waited for her in the folds and shadows of the trees, and when she prayed at the chapel, he lingered in the dusky churchyard.

How long it had all gone on, Gawain didn't know, and at first, like many others, he didn't want to know. But the more they were seen together, the more the court began to speak openly. Gareth and Percival had challenged Lancelot on his conduct, and Sagremor, an old favorite of the Queen, had delicately spoken to her about the effects the indiscretions were having on the other knights. But when he'd finished, she'd laughed and told him not to trouble his foolish head – she was glad of Lancelot's company, that's all. She felt safe, happy ... and the romance blossomed.

During this time, Arthur seemed unaware of what was happening. He went about the business of state as usual, often stopping to chat with Lancelot and Guinevere in the garden, or at court. And never, in all that time, was there the slightest sign of a strain on his friendship or a question of his love for the queen.

This last week had been a long and painful one for Gawain. He had stood by watching amid pointing fingers and hushed voices. The mood in the court worsened until Gawain felt himself spiraling with the others. Like them, he had come to respect Lancelot and even to enjoy his quiet, reserved company. Then, two days ago, the knights had turned to him and asked him to speak with Arthur. Finally, he'd agreed, but on the very day he was set to approach the king, Arthur had awoken him at dawn and asked him to dress and ride.

And now, on this fresh spring day, emerging from the misty woods, Gawain agonized over how he should broach the subject. How could he tell Arthur his newest knight was, even at this early hour, stealing his way to his wife's chamber, there to make love to his queen? Gawain shook his head in frustration, his thick dark hair swinging below his helmet like his vacillating thoughts.

Ahead, past the last few oaks, they broke into a vast clearing. The ground, now dotted with rocky outcroppings, sloped gently to the edges of a long, deep lake. Mist lay across its surface like sheered lambs wool.

Arthur reined his horse allowing Gawain to catch up. They sat side by side for a long minute, the breath of their mounts slowly curling up into the air as they looked out across the lake.

"Colwyn," said Arthur finally breaking the silence. "The birthplace of Excalibur." He pulled off his studded gauntlets and crossed his hands on the pommel of his saddle. "This day I intend to return it. I no longer wish to rule." He said the words simply, without remorse or resentment.

"My lord, you cannot ... "

Arthur held up his hand. "You have no need to speak; you've suffered enough, everyone has." He turned, shifting uneasily in his saddle, his eyes paler than Gawain could ever remember. "I've known of the affair for a long time. I've tried to be patient and wait it out, God knows, as a good Christian, I have, but Guinevere will never give up her love for him. It's gone altogether too far for that." He took a long measured breath. "I cannot be a king and a cuckold in my own court."

"My lord, send her away, if not for your sake, then for the sake of all you've worked for," Gawain said, not realizing just how much he'd prepared for this moment. "If you won't send the queen, then at least send Lancelot away. Order him to Cumberland, to Windermere – there's need out there for the leadership of a strong knight."

Arthur did not reply, instead he gazed silently at the lake. Somewhere in the trees behind them, a brace of wood pigeons cooed and a wind gusted up, swirling through the sedge and knotgrass at the shore's edge.

Arthur lowered his head. "Whatever I do from now on, will be done by a king who commands no respect. Nothing will change that. I cannot stand by and see all I've fought for simply vanish. Things won't get better, Gawain. No matter what I do or what I say-they'll never get better."

"But, my lord, if you were to send them away, somewhere far from court, the people would support you. They'd still respect you. You have endured enough. Your subjects are human. They'll understand – whatever you decide to do," said Gawain.

Arthur frowned at him. "That's my point. I've struggled to raise us above all that. Vengeance and retribution were my father's way, not mine. I've tried to change those things. God only knows I have. I built Camelot with the belief that we could pursue noble ideals and raise ourselves above the frailties of our base nature. If I go back now, we'll end mired in war again. Don't you see, it's time to go on, to go forward? If we falter, we'll be trapped forever like this. It's me, Gawain, I must set the example. Me, Arthur. No revenge, no Druid magic, only reason and faith, the Christian way – that's all." He stopped, breathing deeply after his outburst, then turned back to the lake and added quietly, "Even though I've failed, I've tried to make a difference."

"The fault doesn't lie with you, my lord."

"No," cut in Arthur, "it lies with us all, in our inability to choose the right way. We're still too young in this world, I'm afraid. We don't have the strength yet to overcome the temptations the true path requires, not even Lancelot, poor soul. It's our weakness, our physical needs that undermine us."

Gawain fell silent, then after a long moment, he asked, "What will you do?"

"I'll renounce the throne, tonight – when we return. Camelot will be Guinevere's to do with as she sees fit. I will to go to Glastonbury. There's a small monastery there, on the Tor, a place I've always admired for its beauty and devotion. I'll study there. Perhaps I can achieve a greater measure of success over my spiritual life than I did over my secular one." He fell silent again and Gawain felt the awful significance of what he'd said begin to sink in.

"Don't look so glum, my brave knight. I was too idealistic that's all. Life will go on and you'll not fail me in matters of the heart or honor. In you there is hope to be kept alive."

Arthur reined his horse toward the lake. Gawain nudged Gringolet and followed, a friend without words. The cold air was sharp and the clouds thin. They made their way in silence to the water's edge, horse hooves grinding over the flinty rocks.

At the lake, Gawain watched the thick mist roll along the shoreline. He glanced at the rippling waves and a sudden, inexplicable familiarity struck him. Something ... he couldn't put his finger on it ... something about the lake.

Arthur dismounted and walked to a wide flat rock jutting out into the water. He looked so solitary, standing on the mossy outcropping, water lapping at his feet, the weight of the world on his small shoulders. The wind gathered, gusting around him as he slid Excalibur from its scabbard. He held the Druid sword with its mystical inlaid patterns of silver and gold above his head. As if in response, the wind suddenly squalled and the thick mantle of fog began to furl back from the lake's surface.

Arthur stood on top of the mossy rock watching the water clear. After a moment, he bent and whirled the sword above his head with both hands. The keening whine of Excalibur drowned even the noise of the wind.

As the blade shimmered, the fog began to roll to the far edges of the lake. The horses pawed the ground nervously and Gawain tightened his rein, pulling their muzzles closer to him.

Arthur spun around, once, twice. On the third spin, he flung the ancient sword far out over the rippling surface. The blade whickered through the air, glinting and flashing in the flat light. It carried further than humanly possible, spinning unerringly toward the center of the lake.

Gawain felt the hairs on his neck suddenly rise and from somewhere behind him he heard a booming command.

The sword stopped magically in its flight. It hung in the air, turning slowly end over end, high above the lake.

Gawain spun around.

"Merlin!"

The wizard was striding along the shoreline, Rune staff kicking up gouts of sand. He looked more animated than Gawain could ever recall; hair disheveled, cloak flapping, one hand clasping the staff, the other extended, finger wagging at the king. "Arthur, think! Is this what you want? Is this best for all? Camelot will sink like that sword and never rise again if you do this."

In the distance, Excalibur continued spinning over the lake spearing rays of sunlight up into the sky and down into the gray depths of the water.

"I know what I'm doing, Merlin. This is right. No more Druid magic. The time for that has gone."

"What then? Christianity for everyone. Is that it? Have you forgotten all I've taught you?" Merlin halted in front of the king and thumped his staff in the sand.

Arthur held up his palm. "Enough, we've argued this too many times. Your way is wrong. Magic has had its day, my father's day. Now we go on, go forward. We find our answers in God. Magic is a crutch. It always has been."

Merlin folded his hands over the polished head of the Rune Staff and leaned forward, his bushy eyebrows furrowing. "Do not do this, Arthur. I beg of you. Our worlds can exist together. Druid lore and Christian faith are not that different – with both, we can bring about the peace this land needs. Give it time."

Arthur pursed his lips and turned back to the lake. He pointed across the water to the spinning sword. "No, no more. It is done. I've made up my mind. No more magic. I'll teach by example. Faith will guide me. Now, release the sword."

"Arthur, please, I ... ."

"I said release it."

Merlin hesitated, about to add something. Then, seeming to think the better of it, he shrugged his shoulders, jabbed his staff in the air and barked a single command. Excalibur fell from its shimmering circle like a stone.

The ancient sword plunged into the lake sending waves rippling outward. When the water settled, the fog along the shoreline began to gather at the north, south, west and east ends of the lake. For a moment nothing happened, then the fog at the four points slowly began to rise in gigantic columns.

The northern column curled and coiled until it took on the shape of a great writhing serpent. At the opposite end of the lake, the column flattened out, then bunched up looking first like a rock, then, in the last phase of its molding, materializing into a twenty-foot child, sitting hunched over, knees drawn to his chest, arms wrapped around his shins.

No sooner was that image complete than the western tower of fog began to form – this one into a massive block of shimmering ice. For a moment, it reflected a blinding light, then it suddenly burst into tiny fragments that glinted in the sun like broken glass.

The eastern tower began to form the same time the third exploded. Gawain tore his attention away from the falling crystals and watched it struggle to find a solid shape. It grew and shrank, grew and shrank, as though it didn't possess enough energy to develop.

Arthur, also staring at the undulations of the last cloud, turned to Merlin, face red. "What trick is this?"

"It's not of my doing, your majesty. This is power beyond me." Merlin didn't look at the king when he spoke; his eyes remained locked on the final formation. "See, there," he pointed. "It's an essence omen sent to warn us of something woefully evil." He turned and Gawain saw for the first time, the light of fear in his eyes. "All our lives are about to change. How, I know not, but they will change as sure as night falls."

The wind picked up, breaking the silence, but this time a natural freshness came with it ruffling the grass and gusting over the lake surface. In seconds, the towering columns blew into ragged mist.

Arthur stepped down from the rock and strode to his horse, face suffused with anger. "That's it, the magic ends here, Merlin. From now on we'll write our own history – the way the Lord intended." He took the reins and paused, one foot in the stirrup. "God will provide for us. He will see us through our days of darkness, not your pagan tricks." He swung into his saddle and tugged the horse's head around. Digging his heels into the animal's flanks, he cantered toward the trees without another word.

Gawain swept his back his cloak and vaulted onto Gringolet.

"Wait," said Merlin. "Believe me when I tell you I had no hand in what happened here. Keep close to Arthur; protect him until I find out more." He glanced back across the lake, brow furrowing. "I'll travel south, to Neume. Maybe she can offer some insight into this. I'll return as soon as I can. Be vigilant, my falcon."

Gawain nodded and kicked the horse. "Take Bors with you," he called over his shoulder as he galloped after Arthur.

Mumbling to himself, Merlin clutched his staff and set off to the far end of the lake. At the edge of the woods, Gawain glanced back. The strange feeling of familiarity struck him again. It wasn't the lake, he'd never been here before – it was something else. *What?* He spurred Gringolet into the towering elms, wishing for Athlan, for her steady eyes, for her love to bring some warmth into this growing world of dread.

The ride back was as solitary as the ride out. Only the plaintive cries of pheasants and the cooing of moorhens broke the silence. When they reached Camelot, the lower streets were bustling with merchants setting up striped awnings and market stalls. Ox carts trundled by clanking and squeaking but Arthur remained distant, removed from the ebb and tide of the commerce around him.

At Caerleon, the atmosphere was the same – averted eyes, heads lowered in passing, lips pursed.

The rest of the day continued with little change in routine. Arthur attended the assize court and ruled on points of law. He signed papers and writs and issued warrants, and all the while Lancelot and Guinevere remained conspicuously absent.

Later in the afternoon, he ordered his knights to attend the Round Table before vespers. That evening, in a room lit by countless tallow candles bathing the great table in heavy gold, the knights filed in like processional monks.

Arthur took his seat, noting Lancelot's absence with a glance. He wasted no time on amenities. When all were present, he placed hands either side of the crown etched into the table before him and rose.

"There can be no doubt that the future of Caerleon and Camelot itself are in jeopardy." The words faded and Gawain watched with a growing sadness as the king stood in the golden light, taking on the weight of a dying world as he told them all of the part he had tried so hard to play, and of the failure torturing his Christian soul.

The words flowed easily for Arthur when he touched upon the spiritual meaning of Camelot, and it wasn't until the candles burned low that he finally addressed the issue they had all been waiting for.

Going over the long days when he'd first discovered the truth, he spoke as he had at the lake, without anger or resentment. He recounted the agony he'd endured as the love of Lancelot and the queen had grown. The gloom seemed to thicken at his words and then, at last, his voice gave way and trembled.

"I cannot in all good conscience continue as your king ... "

The words echoed high in the vaulted chamber and in the hushed silence, a glow, a tiny pin pick of light appeared and began burning at a point just above the center of the great table. At first, only Gawain saw it, but soon the other knights shifted their gaze from the king to the spinning particle.

Gawain couldn't recall exactly when Arthur stopped speaking – he was only aware of the speck of light whirling in front of him, growing until it split into two perfect circles of light, one revolving above the other.

The faces of the knights were lit up beneath their chins, making them look strangely dreamlike as they bent forward, eyes riveted on the bright circles suspended above the table.

In the breathless silence, the circles linked then stretched apart and Gawain saw a shape emerging – the top circle formed the rim and the bottom the base of a simple cup. Moments later, when the cup was fully formed, intricate engravings began appearing on its surface. The knights watched in amazement. As the vessel slowly turned, the etchings crawled with life: people planting and hunting, animals he had never seen before, wine-dark seas and turbid skies, stars, planets, saints and sinners. The story of man and the infinite beauty of God's world slowly unfolded before them, never repeating, never ending as the cup rotated. One by one, the knights steepled their fingers and began praying silently.

Gawain bent his head and at that moment a sound as pure as the light bathing the room rose from the center of the cup. It started as a single chime of heart-rending clarity, then it slowly changed into a steady peel of bells that filled him with inner peace.

The celestial sounds faded.

The light intensified to an impossible brightness and then winked out, plunging the room into darkness. No one moved. No one spoke. In the deep tranquility, Gawain struggled with his mortal sin and his growing need to follow the Druid path.

It wasn't until after the knights had filed silently out of the room and had gone to pray in the chapel, that Gawain realized Arthur had not finished his speech – had not yet given up the throne.

Later, sitting by the hearth in his sleeping quarters high in the east wing of the castle, Gawain went over the events of the day. He tried to make sense of his part in it all – the cloud shapes on the lake, the Dark Druids and now the appearance of the mysterious cup.

A sharp rapping at his door snapped him out of his reverie. He rose from the comfort of his armchair, but before he crossed the room, the door burst open and Merlin blustered in. His sodden cloak and wild beard dripped rain. Throwing back his hood, he leaned his staff against the wall and shuffled to the fire.

"What a day! What a day!" he exclaimed rubbing his hands over the flames. "Do you have anything to eat, lad?" He turned his backside to the flames and sighed as steam rose and warmth stole through his clothing.

"I have some of master Renman's roasted chicken, bread and meat pie. Just a moment," said Gawain.

He went to the nightstand and returned with his untouched supper. "Did you hear about the cup?"

"I did, my falcon, I did indeed. Great Christian miracle, that. And I'll tell you something else, it fits perfectly with what I learned today."

Gawain pulled his stuffy armchair up to the fire and placed the trencher on a side table. "You look exhausted; you must take better care of yourself. Here, sit."

"Humph. I should be the one chiding you for being out late and neglecting to eat, not the other way around." Merlin chuckled at his own humor, struggled out of his wet cloak and sat down with a thankful groan. He nestled the trencher in his lap and looked up at Gawain through mischievous green eyes.

"My boy, I do believe what happened today could determine more than just the fate of Camelot – it could change the course of history." He nodded, breaking off a piece of bread and chewing thoughtfully.

Gawain waited. Merlin swallowed and took a long draft of wine. He burped, then took up the chicken leg. "When I left you, I went straight to Neume and told her about Arthur and what happened to Excalibur. She was able to throw a great deal of light on the subject. Did you notice anything familiar about the lake?"

"Yes," Gawain said sitting on the footstool. "I don't know what, but it seemed like I'd been there before ... or somewhere like it."

"It wasn't the lake you recognized," Merlin said, wagging the chicken leg. "It was here, this place."

"I don't follow you."

"Think back to the shape of the lake, my boy. What do you see?"

"Well, it was long, sort of indented where we stood. Further up the left shore it bulged out, then further on past that, it narrowed in. At the far end, it cut back out again. That's about it. That's all I remember," he said, trying to figure out where Merlin was going with all this.

"Not bad, my boy. Your powers of observation are admirable. Must be the Druid in you," Merlin said through a mouthful of chicken. "I knew the shape was familiar myself, you see. But it wasn't until Neume drew it for me that I saw it for what it was. The lake now holding Excalibur is *here* – this land, the shape of our country down to the smallest detail!" He paused, eyes twinkling as Gawain's face lit with understanding.

"Yes!" breathed Gawain, thinking back on the maps he'd seen in his father's study. He slapped his palm against his forehead. "Yes!" The shoreline had followed those ancient tracings with uncanny accuracy.

"The bulge you saw was Wales, my boy. We were standing in the southern part, near the coast."

Gawain marveled at the lake's miniature exactness of the realm. He guessed its length to be five, maybe six miles. Which meant it was perhaps a hundred or so times smaller than the country itself.

"What do you make of it all, Merlin; the magic lake, the cloud forms, the sword? What did Neume say?"

"First things first, my boy, tell me about this cup of yours," said Merlin dropping the chicken bone on the trencher and wiping his hands on his thighs.

Gawain shrugged his shoulders. "It was ... it was ... well, there are no words to describe it really. When it appeared, Arthur forgot all about his abdication. It was a sign sent by God. I've never seen or heard of anything like it before, nothing. The power alone ... it brought every knight in the room to tears, even Bors. For a while we were all ... well, lost," said Gawain. "I've never been so afraid, not for myself, but for my soul. I knew I was in the presence of something greater than anything of Druid making." Gawain realized he was gripping Merlin's arm and let go.

"There's nothing for you to fear, my boy. There was never a truer heart in the kingdom. I doubt your God has come to claim it just yet." Merlin rose, brushed the crumbs from his cloak and paced to the window.

He paused for a long moment looking out at the moon then turned. He struggled with what he had to say next, the sparkle gone from his eyes. "When I was in Uther's mind, I learned more than I bargained for. There was an evil in him far beyond what we ever imagined. One of the things I was privy to while I was there was a short ... perhaps that's not the word for it ... more like a random thought, one he'd had the moment he realized I'd entered him. He tried to suppress it, but I shared it for an instant before it was lost to me."

He ran his fingers through his beard. "He was planning to kill Arthur. At first, I thought he truly was as mad as we believed. Then I probed deeper, seeking answers. Why kill Arthur, his only son and heir? The logic escaped me. Did he want to die and let the kingdom fall into the hands of the barons, most of whom he despised anyway? It didn't make sense. All the time I shared his other thoughts, I tried to find a way, a path to lead me to that one thought again."

He took up his staff from the wall and leaned on it. "The problem was, I always came up against the same jumble of half-hatched schemes: plots of revenge involving just about everyone, lust, lechery, everything and anything, but not that fleeting thought. I never found it again. Try as I might, my boy, I just couldn't figure out why he would want to do such a thing – and yet it was obvious."

His face caught the warming glow of the fire, highlighting his silver hair and thick eyebrows. "He never knew why himself, that's why! I should have known. I should have puzzled it out." He tapped his temple. "You see, after Morganna charmed him, he had no control over what he was doing. She'd instilled the killing of Arthur in him. Poor, stupid Uther, he didn't want it, she did!" He paused, absently polished the top of the staff with his sleeve.

"There's something else too, my boy. This may be difficult for you, but you need to hear it – all of it. Long ago, before you were born, in the time when Uther came to power, I lived in fear of my life as most of us did back then. Bran's breath, he was so unpredictable. You were just as likely to be hanged as receive a barony. We lived according to his whim and that changed like the weather.

148

"Something had to be done if we wanted peace in our future. Your father and I spoke about it many times. Unfortunately, we could never agree on a course of action. So, after one particular display of brutality, I decided to take matters into my own hands."

He cleared his throat before continuing. "You see, I knew Uther's real weakness: women and one in particular, Igraine. He wanted her more than the throne itself, his lust was insatiable. I realized it wouldn't be long before he'd do something stupid, even though she was married to Galois, the Duke of Cornwall at that time. So what to do? I consulted the omens. The moment was right. That very evening I had a message delivered saying I could arrange for him to spend a night with her if he so desired. He sent for me straight away. The fool would have cut off his right hand for a chance to bed her. I had him, my boy. Had him like that." He snatched his bony fist in the air as if he were catching a fly.

"It was so easy. He agreed to all my terms. I arranged for Galois to be absent later that week and took him to Tintagel, Galois' castle. When we arrived, I cast a *Jard* Rune of shaping on him. Anyone meeting him that night, even Igraine, would only see Galois, not Uther. The Runes were strong then, the spells guaranteed.

"Anyway, what I'd planned came to pass. He had his night. And just as the omens foretold, a child was born from the bedding – a boy. Uther kept his promise and allowed me guardianship. I provided the best teachers and the best training for him. I even chose his name – Arthur." At the final word, Merlin turned back to the flames.

"But I'm afraid my plan was not so perfect after all. I don't mean because Arthur grew up to disavow my faith, or because of what we're up against now. I mean because what I did to Uther gave Morganna ideas of her own." Merlin took a deep breath. "You see, she also used Uther to sire children – children *she* could control!"

He waited, letting what he said sink in while he stretched his hands out to the writhing flames. "Neume found out through divination that Morganna had procured four children through him. Athlan was carrying the last of those children the night you killed her." Merlin caught himself and looked up. "I'm sorry, my boy. I didn't mean ..."

"No, it's all right. Please, go on," said Gawain quietly. The day and now the night full of revelation and all the while Athlan buried deep in his memory, secure, hidden away, safe – until the knives came out.

Merlin sighed. "I've not spoken of her before. I know the pain her name carries for you, but she's part of what I have to tell."

"I'm fine, really ..."

The wizard looked at him as if he were trying to read his thoughts. With a sigh and a shrug, he continued. "Neume said she was the last to be charmed. Morganna warded each of the women with a unique Dark Druid spell in order to procure a male child. Afterwards she had them taken far away where they await her orders even as we speak. Just what these orders are, neither Neume nor I can fathom – but as sure as grass grows green, my boy, they herald the dark days your father spoke of," he added shaking his head.

"Nor is that the end of it, I'm afraid. In her divination, Neume also saw the fog on the lake. Each one of its towers, she said, not only showed us the form of Morganna's dark princes, but their location as well. All was revealed to us through the power of the sword." Merlin cleared his throat.

"The fourth tower, the one that never formed, was Athlan's unborn child." He crossed to Gawain and placed a hand on his shoulder. "I want you to understand that what you did spared her and her son a life of suffering, and perhaps, in your Christian world, even saved his soul – what you did was right, the only thing, my boy."

Merlin fell silent. The crackling logs sent a cluster of embers spitting onto the hearth. Outside, the stars blazed. Gawain felt the words rain down, killer that he was, wondering when it would all stop – the taking of lives in the name of peace, or God, or wild Druid plot.

The emotions welled within him and he felt himself slipping from his image like a specter from a shallow grave.

CHAPTER 8

He squinted, surprised at what he saw. The gloom had lightened. Now he could make out the shapes of wide leaves drooping from branches. *Trees? No. Above, a sky, maybe.* He peered. *No, not a sky a ... .* A hand touched the sleeve of his mail shirt and he turned. Before him, barely visible was a woman's face framed by dark, curling hair. *Who in God's ...?* But the words were only thoughts. Then she spoke, her voice muffled, but clear enough for him to make out the words. "Come, we're near now, almost there." And with a gentle tug, she led him away from the dimming beam.

Struggling with the shift back into this world and the ghosting emotions from his past, he followed. Trudging up the steepening hill, he tried to fit the latest pieces together: Merlin's revelations, the appearance of the Grail and now this Neume. Who was she? What part did she play in all this?

To his right, another shaft of Terran light flashed through the tree shapes, cutting off his thoughts. Now he could see what he'd missed before; it was breaking through the gaps between giant fronds. A chill ran down his spine as he brushed aside the thick foliage and made his way to the place where it sheered into a clearing.

The mist shifting around the light hid everything except for a greenish tinge at the center. He puzzled over this for a moment and a Latin phrase his father had often used sprang to mind: 'Quo Vadis.' *I wish I knew*, he thought reaching out.

This time there were no sensations – no queasy feelings in his stomach or dryness in his throat. When he touched the beam, the surface cleared and a wide valley sprang into view. Far to the left he could make out his young image bent over Gringolet, galloping east. Cupping his hands, he peered closer. The rider and horse were skirting a long green lake. He tried to recall the scene, where he was, why the urgency, but this time there were no clues.

He followed the horse and rider until they broke out into open fields again, then, taking a measured breath, he stepped into the light as if he were stepping through an open door. In that instant, his thoughts became those of the younger Gawain and he lost himself in the thrill of the ride as Gringolet thundered through rich meadow grass.

Neume's cave lay ahead, a few miles into the mountains. Merlin had sent him to see the old hermit after receiving information a plague had broken out in the far north – the position shown by the serpent-shaped tower of fog. Merlin hadn't learned the news from any source in Camelot. He had received an image from Neume while he slept. The pictures were still with him days later when Gawain arrived. The wizard had rushed out of the castle barely taking time to greet him before whisking him up to the battlements where he had spent the afternoon, trying to read the winds.

"He's out there, my boy, planning," he said, finger wagging at the rugged mountains as if he were admonishing them. "Neume's divined and she's asked for you. To confront this spawn of Uther's we need her help. I can cast the Runes and fuse the spells, but it's Neume who sees the way," he said, spreading his hands on the parapet and staring into the failing light.

A sudden squall whipped back Merlin's heavy blue cloak and he turned, shielding himself. "You'll need to rest here tonight and ride to her cave tomorrow. She'll tell you what to do when you get there," he shouted above the roar.

The night had been long and full of violent storms. Merlin had spoken little, choosing instead to spend the hours locked in his study poring over maps and parchments by candlelight. Gawain slept fitfully in an adjoining chamber while the winds howled and shrieked outside.

The next morning Gawain had lumbered downstairs bleary eyed to find Merlin in the kitchen sitting on a stool near an open window. A raven perched on his arm was taking small kernels of yellow corn from his hand. When Gawain entered, Merlin stood and placed the bird on the stone ledge where it sat hunched over moodily.

"Some say they are harbingers of death. But to me, they speak only of freedom," he said running the crook of his finger along the bird's sleek wing. "Do you have the Dragon Ring, my boy? I'll charm it with a more powerful essence spell. I believe you're ready for it now."

He took the silver ring and this time when he spoke the binding words, his voice softened, almost as if he were afraid someone might hear him, thought Gawain. When he finished, he looked up, his winter green eyes flashing. "There, fused. The link between us is much stronger now."

Later, when Gawain led Gringolet out onto the drawbridge, the wind had died down and the day shone blue-skied with billowing clouds bright behind castle flags of silver and gold. Merlin shuffled alongside, staff thumping on the wooden slats. When they'd crossed the moat, he bent to the mare and patting its coarse mane whispered in its ear.

Gawain mounted and took the reins in his fist. He looked down at the fretful face. "If we can rid this land of a king, we can surely rid it of his princes," he said. Then he dug his heels into the horse's flanks and galloped down to the plains below.

And now with the sun sinking in the west, Gringolet pounded over the soft earth and through the last of the bowing poplars. Racing time, they thundered out onto the wide slope of foothills leading to the Lait Mountains. Lathered with sweat and streaked with salt, Gringolet sped through the short sweet grass.

Neume's cave lay high up in the lea of the horn-shaped mountain looming above the, a steep climb. Gawain slowed Gringolet to a walk allowing her to thread her way between the hawthorn bushes covering the mid ground of the lower slopes. He relaxed the reins, marveling as she followed an invisible path with unerring certainty. Snorting plumes of steamy breath, she wound back and forth across the steepening slope.

An hour later, they picked their way over mossy rocks and sparse clumps of heather. He bent over Gringolet's sleek neck and ran his fingers through her mane and down her trembling flanks. Ahead lay the high divide. He patted her gently. "Merlin's magic, little one. It drives you too, doesn't it?"

Trekking up the mountainside, he cast his mind back to what Merlin had told him about Neume. "She was born blind," he'd said over a breakfast of boiled oats and thick yellow honey. "Her eyes were the color of fresh milk but she could see in other ways. As a little girl, she learned to survive through her special Druid talents. She was barely six when she discovered she could expand her mind and see in ways different from anyone else. It was like casting a fishing net, she once told me. But when she got older, the net caught more than just the shapes of those it covered – it also caught their emotions and feelings.

"She soon found she preferred to be alone after she discovered the darkness in the hearts of so many. At sixteen, she packed up her few belongings and set out for the Lait hills determined to live a hermit's life. And she did – until the divining."

Merlin's eyes flashed mischievously when he said this and Gawain knew he was in for the best part of the story.

"Once, quite by accident, she cast part of the net above her – into the firmament – and there it spread like lamp oil on water. It went so far and so fast, it left her disoriented for hours.

"Later, when she learned to control this new way of casting, she found she could throw the net directly into the sky without the ill effects. One problem, though, was its incredible lightness. Casting her mind around her may have been like casting a fishing net, but casting it into the air was like spinning a never-ending spider web.

"Once she got over the shock of the new experience, she discovered she could send her mind traveling along the web's threads with infinite ease. From up there she could look down at the shadows of the world passing far below. She also learned something else too: she could feel vibrations in the web every time a death of an evil nature occurred – just as a spider feels the tug of the smallest insect caught in its strands."

Merlin had stopped then to ladle more boiled oats into Gawain's bowl. Waving away the steam curling up from the cook pot, he continued. "Now to the heart of it, my boy. A few weeks ago, Neume was shaken out of her sleep by a disruption so intense it left her fighting for breath. Not knowing what could cause such a disturbance, she traveled along the web with great caution. But when she neared the scene of the death, something happened that had never happened before, not in all the time she had ever divined: she discovered *she'd* been divined! Panicking, she went to turn back, but where could she hide? Nowhere. And, if she returned, couldn't the diviner follow her and find out where she lived? So, she went on.

"The shadow was waiting for her. He was standing in a field littered with the corpses of men, women and children who had died from the plague he carried.

157

"She hovered high above, not daring to let her mind travel down the thread any further – but she may as well have, because the moment the shadow sensed her, he sent a thought bolting up through the web shredding away all the fabric and knocking her unconscious. The only thing she remembered when she came to was a single word-thought that sizzled in her mind for days.

Know this, Druid, I am Argath, harbinger of evil and I am coming for you and yours.

"Later, when she recovered, she contacted me and bid me send you to her with all haste," Merlin had finished.

Riding through the rocky terrain, Gawain mulled over the name Argath, trying to envision what he might look like, but there was no picture.

He broke out from between clumps of purple bracken into a wide upland meadow strewn with bright, wildflowers. The pasture spread before him like a royal carpet running between the horn-shaped summit on his right and the cratered mountain on his left.

He reined Gringolet and stared up at the peaks. In the last rays of sunlight they gleamed like giant Runes. He took off his helmet and pushed back locks of sweat soaked hair trying to recall what branch they came from. But even as he tried to remember them, they faded into pale shades. *Slippery like eels.* Yet the mystical shapes stirred something deep within him. He took a long drink from his water skin. *I saw the wind cut into you with its cold last night, Merlin. Saw you shiver. Is this why everything seems so urgent, because the magic is failing? What else are you hiding from me?*

He buckled on his helmet and dug his heels into Gringolet's flanks. The horse cantered across the fields, happy to be following the invisible path winding its way to the base of the horn.

With less than an hour of light left, the lone rider and panting horse scrambled up the last rocky incline, sending small stones skittering over the ledge into the valley far below. They cut through a cleft between sheer cliff faces, then, as they rounded a final bend, Neume's cave loomed out of the dark mountainside like a knife wound.

Gawain dismounted, tethered Gringolet to a boulder and took a torch and flint from his supplies. Above him, wind fluted through the escarpment and high rocky crags. He walked to the entrance and struck the flint against the rock face. The oil-soaked torch flared into life and he stepped through the narrow opening into the cave.

Shadows leaped back and a sickly smell stuck him as he entered. He lifted his sleeve to his nose and waited for his eyes to adjust. In the distance, something gleamed. He lowered his sleeve and held the torch at arm's length. Near the center of the cave, a figure floated in the air.

Breathing softly, he drew his sword. Nothing, no movement. Heart hammering, he inched forward, ignoring the coppery smell.

Closer.

The torch hissed and crackled, sweeping away the darkness before him. Then he saw the figure for what it was-a woman, arms wide, head bowed, hanging from a wooden cross. Holding up the torch, he went closer. He clenched his teeth. The frail body was skinned from the neck down. It shone grotesquely. Congealed blood and fatty yellow wax glistened in the flame light.

Gawain stood still in the awful silence, staring at the naked figure. *Dear God above.* Sweat beaded on his forehead, trickled down the cords of his neck and crawled under his mail shirt. He drew nearer. The eyes, for all their use, had been plucked out, leaving dark spider lines trailing down the sunken cheeks. Her hair, matted with skin and clotted blood, hung in limp strands. He circled behind her, scanning the room. Nothing, just silence.

Leaving her, he walked deeper into the cave. The torch revealed a circular cavern hewn out of solid rock. A ceiling arched some twenty feet above him. Slats from boxes lay splinted amidst smashed chests and strewn scrolls. An upended straw bed leaned next to what could have been a table or chairs. Whoever had done this had taken either what they were looking for, or had wholly destroyed it.

He returned to Neume and ran his finger through the blood on the cross. Tacky. They must have taken her eyes long before she died because the blood on her face was dry. He set down the torch and hacked through the base of the main stave with his sword. When the cross fell, he levered out the nails with the blade and gently eased the body to the ground. He took a blanket from the ruined bed and wrapped it round the bloody shoulders and legs. Then he lifted Neume's songbird weight in his arms.

Outside, the last of a twilight sky streaked the mountains a cold purple. Shadows lay like dark folds in the earth as he dug out a grave with the hard edge of his shield. When it was deep enough, he drew the circles of joining Merlin had taught him and buried her crouching – ready for the life forces that would run through her earthen womb.

By the time he had finished, night had fallen. He cleared the debris away from the mouth of the cave and spread out a blanket. He would sleep next to the entrance where he could breathe God's sweet air ... and hear anyone approaching.

While he lay on his makeshift bed watching the early stars press out of the night sky, an inexplicable comfort came with the sight of their distant, wheeling patterns. He waited and when the moon finally slid behind the horned peak, the cluster of Orion appeared. The heavens seemed to swirl, then merge, and when they did, he felt the elemental power storming in their heart.

He sought the wizard in the center of the churning furnace and the Dragon Ring warmed. The starry sky swam and his mind filled with brief, clear pictures. He glimpsed an image of the cave as it had been, before Neume's death – the boxes and crates back in place, the shelves stocked with pots and earthenware, two cupboards open, jars of herbs and potted plants set in rows.

Above an incense burner, curled smoke lay frozen in the air, and behind, a small chest of drawers stood against the wall by the bed. At the far end of the cave, a strange mushroom-shaped lamp glowed with dark blue light.

The scene brightened briefly then disappeared. Yet it didn't vanish as a single thought does, but piece-by-piece, as if someone were dismantling it-someone invisible, sneaking each item from the room. And with every missing article the cavern began taking on a deeper and deeper loneliness. He felt it as he saw it-chairs, boxes, yellowing scrolls, everything Neume had collected and valued, all winking from sight.

When the objects were gone, the cavern lay bare for a moment, then it too plunged into darkness. Finally, the picture itself vanished, except . . . except for the small chest of drawers that shimmered brightly in his mind.

"Merlin." He spoke the words as he thought them. "Help me understand what is happening." He pronounced every syllable carefully, willing each one to reach the distant wizard. "Tell me what I must do."

Again a picture, but this time it came in a single shape-a Rune, a scarlet sigil floating in front of him made up of two parts: a curved horn inside a circle. Each part appeared exactly as Gawain had seen it from the meadow below-the shapes of the mountain peaks.

"What does it mean, Merlin?"

No answer.

"What must I do?"

No answer.

"Merlin?"

No answer.

Orion's nebula remained implacable, the dense cloud of stars swirling impossibly fast, impossibly distant. He closed his eyes giving up.

He turned on his side thinking of Athlan, of the night high on the castle ramparts. And when his mind strayed to her death, he forced it back to her face, the curve of her long neck and slim shoulders, her breasts and the love still living within him and he fell into an exhausted sleep with his back to the dark and murderous cave.

The dream came, more vivid than any before, so strong he was there.

He stood defiant in full knight's armor. In front of him, on a wide sandy plain, sat a Golden Dragon perched on massive leathery haunches. Gawain unsheathed his sword and held its shining tip up toward the majestic creature.

"What can you do with that?" the dragon boomed down, sweeping its scaled tail lazily across the sand.

"My best," Gawain replied boldly, looking at the golden eyes above him.

"Not good enough, I'm afraid," the dragon said, his voice rolling like distant thunder as he raised a massive clawed foot to stamp out the little annoyance standing before him.

"Stop, or I will cause you grief," Gawain said.

"How so?" The foot above him hesitated, blocking out the sun and throwing a curved shadow of a claw over him.

"I am Gawain, Arthur's knight, and this charmed sword will be the death of you," Gawain replied.

The huge foot came crashing down at his side, showering up sand. The dragon's head shot to within inches of Gawain's face.

"Charmed! You know magic?" he breathed.

"Yes."

"You know of Druid magic-Runes?" he asked, barely able to contain his excitement.

"Indeed." Gawain pushed the sword tip into the sand and leaned over the hilt, his gaze riveted on the swirling flecks in the dragon's eyes. "I know two very secret Runes-each one has power beyond your knowledge," he said, emboldened by the dragon's newfound respect.

The golden creature arched an eyebrow. Flaring scales caught the sun as he shifted his weight and flopped down, exploding the sand around into clouds of dust. "Tell me what they are. You know we dragons thirst for knowledge-especially the Druid magic."

"The Runes are *thea* and *mor-banna*," Gawain answered without hesitation.

"I have not heard of these, not even in all my travels," said the great dragon expansively. "Are they Far Druid Runes?"

"They were taught to me by Merlin."

"Ahhh, that one! I know of him," the dragon declared reverently. "He once helped cure a Luck Dragon of a rare malaise. Foolish creature wouldn't leave his treasure, not even to eat. It happens sometimes." He shook his great golden head. "He would have died in his cave, slowly starving to death while he guarded his treasure, but that one, Merlin, he filled him with a spell of wonder and he abandoned his treasure and left the cave for the skies. I don't think he ever returned-the spell was that powerful."

"Merlin told me of this dragon."

"Ummmm, and the Runes, what did he tell you of them? Show me what you know, brave knight."

Gawain pulled his sword out of the sand. "They look like this."

The Golden Dragon watched, eyes wide as Gawain drew the images of the horn and the crater in the sand with his blade. When he'd finished, he stepped back into the dragon's shadow, curious to see what his work would bring about.

For a moment, nothing happened. Then the sand inside the Crater Rune began to tremble. A hole as black as night slowly appeared at the center of the circle and the sand began to funnel down into its depths.

Gawain looked up but the dragon was too intent on the events to notice him. The hole widened until it reached the circumference of the Crater Rune. When it touched the edge, the sand trickled to a halt. A gaping pit stood before them like an open wound.

Gawain tugged on one of the scales of the Golden Dragon's great curved belly and they backed away. But before they had gone a few yards, an ancient bell pealed from the abyss. It rang with such intensity that Gawain clapped his hands to his ears and the great dragon buried his head under his tail in an almost comic attempt to hide.

Silence, piercing silence. The bell rang again, clanging far out over the desert. It tolled two more times and then a reed thin voice spoke from the depths of the pit.

"Who summons me?" it quavered.

Gawain didn't answer but crawled forward. The Golden Dragon unfurled his tail from around his head and stretched out his long neck until he was level with Gawain.

"Who woke me from my sleeeeeep?" the voice wailed from the depths.

Silence.

"Where are my tears?"

Gawain inched further forward.

164

"Closer, come to the other side. Know the secrets of the tower and learn why your magic fails. See the heart that feeds."

Spreading his arms wide for balance, Gawain peered down. A pale outline swam in the darkness far below. Flat silvery eyes like those of a fish stared up out of a bone white face. Two thin lips opened as if to speak but no words came. Instead, Gawain saw tongues of flame licking in the depths of its furnace mouth. And that was all, because the sand beneath him suddenly gave way.

He flailed desperately, trying to wriggle back from the edge but he lost his balance and tumbled head first into the yawing pit. Just as he felt the terror and the air take him, he was jerked to a sudden halt.

The Golden Dragon had caught him, his great curved teeth driving through the back of his breastplate like spikes through worn tin.

Gawain dangled, swinging perilously, his armor squeaking as he rocked gently back and forth. He twisted his head and looked up at the fabulous beast holding him.

Those eyes.

He stared into the golden flecks. They were like suns, distant constellations, whirling and swirling in great slow circles.

Orion.

Merlin had spoken.

The ground opened and this time, in his dream, he fell forever.

Yesterday's Falcon

CHAPTER 9

G awain woke with a start as a ray early morning sun crept between the high crags, across the rocky path to the cave entrance and touched his cheek. His hand went instinctively to his sword. It was half way out of its scabbard before he realized there was no danger. He struggled to his feet, stiff from the damp wind blowing down from the mountains. He stretched. Behind him, the curved wall of the cave glimmered in the weak sun. Pulling on his boots, he went back over the horrors of what he had found earlier, and to his dream: the Runes, the chest of drawers and the image of the Orion constellation.

He laced up his surcoat and went to tend to Gringolet. When he'd finished, he took a loaf of cocket bread and a wheel of cheese from a leather pouch and sat on the barren rocks. Thin fog wisped around him as he chewed and sipped water from a flagon. He looked up at the sky thinking how much he wanted to get away from this place and back to the warmth of Arthur's court, to sit in the company of Percival and Bors and hear laughter once again.

The wind picked up, blowing through a nearby crevasse with a deep fluting cry and Gawain subconsciously rubbed the ring on his finger. If only his own abilities were stronger, he might be able talk to the wizard without all the dreams and baffling images.

When he'd finished the sparse meal, he led Gringolet to an outgrowth of sedge and tethered her. He decided to explore the cave one last time before he left. If there were answers, he would find them. He lit the torch and ducked into the darkness. He began with a hunt for the chest of drawers, or at least a search for where it was once located.

Passing the spot where Neume died, he made his way to the back of the cave. "What now, Merlin? I see your pictures and try to write your Runes, but why is it I feel I'm only the instrument of your bidding-your falcon, as you so often call me?" he muttered, his voice hollow in the bare cave.

When he reached the wall where the chest once sat, a strong smell of lavender drifted up from the ruins of a smashed vase. His heart skipped a beat.

NO!

Forcing his mind away from Athlan, he crouched by several broken pieces of wood and twisted iron hinges he suspected might have once been the chest itself. He brushed the area clean with his fingertips examining the ground.

Nothing.

He looked around, holding the torch at arms length. "I am on top of a God-forsaken mountain, inside the tip of some immense Rune. I've buried a poor, crucified Druid, skinned from neck to toe and I've spent a night staring into a dragon's eyes and still I have no idea where to go or what to do."

He dropped forward onto his knees tapping a broken length of wood on the ground as he ran through his choices. He could leave and take the long ride back to Camelot and find Merlin; he could try to clear his mind and wait for more picture puzzles, or ... or, *try drawing the Runes from the Dragon dream!*

He stood up, moved away from the wall and focusing on the Rune shapes he'd seen in the dream, scratched the Crater Rune on the ground with the stick. He'd barely finished the inner circle when a jolt snapped his wrist back and sent the wood spinning out of his hand. It flew through the air and caromed off the nearby wall, bursting into flames and sending a shower of sparks around the cave.

He waited, not daring to move. A long moment passed then a thin green light began tracing the Rune he had drawn. When it was complete, it expanded outwards rippling across the floor like waves on a wind-tossed lake. It highlighted ghostly chairs and tables, books and parchment stacks, globes, cupboards and tapestries, all in precisely the same position he'd seen them in Merlin's dream picture. Then, in its wake, each object lost its transparency and became solid.

Gawain stared around at the magically transformed cave. The chest of drawers, the last image to appear in the picture, stood directly before him. It looked real enough. He ran his hand over the knotted wood. It felt solid to the touch. He rapped the top with a knuckle. The sound echoed in the cave.

The chest stood waist high. Each drawer had a small set of handles carved from animal bones. He took hold of the top pair and pulled. The drawer slid open. It was stuffed full of shells and stones. He tunneled through them letting the smaller items slip through his fingers. Nothing unusual.

Frowning, he bent and pulled the second drawer open. It was similar, except here the stones and shells were larger. He tugged open the third drawer. More of the same but this time when he burrowed under the rubble, he touched something smooth – so smooth it felt wet. Grasping the stone gingerly, he pulled it out. Even in the torchlight, it looked extraordinary. It was flat, perfectly round and so dark he though for a moment there was a hole in the palm of his hand.

"Merlin, is it this I was supposed to find? Is this what you've led me to with your dreams and pictures?" he muttered, turning it over and inspecting it. On the underside, fine white Runes horse-tailed across a slick surface. He rubbed them with the ball of his thumb but they were etched into the stone.

"They cannot be stopped easily."

Gawain spun around at the sound of the voice and drew his sword. He stood still, squinting beyond the torchlight. Wind blew in from the cave mouth making the flame waver. He strained his eyes, combing the darkest reaches where shadows played off the walls.

"Show yourself."

His words echoed back.

He turned his head slowly. "Show yourself!"

He waited, listening for any sound that might give the intruder's location away – but the cave was as silent as a pauper's grave.

"If we're to be rid of them then we must act soon. As they grow, they become stronger and they're growing at an alarming rate."

It was a woman's voice, the words uncannily clear. He scanned the cave again, searching the places she might be hiding.

"Merlin, we face men not children. Even you will not be able to hold up against their combined strength."

Merlin? Then it struck him. The voice was not coming from the cave. He was not hearing it. It was in his mind! He sheathed his sword and turned the black stone over. He ran the ball of his thumb across its silky surface again.

"Your Gawain must leave for Northumbria immediately, before the festival of Lughnasa. After that, Argath will be too strong."

He took his thumb off the stone and the words ceased. *Merlin, I swear. Is there no end to this magic?*

He ran his thumb over the white etchings again.

"Tomorrow I journey to the Terran Stone at Wayland to find out more about Argath. I dare not use my web."

This time there was a long pause.

"The Wayland Stone has shown me. Listen, when Morganna charmed Argath's mother, she used a Dark Druid Rune of unknown origin. Where or how she discovered it, I have no idea, but it's more potent than you can imagine. Perhaps she found a Far Druid artifact we know nothing about. I'm not sure. We've neglected her too long, Merlin – far too long."

Pause.

"I'm returning through Cornwall, along the coast. I'll use the Stone at Ashbury to find out more. There's also a chance I can get further insight into this from Mabs. She has access to Brannast powder. It may not be as good as the Stone but it might turn up something new."

Pause.

"We're worse off than I thought. I've just left Mabs; she's getting so old, it's hard to converse without constant invocations. The Brannast helped but there's still much more to uncover. She's become so forgetful these past years, poor soul."

Pause.

"The name of the second son is Eyenon, sometimes called the Dreamwalker. He's still a child. He hasn't grown like the others. I don't know why. Perhaps Morganna got the Rune casting wrong or perhaps the Dark Rune she used only developed his mind not his body. I cannot say for sure."

Pause.

"The Ashbury Stone revealed more about Argath: he's gathered an army-right now it's small but it's deadly all the same. He's already planned a campaign that will bring him to Camelot. Last week he took his first village, Thurlstone. Little or nothing stands in his way. He uses a weapon of such destruction that he's assured victory. He's learned to control a deadly plague, which he spreads before him through rats he commands. It's like a *sylvan* Rune, remember? Can anyone hold that now? Dear Bran, things have changed. Listen, old friend, right now, he is assailable and so is his small army-all we have to do is find a way through the plague rats.

"I said he must be killed before Lughnasa; this is because his strength grows daily. Many threatened by the sweeping death choose to join him, rather than fight. He may even reach Lothian before the festival. You can guess what will happen next, either hundreds of deaths, or hundreds of converts. We must move fast, before the tide turns against us.

"You have so much faith in this Gawain of yours. I hope it's justified. Argath is cunning and ruthless. It would not be easy to defeat him with a practiced army, let alone a single knight. Damn Morganna! Don't you love these Christian curses, my old friend?"

Pause.

"There's a third son but all is denied me. Neither the powder nor the Stone have helped. All I know is, he waits in darkness – make of it what you will but this one frightens me more than the others."

Pause.

"I got back this morning. I'm too old for all this. I doubt I'll venture out again. I must confess I've been uneasy since my return. When I used the Wayland Stone, I had a feeling that someone was aware of me, of what I was doing. It was uncanny, enough to make goose-bumps dance on this old flesh of mine."

Pause.

"I was right. There is danger. I've divined it, an evil presence and it's close – perhaps as near as the meadows below. I'm casting a glyph on this speaking stone just in case. Only you, who know the correct *Mor Banna* Rune, can make it appear."

Pause.

"The third son. He's the one who detected me. Why do I feel so cold? I must hide."

Pause

"The gods are not with me. I've cast the *Mor Banna*, but the Rune I need for the shadow glyph evades me. It's gone clear out of my head. I can't even name it, let alone cast it. How long before they all go like this – butterflies at our summer's end. I should have carved a Rune Staff, my old friend, you were right. Now I must face the one that comes."

Silence.

Gawain took his thumb from the smooth surface. In the dying torchlight the swirling Rune lines faded and the stone became pebble rough. An indefinable sadness gripped him and he placed the stone reverently back in the drawer. He crossed to the cave entrance.

"Sweet Lord," he muttered, leaning against the wall and staring up at the pale sky, "Speaking Stones, Argath, Dark Druid Runes, Morganna, and now these Terran Stones. Merlin, we need a long talk. Indeed, we do." He walked out into the brisk morning air. "If I'm to help in this conspiracy I need to know all you know, everything."

He untethered Gringolet, hung his tower shield on the saddle and mounted. Behind him, the cave loomed lone and bare. He crossed himself as he passed Neume's grave. "In aeternae salvationis partem restitue." His breath curled up in thin ribbons with the words and he rode on without looking back.

As he guided Gringolet down the narrow trail, a new thought occurred to him. Whoever killed Neume could just as easily divine and track down Merlin.

He spurred Gringolet over the rocky terrain.

173

CHAPTER 10

When Gawain rounded the last bend opening onto the grassland meadow, Gringolet pulled up short, almost unseating him. In the center of the rocky path, staff in hand, stood Merlin, wisps of hair framing a face creased with riverbed lines of worry.

"I've been waiting for you, my boy," he called out wagging his staff. "I felt Neume's death yesterday. We have precious little time, it seems."

"Merlin, what in God's name is going on?"

"Time enough later," he called over his shoulder as he hurried toward a nearby grove. When he reached the circle of spruce trees, he beckoned. "Let your horse free, you'll not be needing her anymore."

"The Dragon ring, I felt it last ... "

"Later, lad. Here's a good spot. Stand behind me, now."

Merlin stooped with effort and brushed away twigs and fallen pinecones from the ground before him. He drew a small wooden box from his robe, placed it on the patch he'd cleared and propped open the lid. He took out a thin piece of wire with a red tip and a brass triangle etched with Runes. Next, he carefully set down the triangle then balanced the wire on the apex. Nodding with satisfaction, he stood and dusted off his hands.

"There's a force beneath us, around us, that you cannot see. It guides the wire. See how it obeys the energy it receives?" he said as the red tip swung lazily to the north.

"We can travel with that energy, along the same stream it follows. We just need to become light enough for it to influence us. I can do that by casting a *Gast* Rune. This will allow us to become part of the elements for an instant-long enough for the energy to affect us. When that happens, we're simply fluxed from one point to another, swept along the stream if you will."

He stepped back as if the conversation had fully explained everything and drew the *Gast* Rune. At the final slash, he began the invocation. Gawain, too confused for questions, simply watched – faith enough.

The dry crackle of Runic energy sounded like wood snapping in an open fire and Gawain felt himself, saw himself getting thinner, fading. He glanced at Merlin who stood by, yew staff clenched in his white-knuckled fist, eyes closed. The wizard's lips moved rapidly but Gawain didn't hear any words; instead, he felt a wind that seemed to pass through him and a second later there was an unearthly tranquility and he *was* the wind.

He traveled – he saw the grass bend and the trees sway and speed by. Then all sensation ceased as the world collapsed in a meteor storm, and for a moment, the briefest moment, he truly ceased to exist.

When he came to, the wizard was leaning over the top of his staff peering at him with a concerned expression. Gawain thought he'd passed out and that Merlin had revived him, but when his eyes focused, he saw the stone pillars and hard gray walls of Tintagel's war room. They were alone.

"Merlin," he gasped like a swimmer coming up for air, "amazing ... "

"Steady, my boy. Here, drink this. I don't know why, but fluxing always leaves me thirsty," Merlin said, holding out a silver goblet. Gawain took it in both hands and drank deeply.

"Better?"

"Yes, but my head's pounding like a battle drum."

"Here, sit down."

Merlin propped his staff against a suit of armor standing by the window and drew up a chair. "The dizziness will pass shortly," he said patting Gawain's shoulder and seating him. He shuffled over to a scroll rack and pulled out a parchment from one of the wooden honeycombs. He unrolled it and flattened it out on the war table and then he placed brass candleholders on each corner. He hummed quietly while he studied the map and waited for Gawain to recover.

"I heard all you did through the speaking stone," he said when he felt the young knight looking over his shoulder. "As Neume says, in less than a week Argath will reach Lothian and when he enters those city gates, he'll kill everyone who refuses to join him." He paused, pointing at the map. "He must have already swept through these towns, here, here, and here," he said, tapping three groups of tiny red buildings inked on the parchment. "Make no mistake, once he takes Lothian, nothing will stop him reaching Camelot."

Gawain rubbed his throbbing temples. The map revealed remarkable detail – rivers, towns, hills, even lakes. He was amazed. Not even his father had maps of such richness and that had been his lifelong passion.

"We must confront Argath here," said Merlin, tracing a finger over a jagged mountain range. "Stop him before he gathers momentum – that's the key."

"What does he want with Camelot?" said Gawain, his head finally beginning to clear.

"A good question. All I know at this point is what Neume learned: each of Uther's dark princes is bent on taking the city."

"Why?"

"Your guess is as good as mine, my boy."

"When will they get here?"

"I have no intention of letting any of them get this far. If we move quickly and strike before they have time to unify, we'll end any plans they have long before they get to our gates."

"Unify?"

"Yes. I believe that's what Morganna wants – to have them arrive at the same time. Battling against three specialized enemies together could prove too much for us. We have to defeat each one separately, before they join. First, we deal with Argath. Unfortunately, we have no time to raise an army then march all the way north. Besides, Arthur is in no condition to make such decisions."

He leaned over the war table, the wide sleeves of his robe making his arms look like hazel twigs. "For that reason you must go alone. It's the only way. How to get you into Argath's camp, though, that's the question," he muttered. "I can help guide you. I can even help prepare you for some of the dangers you'll be up against but I cannot travel with you and risk leaving Camelot undefended."

"I'm not afraid of facing Argath alone but how can I get far enough north in time to stop him taking Lothian?"

"The same way as I got you here," Merlin answered simply. He walked over to a banded chest in a far corner of the War Room and brought back one of the small brass triangles and another strip of wire.

"Here." He placed the triangle on the table and carefully balanced the wire on the apex. The red end remained motionless for a moment then began to turn like some ponderous insect until its tip faced north. Merlin waited until it steadied then glanced up.

"Good, a clear path. There are two drawbacks to this kind of traveling; first, you can go only with the stream, which means traveling north. That's why we came from Neume's cave here – Tintagel is directly north of the horned mountain. The second drawback is more serious. Since I began traveling this way, I've experienced unaccountable aging. For a long time, I didn't notice anything but after the last few journeys, I felt a marked difference. If I were to travel again, I would age perhaps a year. The time after that more, maybe two years. Unfortunately, I have no way of preventing this, nor can I reverse it. I've traveled a great deal since our visit to the lake, and I've set up many triangles on my way north when I was mapping. As you can see," he said, tapping the scroll, "I've gathered a wealth of information."

Gawain opened his mouth and Merlin held his hand up staving off the next question. "All in good time, my boy."

Gawain nodded.

Merlin sighed, wrinkles nesting around his keen eyes. "Sometimes I see so much of your father in you, your build, your serious nature, but most of all this insatiable need you have to find answers for everything. Let miracles be, lad, learn the virtue of patience and for Bran's sake let me finish a thought."

"I still miss him, even the Bible study."

"When he was your age, I spent many hours at his side. Not so many as I seem to spend with you, however," Merlin added shaking his head and turning back to the map. "Times were a lot simpler then; Runes a lot easier to hold. I didn't have a king to protect or Dark Druids nipping at my heels."

Harrumphing, he smoothed out a section of the map. "Now, getting you here," he said, pointing at Lothian, "won't be a problem but arranging for you to meet with Argath before Lughnasa will present some difficulties. The village of Tarn lies roughly a day's ride from Lothian. I can flux you to a small room in a holding I secured when I was mapping there. On arrival, you must arrange for a horse and then ride east through this long valley. At the northern edge of Lothian, you'll find a tavern, *The Mantrap*. That's your goal. When you arrive, you'll need to get Argath's attention. It shouldn't be too difficult. I'm sure he has spies everywhere by now. All you'll have to do is perform a little wizardry; he'll soon get to hear about it."

"How do I ... ?" Gawain began but quickly checked himself.

Merlin rummaged through the folds in his robes and pulled out a leather pouch. "At some point during the evening, when the place is crowded, you must make your presence known; perhaps start an argument or pick a fight. That's where the *Sith* powder comes in."

"Like the Sithean web?"

"In a way. They both derive their name from the Sidhe, the ancient Gods. I have a theory on that, but later. Now, once you've found your target, open the pouch and rub the tips of your fingers in the powder, like this. When you're done, make your move. Remember, the purpose of the fight will be to show off your magic, not your strength. Argath won't pass up the chance to meet with you once he learns there's someone nearby with Druid powers.

"So, when you've got everyone's attention, step back two or three paces and draw this Rune." Merlin slashed the air.

Gawain stared blankly.

"Nothing?"

"I ... I ..."

"No matter. I suspected as much, so I prepared a little something extra."

Merlin fussed with the folds of his robe again, this time he pulled out a small vial. "A distilment I made," he said holding the glass tube up to the light and swilling around the dark liquid inside. "It should last two or three days if we're lucky. Here, drink. Then see what happens when I draw the Rune."

Gawain took the vial and pulled out the stopper. He held it under his nose and sniffed at the contents. He glanced at Merlin, tipped his head back and swallowed. He shuddered at the taste and Merlin huffed then redrew the Rune. Gawain gaped. Now the strokes he made trailed with vapors of sparking light.

"Close your eyes. Tight now. Can you see the Rune in your mind?"

"Yes, it's glowing the way the sun does after you look at it."

"Good, now see if you can draw it."

Gawain opened his eyes and drew the Rune with ease.

"Good. Again."

Gawain did as he was asked.

"Very good. If you do that with the *Sith* powder on your fingers, the elements will absorb your opponent instantly. I'm afraid you don't quite have the talent for fusing the *Danna Gast* Rune yet, my boy, hence the powder. It will do that nicely for you."

"What happens to the challenger?"

"Don't worry; he'll return soon enough, the elements can't contain him for long. It should cause quite a commotion though," he said. "To be doubly sure, I've also added some other effects."

Merlin dipped a finger into the pouch and flicked the powder toward the hearth. A crackling trail of sparks leaped from the tip of his finger and arced toward the far wall where it exploded with a boom that shook every piece of furniture in the war room, showering them both with dazzling light.

Gawain gasped, ears ringing.

"Effects, my boy, merely effects. I mixed some *allatote* in with the powder, that's all." Merlin shrugged as if it were nothing then he began rolling up the map. "The next trick will be to trap Argath. For that I have something rather special." He slid the map back in the scroll rack, rummaged through a drawer and withdrew a small band that swept the floor and walls with prismatic rays of light.

"This," he announced, dangling the thin circle of wire from his finger.

"What is it?"

"The Druid word for it is *shorn*. It's charmed to attune to you, so when you wear it, nothing will happen. Shouldn't anyway," he muttered as an afterthought. "Go ahead, try it on."

Gawain slipped the wire over his wrist; the brilliant colors dulled then disappeared.

"Anything?"

"No,"

"Right you are then. But put it on Argath and he'll become docile, even obedient if we're lucky. Of course, the secret is to get close enough to him. Remember, as long as he wears it, he'll be in your power. If it's possible, bring him back here, I can learn a great deal from him. But if that proves too difficult, then you must kill him. He cannot be allowed to go free." He held Gawain's gaze steady. "Not under any circumstances."

"I understand."

"Good. If you need to contact me, you have the Dragon Ring. Open your mind – use your stars. You know how. I'll feel your presence when you do."

He paused, green eyes almost predatory in the dusky light. "Perhaps one day, with enough training, we'll be able to communicate without the pictures and dreams. Maybe we'll even walk the Far Druid path together, my boy."

He retrieved a long dark robe hemmed with Rune symbols from the back of a chair and held it out. "Here, change into this. It's more fitting to an acolyte's station. In the pockets you'll find some gold coins and a *Pence* dagger."

Gawain stripped off his knight's tunic and pulled on the robe. He searched the pockets and pulled out a slim leather-sheathed dagger.

"Be careful, it may look innocent but if it breaks the skin that's another story. The blade was forged in the first Beltane fire. It takes easily to charms. Last night I glyphed it so that any blood it touches will turn to powder – not a pretty sight but then neither is someone dying from the plague. Use it only as a last resort. Right, that's about it. Let's get you ready."

Gawain adjusted the *shorn* wire and Merlin stepped back and checked him over.

"You make a handsome Druid, my boy. Remember the day we set out to kill Uther? You asked your father on Barras Point if we'd succeed. Well, I'll repeat now what he said then. We fight and we go on. We will find triumph in adversity." Merlin clapped him on the shoulders and pulled him close.

"I'll not fail," breathed Gawain.

"I know. I know, my falcon. May the great Bran and your Christian God follow in your footsteps."

The two stood facing each other for a moment, Gawain feeling the loss he must bear if anything were to go wrong. Young knight and old wizard – the love in their smiles chasing away the doubt in their hearts.

"Time," said Merlin stepping back and straightening his robe. He raised his hand to slash the *Danna Gast* Rune, curled his two fingers then hesitated. He frowned, staring up at the rafters, lips moving. Finally, huffing to himself, he snatched his staff from the fireplace, closed his eyes and ran his fingers over one of the carvings.

Gawain watched, puzzled. *I've never seen ... .* But his thoughts were cut short because Merlin's eyes suddenly blazed open and he slashed the Runes he needed. Gawain felt his head peel open and the world vanished.

183

The room that materialized around Gawain smelled of rich earth. It was damp, despite the afternoon sun slanting in through a cobwebbed window. He waited for his stomach to settle and the room to stop shifting, then he made his way to the casement and threw open the window. He drew in a deep breath of cold air and stared at the unfamiliar landscape of hills and snowcapped mountains.

In God's name how far have I traveled – half the length of the realm? He fingered the shorn wire on his wrist. "One day, old wizard, we'll sit down under the boughs of an oak tree and you will tell me all you know of your ancient world and your wondrous spells and you will answer all my questions," he muttered.

Gawain opened the door and crossed a deserted yard to a muddy paddock where two dappled mares stood snuffling at heaps of straw. A cold wind gusted and he pulled his thin robe tight around him, trying to find some measure of comfort in the worn cloth.

"As sure as the stars shine, Merlin, I'll learn to forgive myself and find love again. And one day, after I've done your bidding and we rid ourselves of these bastard sons, I will find a place to settle down and finally live in peace."

It was a long uneventful ride to Lothian and he didn't arrive at *The Mantrap* until well after sunset. Checking he still had the pouch within easy reach, he pulled up his hood and entered the weathered tavern.

The warmth melted the ice from his bones. A cluttered bar stood at the far end under smoky oil lamps. The black timber beams holding up the low ceiling sagged from age. Merchants, farm hands and pockets of guild workers occupied most of the tables scattered about the noisy room.

Gawain looked for anything out of the ordinary. His Druid robes caught the attention of a few nearby customers but aside from an odd glance, no one seemed to show him much interest. He chose a table with a view of the door and took a seat.

A fire burned brightly in a wide hearth to his right. His was considering moving closer when a smiling buttress of a woman in a food-stained apron strode toward his table with a mug of ale in her sizable fist.

"Here ye are, handsome," she said, slopping down the drink and wiping her hands on a small towel tucked in her waistband. "Will ye be wanting supper?"

"No thank you," said Gawain dropping a coin on the table. She gave him a toothy smile, swept up the coin and headed back to the bar. He raised the mug to his lips and scoured the room over the brim. A group of men playing sevens near an alcove caught his eye. At the far end of the table, a loud redhead with a thick tangle of hair and a beard jutting out like a spade was cursing the thrower. The dice settled and his companion, an angular man dressed in black wool-spun and threadbare pants, pocketed some of the coins from a nearby stack. Gawain fingered his mug thoughtfully.

He sipped at the foam and stared at the redhead. The man shot back a brief glance. Gawain held his look steady. A few moments passed and the redhead glanced up again. This time when he caught Gawain's stare, he glowered. Gawain kept gaze fixed. Kicking a chair aside, the redhead lumbered over.

"Ye have a problem, Druid?" The voice was thick with ale.

Gawain stood and taking time to straighten his robe spoke in measured tones. "First, I'd suggest a change in attitude when you address me."

The redhead's eyes widened in surprise then his face tightened. He drew back a scarred fist and threw a wild, looping punch. Gawain stepped back and away in a single movement. The redhead stumbled and Gawain pushed him between the shoulder blades sending him sprawling into a table.

The chatter stopped. Chairs scraped back.

Gawain drove his hand deep in his pocket, dug open the pouch and moved into the light of an oil lamp hanging from a roof beam. He ground his fingers into the powder.

The redhead struggled to his feet, face burning with shame. He groped for his sword. There was a sudden movement to his left as his blade cleared the scabbard. He turned, but too late. A small ferret-faced man slid from his seat. In a single deft movement, he thrust a gutting knife deep into the redhead's stomach.

The gambler slumped over the assassin's shoulder with a grunt and the broadsword fell clattering from his fingers. The face below broke into a yellow toothed grin then the killer reefed the blade up and across, opening the redhead's stomach like a sack of warm fish bait.

Falling to his knees, the redhead tried to stop the slippery blue rope from spilling out of the gaping wound. He looked up at Gawain, confusion clouding his pale eyes. His lips moved once, twice, then without uttering a word, he crashed to the floor.

"I think ye owe me, Druid. That turd would have unseamed ye, like as not," said the assassin, wiping the blade on his sleeve and nodding at the body.

"I could have taken care of him," said Gawain coldly.

"Perhaps, Druid, but I wouldn't have fancied yer chances-besides, I had me orders."

"What orders?" said Gawain as the room began to fill with sounds.

"Orders, is all."

"I don't understand."

"Ye will."

The assassin jammed his dagger in its sheath and stood aside as two guildsmen set to dragging the body away by its heels.

"Me lord'll be right pleased I culled me a wizard – even a nearly dead 'un. Now, if ye value what skin ye have under them fancy robes, ye'll be following me right smart and no questions asked."

"Where to?" said Gawain.

"Don't fret none, Druid. It'll be somewheres ye'll be safe. Now, quick's the word and sharp's the action – or these people here will be stringing ye up before ye can say Tom Shorty. Which is the name of yours truly," he said, tapping his blood-spattered chest proudly.

Outside they mounted two horses. Shorty led and Gawain followed. The trail they took wound its way toward the snowcapped mountains Gawain had seen from the window of the holding. On either side, fields of lowland farms spread wide skirts over a rich, fertile valley that in turn stretched out toward a distant lake.

They rode in silence, Shorty's gelding snorting into the cold night as it cantered over the grass. After a few hours, they came to a riverbank and followed its meandering shore to the foothills. A horned moon broke out from between ragged clouds, bathing the landscape in ghostly silver. Making their way north, Gawain took careful note of the route.

The horses slowed to a walk as they pushed on through a heavily boldered pass. The air grew thin and the cold mountain wind cut between the sparse trees, chilling Gawain to the bone and leaving him cursing the flimsy robe.

Once they reached the sheltered lea of the mountain, they set up camp. Gawain lit a small fire and they fell to sleep long before it burned out. In the morning, they rose with the sun and rode on, climbing steadily until they reached small islands of snow high up on the alpine ridge.

By late afternoon, the horses were slogging their way through heavy drifts clogging a narrow passage at the summit. Both riders urged the animals forward, not wanting to set up camp in the forbidding terrain. But it wasn't until the sun began to set that they finally broke out of the snowbound pass and began the descent toward the lowland basin far beneath the other side of the mountain's jagged peak.

That night they camped on the open mountainside where lonely winds howled and moaned. Despite his questions, Gawain could scarcely get a word out of his companion, who seemed to get quieter the closer they got to Argath's camp.

The following day, under the sparse warmth of an early sun, they wound down the rocky path until the land flattened out onto a plain that Shorty said led to the fens and Argath's army.

After another long ride, they saw the first signs of Argath's presence near a wood. In one of the fields bordering the trees, a herd of cows, twenty or more, lay dead and bloated in the long grass.

Gawain fought back the urge to gag as he neared the rotting corpses. The gnawed hocks of the cows left them in grotesque contrast to their huge swollen bodies. Flies glistened in moving patches. Tongues lolled out of leathery mouths. He nudged his nervous mount around the carnage toward the smoldering remains of a farmhouse. This time he found a dog and a small herd of sheep and by an enclosed pasture an old horse; all lay bloated in the late sun.

"Master's 'bin close about, I'd say," Shorty whispered as they skirted the corpses.

Further on, after rounding a break of poplars, they saw the army. Men, old and young, perhaps two hundred or more, were busy erecting tents and building makeshift shelters. Horses stood nearby, tethered or corralled in crude pens. At the center of the camp Gawain could see a dark rectangular tent. Above it flapped a large red flag. Even from this distance, Gawain could make out the shape on the background of the standard – a black cross, broken through the middle.

"That'd be him," Shorty said, following Gawain's gaze. "I expect he'll be waitin'."

They rode through the camp to Argath's tent. No one stopped working or glanced in their direction until they dismounted before two guards posted at the entrance. Both burly men, wearing leather cuirasses and high boots, looked more like farmers after a day's work than guards of a dark prince.

They stood to attention pulling halberds into their chests when Gawain and Shorty dismounted and approached. The tent flap swung between them. Gawain cast a look at Shorty and ducked through.

Inside, strong earthy smells of old bark and compost thickened the air. Through the gloom, Gawain could make out something or someone sitting in a chair. Shorty stepped forward bowing deeply.

A reed thin voice spoke from the center of the tent. "Well, my little ferret, what have you brought me this fine morning? Tell me things. Things I want to hear, things to cheer me up this fine day."

As his eyes began to adjust to the gloom, Gawain could make out a willowy shape languishing in a high-backed chair.

"Come closer, I see you well enough, wizard, but perhaps you would care to get a better look at me? *Narth ram.*"

At the strange command, Shorty tugged Gawain forward, then bowed again and shuffled back into the deep shadows.

"Argath at your service, or should I say, considering where you hail from, at your peril," the thin voice said nonchalantly.

When Gawain's eyes finally adjusted, he had to resist the temptation to rub them. The figure before him may have been a man in form but he looked far more like a serpent from the fens. He would be the height of a man if he stood, thought Gawain, even taller, but the head, smooth and flattened like an adder's, ended any further similarity. His nose and mouth protruded and Gawain could see the curve of fanged teeth and the leathery tines of a split tongue darting behind them.

"You seem distressed, wizard." Argath hissed. "What was it you expected, a noble prince? A winning smile? Phaaa!" he spat.

Argath placed his long thin hands on the arms of the chair and pushed himself up, writhing almost sensually as he stood. He bent forward with an extraordinary subtle movement, yellow eyes glowing in the dusky tent. "You seem all too quiet and far too poor for a Druid of any esteem. No matter, perhaps you'll serve to entertain me, rather than help me. Speak. Tell me why I should let you should live."

Gawain subconsciously fingered the *shorn* wire as he answered. "I don't possess the Druid skills required for casting spells. I'm merely a bard, a priest on my way to Column Hill to worship at the Sensacharach ceremonies," he said, trying to sound unruffled, hoping to allay suspicion by his casual answer. "I have only rudimentary knowledge of Runes."

"My, my, a wordsmith – *rudimentary*. I *shall* enjoy having some chat with you after conversing with these imbeciles all day. But you may just find yourself in dire need of some of that *rudimentary* knowledge of yours when I'm done," he added. "*Anna Kast*." Shorty sprang forward at the command and Argath settled back into the tall chair with languid grace. The audience was over. Shorty escorted Gawain to the entrance.

Outside, Gawain put his hands up to shield his eyes against the dazzling light. But the after-image that burned in his brain then was not the corona of the sun, it was the slinky outline of Argath.

Shorty led him passed a group of helmeted soldiers practicing with claymores and on to a makeshift storage depot in the middle of the compound. The two guards on duty at the entrance saluted and Shorty left. The guards ushered Gawain inside without a word. His position was clear: he was a prisoner.

Gawain spent the rest of the day inside the compound sitting with his back against a stack of kegs. He watched from under the folds of his cowl as workers in hard leather tunics cut staves and pegs and erected more tents. He guessed the camp would be in use another fortnight then dismantled and moved to the edge of the next town. With its ranks swelling, it would advance again, becoming stronger, more powerful, until it finally became unstoppable – long before Camelot.

One of the guards fed him a bowl of watery thin gruel in the early afternoon and again when the sun set, but he never spoke to him or answered any of the questions he asked. Gawain waited while the evening shadows melted into darkness and the stars slowly powdered the heavens. Somewhere in the distance, a dog howled and he heard the hungry cry of distant rooks.

Out in the east, the misty haze of Orion appeared and thoughts of Merlin filled him. An hour later, he surrendered to the power of the great constellation. He emptied his mind of the day's events and found the heart where the white light burned the brightest and slowly, the warmth of the Dragon Ring began to intensify, clearing a path to the wizard.

CHAPTER 11

*D*eath.

Gawain's head snapped back as if an invisible hand had struck him. His stomach churned, ripping him away from the tranquility of Orion's spell with a force that left his mind reeling.

He sat up blinking, skin crawling. Argath was near. He struggled to his feet, checking for the *shorn*, but the ridiculously thin wire brought little comfort. Moments passed then he heard the sentries' challenge.

The slinky figure of Argath rounded the entrance to the compound, flanked by six guards. He was a head taller than they were and walked with a willowy, swaying rhythm. As he neared, a flash of moonlight glinted off his flat skull. The arms swinging at his sides were no thicker than tallow candles and ended in ludicrously long fingers. The odor of old leaves and compost billowed around him. When they reached the depot, the entourage halted and Argath stepped forward.

"I have come for some chat," he said in a low, seductive voice. "Tell me of your Druid days. *Tannath arrat rath.*" Argath's head swiveled and the guards stumbled back. He leaned forward, pale light shimmering on his skin like moonlight on still water.

"Speak your clever language to me. Tell me things." At the last word, a forked tongue flicked out, tasting the night air before disappearing into the wide mouth in a single, impossibly quick movement.

"I have little to add to what I've already told you," Gawain said trying to keep the shock of what he was witnessing out of his voice. "I was staying at Lothian on my way to Falfax Coome when ... "

"First, you will address me as lord. Then you will prove yourself useful to me with your next words or I will dine on your liver." Argath hissed the threat, his subtle body swaying from side to side.

In that moment, Gawain fully expected him to coil and strike. "My lord," he said quickly, "I'm no great wizard; I'm not even a passable one. The only way I can cast Runes is by using this small band I wear, which gives me the power I need to create the spell."

He held out his arm so Argath could see the *shorn*. The serpent head shot forward, pupils elongating as they inspected the wire.

"Shape me some Runes, Druid," he said, eyes locked on the *shorn*.

Gawain took a measured breath, watching the head wearily. "The only Runes I know were taught to me for protection, in case I was attacked on the road, lord."

"What are you trying to say?"

"I'll need a volunteer if I'm to demonstrate, sire."

"There are no volunteers in my army. I command, they obey," Argath said simply.

"Then lord, command someone to fight this unworthy Druid."

Argath's thin lips wrinkled in a hint of a smile and the slits in the center of his yellow eyes relaxed into dark, silky rings.

"As you wish. See you do not disappoint me, wizard. I'll be watching closely, and believe me when I tell you, these eyes that seem to fascinate you so much, miss nothing. *Rath ara carn.*"

At his command, one of the guards from the entourage stepped forward.

"My lord." He was broad-shouldered and muscled like a smithy. He bent to one knee and bowed deeply, his long braided hair sweeping from behind his neck to the ground. Argath turned to Gawain.

"Speak to him."

"My name is Orts," Gawain lied. "I'm a Druid bard. I've come here to show your master how to . . ."

"You're too long winded. Grattan, rid me of this excrement," Argath said stepping back. "*Dunna rav!*"

The muscle bound guard jumped up at the command. He snatched the long sword from his scabbard in a movement so quick it barely left Gawain time to dig for Merlin's powder. The chiseled face showed no strain as the hands whirled the weapon in a controlled arc.

Gawain drew the Rune, cutting the air with a fluid motion. The strokes were exact – but nothing happened. The guard grunted then swung the sword.

Gawain looked up to see death.

Athlan's words flew through his mind as moonlight streamed off the blade: *The magic is fading. One day I think it will simply vanish, you know ... .* The sword arced down. Then Gawain watched in horror as the blade cleaved through his skull and body and disappeared harmlessly in a shower of vaporous light.

The guard before him registered utter shock. His jaw dropped then he too shimmered and vanished. Gawain staggered back from the blow, feeling his neck and chest with disbelieving fingers, shivering from the effects of the ethereal sword. *Bless you, Merlin.*

"My, my. This trick I like," Argath whispered pensively. "Show me how to draw those Runes, Druid."

Gawain turned as the guard materialized, the stunned expression still etched on his face. "I can show you how to draw them, my lord, but I cannot make them work. For that," he hesitated long enough to show his reluctance in having to give up his treasured possession, "you need to wear the *shorn.*"

Argath's eyes narrowed to knife slits and Gawain felt his throat tighten as the head shot forward. It hung in front of him, motionless, taking in every inch of his face.

"*Rath ara carn,*" Argath spat, gusting foul breath. "Do your trick again, Druid. This time without your precious band, I think."

A second guard, tall and grisly, wearing a boiled leather cuirass studded with rivets, stepped forward. A huge double edged axe swung from a thick cord bound around his wrist. With a flick he caught the haft and ran his fingers along the crescent blade. He grinned showing brown streaked teeth.

"*Dar Kath.*"

At Argath's command, the grim figure thrust out a hand.

"Give him the trinket, Druid," said Argath.

"My lord, if you do this, I'll surely die," said Gawain taking off the band and reluctantly handing it over.

"Then do so. I'm getting hungry. *Da Grat Katha.*"

The guard passed the *shorn* to Argath, tossed the axe into his right hand and stepped aside. Gawain glanced to his right praying Argath was slipping the band over his wrist. His stomach dropped. The *shorn* was dangling from his ropy fingers.

The guard leaped forward long grey hair flying out behind him. Gawain backed up, forcing himself to act clumsily. He stumbled to one side, slashing wild Runic arcs and lines trying to avoid the wheeling blows. No matter the cost, he had to convince Argath the *shorn* was his only source of power.

The guard read Gawain's next move easily and intercepted him. The crescent blade flashed as he swung at the Druid cowering before him. Gawain closed his eyes. But before the axe finished its thrumming stroke, Argath struck.

If the guard was fast, Argath was lightning. His head blurred and his leathery mouth scissored open impossibly wide. He snapped the guard's neck in his curved fangs with such force he swept the body off the ground. Blood spattered through the air like molten rain and the hapless victim jerked so hard his right boot flew off and clattered into the nearby barrels. The Serpent Lord twisted viciously pinning him to the earth then ground his fangs into his spine.

Gawain staggered back, stunned by the unexpected display of speed and ferocity. He felt his stomach rise at the sound of Argath's excited breathing. Then he realized he had instinctively reached for his own sword. He glanced at Argath but he hadn't noticed.

"Always enjoy that," said Argath, finally straightening. "Keeps me sharp, on top, if you know what I mean," he added, his distended mouth slowly shrinking to its former size.

He paused swinging the *shorn* lazily from a slender finger. "Why does this look so much like a weapon to these poor eyes of mine, umm? What else does it do, Druid?"

"It's glyphed to help channel essence, my lord, that's all," said Gawain, keeping his voice even. "I can't hold it like some. My master kindly gave it to me to help intensify my poor powers in times of trouble."

Argath grinned, the guard's blood still clinging in threads to the cusps of his fangs. "I'd say times of trouble are already here, wouldn't you?" He rocked the *shorn* back and forth. "Draw me those Runes again," he said, inspecting the wire.

Gawain squatted and traced a Rune in the earth near Argath's feet. When he'd finished, Argath stabbed at the Rune with his boot. "Let me see if I have this straight. I wear this trinket, draw this Rune and then I'll have the power to make my enemies vanish-even if I do risk losing my supper." At the last words, his head swiveled, eyes boring into Gawain.

"Yes, my lord," said Gawain, warily.

"Then, I think I'd rather dine while I can," he shot back. His forked tongue flicked out and he threw the *shorn* high over the supply tents. Turning back, he stubbed the toe of his boot into the earth and erased the Rune.

Gawain was stunned.

Argath's silky pupils narrowed to pinpoints. "I can taste your lies, Druid."

"My lord, I . . ."

"*Annassss Man.*"

Guards materialized out of the shadows and flanked Gawain with a clattering of swords and shields.

"Take him to Squee. I want to know all things. Who he is, where he's from, what he eats and how he sits to shit. All. Everything. Understand? *Nacht Batta.*"

The tallest guard stepped out of the formation, a man with thick graying whiskers and cheeks chafed red from the northern winds. He seized Gawain by the arm. Argath held up his hand. "Be sure to tell that idiot Squee not to damage his liver. I hate people spoiling my food."

The guard saluted and without another word, Argath turned and ambled off, swaying rhythmically between his troops.

The Guard shoved his prisoner ahead. Gawain tried to figure out what had caused things to go so horribly wrong. Argath seemed to know about the *shorn*. It was if he had sensed its purpose. *My secrets are thin in his presence. A*

198

stubby finger pointed to a group of tents cutting off his thoughts.

"There," husked the guard.

Gawain raised his hand to his eyes squinting as if he couldn't see that far. He needed a diversion.

Another shove sent him staggering. The compound lay in a pool of darkness. The tents on the far side glowed from lanterns within but they were as silent as winter trees.

"Through here," the guard grunted, grabbing the cowl of his robe and forcing him between two stacks of barrels.

Gawain considered using the Rune but changed his mind. If he did that, it would only be a matter of time before Argath discovered he was lying about the *shorn*. Somehow, he had to find a way to contact Merlin.

The single tent ahead loomed over the others. Voices rose from inside the thick canvas, someone yelling, then silence, then yelling again, higher pitched this time. *Squee?* If Argath managed to find out what he really knew, he would be free to move at will. And if he ever discovered the secrets of the triangles and Merlin's ability to travel ...

Twenty paces before the tent, they passed close to a supply depot and Gawain slipped the *Pence* dagger from its small sheath. To his left lay a coil of rope and an open sack of scattered tent pegs. *Let this work, Merlin.* He caught his foot in the rope and stumbled to his knees.

"On yer feet," the guard growled, lashing out with a muddy boot.

Gawain caught the ankle. He twisted and drove the *Pence* dagger up deep into the man's groin. A look of disbelief swept across the face above him. The mouth opened but before a cry could escape the lips, the body stiffened and the neck snapped back.

Gawain pulled the charmed weapon out, expecting to see blood gush from the wound – it did, but not in a stream, in a flow of fine dry powder. The guard toppled and hit the ground. He smashed open like an earthenware gourd – the blood powder spilling into neat little pyramids as the broken cavities of his body emptied.

Gawain looked at the *Pence* dagger with newfound respect. It gleamed ominously in the moonlight. There was no trace of blood or powder on its thin, narrow blade. He slid it into its sheath, tucked it into his pocket and slipped back into the shadows. He waited, breathing deeply. The voices in the distant tent held steady. Safe.

He stole behind the supply awnings and skirted two guards crouched by a fire, hands spread over the low embers as they talked. The wind blew in his direction carrying with it a smell of roasting meat and his stomach growled. Somewhere off to his right a dog barked. He backed away, tracking west in a wide arc. Another bark, this time followed by a low, throaty growl. He hurried now, slipping deeper into the shadows. He had to find a place to let Merlin know of the shorn's failure and find out what to do next. In the night sky, the moon was both a boon and a curse – bright enough to see by but also bright enough to make him visible.

Threading his way between the final tents, he used the high passing clouds to his advantage, crossing the open spaces when the shadows lengthened. Every minute counted; he had to clear the encampment, let his scent fade in case they used the dogs.

When he reached the perimeter of the camp, the wide fields lay bathed in pale light. The clouds had cleared. He felt the skin on his back crawl as he slipped away from the last tent and sought what little cover the tall grass offered.

He followed the path for another hour until he came to a rocky knoll marking the entrance to the mountain pass. At the outcropping, he stopped to catch his breath and look back to the distant humps of tents and faint dots of campfires. Everything seemed calm. He peered up into the night searching for Orion. It wheeled high in the western sky, partly obscured by smoky thin clouds. An owl hooted and he heard vague sounds of rustling and scurrying in the bushes below.

Exhausted from his narrow escape and the long trek, he cleared away a place between the rocks and lay down thankfully on the mossy ground. He focused his mind, trying to push aside the images of Argath but it was a long time before he could rid himself of the nightmare face that had so effortlessly distorted into a serpent's head, or the eyes, the narrowing pupils, that seemed to bore right through you. He stared up into the lonely vault above, willing his mind to escape, to find its way to the impossibly distant stars and there find peace and safety in Orion's glowing heart.

At length, the images of Argath faded, scattering like charred scraps of paper and Gawain found the center he sought. The Dragon Ring warmed. A dull image of Camelot swam into view and suddenly Merlin's Rune staff burst in his mind in a single bright flash.

The staff slowly rotated. On the third turn, it transformed into the image of a snake. Moments later the image split and the snake and staff pulled apart facing each other. The staff lashed out, striking at the snake's head. The snake reared back and struck with uncanny speed, snapping fangs glistening with ropy green fluid. The staff swam with Runic magic and struck again. This time it hit true and the snake vanished in a storm of stars.

Darkness.

Then, from the velvet night, the most glorious sunrise Gawain had ever beheld broke over the land bathing him in white light. And all around, stretched out as far as he could see, tiny, blood-red pyramids of sand, dotted the land.

CHAPTER 12

And then the star strewn firmament was blazing above him. He struggled to his feet. Nothing had changed; the owl still hooted into the night sky and far away, the soft yellow glow of tent lights and burning campfires winked in the darkness.

Gawain rubbed his temples. Maybe Merlin was right and his Druid strength was increasing each time he used the stars. *I need to understand what this means, Merlin. What's the connection between your staff and Argath? And what of the sun burning in a clear blue sky? What does that mean?* He pulled his thin robe tight for warmth and he set out for the sheer cliffs at the mountain base.

He weighed his chances – he couldn't leave Lothian to Argath. Merlin clearly said, 'if you can't *shorn* him, you must kill him.' But how in God's name could he do that with all those guards and the speed of that creature? Even Lancelot at his best couldn't hope to defeat him.

He picked his way between boulders that had tumbled from the ridge high above until he came across a small patch of bracken growing at the base of the cliff face. He tore up the springy bushes and laid them on the earth. At least here, in the lee of the mountain, he'd be out of the open and sheltered from the biting wind.

The answer lay in Merlin's message – the pictures. He bent and tested the crude bed. *The staff ... Magic. What magic? The Pence dagger! The tiny pyramids of red sand –*

Argath – his drying blood after I've stabbed him. That fits. And the sun . . . Yes! The sun's tomorrow. It has to be done then! Somehow, I have to find away to get close enough to him ... .

He decided to make his way back to the camp at first light. No one would expect that. They'd assume he'd try to flee through the mountains but he would circle round and approach from the east. He smiled in the darkness. If he could kill a guard and use his clothes – maybe, just maybe ... .

He lay down on the bracken breathing in the aroma of heather and lilac and searched for Orion again, but it had long since wheeled away on its lonely journey across the heavens.

I'm no more than a pawn in this game. Here in this land, pitted against a beast before whose power I lie so helpless, I'm forced to await mysterious pictures sent the length and breadth of this wild land in a fashion only God could fathom, while you lie abed at Camelot, Merlin. If I could comprehend your strange intelligence I would, I'm sure, find deeper, darker purposes in what you've wrought and I'd come to a greater understanding of the Druid lore that drives you so relentlessly. So tell me, wise wizard, are you truly my friend or are you only finding in me desperate solutions to fix those things you've set in motion that are now so out of control?

Above him, perched high on a branch of a lone pine, a mousing owl hooted – the same familiar note that had followed him when he first left the fields below.

His sleep was deep and dreamless and when he awoke, he was shivering from the cold. A light rain fell from heavy skies. He looked toward the camp hidden now by a veil of drizzle and fog. He pulled the thin Druid robe tight and set off to the plains, skirting north. It would take the better part of the day to sweep wide enough to approach the camp from the rear.

The one thing troubling him as he clambered over the rock outcropping was the weather. Where was that fierce sun burning against a blue sky? He looked up into the straining belly of the low clouds. Would they clear by the afternoon? Would there be such a day today? In his heart, he doubted it.

Marsh covered the land to the north and he had to thread his way carefully between tufts of tall reeds and bulrushes growing in the swampy patches. He stopped frequently to listen for any signs of a search party but there were none. Perhaps Argath would believe by now he'd truly made good his escape and wouldn't bother tracking him.

Shivering and holding back fits of coughing, he slogged through the endless fens and boggy fields until early afternoon when he judged it time to cut east toward the camp. Another hour and he reached the fringes of the valley where he could see the distant hump of tents. Weary and cold, he sought rest and shelter in a grove of elm and ash trees.

He sat in the bowl of a blasted trunk and looked up at the leaden skies. He hadn't eaten in two days and he could feel the effects. He coughed deeply hugging his knees to his chest and blinking away the rain running off his lank hair and dripping down his neck. "Where's your sun, Merlin?" he muttered into the steady downpour. "Where's your magic to take this cold from my bones and fill my stomach?" Then he hung his head between his knees, and spoke again, this time quietly, "Will I ever be free of this guilt, Athlan? Will I ever see you in heaven?"

Hope waned at the memory that dogged him so tirelessly. And when his mind sought comfort and shelter from the downpour, he found her again-there, where he always kept her, safe in his heart.

Rain sheeted across the clearing soaking through his flimsy robe, plastering his hair to his face and sluicing down his cheeks. He closed his eyes and she came to him-soft pale skin, smile showing tips of white teeth and in the spiraling depths of her blue eyes, he felt a strange duality. Slowly, he drifted.

No!

He separated from his younger self-shifted, floated, wavered like a lost soul and for a moment, he saw himself from up high, a bird's eye view-a pitiful figure huddled against a thunder-split elm, sodden and friendless. Behind him, night yawned and a narrow path wound its way to where the tip of the Terran Stone beamed steady rays of light above a hilltop.

NO!

He fought the welling emotions. He'd been the younger Gawain for so long this time, the awakening terrified him.

NO!

He snapped his eyes shut.

NO! I HAVE NOT FINISHED.

He fought to stay with all his strength. *Seek ... the cold, the trees, the rain ... .* Then, suddenly, he was back, shivering, empty stomach rumbling, head pounding. Above him, grey clouds lumbered across a bruised and sullen sky.

Later that afternoon he neared the first humps of tents poking through the mist and hissing rain. He moved cautiously, although he doubted anyone would see or hear him. When he gained the first tent, he put an ear to the dripping canvas.

No sounds came from within but he still felt uneasy. He peered around the side of the awning. The camp seemed deserted. There were no soldiers or guards, no one, not even a stray cur.

He edged around to the front. The tent flap hung open. He unsheathed the *Pence* dagger and peeked inside. Empty.

He slipped in, thankful to be out of the incessant rain. He stood in the gloom stifling a cough, waiting for his eyes to adjust. Clothes and the remains of a meal lay on an unmade bed.

Sheathing the dagger, he quickly changed into the padded shirt, wool – spun coat and heavy pants. He ate the dark bread and hard cheese, forcing himself to chew slowly.

Swallowing the last dry mouthful, he crossed to the entrance and peered out. Still no one in sight. He slipped into the rain and stole to the next tent. No sound. He ducked inside – more food, this time potatoes and mutton half eaten. He stuffed them into his coat pocket.

Keeping to the awnings, he threaded his way to Argath's tent. If the Serpent Lord were there, unguarded, then he'd have a chance. He was already beginning to feel stronger after eating. He fingered the sheath of the *Pence* dagger.

When he reached the last row of tents, he could see Argath's flag with its broken cross hanging limply in the center of the compound.

It's too easy.

The words thrummed in his mind as he inched forward but there was no choice.

Heart racing, he slipped past the final guy ropes. Twenty paces across the muddy grass and he'd be at the awning. The rain danced off the ground, sending a fine mist swirling around his feet. He crouched low and ran the final yards. Rolling thunder boomed in the air and a scar of jagged lightning ripped across the eastern sky.

Even before he reached the tent, he knew it was a mistake. Foreboding, heightened by the ancient power in the thunder, caused him to pull up short. In that instant, the flaps of the entrance flew open and a voice drifted out from deep within.

"So nice of you to come back and visit, Druid. Please, do come in. *Arreth barr*."

Guards materialized from either side of the flaps. Gawain grunted as hands grabbed his arms and shoved him inside.

"This time I'll accompany you to Squee myself. I really am quite anxious to learn the Runes that turn a man's blood to powder. Just imagine how creative I can be with those. Come now, Druid, I won't bite – well, maybe once." He hissed what could have been a laugh, and the guards forced Gawain to his knees.

The Serpent Lord stood over him pointing. "If all my enemies are as stupid as you, I'll have Camelot before the spring thaw," he said.

Gawain started at the mention of Camelot. Argath was close, maybe close enough. Gawain stayed on his knees, fingers stealthily searching for the Pence dagger in the folds of his borrowed clothes. If he could inch closer, perhaps pretend to cough, then .

"*Rath a gar set, set.*"

The guards sprang forward and hauled him to his feet. Argath bent his head so close Gawain could hear the air hissing through his flattened nostrils.

"You're thinking of some way to harm me, Druid." The voice rumbled with menace. "But let me tell you, it will never happen. My army is already on its way; in a few days, Lothian will fall. But of course, you won't see it. You'll die long before then and I'll have your Runes to play with. Understand me; you pose no threat. You're merely entertainment."

Gawain's mind raced. Can he read thoughts? Panicking, he forced himself to cut off the picture of the Pence dagger and seal away all thoughts of Merlin, Camelot, even Athlan. He closed his mind to them successively, locking each one away. Then he called up an image of Orion and sought safety in its swirling center.

Argath reacted visibly. His eyes narrowed and he slowly retracted his head. He turned to the guards.

"*DAR, DAR, GRAT!*"

The tall guard to Gawain's left drew a long knife; the other grabbed his hair and yanked his head back exposing his throat.

"*Naaaar brac.*" The guttural words hung in the air and the cold blade pressed against the skin below his Adam's apple. He closed his eyes.

"I don't trust you, Druid," Argath hissed, breaking the tension. "*Brac set.*"

The guard let the fistful of hair go and the other withdrew the blade.

"You'll wait for me – outside. I'll come when I'm ready and woe betide you when I do." He shot a look at each of the guards. They bowed deeply and backed away dragging Gawain between them. Outside, they tied his hands behind his back and looped the end of rope over the tent pole. The smaller guard strung a cord around his neck and secured it to the same pole. He stepped back grunting his satisfaction. Gawain blinked away the rain dripping from his hair. Cough and the cord would cut into his throat; move his arms and it would choke him.

The afternoon had receded into a dreary dusk by the time Argath emerged. He was wearing a long dark cloak that swirled around his feet. His hood lay in folds over his shoulders leaving his head glistening in the light of a lamp held by a guard. Rain cascaded off tent awnings in streams as the two soldiers freed Gawain. This time there was no chance of escape.

Stiff and sore, Gawain splashed through the sodden grass and muddy puddles. When entourage reached Squee's tent, the flaps furled back and a squat, heavily muscled dwarf stepped into the lamp light. Although his bandy legs and bulbous eyes gave him the appearance of a toad, a malevolent twist at the corners of his obsequious smile made Gawain wary. He was more than dangerous; he was a coward.

"My lord," Squee said bowing low.

Ignoring him, Argath ducked into the tent.

"You honor me with your presence," Squee bleated behind him.

"I'm sure I do," said Argath spinning around. "I have the Druid that you let slip out of your greasy little paws. *Nargat*." A guard pushed Gawain forward. "This time perhaps you can manage to finish what I ask."

Squee's lids slid over his bulging eyes in an owlish blink. He took an awkward step back and bowed again. "My Lord, as always, I am at your command. You will learn all this creature knows. I promise you, I will do . . ."

"Yes, yes, I know very well what you *think* you can do." Argath waved a frail hand. "I want the Runes this Druid knows. Send someone when you're through. I have work to do. *Vast grath*." Casting a last look around the tent, Argath spun on his heel and disappeared into the night.

When Gawain met Squee's eyes, he saw a look of such cunning in them that despite his own training as a knight, he felt his stomach knot.

"Bring our guest through. This way, Dakkar," the toad said grinning openly now Argath had gone. A burly guard with a pock-scarred face stepped forward. His long hair fell in braids to square shoulders. He gripped Gawain by the arm and almost lifted him through the opening.

The tent was rectangular, the size of a barn. Light from low-slung lamps cast a dull yellow pall over the interior. Barrels, casks and rows of crates nested with straw, filled the place. Three iron barred cages stood at the far end. Two of them held prisoners, each tied to a thick cross. One stood upright, his head slumped on his shoulder; the other hung upside-down. Gawain gritted his teeth. The skin of the last man lay like loose clothing at the bottom of the cross. Neume. The air was redolent with the smell of blood.

"That one's for you, Druid. Just waitin,' it is." Squee gestured to the empty cage. "And I might tell you here and now, any Runes you cast, or magic spells you might think of using once you're in there, will probably blow off your arms or legs, because a wizard far more powerful than you warded the bars against magic of any kind. Off you trot now. I'll be along shortly." It was a poor imitation of his master but its threat was no less serious. Squee rubbed his bristly head and nodded to the jailor. "Why don't you show him his new home, Dakkar."

Dakkar shoved Gawain toward the cage entrance.

"Wait." Squee's face tightened. He grabbed Gawain's arm and spun him around. "Just in case." He patted down the sides of Gawain's coat. When he ran his soft pudgy fingers into the pockets, Gawain pushed his hands away.

"Bards don't carry weapons," he said fixing him with a disdainful look. "It's against our beliefs. We are men of peace."

Squee hesitated, running a tongue over a row of mossy teeth. Then he broke into a smile. "Makes no mind to me, Druid. I'll be learning everything I need soon enough." He nodded to Dakkar who jangled through an iron ring until he found the key he needed and unlocked the cage. He reefed open the door.

The barred cell was bare, save for a wooden bowl of water, a joint stool and a thatch of straw layering the ground. Dakkar shoved his prisoner inside and turned the lock. Squee grunted and waddled back to the creates at the far end of the tent.

Gawain waited until it was safe then went over to the cage next to him. The wretch hanging from the cross was barely conscious. He judged the man to be around the same age as himself. Rope bound his arms fast to the beam and his feet to the center post.

When Squee's back was turned, Gawain tossed the crude bowl of water over the prisoner's head. The man's eyes flicked open.

"Don't be alarmed," Gawain whispered urgently, "I'm a prisoner too. Quiet now. There's a way out of here, if you can help."

The man hung still, mouth slack, dried blood caked on his lips, tongue lolling. His glazed eyes slowly shifted to Gawain, then flickered toward the far end of the tent where Squee was busy unpacking one of the crates.

"Who are you?" whispered Gawain.

The prisoner coughed. The ragged clothing he wore seemed the only thing holding his body together. He was small, with close-cropped blond hair. His eyes were the pale blue of distant skies. When he tried to speak, Gawain saw bloody gums where his teeth had been torn out. "My name is . . . Cullen," he managed thickly. "I was put in here . . . five days ago." His voice faded and a long moment passed before he summoned the strength to go on. "Who are you?"

Gawain took a chance. He pressed his face against the bars and whispered. "My name is Gawain. I was staying in Lothian. One of Argath's men brought me here. What do you know of him?"

"He's . . . he's the devil's own." Cullen's head dropped.

"Cullen," Gawain said urgently, afraid he'd slipped into unconsciousness "Listen to me, we can escape. There's a way, but I need your help."

The eyelids fluttered open again and Gawain saw in that instant all he needed-there was still fight in them.

He dug Pence dagger out of his inside pocket. "Listen, my friend, I'm going to reach across and cut your ropes. You must stay still though; the blade I'm using is charmed and truly dangerous. I'll free only one of your arms but you must continue to hold onto the beam as if you're still tied up. Do you understand me?"

The bloody head nodded.

"I'll get the dwarf's attention. When he comes into the cage, I'll move so his back is toward you. All you have to do then is throw this dagger. You don't have to aim to kill, just to cut; if his skin breaks, he's as good as dead. Have you got that?"

"Aye," Cullen croaked.

"Remember, a simple scratch will do the job." Gawain gave him an encouraging smile. Then he unsheathed the Pence dagger and slid his arm through the bars. Cullen held still as Gawain feathered the deadly blade across the ropes. The parted strands broke away in brittle slivers that shattered on impact with the cage floor. A few more strokes and Cullen's arm swung free.

"Here, take it. But be careful." Gawain emphasized the last words.

With a struggle, Cullen managed to grasp the smooth leather handle between his outstretched fingers. He inched it into his palm and then tucked it between his legs. The effort cost him and he swung helplessly for a moment, dangling like a corpse on a gibbet.

Gawain cast an anxious glance toward the end of the tent. Squee was talking to Dakkar, hands waving. The guard bowed then ducked through the tent flap. Squee turned back to the crate and began tossing out handfuls of straw.

"Steady now. Wait until your strength returns, then try to swing and catch the beam." Gawain held Cullen's gaze, willing the strength into his limbs.

Cullen's head dropped again. Then, he swung his free arm from one side to the other, slowly gathering momentum. When the arc reached its greatest height, he gave a final lunge and grabbed the beam. Gawain drew in a deep breath as he watched him curl his fingers over the wood. Sweating, Cullen closed his eyes and nodded weakly.

"Squee, I have something to tell your master," Gawain called. The dwarf's bloated head popped up from the crate. He kicked a path through the straw and waddled to the cages.

"What?" he growled nearing the bars.

"I need to see Lord Argath. I have something important to tell him," Gawain said, feigning urgency.

"What?"

"I'll tell it to him only."

"You'll tell me first or I'll make my work on that one seem like a love making session." Squee spat, splattering the bars of Cullen's cage with a wad of phlegm.

Gawain backed away feigning cowardice. "I want no part of all this. Please, I just want out of here. If you let me see Lord Argath, he'll reward you after he's heard what I have to say. He'll let me go, I know he will."

Squee smirked. He seemed buoyed by Gawain's fear and unhooking the key ring from his belt, he opened the cage door and tossed in a crude pair of wrist braces.

"Put 'em on."

Gawain clamped the clumsy device over his wrists and backed up against the end bars. Squee scanned the cell then stepped inside. He glanced at Cullen then around the cage. For one heart-stopping moment, Gawain thought he would see the missing rope, or the strands on the ground but the bulging eyes rolled back to him.

"Tell me what you know," Squee said.

"I can show him Far Druid Runes," Gawain answered, maneuvering so Squee's back was toward Cullen's cage. "I can't show you in here because the bars are warded."

Squee frowned studying him long and hard. Behind his broad back, Cullen let go of the cross stave and swung loose. His bruised face flashed grotesquely in the yellow light-but his eyes remained focused.

"If there's a trick in this, you'll be a long time dying," breathed Squee jabbing a pudgy finger at him.

Cullen inched the *Pence* dagger down his palm until he held it by the blade. Gawain forced himself to hold Squee's glare. He was about to speak when he saw a sudden flash of understanding race through the dwarf's pupils. Squee spun around scowling. Gawain had no time to react. The dagger glinted as it flew but Squee's hand shot up with uncanny speed and caught the blade in front of his chest. Gawain froze.

"Druid bastard. Trick me would you ... . " But he got no further; grains of red powder trickled from a small nick in the palm of his hand.

The eyes.

Gawain stared. The bulging irises glazed over and began cracking. He could hear the sounds as spidery white fissures ran rupturing patterns across their solidifying surface. Then pieces, small chips of marbleized eyeball, simply broke away and fell smashing to the ground like frozen tears.

Squee's face contorted, turning stony gray as a steady flow of blood powder poured from the empty sockets. Then the thing that had looked so much like a toad toppled over and shattered into tiny clay-pot pieces.

"Dear God above," said Cullen in a faltering voice. "Sweet mother of Christ. Did the knife do that?"

"I doubt you'll be putting it between your legs again," quipped Gawain and gave him a broad smile. "Come on, my friend. Let's get out of here."

Gawain took the keys from under the powdered blood and clicked open Cullen's cage. He loosened the ropes binding his feet and lowered him from the cross.

"We have an hour, two at most." He looked at the beaten figure, doubtful he could survive for half that long in the chilling rain. He slipped his arm around his waist and took his full weight. They lumbered to the entrance, stopping when Gawain spotted the remains of Squee's supper. He grabbed the bread and meat from the trencher and jammed them into his pocket.

"Perhaps I can surprise Argath before he finds out what we've done. There won't be any extra guards on duty. If I can get to him, I may be able to use the *Pence* dagger."

"No, we can't risk it. The minute we're seen, he'll know-even the smallest animals carry messages to him," said Cullen weakly.

"How do you mean?"

"Later ... we must get away from here, far away."

Gawain grabbed a thick blanket from a makeshift bed and pulled back the tent flap. He peered into the heavy night. All clear. He draped the blanket over Cullen's shoulders and they ducked out into the hammering rain. He made to go west but Cullen tugged at his coat.

"No, horses ... this way." His voice was barely audible above the rain but Gawain understood and followed in the direction he pointed.

They squelched through the thick mud between rows of sagging tents, Gawain thinking over the comment about the animals. It seemed to fit Argath's pattern. Although he hadn't seen any rats yet, he'd witnessed their work in the fields, if Argath could control them and the men surrounding him, why not other creatures.

Cullen tugged his sleeve. Gawain bent to catch his words.

"Behind ... those tents."

They found the horses standing still in a fenced enclosure, rain splashing off their broad backs. Gawain picked out two of the strongest geldings and saddled them while

Cullen leaned against the gate clutching the blanket tightly around him.

"We'll make our way over the mountains to Lothian. If we're lucky, we can rally the townspeople and surprise Argath when he arrives," Gawain called through the squall. He tugged on the reins and brought the horses over, their great brown eyes blinking away the sheeting rain. "Can you make it?"

Cullen looked up nodding, dried blood running in watery streaks down his face and neck, his bruised and swollen eyes barely visible.

"That's the spirit. Come on, give me your hand. Once we get to the mountains, we'll find shelter and rest."

Gawain took his arm and helped him into the saddle then he swung up on the other horse. They rode out through the muddy paddock, Gawain leading, circling to the west.

The rain swept across the fields in roaring gusts, making communication impossible as they splashed their way out of the sodden camp. Thunder rolled in the low clouds and jagged lightning ripped across the eastern sky. Gawain glanced back. Cullen lay over the horse, head lolling across the animal's coarse mane, arms draped around its neck. He was in danger of falling but stopping now was out of the question. Gawain bent into the wind and rain muttering a prayer.

They rode steadily for the next few hours, thunder and lightning silvering the night and Gawain realized neither horse had so much as neighed or whinnied since they'd left Argath's lair.

Dawn broke when they reached the foothills. Miraculously, Cullen had managed to stay on his horse but it would be a different matter once they started up the mountain pass. Gawain knew he had to find a place to rest and make a fire to dry him out or he would be continuing alone.

217

Riding ahead, Gawain scanned the looming cliffs for signs of shelter. It wasn't until they reached a knot of bedraggled pines that an opportunity presented itself. Behind the thin branches, a dark opening split an almost perfect cliff face. Thanking God and Bran in the same breath, Gawain nudged the horses toward the rift.

CHAPTER 13

The cave proved small, but with ample room to bed down. Once Cullen was safely inside, Gawain went back out, tethered the horses in the tree grove and gathered an armful of driest twigs he could find. Then he picked up a couple of rocks containing enough flint to light his precious fire. It took him almost an hour to get the kindling going, but when he did, warmth spread through the small cave like a smile from heaven.

Leaving the fire, he went out a last time and collected all the thick branches he could carry. When he returned he stacked them close to the fire to dry then he roused Cullen and forced him to eat. They spent the remainder of the night and the second day resting while the storm raged and blew wild gusts of icy rain across the entrance of the cave.

During those long hours, Cullen slipped in and out of consciousness but by the morning of the third day, his strength was returning.

"If you hadn't rescued me when you did, I would have ended up like Harn, the poor wretch in the next cage," he said sitting up.

His voice was stronger after the long rest and now the rain had washed the blood from his face and some of the swelling around his eyes had gone down, he looked a lot better. "We must cross the mountains as soon as possible. For certain he'll know where we are by now."

"Are you strong enough?"

"Aye, I'll no be a hindrance to you."

"I know, but the mountain pass is high; it'll be a danger-ous journey and this rain hasn't made things any easier," Gawain said, nodding to where the muddy trail wound up to the mist-shrouded peak.

Cullen struggled to his feet. "I'll be all right."

Gawain watched him limp to his clothes. He was short, his hair nothing but a mass of tiny blond bristles except for the islands of welts and newly formed scabs dotting his scalp. His round features and light blue eyes gave him a boy-like appearance, making it impossible to guess his age.

"Then, my friend," said Gawain, "we'll give it our best."

Outside, the rain had stopped but low clouds hung in great misty rolls. Gawain brought up the horses and they set out.

Once they were clear of the cliff, Cullen talked freely. "You're a traveler you say, me too. I came to this forsaken land looking for herbs and relics; instead, I found that half-crazed serpent. I was on my way up to Lothian from Glen Allen. One sorry mistake, I can tell you."

They rode round a craggy ledge and the path before them rose sharply.

"Even now he knows where we are," said Cullen, eye-ing a hawk weaving in and out of the mist above them. "We'll be safe a while though. He'll choose to go round these mountains and follow the valley route. He'll not attempt this. Before he died, Harn told me he can't abide the cold."

They managed to guide the horses around the tangled roots of fallen tree and safely back on to the steep path.

"How did you get caught?" asked Gawain, over his shoulder.

"As I said, I'm a traveler like you, though I'm a mer-chant, not a practicing Druid. I was on my way north trading some of the rare herbs I'd acquired from the coast when I first encountered his work: the dead cattle, horses, even wildfowl." His voice took on a hard edge. "Later that day I arrived at Glen Allen and found everyone talking about the plague rats. It was the only thing on their minds. By evening, they were out boarding up houses, digging trenches and filling them with oil-soaked wood. Poor sods were terrified. I didn't know what to do – try to leave and risk running into the things in the dark, or stay and help defend the town. I did what you'd have probably done, right? I stayed."

"There could be a place for you at The Round Table."

Cullen broke into an infectious smile and for a moment, he looked no older than twenty. But as quick as it came, the smile vanished and he grew solemn again. "Early the next morning, the rats showed up. It were the darndest thing. A few came ahead, scouts, I suppose. The people who first spotted them ran through the streets yelling fit to wake the dead. Then the rest arrived, the main army – that's how I came to think of them. They *marched* into the town and down the main street like soldiers, lined up in rows, right as you please.

"God's teeth, it were a terrible thing. People panicked, scattered everywhere when they saw them. But it did no good. Not a soul escaped. After a while, the little bastards broke formation and gave chase. I've never seen the like. Within the hour, they'd bitten every last man woman and child-including me. After that, puff, like magic, they disappeared, vanished like they *knew* their job was done." He stopped and shook his head in wonder.

"What happened then?"

"Well, I'm sure you've seen your fair share of horrors in this world, traveling like you do. But this was the devil's own work, my friend. The next morning people lay dying everywhere, dropping like flies. Dear God, what a sight. In a few hours, the bodies had turned blue, great red welts on their arms popping open. By noon, half the town had gone. They didn't stand a chance, poor sods." He shook his head. "When darkness fell, I was the only one left."

Gawain reigned up his horse and turned. "The only one?"

"Aye. Oh, I was sick right enough, throwing up, sweating, coughing 'till everything was stars. I stayed in my bed at the tavern for three whole days. It's all a blur now but somehow I hung on. I thought maybe the good Lord wasn't ready for this sinner just yet.

"On the third day, I awoke and I started to feel better. I was still feverish, mind, but I could stand and had an appetite. By the fourth day, I was able to leave my room and venture outside. What I saw there ... ." He closed his eyes swallowing thickly.

"The smell hit me first. Remember, the fields we crossed? Like that. Death everywhere. The bodies of those poor sods who'd died from rat bites were swollen up the size of rain barrels. You couldn't recognize a soul. Sweet Lord, you could hardly tell if they were human, they were so blotched and bloated.

"Even though I knew I was over the sickness, I still couldn't bring myself to go near those bodies – not even to say a prayer. I just took my things and set out for Lothian." He stared up at the mountain peak. "It weren't right, Gawain. It weren't right, I know."

"What happened then?" said Gawain softly.

He took a deep, breath. "That's when I got caught. I was no more than a mile outside the town when the lizard's men spotted me."

"You mean Argath?"

"Aye, the damn Night Crawler."

"Night Crawler?"

"Sure, that's when he's up and about, after the sun's gone. Like Harn used to say, he's does the devil's work in the devil's own time."

The simple statement left Gawain speechless. *Of course, the snake part of him avoids the sun. That's why he stayed in his tent when I arrived ... why he tied me up outside and didn't go to Squee's until after sun set. And Merlin's message! The wizard's staff attacked then the sun shone. It didn't mean something was going to happen the next day. It meant the sun was the weapon!*

"... soldiers, if that's what you can call that sorry lot, put me in chains and took me to their camp. That was five days ago."

"And that's when you first saw Argath?"

"Aye. They took me to him the very same night. He said I must be a Druid, or how else could I have survived the plague. He probably asked you the same thing, right? He wanted to know what spells I'd used. I told him who I was and where I was traveling but he didn't seem to care. He just kept on about what Runes he thought I'd cast to protect myself. I showed him the scar where I was bitten, see, here."

He pulled up his pant leg and pointed to the puncture marks in his calf – purple rings with small white indentations in the center. "But it didn't matter, he just kept right on about the magic. When I said I didn't know what he was talking about, he got all mad and squinty eyed. I just told him I knew nothing about Runes. I can't hold them anyway, never could."

Cullen rolled down the pant leg and rubbed his hands together, blowing in them, trying to gather a measure of warmth from the thinning air. "Mother of God, what a week."

Gawain waited but when he saw Cullen wasn't about to continue, he asked, "What happened next?"

"Well, there's not much else to it really. No matter what I said, he wouldn't believe me. I told him my grandfather was a Druid and that was all. My father adopted the Christian faith long ago and brought me up in the name of our good Lord. We've never observed Druid rites in our house not even Beltane. But that didn't seem to matter; he was certain I'd used magic to avoid the plague and nothing I could say was going to make him think otherwise. So he turned me over to Squee and I spent the next two days watching him torture poor Harn." He stared at the mountains sawing up on either side, tears glistening in his eyes.

"You want to know something else? The Night Crawler, Argath, as you call him, he knows everything that happens. He reads minds for one. He commands everyone in his camp, not just the men, but the dogs, the rats, every living thing obeys him."

"Then why don't we?"

"I don't know. Maybe it has something to do with who we are."

"What do you mean?"

"You've seen how everyone there walks around terrified of him right? Have you had a good look at them? At their eyes, I mean. They're vacant, empty. All the time I was there, I've only seen three people without that look – Harn, you and me and I believe we all have some of the Druid in us."

Gawain nodded. "So he resorts to torture to get his answers from us? His power's no good?"

"Exactly. If it was, all three of us would be standing outside his tent right now, waiting for him to hiss out one of his damn commands."

"You said he only comes out at night. How does he control the others while he sleeps?"

"As far as I know he doesn't. He just stays there in that tent of his until the sun sets."

224

Gawain nudged his horse around a bolder blocking the center of the path and called back. "I think I know how we can kill him."

"How?" said Cullen.

"In good time, my friend."

It took them the better part of the day to get to the high pass. At the summit, fresh snow had fallen and the horses struggled to find sure footing. By the time they were half way through the pass, Cullen began to worsen.

They slogged through another mile of dangerous terrain in silence, the light fading. If they were to find shelter and gather wood for a fire, Gawain knew they had to make the descent, which lay hidden in folds of ragged clouds on the other side of the divide.

Neither spoke during the next grueling hour. Any distraction could spell disaster. Even though Cullen's horse nosed Gawain's, he was only visible for short intervals between the churning mist.

Darkness had fallen by the time they stumbled out from the two vast overhangs marking the end of the pass. In the stillness, Gawain could hear Cullen shivering as the horses wound their way down the leeward side of the mountain.

When they reached the tree line, they dismounted and made camp at the first sheltered place Gawain could find. He tried to get a fire of pine needles and twigs going again but this time he failed, and finally, tired and cold, he crawled under the blanket and huddled next to Cullen to keep him warm.

Lying there, holding his friend, Gawain shared the pitiful warmth. In the distance, rocks rumbled and fell crashing to places far below. Lonely winds keened through high escarpments. Just before he fell to sleep, a bright star winked into view. His mind instinctively sought its ancient source but he was so tired he found there only the endless void where dreams begin.

In that slow time, he didn't feel the glow that came, or the soft warmth spreading from Merlin's magic as the Dragon Ring thrummed its warning of the new danger in the distant valley.

They awoke to a clear cold dawn, the weak sun washing the jagged peaks with pale light. The mist had cleared. The day would be good for traveling. But when Gawain shook Cullen awake what he saw made his heart sink: his friend's eyes were rimmed a deep red and he shivered in fitful bouts.

"Can you go on? We can rest longer if you need."

"Don't wa, wa, worry about yours truly, Ga, Gawain. I'll be right. Just get me off this ki, ki, cursed mountain," he chattered.

They broke camp and Gawain helped Cullen onto his horse. He sat in the saddle swaying for a moment, then he draped his arms around the animal's neck and dropped his head into the flaxen mane. There was nothing for it. Gawain just hoped he had the strength to hold on.

Gawain led, taking the reins of Cullen's horse as they wound their way down to the flatlands leading to Lothian. They broke out into the valley in the early afternoon but despite the warmer temperature, Cullen still shivered, drifting in and out of consciousness.

They rode south to where a wide river flowed out of the mountain range toward the distant town. Gawain scanned the valley. If he didn't find shelter soon, Cullen would surely die. At their present rate of travel, they wouldn't reach Lothian until well into the night and one more drop in temperature would certainly spell the end for Cullen. The best bet was to follow the river, Gawain decided. Sooner or later they would come across a holding or small farm and when they did, he could leave Cullen in good care. Alone, he should make the town in five or six hours.

Gawain encountered the first signs of trouble in the early afternoon when they crested a small knoll a scant fifty yards from the riverbank. In a wide pasture, a cow lay toppled in the grass. This time there was none of the bloating he'd witnessed earlier. He rode down the slope, dismounted and walked to the carcass. The gnawed legs looked the same as those near Argath's camp but here the blood was still a bright red and there were only a few flies.

He scoured the distant fields. How had the rats managed to make it this far? How had they covered so much ground in such short time? It was impossible for them to have traversed the mountain pass. The snow would have stopped them. They must have taken the longer route through the valley – but that would have been a journey of four or five days. Argath's soldiers were all on foot, except for perhaps a small expeditionary force. There was no chance they could have covered that distance in such a short time. Had Argath other powers?

Baffled, Gawain returned to the horses and found Cullen struggling to sit up in the saddle. The rings under his eyes sagged in pouches. He coughed, hacking deep in his chest as he tried to speak. "Gawain ... listen carefully. Leave me ... you can't fight this ... taking care of me." His head lolled from side to side.

"I'll find a safe place ..." began Gawain.

"No, look." Cullen pointed with a shaking hand to a spot over the river. "See there ... he guides them."

Gawain followed his gaze. High above, two hawks circled, swooping in and out of the clouds. The patterns they flew were unnatural, far too measured – too precise. Instinctively, he realized they were communicating, perhaps relaying Argath's commands to the rats.

"I must get to Lothian. I have to warn the people about this, organize them to fight."

Cullen grasped Gawain's collar, feebly pulling him closer. "Remember, there's no surrender. This time he won't bargain ... . He's sent the rats ahead to finish the town so he could be sure we'd die as well. When they find us ... it won't be just a bite ... ." His eyes filled with water from the effort of speaking.

"I'll get you help," Gawain said. "No more talking now. Here, give me your arm."

Gawain eased him forward in the saddle and taking the reins, set out walking the horse toward the water while he kept an eye on the hawks. What was it in those patterns? He frowned, hand up to shade the sun as he studied them. Suddenly he knew where he'd seen them before. They had the same shapes as some of the Runes on Merlin's staff!

After journeying through thinning meadow grass and patches of bracken for the better part of the clear, dry afternoon, Gawain saw the first signs of life ahead – the dark contours of a small holding backing on to an elbow of land jutting out into the river. Strain as he might, however, he couldn't see any smoke rising from its chimney.

An hour later, exhausted from the effort of keeping Cullen steady on his horse, he arrived at a makeshift fence running around the side and front of a small holdfast. He helped Cullen down and tethered the animals.

"Hello."

His voice sounded flat and tired. He heaved Cullen up the few rickety steps to the door and shoved it open with his hip.

"Hello," he called again. "Is anyone home?" He half-dragged, half-walked his friend inside. He spotted a small cot-sized bed next to a hearth. Grunting, he lugged Cullen the last few paces and with a final heave, rolled him onto the worn mattress, tumbling after him as he lost his balance. He lay there for a moment, head spinning. He had to eat and rest if he hoped to fight when he got to Lothian.

Cullen tossed in fitful sleep while Gawain prepared and lit a fire. He found dried meat and wheat cakes in the pantry and ate. By the time he'd finished, the sun was setting. He made up a makeshift bed from cushions and spare blankets and lay down thankfully next to his friend.

That night he slept a deep and dreamless sleep, and in the late morning he awoke to another blue sky, this one dotted with white handkerchief clouds drifting lazily over the snow-capped mountains. He checked on Cullen, only to find him clammy with perspiration. He'd need at least another two-day's rest before he'd be able to walk again. Enough time. He could get back from Lothian by then, if he was successful – if not, what would it matter?

He left food by the bed and stacked up wood next the hearth in case Cullen needed warmth when he woke. With everything in order, he took a last look around and went to the door. He grabbed the latch and ... hesitated.

Something ... . He stood there, hand on the wooden bobbin, a heightened sense of danger roughing the hairs on the nape of his neck. Carefully sliding back the latch, he inched the door open.

His stomach knotted. Between the fence and the holding sat a large a group of shiny black rats in a semi-circle. He eased the door closed and leaning back against the wall, let out a deep breath. They numbered fifty or more. How long had they been out there?

Eyes – for the brief second he'd seen them, he was unaccountably drawn to them. It wasn't their bulging grotesqueness or the coal red glow that captivated him, but the intelligence behind them – it was palpable. They seemed to understand his predicament.

He stole to a window at the side of the cabin and peeked though the curtains. On a bare patch of dirt, ten feet away, two more of the creatures were sitting back on thick haunches. Bloated to the size of piglets, they reminded him of sentries on duty. Scabs festered the black skin stretching tight across their underbellies. He suppressed shiver. Their eyes held his with unwavering comprehension.

He crossed to the other window at the far end of the cabin. Outside, three more rats sat in silence. He knew if he attempted to escape they would alert the others in front, then the whole pack would be on him long before he could make it through the casement and drop on the other side. He scanned the area behind holding. A hundred feet away, the sun reflected off the high riverbanks.

Yes.

He clenched his fists. He could use the river to get to the town. Depending on what happened there, he could come back for Cullen later. If the rats followed, his friend would be safe. But could he get to the river before they attacked? One bite would spell the end.

He checked the place for weapons. He found only a bundle of sticks and some short staves, but in the corner of the kitchen, he came across a crude cudgel and pouch of flint-stones. He took the cudgel, tucked it into the belt and slipped the stones in his pocket.

Next, he went to the table in the kitchen. He rapped his knuckles on the top – sturdy. A round solid slab of beech wood, at least four feet in diameter, one, maybe two inches thick. He upended it, snapped off the legs and hoisted it over his head. Heavy, but if he could get it to the river it would help keep him afloat.

He propped the makeshift craft against the wall by the back window and took a spare blanket from a closet. He tore it into three strips and wrapped one strip tightly around each of his legs, starting at the ankles and working up to his knees. He poured oil from a lamp on the wall over the remaining strip then knotted the end to give it weight. It would make a good diversion. A hundred feet to the river. An easy run-no obstacles, not so much as a fence. If he could get thirty, even twenty feet before they set after him, he'd make it.

He returned to the front door and inched it open. Dear God. Outside, the number of rats had almost doubled. Worse, the hawks were now prescribing their endless Runic patterns at tree top height, directly above the creatures.

He crossed to the hearth and casting a last look at Cullen, thrust the blanket into the burning fire. It burst into flames. Dense, black smoke curled around his arms. Grabbing the half-empty lamp, he ran to the entrance. He pulled open the door and hurled the lamp out. It smashed in the middle of the rats, dousing them in slick oil and sending them scrambling back, squealing indignantly.

Wads of black smoke billowed up from the knotted blanket, obscuring his vision and filling the cabin. Coughing, he stepped outside, whirled the blazing cloth high over his head and cast it into the thick of the pack as they regrouped. Seconds later, oil-drenched fur began to splutter and spark into flames.

Panic swept through the rats and they bolted, creating whooshing arcs as they fanned the flames into white-hot fire. The squealing rose and the terror spread.

Enough.

Gawain slammed the door closed and ran to the rear of the cabin. He grabbed the tabletop and pushed open the window. The sentry rats had gone. He tossed out the table-top and jumped after it. Still no sign of the creatures, just the smell of smoke and sounds of squealing coming from the front of the holdfast.

He scooped up the makeshift vessel and raced across the short grass.

What?

A wave of premonition swept over him. He hesitated, spinning around. He expected to see rats rounding the corner, but the path was clear.

The puzzled expression was still spreading across his face when the diving hawk struck him. Jagged pain ripped through his shoulder as two sharp talons gouged into his flesh. He grabbed frantically at the bird trying to dislodge it, but the flapping wings prevented him from getting a firm hold. It cawed and screeched, and the more he struggled, the deeper it sank its claws. The pain blurred his thinking. He felt the blood pulse behind his eyes and faintness begin to fog his mind.

And that's when he saw the first smoking rat. Even with the bird tearing at him, he froze. The oils in its skin bubbled, hissing like water on hot coals. Crying out in anger and pain Gawain seized the tabletop. He ran lopsidedly, the hawk tearing at him, ripping away flesh, gouging open muscle. Behind him, the other rats washed around the holdfast in a smoking wave.

A few yards from the river, he heaved the tabletop over the embankment. It had barely left his hand when he saw the charred head of the first rat from the corner of his eye. He leapt as it lunged and sank his teeth into the thick blanket around his leg.

The strange montage of man, beast and bird, tumbled over and over, flailing as it fell toward the waters far below. Then the smash and bitter chill of the icy river. Gawain sank deep beneath its surface. Suddenly the pain vanished – the tearing, clawing pain, blessedly gone. And he didn't care if he stayed there in the rush of bubbles because he was safe from fangs and claws and the terror of rats that smoked and hissed and burned with Satan's very breath.

CHAPTER 14

Gawain floated upward in a wreath of silver bubbles. When his head broke the surface, he saw the cliffs above bristling with dark shapes. He turned, spitting out a mouthful of water as the tabletop bobbed into view on the choppy waves.

He struck out for it but his left arm refused to obey and the table spun almost lazily away toward the middle of the river where the faster current ran. He kicked with failing strength, trying to find the same current but an eddy caught him forcing him back. For one desperate moment, he thought he'd be drawn out to the shallows where the river pooled in wide slow circles and he swam harder.

Long moments passed. Finally, the table top bobbed into view on his right. He lunged for it, too far gone to judge its path and for the first time since he arrived in this God-forsaken country, he considered himself lucky – his hand hit the hard surface of the beech wood and his fingers locked on the edge with a terrier's grip.

Whirling and dipping, the top continued to spin with Gawain hanging on. The hard wood slammed against him, then twisted away repeatedly but he somehow managed to keep his grip. Then, as quickly as the raging current began, it abated changing into a gentle steady flow where the river widened. Blinking water from his eyes, he hauled himself up onto the flat surface.

Exhausted, he rolled on his back and let the river take him. He closed his eyes and drifted with the dark, slow current.

He must have passed out, because he was suddenly jarred awake when the tabletop scraped against the low branches of a willow tree. He started, not knowing at first where he was. Then he winced. His shoulder throbbed with pain.

Teeth chattering from the cold, he kicked his feet bringing the little vessel closer to the bank. If he could get ashore here, there would be enough wood to make a fire and dry out and God willing, he could rest for a few hours. He'd need to build the fire in a semi-circle with his back to the water. If the rats caught up, they wouldn't dare cross the fire line, not after their last encounter. Besides, if trouble started, he could always escape on the river.

The numbing water had chilled him to the marrow and by the time he found a break between the trees, he was shivering uncontrollably. He dragged the battered craft ashore and staggered up the sandy bank. Too exhausted to check for rats, he set about collecting driftwood for the fire.

An hour later, he sat before crackling flames, arms out gathering the heat. By the time the fire had warmed him through, it was starting to die down. He rose reluctantly and began to prepare for the long night ahead. First, he piled up ten large stacks of wood in a wide arc, cutting off his section of beach. Then he bent stiffly and lit each of the piles. If the rats came, they wouldn't get through without paying dearly.

After he'd lit the last fire, he roughed out a bed in the sand and curled up, worn out. Lying on his side, he looked across the gliding water where bright yellows flames from the fires shimmered and waved like flags on a distant battlefield. He crossed himself mumbling the *Kyrie Eleison*, but before he had the chance to finish the prayer, he fell into a deep sleep.

Hours later, in the dead of night, he awoke with a start. The first fire had gone out and the others had died down to humps of glowing embers. Something was wrong. He sensed it. His skin felt clammy. He lay still, listening.

Silence.

How long had he slept? There were no sounds. None. Above him, the stars winked in a clear sky.

Orion, where are you?

The Dragon Ring. He ran his fingers over it. It was warm. Had Merlin awoken him? His mind raced. It was too quiet. His ears rang.

Then he heard it, a soft rustling high up in the branches of one of the willow trees. He turned over slowly, peering into the dark as he did. His eyes, unhampered by the dull glow of the fire circle, took in a sight that made the hairs on his neck stand up. The tree was alive with rats!

He watched from the corner of his eye, mesmerized by their craftiness. A single creature had ventured out along the branch hanging over the fire circle. The ones behind were inching forward, their movements almost imperceptible in the shadows of the high canopy.

He lay still, watching as rat after rat crawled with frightening purpose over the flattened backs of those in front, their hard claws softened by fur as they stole along the branches.

The creature at the far end waited patiently for the others to catch up. A few more yards and they would all be clear of the fire circle-then they could drop down safely from the branch into the sand below. Gawain broke out into a full body sweat. One bite that's all. He had to do something fast.

He coughed fitfully and rolled over, feigning sleep. The tabletop lay between him and the river, its edge half buried in the sand. He moved again, this time drawing his knees up and curling himself into a ready position. High above, the rats halted their advance and the tree became as still as the night air.

They know!

He sprang up, feeling the pain and stiffness in his shoulder melt as adrenaline blasted through him. The tree exploded into life.

The rats squealed in their fury. They hurled themselves out of the branches heedless of where they fell. He heard the dull thud of bodies raining down, then a series of whooshes near the edges of the fire circle. He glanced back. Half a dozen rats were bursting out of the ashy clouds like ghosts from a graveyard.

He grabbed the tabletop, flung it into the water as far as he could and dove in after it. The cold took his breath away, but the rabid squealing behind him drove him on. He surfaced and struck out, kicking for the vessel. Above his efforts, he heard a clear, distinctive splash-then another and another.

His hand bumped against hard wood. No time to climb on. He grabbed the edge. Behind him, small silvery wakes veed out from the rats. Ahead, he could see the ripples where the current became stronger. Ten, twelve more feet. He held his breath, ducked his head under the water and kicked with all his remaining strength.

His lungs burned, his temples pounded, but he didn't surface. He forced himself to keep on kicking, certain in the knowledge he would surely die if he didn't make that current. Blood pulsed and boomed in his ears but he continued driving his legs until he felt the rushing force take him.

He gulped air when he broke the surface. Slewing to his left with the weight of the current, he summoned up the last of his strength and heaved himself onto the craft. Spluttering out a mouthful of water, he lay panting on his stomach, cheek pressed against the rough wood as the river bore him safely west. He blinked away water running from his hair and watched the glow of the fire circle and the grove of tall willow trees fall behind, receding into deep shadows, taking the terror with them.

Now Lothian. Two, maybe three hours. He turned his head to look down river and froze. Directly in front of him, two red eyes smoldered like dying campfires in the night.

The rat stood perfectly still, at the far edge of the table, water dripping off its sleek fur. Obscenely patient, claws sunk into the thick beech wood, it stared at him. Gawain slowed his breathing. He remained perfectly still, arms spread, chin digging into the tabletop, eyes level with the rat.

How much time they spent looking at each other like that, he didn't know, but gradually, as if some malicious thought had flickered across its primitive mind, the rat's lips writhed back, revealing curved yellow teeth. Slowly, it retracted a clawed foot from the wood with a squeak and took a deliberate step forward.

Gawain yelled. The creature flattened its ears and halted. Gawain drew in a deep breath and yelled again. This time the ears trembled but didn't flatten back. When he yelled a third time, the rat merely stared at him impassively. Retracting a claw, it took another methodical step forward.

Gawain tried to rock the little craft from side to side and dislodge it, but the rat held firm. When he stopped rocking, the creature lowered its swollen belly to the wood, pulled another claw loose and took another calculated step toward him.

There was death in those red eyes and Gawain realized there was nothing he could do but abandon the vessel. He let one hand slip from the edge of the tabletop and was about to release his grip with the other, when the rat sprang.

Gawain flung up an arm to protect his face and the next instant he felt vicious teeth slice through the soft flesh of his wrist and grind against bone. Pain exploded in his head but somehow he found the strength to grab the gnawing rat by the neck and tear it loose.

And he never let go, not even when they both spilled off the tabletop and sank beneath the icy current. He continued choking it, continued to squeeze it with a strength that forced the creature's eyes to pop out of its head one after the other and float up past him like two red bubbles.

The same deep, icy cold that had almost killed him earlier, now served to save his life. It numbed his pain and cleared his vision. He kicked his way up to the surface and heaved himself back onto the little craft. He examined the two puncture wounds in his wrist where fresh blood continued to seep out. Was he infected? He tore off the hem of his sleeve and bound the wound then he lay back exhausted.

And there he stayed, half awake, half asleep. Throughout the remaining hours of the night, he faded in and out of consciousness, fighting the growing nightmares, crying out to Athlan, to Merlin and to his father-the words lost but the love and faith in him never faltering.

Lazily turning and dipping, the craft moved at the pace of a man walking. The steady current ferried Gawain along gently. And when dawn broke and the sun's weak rays sifted across the river, he stirred. Blurry images of passing banks greeted him. He tried to blink away the fuzziness throwing a strange, hazy veil over his world but he couldn't. And when he raised his head to see what lay before him, a ring of pain rippled from the growing stiffness in his neck.

He knew.

Cullen had spent time on their journey telling him about the symptoms of the plague-the dizziness, the dry throat, the headaches-he had them all. Lying there, floating along serenely under a soft golden dawn, he had survived so much. His mind reeled-to know the swelling would soon start and the black welts would follow, the dark bruises that were the shadows of death. To die here, too weak to leave the river. Then to float on, far away, until the cold North Sea took him with her boundless waves.

He grimaced. The smell hit him with stomach churning power, waking him from his delirium. At first, he thought it was his own flesh. Then he realized he'd drifted into the dying town of Lothian. The stench blew across the river like smoke. He blinked and went to rub his eyes but the effort hurt too much.

The small craft that had carried him so far and had withstood so much bumped gently against a mooring post propping up a sagging wooden pier. Gawain groaned. He clambered off the little vessel and stumbled onto the loose slats of the landing. He stood on shaky legs gripping the weathered railing leading up to the docks. He winced with the pain pounding in his ears and forced himself up the rickety steps.

Almost keeling over at the top, he somehow managed to hold on to a head post and steady his swaying with a hand already turning gray. He peered across the hazy street to where a large wooden building ballooned like a forge bellows.

Inside, there might be food and perhaps the warmth of a fire. And if he were really lucky, and God alone knew he deserved to be after what he'd endured, he might even find a blessed bed where he could rest and put a stop to the aching that seemed to grow with each passing minute.

He staggered across a street strewn with blackened corpses. At the bottom of the stairs leading to the inn, he almost trod on a child's tiny outstretched hand. More wavering steps and he lurched through doors that hung open.

Lumbering into the dim tavern, empty and as quiet as a winter night, he staggered between more corpses, bumping into a table and knocking over a stool. The world wavered for a moment, darkening at the edges and he clung onto a timbered upright for support.

Burning with fever and shivering from cold, he had neither the energy nor the wits to throw the few branches and logs laying near the hearth into the fireplace and light them. Instead, he let go of the timber and tugged down a heavy curtain from a nearby window. He wrapped it around his shoulders and pushed a bench to the wall. Then he thankfully, blissfully, lay down to rest.

His dreams were all too real.

In them, he spoke to Merlin who seemed to have aged yet again. His hair had grown sparser, his skin thinner, like parchment, and his eyes had become more faded than summer lichen.

"You have been traveling again, haven't you?"

"I won't have to any more, my boy, my mapping is complete." Even his voice sounded older, carrying with it a faint tremble-the onset of the age that comes before death.

"Do you know what has happened, Gawain? What you are doing at this very moment?"

"I'm here, talking with you."

"And how do you feel?"

"Strange, I can't explain it really. It's as if I'm floating somehow. I'm tired perhaps. Why do you ask?"

"What do you see?"

"You."

"What else?"

"Your room, your books about to tumble off their shelves. The tapestry Lanacoom made you."

"Interesting."

"Please, Merlin, tell me what is happening."

"What you say is indeed accurate. I am in my room, but for you to actually see me, should be quite impossible. At this moment you're still in the far north and I'm at Camelot."

240

"What does it mean?"

"That you have somehow opened your mind, my falcon. I have always had to come to you before. But now you have come to me."

"How is that possible?"

"I don't exactly know but I'd like to try something. Are you willing to help?"

"Yes."

"Remember when we were together and traveled into your father's mind when he lay on his death bed?"

"Yes."

"Well that journey forged an inextricable link between us – a bond that will remain until one of us dies. I believe it's provided the connection that's allowed us to communicate the way we do now. You see, the Dragon Ring, in a mild sort of way, has only served to make my own thoughts stronger. Charmed though it may be, it couldn't affect any increase in clarity without the bond. And, as your Druid strength grows, so does that bond, my boy.

"What I propose is this: I want to try to join with you again, if I can. With this new strength, I'll not only be able to find out what's happening but I may be able to help you defeat Argath. What do you think of that, Arthur's champion?"

"Let it be soon. I don't know ... I feel there's something wrong – with me, I mean."

"I too feel this, so we will act quickly. You must open your mind even more. It will not be difficult – try to see me, not as you do now, but as you've always thought of me. See me with your heart; find my essence. When you do this, I'll know and I'll be able to join you."

And he did. In the dark of his delirious dream, Gawain saw his father's old friend as he had first seen him – strong and vibrant, striding into the Great Hall at Llansteffan. He saw him as clearly as he would see a moon rising over a summer lake. He smiled, and Merlin turned and threw his arms wide, cloak billowing in the wind blowing from an open window.

Friendship and love suffused Gawain, filling him, burrowing into every lonely cranny, chasing away the ghosts of failure: Athlan, Morganna, the rats, even Argath himself – all banished. He felt love and understanding sweep through him with a fusion of such strength, he thought he would burst with gratitude. But through all the light of joy, he saw a shadow Merlin could not hide – a speck, a mote of blackness piercing the light like a cancer. And in that moment, Gawain beheld both living fear and dire revulsion. He saw fatality and he saw Merlin's weakness, but above all, he saw the dread the wizard felt at knowing the truth about his friend – that death had laid its hand upon him.

Then, without warning, thought words exploded, raining over him, drenching him like a spring storm – Druid words, the harmonious sounds he had found impossible to master. They cascaded in shimmering complexity, each word-drop a rainbow, dazzling, spinning, leaving fire trails of music in his mind.

Finally, the onslaught stopped, leaving behind a silence ringing with purity.

Then another torrent of Druid lore, this time a series of brilliant shapes flared out of the dark like Caerleon's Yule Tide beacons and a collage of Rune strokes came angling and slashing though the air that was his thought.

Silence.

Stillness.

"Gawain?"

"Yes."

"Listen. Do you know? Know you're dying."

"Yes."

"I've given you all that is Druid in me. From the mountains and from the vast salt seas, from the cold streams that have sunk their fingers deep into the tender flesh of this earth, I have found, and given you, all the power of our race. But it will last only a short time. Use it wisely."

"But what must I do, Merlin?"

"For now, but two things. Will you try for me?"

"Yes."

"It will take all your strength, but if you do not do these things you will die as surely as the day ends – not from the plague in your blood, but from the cold growing in your lungs.

"First, you must light the fire near you, and then you must take off your wet clothes. Get the clothes from the man near the sea chest and put them on, then wrap yourself warmly in the covers you'll find lying on the chair by the far window. When you've done this, you must lie down by the fire and rest, my falcon. The Druid lore I have inculcated will do the rest. I'll be close, looking over you at all times. Never fear."

Gawain rose; up from the warm to the shivering, teeth-chattering cold. The room was awash with floating color and mist coiling about him as he moved. Lurching from side to side, he took wood and oil-soaked staves and threw them in the open hearth. And then, as the fog began to thicken, he lit the fire making the gold flames chase away the sinewy fingers of death.

He moved to the corpse curled on the ground. Bending, he picked like a vulture at its clothes, tugging in the haze, pulling off, pulling on, staggering to the Merlin words. One shaking step after the next, he made his way to the chair by the window. Blankets of wool. And back to the gold. *And bless you, Merlin.*

As the flames licked greedily at the wood, he collapsed, swaddled in the warm roughly spun wool. Out of the entombing silence, a voice whispered like wind blowing through dry reeds, "I'm here. I'm still with you, my falcon.

You have done well, all I've asked. Rest now; let the lore do its work."

Long shadows reared, curling heavenwards like smoke. His very bones ached and his skin burned but he felt the faintest tremble of hope.

And he slept.

The day passed under a cloudy sky. Outside, the corpses in the streets and in the shelters of the homes where they had once lived, lay rotting while light rain fell. The rats had done their work well. Only a thin wind moaned through the streets. Windows rattled and somewhere distant, a solemn bell knolled in an unattended belfry as the gusts blew through weathered slats. Then silence.

Lothian was a grave. The pestilence had struck and spread with a force that had claimed all life. He slept on while the bell tolled and the decaying corpses slowly turned back to the earth. He slept on through the night and all the unnatural quiet of the next day and on again, until the second morning. And for the first time in that chilling month the sun shone in a clear blue sky.

In the graveyard of Lothian, the rays sought out the silent streets and the damp, ancient docks and bathed them in a brash light. It sent beams spearing down into the dreary alleys and the foggy marketplace and flooded the town with a warmth that would have brought a song or whistling ballad to the lips of any the week before.

Later, as the sun climbed higher, golden rays sifted through the dusty panes of the inn, inching slowly through the gloom until they chanced upon the sleeping figure near the fireplace. Slowly, almost lovingly, they caressed the sunken cheeks and pale skin with a gentle warmth.

Gawain awoke from far healing depths. His eyes burned, his throat ached and his body cried out for food. He sat up, light headed. Before him, the room swam for a moment then slowly settled. Perhaps it was at that point he first felt the world had changed. He didn't know. But somewhere deep within him a new sense of awareness grew from Merlin's temporary infusion of essence and a feeling of peace greater than he had ever known filled him.

Even in his present condition, he could feel the strands, invisible fibers that seemed to reach out like hairs from his skin to the air around him and the ground below. It was as though every tiny Druid sense he'd ever experienced was intensified a thousand fold. *Dear God and all the saints, is this how you feel, Merlin? How you see life every day?*

His new intelligence spoke through those fibers, of the death and suffering. He looked around and from the air, his new tactile sense experienced the first signs of healing; he knew the plague had run its course.

He stood up shakily, marveling at his new awareness. He walked to where he *felt* food would be rather than having to look for it. The world hummed as if a lightning storm was pending. The very air sang with Druid power.

He took what few supplies there were in the pantry and wolfed them down. Then he drank long and deep from a flagon of cider. Renewed strength coursed through his limbs.

He sat and rested, enjoying every moment of peace and growing well-being. He reached back to his shoulder where the hawk had ripped at him. The place was tender but that was all – the wound had healed. He inspected his wrist where the rat had bitten him and saw only a ring of pinkish puncture spots.

Merlin, this is your doing. This, the power, everything. Sometime during my sickness, you came to me. He racked his brain, trying to piece together the dream fragments of the last two nights, but the fever had left only ghostly tracings.

He made his way passed corpses lying on the floor. Outside, his new awareness amplified the light wind and the warmth of the mid-day sun. For a long while, he simply stood there, oddly out of place amidst the dead. He closed his eyes, turned face up to the sun and drank in its power.

While he was surrendering himself to the new experience, he felt a sudden cold jolt. It was not so much violent, as intrusive. He opened his eyes. The streets were empty save for the blackened corpses. He tried to think in terms of direction. He turned slowly, looking for any signs of life. None. But it had been a life force he felt, he was sure of that. He walked to the center of the street and closed his eyes again, searching the elements with Merlin's temporary power.

Cold.

Jolt.

This time he did not break the connection but let his mind follow its source. The cold grew from the west. He tracked it further and as he did, the restorative power of the sun and fresh wind receded and the cold began to expand. He stopped, because he knew intuitively if he traveled too far he might not be able to come back.

When he opened his eyes, he found himself facing the docks. He looked beyond the gleaming river to where one or two holdings and then a series of wide-open fields lay. Somewhere out there was the source of the cold he'd encountered – Argath.

He returned to the inn, the sun on his shoulders, his mind clearing with every step. If he was to defeat him, it had to be now, while he still had Merlin's powers. But a weapon-he needed a weapon. The *Pence* dagger was long gone, lost somewhere at the bottom of the river he reasoned. He needed something else – but what?

He checked the pockets of his new clothes but they were empty save for a few bronze coins. He returned to the inn, covering his nose against the smell as he rummaged behind the serving shelves. In one of the draws, he found a broad-bladed knife, well balanced, with a keen edge. He tucked it into his belt. On the way out he stopped in the doorway – the sky outside was a perfect blue and the sun – the sun was the same as the burning image Merlin had sent when he'd contacted him through Orion the night he'd escaped. This was the day! He cast his mind back to the other image: the staff striking the snake. And it came to him. *Yes!* Now he had Merlin's power. That's what the staff represented. His power was the way to defeat Argath. The red sand? What did that mean? Powdered blood? But he'd lost the *Pence* dagger – *dear God*. What if he was meant to use it on Argath? What if that was the only way to kill him? *No.* He focused his mind. *This is the day. I will find a way.* Hefting the broad knife into his hand, he ran down the stairs and across the street toward the river.

The sun blazed. As he approached the docks the smell of rotting corpses faded, and by the time he reached the rippling water, he could breathe deeply without gagging.

He untied a rope mooring a small coracle and climbed in. He knelt, took up the paddle and rowed the rocky craft across the river. Behind him, he caught a glimpse of the tabletop bobbing against the wharf as if it were obediently waiting for him to come back and continue some other wild adventure. He still felt weak but he knew he had more than enough strength to make the crossing.

Argath.

The cold grew as he neared the far bank. He didn't need his heightened senses to find the source, the chill radiated outward from the fields like a winter wind.

When he steered the coracle to a small reed patch and stepped out onto the shore, his new senses made him aware of something else too – the elemental power in the earth and air surrounding him seemed weaker the closer he got to the camp. Was Argath draining the essence?

Puzzling over this, he stood on the muddy beach, searching for signs of life ahead. He sensed people moving to the west. Each one appeared in his mind as a small black dot, then, with concentration, a cold pinprick hole.

He dragged the boat to higher ground and climbed up the embankment. Near the top, he kneeled and peered over the grassy edge. Ahead, a mile or so, he could make out the white humps of tents. Even from this distance, there was little doubt: Argath had come fully prepared.

The best approach would be from the south. A heavily wooded area there cut off the river. All he needed to do was follow the riverbank, come up on the other side of the tree line and he'd be impossible to spot. He glanced at the cloudless sky. The sun was still high. It wouldn't take long to make the trees.

He set out splashing along the river's edge and wading through tangled weeds. When he came upon a marshy area too difficult to traverse, he clambered up the embankment to get his bearings.

In the distance, he saw two men riding in his direction. He slid back down the muddy bank, hoping they hadn't seen him. He'd need all his strength for Argath.

As they neared, he *felt* their presence through Merlin's senses. He closed his eyes concentrating. The two pinprick holes were growing, eating away at the fabric around him like dark blights. Slowly the holes expanded into jagged tears, then Merlin's Rune power suddenly flared. It drew on the elements and slammed both gaping holes shut as easily as child would close a door.

The actual result was no less amazing. Gawain rose. Both riders had pulled up and were looking at each other. *Looking!* He watched as they slowly turned and stared across the fields. The smaller rider pointed north. He said something and the other nodded. Casting a quick glance over his shoulder, he kicked his horse and headed toward the mountains. The other bolted after him, low in the saddle, face hidden by the horse's flying mane.

Gawain sank back. What had he done? Somehow, he'd used Merlin's temporary power to dispel Argath's hold. If he could release those two that easily, then he should be able to free the others the same way. *Now, while I've got the power.*

The sun blazed high in the open sky as he planned the next step. No matter what he decided, he knew it would come to two things – how many soldiers there were and how long he would retain Merlin's power.

He scrambled down the embankment and tracked along the river to the tree line. Near the first saplings, he splashed up a shallow stream cutting between mossy rocks. Where the water sluiced against the bank, he found easy footholds and hauled himself into a position where he could see the camp. Despite the trees, he had a clear view.

The tents stood in neat rows. He guessed twenty or thirty, probably half the number of the previous camp. The other soldiers would arrive soon but if he could kill Argath here and now, that wouldn't matter. Without his control, there would be no reason for anyone to continue.

He pushed aside a leafy branch. Men were unloading wagons and hauling goods into the large gray awning of a supply depot. Behind the area stood four more tents arranged in a square. In the middle of the square a round, heavily canvassed dome rose up, a dark flag waving from atop a tall standard placed outside. The cold emanating from the tent pulsed in icy rings.

Gawain scanned the rest of the camp. Here and there, soldiers dressed in dark tunics and boiled leather cuirasses milled about feeding horses, cooking or seeing to their weapons. Everything seemed normal.

Gawain focused on three men standing near a forge. They were watching a smith in a leather apron hammering a glowing blade. Gawain closed his eyes. Through Merlin's senses, three black holes shimmered into view. The Rune power flared; the holes slammed shut. He opened his eyes. The reactions on the soldiers faces were the same as those he'd seen earlier – gaping surprise. They looked around then began backing away from the forge. When they reached the water trough, they dropped their weapons and bolted for the fields.

Gawain crossed to the edge of the tree line, singling out other targets. One by one, he sealed the breaches and freed the soldiers. Eyes blinked, heads snapped back and awareness flooded in.

Leaving cover, he strode toward the camp, eyes fixed on the black standard, knowing he could deal with anyone who might try to stop him. He felt invulnerable. He passed the paddocks and supply depots, closing each breach he came across. By the time he reached the compound, the camp was deserted – only the searing cold of Argath's image remained.

When he entered the clearing, he saw the outer flaps of Argath's tent swinging lazily in the breeze. He drew out the blade he'd taken from the inn and ran his finger along the honed edge. The innkeeper had looked to his weapons well. If he cut the two main guy ropes staked to the ground, he would be able to rip the tent away and expose Argath. He glanced up, squinting at the clear bright sky. The sun would do the rest.

The first rope was the thickness of his finger. He knelt and began carefully, quietly cutting. The threads parted easily. He moved to the next rope. When the main guys were cut, he stepped back and took the two ends in his fists. He jerked and the awning collapsed, toppling over the poles propping up the tent.

Argath had tried to prepare. A dark green cloak covered him from head to toe. Bursting out of the collapsed canvas, he whirled on Gawain.

"Sar goth," he snarled, the strange material of the cloak reflecting the sun like mirrored water. He grabbed for his weapon but as soon as the daylight touched his hand, he snatched it back.

"Sagath bratan goth," he cursed, turning to the supply tents.

Gawain stepped in front, cutting him off.

"Druid spawn. Just blind luck you survived my rats," Argath spat from deep inside the hood. "But even now they come. They hear my pain. This time they'll finish what they began. In an hour there'll be nothing left of you, knight."

Gawain started. Knight, how did he know that? Argath shuffled backwards, careful to keep his feet within the shadow of the shimmering cloak. Gawain pressed ahead. "Maybe, but you'll be long dead before they do." He raised the knife.

Argath spun and made to dash for the open tent but Gawain grabbed the shiny hood of his cloak and ripped it back, exposing the long neck and thin shoulders to the dazzling sun.

Argath twisted. He writhed and contorted his sun-warmed body in a vain attempt to rid himself of the spreading agony. He hissed and howled then he suddenly dropped to the ground and began trying to burrow into the earth. Gawain stepped back. Argath shoveled up clods of soil as if he were obeying some primal urge of self-interment.

Gawain watched in astonishment as Argath smashed and battered his head into the ground, his slender, transparent hands clawing at the earth. But before he'd dug more than a foot, bile spluttered from his mouth. Gawain backed away as flecks and curds of the stringy liquid flew from his lips.

The sun burned on and Argath slowed his frantic pace. The bile began pouring freely from his nose and flattened ears. Then the hissing faded and he began convulsing. To

Gawain's surprise, he ceased his efforts and spreading out his pale arms in a lover's embrace, fell forward and hugged the earth that had denied him sanctuary. Thin tendrils of smoke rose from his exposed neck and hands in spiraling columns and for a moment, Gawain thought the skin would burst into flame. Argath gave one last shudder as Gawain went to him and then he simply, quietly, died.

A raw gust of wind blew across the empty fields. Gawain stood quietly looking down at the smoking corpse, black flag atop the standard snapping behind him. Tucking the knife back into his belt, he dropped to one knee. He pulled the shimmering cloak back over the corpse and drew the sign of the cross above it. Then he rose, glancing up at the glorious blue sky, reveling in the last vestiges of Merlin's power. Feelings of distant Camelot and the need to see his friends welled within him and without looking back, he turned south and made his way through the deserted camp.

He picked out a workhorse from a temporary stockade and freed the others. In a nearby tent, he found enough food for his long journey home and spare clothes for Cullen and set out for the river. If the rats were coming they would find no master here – only the calling of their own dark kind.

Out across the low land, he followed the wide river flowing into the heart of the silent town. The surefooted garron bore him safely across low hills and dales filled with spring flowers. On the second day, he saw smoke pluming from the small holdfast. He forged across the river at its shallowest point and urged the steaming horse up the embankment and across the last wide field to where his friend stood waving from the doorway.

So much to tell that cold evening by the crackling fire. And the next day moving on, Cullen traveling north and Gawain south. Saying goodbye as the sun rose above the hulks of hills – knowing that in all the years to come, a friend was with you, no matter how far away.

The journey south took weeks. Gawain spent the nights searching for Orion but not once was he able to contact Merlin. Then, near the market town of Hereford, when he sought the wizard late one night, he felt the earth tremble. And for a brief moment he thought of death, then he saw the blood – the red blood of his earlier vision. There, stretching across the empty northern land, lay heaps of little pyramids and he knew with certainty all the rats had died. And the words that came to his lips before he felt the world stir were full of love, *Merlin*. And that was all, because he was moving, leaving his younger self once again.

Yesterday's Falcon

Chapter 15

He could see the path clearer now. The gloom had lightened. And this time when the hand gently tugged him, he held it tightly.

"You know I'm here, don't you?" the shadowy guide whispered, searching his eyes for signs of recognition.

He nodded. The words were there to voice now, but his lungs burned when he tried to talk.

"No. Don't speak; it will only bring on the coughing. Wait until we get to the Stone. We're almost there," the gentle voice urged.

The figure led, turning back and glancing anxiously at him with each step. Just before they crested the hill, a beam from the Terran Stone broke through the last of the giant fronds and Gawain went to it instinctively.

He reached out to the mist playing on its surface determined to unravel the rest of Morganna's plot and see an end to her plans. When it cleared, he saw a scene with himself standing in the hall outside the Chamber of the Round Table next to Guinevere, Merlin and Arthur. Puzzled, he watched the figures talking soundlessly. Then, suddenly, he knew what was about to happen. *Dear God, no.* He rushed forward into the magic of the Terran light and into his younger self.

". . .'s why you must send Lancelot. You cannot go alone," The wizard was saying to Arthur in the Shield Hall at Caerleon.

255

"Merlin, this is God's gift. I will not pass up the chance to bring the Grail back. I've made up my mind and as king, there's nothing you can do about it."

Merlin turned to Guinevere, face red, knuckles like little white islands on the glowing Rune staff. "My lady, I beg you, talk to him. He cannot leave Camelot now. It's far too dangerous. We still have Uther's sons to deal with – they're out there planning even as we speak. Please, ask Gawain. Argath alone could have brought down this kingdom. My oath, who knows what the others can do?" He turned to Gawain. "Tell him, Gawain. Tell him what we're up against."

"My lord, what Merlin says is true. If the others have half Argath's powers, we're in mortal danger. We must prepare. You must lead us."

"We know about Argath. We've listened to your brave exploits with great interest but this is another matter: this is the Grail. If the Lord did not mean for us to seek it, then why did He bring the vision to Camelot?"

"It was a vision for everyone to see," Merlin cut in. "All the knights."

"But it was in *my* presence, in *my* castle." Arthur slammed his goblet on the table, splashing red wine across the light blue weave of his tunic.

"My lord. Merlin, please," said Guinevere. "We're getting nowhere like this. Gawain's right, we must prepare. We can discuss the Grail later, at the Round Table," she added, turning to the wizard. "Merlin, what other news do you have?"

"I've finished mapping in the north, your majesty, but I haven't had a chance to go far enough south to find out more about the second son. The trouble I've discovered there is sketchy at best. My sources and poor attempts at divining have revealed little more than what Neume told us. However, I'm expecting another Speaking Stone to arrive shortly and when it does I should be able to find out more. I've also prepared a spell that will allow me to experience the impressions of her thoughts while she spoke to the Stone."

Arthur scowled. "More Druid meddling." He pushed the wine aside and rose. "Sweet Jesus, I'll be glad when the Runes disappear once and for all." He glared at Merlin, snatched his crown from the table and stormed out, leaving the others standing in silence.

Moments later an old retainer entered the room, a wine jug cupped in blue veined hands. He took a quick look at the faces before him, bowed stiffly and shuffled back into the hallway. Gawain turned to Merlin. "How can I help?"

"Fetch Bors and Percival and meet me in my study after vespers." Merlin bowed to Guinevere and went to the doorway. "You'll need to pack, Gawain – you'll be traveling. At least there are Runes enough for that much meddling," he added disappearing down the far stairwell, the Rune staff spearing rays of light into the dusk of the hallway.

Gawain took his leave of Guinevere. Crossing the courtyard, he wondered, not for the first time, if Arthur was right – that all this was truly of Merlin's making. Now, Bors and Percival were to play a part, rooks? Pawns? Or the knights they were?

He left the castle grounds thankful of the long walk to the town's armory guild where his friends were working on the construction of a new crossbow. When he entered the timbered hall, he found Bors by the far window bent over a scroll. The big northern knight was muscled like a bull, his great moon of a face creased in deep concentration as he tried to decipher the French written on the plans. To his right, Percival, dressed handsomely in the king's white and gold colors, sat in a chair, feet up on the desk, head back resting in delicate fingers. Gawain approached grinning.

Bors glanced up and the cloud of frustration vanished from his face.

"By the Saints, if it nay be our Gawain!"

Percival rocked upright on his chair, blue eyes sparkling. "O knight nonpareil, what brings you to these haunts?" he asked in a voice as cultured as Bors' was rough.

Gawain told them of Merlin's request. When they tried to pry more out of him, he laughed and clapping Bors on the back told him he would likely get them both turned into dwarfs if he uttered another word.

After supper at a cozy inn near the Usk Bridge, they made their way back to Arthur's castle. Rain fell in heavy drops, forcing them to run the last few yards across the courtyard. Gawain feared they were late as they wound their way up the long flight of stairs to Merlin's study high in the west tower. When he found the place empty, he breathed a sigh of relief.

He lit the fire while Bors and Percival pulled up chairs and set goblets on the rough little table. The logs had scarcely caught when the door flew open and Merlin burst in, breathless after the climb. He waved his hand in the air as the knights rose. "Sit, sit," he panted.

He shuffled across the room and taking a taper from a conical holder at the side of the hearth thrust it in the fire. He lit the candles on the mantle. Then he pushed aside a set of bronze scales on his desk and leaned his weight on his fists. "It comes to this. If Arthur won't help, then we must take the matters into our own hands. Gawain, we'll need more candles for what I have to do. Not these mind, the tallow ones."

Gawain left and went down to the supply room. When he returned, Merlin was finishing the tale about the clouds they'd seen at Colwyn Lake.

"The enemy you face in Eyenon grows more powerful by the day – or rather, night," he was saying when Gawain entered. "He's able to control those who sleep and, from what I've been able to discover, somehow enter their dreams."

Merlin took one of the candles and placed it on the desk. After lighting it with the long taper, he continued. "I've little understanding of the dark magic that affords this dream-walking, and I've no way of knowing the extent of his power. Somehow, he's managed to evade or deflect my attempts to discover his whereabouts. However, I've received some recent reports of strange events occurring near Bodmin – where you'll be journeying. If I can't find our enemy, then I can't get to know his weaknesses and that means I won't be of much help to any of you."

He pinched out the taper, blew away the smoke and dropped it back in the copper holder. "As I see it, there are only a two things I can do for now: charm your weapons, and teach Gawain more about the Sithean Bauble – but I can't guarantee the success of either in Eyenon's presence."

He paused, taking a long look at the intent faces before him. "I may not know a lot about our enemy, but I know enough to have chosen the very best of Arthur's knights." His gnarled hand seemed to command the power of wisdom as he wagged a finger. "And I'll not see one of you alone in this."

He crossed to an oak chest, threw back the lid and rummaged inside. He returned carrying a pouch and a small crucible. "To that end, I've prepared a little something while you were out gallivanting around the town."

He took a knife and pricked the ball of his thumb, then the thumbs of each knight. Holding the crucible, he caught a single drop of blood from each of them. Muttering something under his breath Gawain couldn't catch, he swirled the crucible over the candle flame. That done, he carefully tipped in the contents of the pouch A few moments later, he emptied a pile of red crystals onto the table.

"Now, Bors, stand yourself at that end of the table. Gawain, you the other. Percival opposite me, over there. Good."

Leaning forward, he smoothed the crystals flat. When he was done, he glanced up, a mischievous smile touching the corners of his lips. "You'll like this."

He furrowed a circle through the crystals with his fingertip. When the channel was complete, he repeated the motion, stirring faster. Within seconds, the surrounding crystals had deepened into a scarlet paste. The knights watched, jaws dropping as the paste began to liquefy and flow into the clear trench.

Merlin lifted his finger, stirring all the while. The liquid followed, flowing around it like a bloody noose. Without taking his eyes off the reeling arc, he raised his finger above his head. In response, the crimson circle followed, widening as he spun faster. When it reached just beyond the knights, Merlin chanted under his breath and jerked his finger away leaving the circle spinning above them.

The knights stared up. The circle slowed then broke into tiny blood drops, each one perfect, revolving, shining in the glow of the tallow candles. A moment later, the delicate drops began evaporating, but not before bathing each knight in the purest incarnadine.

"There," said Merlin rubbing his hands together once the air was clear. "We're linked, fused through the Bloodline. From now on, your wound is my wound, your pain mine. We share a common life force on this journey. We may not be as lucky as the proverbial cat, but for a while anyway, you'll each have four lives."

Bors and Percival erupted into questions but Merlin dismissed them with an impatient wave. Gawain smiled. For the moment at least, someone else was at the mercy of his mysteries.

The candles were spluttering by the time Merlin finished outlining his plan. When Bors and Percival left to prepare for the journey south, he took Gawain aside.

"This time I might not be able to come to you through your stars, my boy. I can't trust my thoughts. If Eyenon has knowledge of Dark Runes, who knows what he can do. He maybe able to block, even change the messages I send. Here." He took out the Bauble. "I've altered the Sithean web. It still requires an invocation but this time you won't have to sustain it. There's one spell to start the effects and one to end them, simple as that."

"What if ... "

Merlin raised his eyes to the dark ceiling and clucked his tongue against his teeth. "Bran, give me strength," he muttered, brow furrowing with lines as deep as ruts in a winter field. "To continue, because Eyenon has the ability to move in and out of dreams at will, we must assume he can also change his shape or form. To see who he really is, would require a powerful spell indeed – one far beyond your learning at this stage, that's why I'm giving you the Bauble. I've glyphed it so you can use your essence. When you release it into the Sithean web, it will reveal his true nature, even his true form, if you're receptive enough."

He smoothed the indigo surface with his fingers, leaving light blue trails swirling behind his touch. "Here, take it, store it safely – it may well prove our best weapon." He handed over the Bauble almost reluctantly. "When you invoke its power you'll feel the energy leave you – remember how you felt in Lothian? It will be much the same."

He pulled the cord tight around his robe and blew out the candle on the desk. "When the energy is released, you'll tire significantly, so be sparing in your use. I doubt if you'll be able to control Eyenon for more than a few moments. Hopefully, that's all you'll need. Now for the spell – out of

Arthur's hearing of course," he said, slipping a bony arm around Gawain's shoulders and walking him to the door.

Downstairs, in the safety of the castle keep, Gawain practiced until he could invoke the new Sithean web. And when the magic flared about him like dry leaves caught by autumn flames, Merlin smiled and nodded enough.

They ate together in the castle kitchens then returned up the winding staircase to Merlin's study. The wizard crossed the room to a honeycombed scroll rack next to the window. He carefully extracted a parchment and blew away the dust.

"Now, for my part, my boy. After you leave, I'll convince Arthur to send Lancelot in search the Grail. The key lies in the Christian faith. The glory of finding the Grail is better shared than earned alone. Arthur's own words. Maybe with a little help, our king might be made more sympathetic to our suggestions. It won't be easy though – he's so single-minded. But, with the *Shard* Runes and the right timing, he could be made to listen, *really* listen."

He untied a faded red ribbon and flattened the parchment out on the desk "These are the only Runes too delicate to carve into my Rune Staff. They go back to the beginning of our time. Some say they're the only true Far Druid Runes left; perhaps that's why they are so complex. The *Shards* can ruin a life, as easily as improve it. I've only used them once, when I first came to Glamorgan as a boy."

Their elegance struck Gawain the moment he saw them. Each Rune ended in a half moon stroke of such painstaking beauty, he swallowed dryly.

"You see them in the shapes don't you? Your stars, the planets, that's what draws you to them, isn't it?" Merlin said thoughtfully.

Patting Gawain on the shoulder, he turned his attention back to the parchment. He traced one of the *Delf* branches. "See these lines, here? How they flair? They look the same, don't they? But you couldn't be more mistaken. One wrong stroke, one wrong angle from where the line leaves the circle and the Rune could cause the victim to loose all capacity for love instead of being infused with it."

Merlin shook his head ruefully. "Great art is seductive but also dangerous."

He looked at Gawain, green eyes luminous in the dusky room. "I'll see Guinevere tonight, my boy and tell her of our plans. During the next full moon, when the *Shards* are most potent, I'll cast them. She'll need to be strong, not only will she have to persuade Arthur to stay – but convince her lover to go."

"What about the Dragon Ring, can we still use it?"

"Better lad, the Bloodline will provide a stronger connection for us." He began rolling up the parchment. "I'll come to you after I cast the *Shards*." "Now, I have more work to do. Tomorrow we face our new enemy," he added dismissively.

The next morning the knights left Camelot for Bodmin. They rode the better part of the blue-skied day through the open fields quilting the countryside. Once they reached the rugged coastline, they traveled south. The three of them, bearing Arthur's banner embroidered with golden lions, never failed to draw looks or reverent bows from the farmers and merchants they met.

Toward the end of the week, they came to a river widening into the tossing waves of the Celtic sea. They scouted the banks but could find no safe place to cross. Percival lobbied to follow it inland until they could find a bridge or at least shallow rapids and the others agreed. A late morning mist lay still and white across the fields bordering the rumbling water. As the horses trod warily through fog curling up about their forelocks, the knights searched for a safe place to ford.

They traveled inland the rest of the morning with Gawain's deepening sense of danger mounting the further away from the coast they rode. They journeyed cautiously, cutting through the thickening mist, no one speaking. The damp stole through their armor and tunics leaving even Bors shivering in its wake. Above them, a sullen sky brooded over the dismal land. Only the horses' occasional snuffle broke the silence.

Bors saw the bridge first. He called to the others and pointed. They rode up to weathered head posts, noting the splintered planks stretching across the chasm.

"I dinna ken if a horse could cross it safely, but maybe I could," said Bors.

"I think a horse is lighter," quipped Percival.

Gawain smiled, nodding up ahead. "Safer to continue along the river. It's bound to narrow or change direction. We'll get across sooner or later." He looked down to the water churning through the fog and grimaced. "Come on, Arthur's best – or Merlin's fools."

They followed the river until early evening but still couldn't find a safe place to cross. The fog thickened until it swilled up around the bellies of the horses. Then, as Gawain was about to suggest they make camp for the night, he caught sight of the hump of a second bridge in the distance. As they neared, he started. It was identical to the first! He turned to Bors.

"What do you make of it?"

"I dinna ken. Maybe we've traveled in a circle?"

"I don't think so."

"Whatever ye think, my friend, but that there's near the spitting image."

"True enough."

"I've nay love for this place, my friend, nay love at all," said Bors, his voice tapering off as he glanced around at the bare trees and white mist.

"Here, hold the reins," said Percival, dismounting. He jumped down into the soupy fog and strode up the embankment to the bridge. He grabbed the securing guy ropes and rocked them. The bridge creaked and groaned but held. He called over his shoulder, his voice oddly hollow as it reached the others.

"I'll try and cross. It should take my weight. Bors, put those muscles of yours to good use and steady this thing would you."

The big knight and Gawain each grabbed the ropes staked to the ground and Percival took a tentative step onto the bridge. Far below the river raged in a muffled roar.

They watched him move cautiously from one plank to the next, his armor clanking dully as he tested each slat. He was half way across when Bors boomed, "Is it safe?"

Percival answered without turning. "It should hold us. I don't know about the supplies, though. Bors, you come over next. Maybe we can find a way to strengthen this thing. I'll steady it from this end."

Percival continued shuffling ahead, hands wide on the ropes for balance. When he finally stepped onto the far bank, he turned and beckoned. "Seems safe enough. Just keep your feet spread and use the ropes."

He didn't see the fog thickening around him. He called to Bors again. And that's when it took him. One moment he was there, the next he was gone – no Percival. No sign he'd ever crossed the bridge.

"Percival. PERCIVAL!" Gawain's voice floated flat and lifeless through the gloom. He turned to Bors. The big knight was peering down the length of the bridge, his great honest moon of a face struggling to come to terms with what he'd just witnessed.

"Stay here, I'll go across. The minute you see any movement, anything, call and I'll come right back," Gawain said.

"Nay, I'll go, I'm stronger."

"You're also heavier," Gawain reminded him. "Wait with the horses, I won't be long. Here, take my breastplate and mail. Hold, the ropes steady."

The bridge creaked and swung lazily as Gawain stepped from slat to slat. Far below the rushing river crashed over rocks. *Why couldn't I hear that before?*

Halfway across, he heard Bors call out. "Something's happening, Gawain ... I ... I canna see ye very well ... I ... "

Gawain spun around. This time it was the big knight disappearing. Thick fingers of fog were wrapping around him like smoke. They seemed to be eating him alive.

"Bors. BORS!"

Gawain hung onto the swaying ropes helpless to do anything but watch his friend and the horses vanish one after the other. When it was over, the fog swilled back, like soup in a bowl.

Gawain turned. The shifting fog swirled ahead and behind him as if it were waiting for him to make up his mind – here, there, it's all the same to us it seemed to say, you'll be ours eventually.

He glanced to where he last saw Percival and then to where Bors disappeared. He could barely make out the trees on either side. He looked from one to the other again and a new understanding dawned on him. *The two groups of trees are the same – no, not the same, they're the reverse of each other!*

Desperately trying to fathom what was happening, he squinted along the skyline toward the hills rising in the distance, then back to the other side of the river. *The same hills. A mirror image! The bridge is the midpoint between the two lands. It's as though I'm at the center of something, in the middle of some looking glass – that's why the fog can't touch me.*

Below he could see the path the river cut through the rolling fog. It fissured its way north and south. He could follow it clearly, as far as the eye could see, but there was no way of climbing down to it. The embankment sheared off to white tips of rocks far beneath his feet.

He looked ahead and then back again. *Which way, Merlin?* He felt deathly tired. Slowly, watchfully, he inched to the bank where Percival disappeared. *I wonder if I'll see the fog when it takes me.*

He didn't.

The world turned pearly white when he stepped off the bridge, then he too was gone.

Yesterday's Falcon

CHAPTER 16

The fog swaddling Gawain slowly dissipated and from its milky vapors four gray walls materialized. Above him, a stone ceiling shimmered into view. Ahead, a stout door studded with iron bands stood all too real. He was in some sort of dungeon. Instinctively, he turned to see where the bridge was but all he saw were the sagging slats of a wooden bed.

He paced the cell puzzling his situation, what had happened? He tapped the walls. They were real enough. He crossed to the iron-banded door and ran his hand over the bolts. They felt rough and hard. He tried the handle, locked, as he somehow knew it would be. The hinges were solid and rounded at the edges – no chance of pulling out the pins. He went to the cot, worked one of the slats loose and used it to hammer on the door. The booming echoed in hallways beyond.

He stopped and listened. Nothing. *No,* something – the sound of water. He pressed his ear against the door. Some way off, water dripped onto a stone floor. He knelt and peered under the sill. A faint light glowed, probably cast from an oil lamp in the hallway beyond. He rose and explored the rest of his room. There was no means of escape. Going over his options, he returned and sat on the bed. Maybe Bors or Percival would come, though he doubted it.

He lay back on the wooden slats and folded his hands behind his head. All he could do was wait. He closed his eyes. *Merlin, just where in the four corners of this realm am*

269

I? How do I use this bloodline of ours? He touched the Dragon Ring twisting it around his finger but it remained as cold as moonlight.

His dream was short. He was there in the dungeon, sleeping, dreaming. The cell was the same, except for one thing – in his dream he rose from the hard slats and opened the door. It was ridiculously easy.

He awoke a short while later, feeling weaker – as if the sleep had somehow taken away his energy instead of restoring it. He yawned and sat up. The door before him hung wide open; the way he'd left it in the dream.

Rising from the bed, head pounding, he crossed to the doorway and went out into the hall beyond. It was narrow, lined with oil lamps hanging from long chains bolted into an arched ceiling. The passage ran some fifty paces in each direction and ended in doors identical to the one in his room. "Now, all I have to do is fall asleep again and open another door," he muttered to himself. "Do I have to do this ad infinitum?"

He chose to go right for no other reason than he'd looked that way first. As he neared the banded door, he heard the dripping water. He tried the handle. It turned but the door remained shut. He walked down the passageway to the other door and listened. The same sounds of dripping water. He tried the handle. It turned. The door opened onto an identical hallway beyond. Another banded door loomed at the far end. He noted the stones in the wall near the doorway where he stood. A dark one jutted out near the lintel. He walked down the new hallway to the other door. The handle turned and the door opened. He looked at the lintel. A dark stone stared down at him.

He tried something else. He reached up and scored the stone with his sword. He stood back. The scratch looked as crooked as Merlin's staff. He retraced his steps to the other door ... only to find the same mark scored in the stone there.

For some reason he was not surprised. *So, whatever direction I take, whatever choice I make, I'll still be doing the same thing.* With a last look behind him, he returned down the passage and through the new door.

He found himself in a large square room with the now-familiar banded doors set in each of the four walls. He looked up to grating bolted into the ceiling some fifteen feet above him. Through the large squares, he could see gray clouds slowly moving. He reached his hand out to the water dripping through the bars. Yearning for the freedom that was so close, he stood under the drops, letting them patter onto his face as he breathed in the fresh air.

There was no way to reach the grating, but he would remember this room and use it as a marker. He went down another series of hallways until he reached another square room. He crossed to the door on his left and tried the handle. It turned. He pulled. The sight that greeted him shook him to the core. He stood transfixed, love and anguish tightening his throat until he found breathing almost impossible. He was looking into his father's study, replete with books, globes, scrolls, even his beloved maps. At the far end, a fire burned evenly, crackling as if Jules, the old retainer, had just finished lighting it.

Heart thumping, Gawain entered. He walked around the room running his fingers over the desktop, partly from nostalgia, partly from the need to feel it once more. *How ...? Why ... ?* The questions trailed off as he crossed to the fire. Absently, he stretched out his hands to the warmth, trying to make sense of it all. He drew back, frowning – there was no heat. Curious, he crouched down and held out his palms to the flames. Nothing. He reached into the heart of the fire – still no warmth. He could feel the logs but it was as if they were unlit.

"In God's name, what's happening?" he mumbled.

He went to the window looking out onto the courtyard and leaned against the casement as he'd done so many times before. "Am I losing my mind? Fog, bridges between worlds, locked doors that can only be opened by dreams, and now my father's study. What next? Squee? Lothian?"

He left the darkened window and went back to the square room. He gingerly opened the next door. He was prepared for another shock but what he saw stunned him all the same – Uther's chamber! His eyes flew to the bed but it was empty. And *dear God*, he tried to stop himself, but he couldn't. He stole a glance to the side of the massive four-poster, to the spot where Athlan had died.

The stone floor was bare.

With a heavy heart, he walked over and stood on the spot where his life had changed so irrevocably. He knelt, tracing his fingers over the place she had bled. Head lowered, he stared at the fatal spot, wondering if he could somehow dream her again. And if he did, would she too feel cold, like the logs in the burning fire?

He rose and closed the door quietly, afraid he might disturb her spirit. In the outer room, he went to the door on his left.

Locked.

What now? He rattled it in frustration, wanting to go on – to get away from this place with its all too real memories.

He knew the answer: he had to dream it open. Sitting with his back to the wall, he tried to direct his thoughts away from the murder and shut out the nightmare of the room beyond. Then he waited for the pain to go and the sleep to come.

And it did, after a long, long time. Again, he dreamed himself to the door and opened it. Later, when he woke, he found himself staring at a long hallway disappearing to a pinpoint of darkness. Fatigued, he set out on unsteady legs.

The hallway was longer than he'd thought. In his present condition, he felt as if he'd been two nights without sleep. His boots echoed dully on the stone floor, the clacking rhythm almost lulling him to sleep. He couldn't afford to dream open doors anymore. If he did, it would impair his ability to reason and he would never be able to find his way out of the growing maze.

His mind turned to the fire in his father's study. *Fire without warmth.* Why was this so important? If he could touch the logs but not sense warmth from the flames, why could he feel the rain coming through the grill? Was it cold to the touch? He couldn't remember. Tiredness muddled his thoughts.

The lamps above him burned with an even glow, casting perfect shadows as he passed beneath. *If I could touch them, would they burn me? If I covered them, would they go out?* The questions grew as he trudged down the endless passage.

At last, he reached another banded door. He hesitated at the threshold, hand on the latch. Let it be open, he prayed. The latch came up and he pushed the door wide. He was prepared for just about anything at this point but what he saw still surprised him. Writhing in the center of a dark cave, in all his terrible glory, stood Argath. His head swiveled as the door opened. The yellow eyes narrowed then flared with hatred.

"So, we meet again," the familiar voice hissed.

"Y ... You're dead," Gawain stuttered.

"In your world maybe."

"In my world?" queried Gawain dumbly.

"I think I'd rather ask the questions, Druid. First, I'd like you to know I can strike from here. A simple thing for me. You'd die before you got ten paces up that hallway. I might also add that your death would not be pleasant. My venom has a tendency to be rather caustic, you know."

"I killed you once, I can do it again," said Gawain, his wits returning.

"Tssssss, hardly the same circumstance, I think."

Gawain blinked. Somehow, Argath had closed the gap between them.

"Two things, just two simple things that's all I want, and you can be on your merry way, questing about, killing to your heart's content." The luminous eyes swam with yellow light.

"Think of it like this: right answers, on you go, wrong answers, dead Druid. Simple. First question. Ready. Who's Merlin? Second, what's this Grail thing?"

Gawain's mind raced. *His voice is the same but the diction is different, more childish somehow. And Merlin, how did he even know the name?* He looked at the monster, wondering, in a fleeting moment of intuition, if he could kill him by sleeping and dreaming him dead. *No, but there was something else.* He stepped into the room. Argath reacted visibly and backed up.

"Fire isn't hot."

"What?"

"I said fire isn't hot."

"What are you gibbering about?"

But Gawain could see worry in that face.

"Answer my questions, stupid Druid. DO YOU HEAR ME? ANSWER!"

Gawain dug his hand into his pocket and pulled out the Bauble. He began the invocation. Argath froze and the light dimmed. Magic erupted around Gawain in flames of burnished gold. Argath's head and neck flattened and he spat a hissing stream of venom at the knight standing before him. It shimmered like moonlit rain as it raced through the air. The Sithean Bauble crackled with dark lightning and the venom dissolved into mist. A moment later Argath wavered and he too began to break up.

Silence.

Gawain was alone in the cave. Exhausted from the loss of essence, he tried to put things in perspective. Argath was there, yet he wasn't. The Sithean power had helped reveal the truth as Merlin said it would. It showed the monster for what he was, a phantom. But why was he so interested in Merlin and the Grail?

Gawain found the next door at the back of the cave. It was unlocked. He walked into another square room with doors set in each wall. He opened the door to his right and went through. He plodded down a vast hallway, then through more empty rooms. At the fifth or sixth door, he found a staircase winding up a single flight of stairs. At the top, everything seemed to repeat itself-the long halls, the empty rooms, the banded doors.

He didn't know when despair set in but the effort of fighting fatigue and the endless struggle to find a means of escape began to take its toll. He started to give up hope.

At the end of yet another long hallway, he found a small room. He desperately needed rest. He had to risk sleeping no matter what it did to him. He took off his boots, and using them for a pillow, lay down. Above him, loomed the same arched ceiling he'd looked at for what seemed a millennium. Where were Bors and Percival? Were they, like him, wandering through this endless nightmare of doors and halls? Were they also glimpsing into their past, seeing ghosts that talked as if they were there, in front of them, part of the living present? Exhausted, he slipped into the vastness of sleep with two questions still plaguing him – what was Argath's interest in the Grail and what did he want with Merlin?

There were no dreams this time, only emptiness – a total void where he rested peacefully. But just before he awoke, a brief image flared in his mind. It was like a flash of sunlight highlighting golden threads in a tapestry or

275

arras, then he saw it for what it truly was, a map! A detailed map full of lines and interlocking squares. At the center, a small circular chamber glowed in the faintest of yellows.

Merlin, again you come to me. Gawain rose, feeling the cooling warmth of the Dragon Ring. This time the sleep had refreshed him, not left him weaker. He set out, working his way through the halls and rooms keeping to the vision-map. The going was easier. His steps were stronger, his hope greater.

When he came across the hallway leading to the circular chamber, he found it wide and carpeted. Thick yellow candles set in the extended hands of earthen gargoyles lit the way. The door at end was different too. It was banded like the previous doors, but not with iron, with gleaming silver. Even before he touched it, he knew this one would be open.

He was right.

The room was a duplicate of the Round Table chamber, except there was no table in the center. Instead, his gaze fell upon the Golden Dragon of Neume's cave sitting back on its haunches.

"Ahh, Gawain." The voice rumbled. "It's good to see you again after all this wild adventure."

He uncurled his tail lazily and rose. The stately head almost touched the ceiling. A blaze of gold lit the chamber as he moved and when he turned his great yellow eyes with their coruscating flecks of gold upon him, Gawain had that familiar feeling of looking into the heart of the Orion cluster.

"My little knight with the Runes, are you going to do me harm today?" the dragon rumbled, cocking his huge head curiously to one side.

"Perhaps."

"Ha. Ha. Ha." His jowls shook, and a shower of tiny golden scales floated down. Gawain stared up at the massive face and felt for the Bauble.

"Do you wonder where you are, little one?"

"Where?"

"If you answer two simple questions, I'll tell you," he said expansively. "Who is Merlin? And just what is that Grail thing all about?"

"You know who Merlin is. He helped the Luck Dragon. You told me the story yourself."

"I'm not up to games."

Gawain stepped forward. *That same childish tone.* "Neither am I."

The golden creature puffed out his chest and Gawain heard the scales stretching then saw them flash iridescent in the light of the candles as they expanded. The dragon drew back his head and arched his neck. Gawain invoked the power of the Bauble.

Light on light.

Magic on magic.

The air crackled and spat as the Druid elements countered the Dark essence in the cavern. Under its power, the Golden Dragon flattened out like cloth, then with a rustling sound, he vanished in a shower of colors. Gawain blinked. In the dragon's place sat a small boy, cross-legged, floating in the air at eye level. All the light in the chamber now radiated from him.

"You're much stronger than the others you know, Bors and Percival." His voice was pure, serene. Gawain watched the soft dark curls and cherubic face warily. He judged the child to be five or six years old and no higher than his waist if he were to stand. His mouth was wide, almost sensual when he spoke and he had the whitest teeth Gawain had ever seen.

"I should apologize for putting you through all this." He waved a small hand in the direction of the hallway behind Gawain. "But you did very well, you know. I really must say that." His voice had more of a real edge to it than either Argath's or the Golden Dragon's but Gawain sensed a similar petulance behind its friendliness. He had the sinking feeling that if he tried the invocation now, it would have no effect.

"I wondered how long it would take you to get here. Please, let me introduce myself, my name is Eyenon. But then, I'm sure you knew that."

The diction and correctness of his speech was unnerving. He sounded more like a Glastonbury scholar than a small child.

"Yes."

"A simple yes. Ummmm, guarded, aren't we? Well, let me help you. Any questions? Like, where do I come from, what do I want – that sort of thing?" A faint note of frustration had crept into his voice.

"Where are Bors and Percival?" Gawain said moving forward.

"That one I don't care to answer. Ask another," Eyenon replied, thick dark curls hanging in his eyes.

"Are you Uther's son?" It was a stab in the dark. Eyenon blinked behind his locks.

"That hurt. He couldn't rule a scullery, let alone a kingdom. He was weak and *stupid*. You should know, even you managed to kill him. By the way, please accept my thanks for that." The child before him grinned, his mouth opening abnormally wide – like Argath's!

"My turn. Who's Merlin? What's the Grail? Help me now, I only have small pictures," Eyenon said tapping the side of his head with a stubby finger.

"Why is this so important?"

"You don't answer questions with questions. Didn't that busy body of a father tell you that?" The child Eyenon folded his arms across his chest and huffed.

"Merlin is a friend, that's all, a family friend. As for the Grail, it's a Holy relic, a cup Arthur once saw in a vision. No one really knows what it is. When he saw it, he was suffering from an illness – we all were ... there was a malaise in the castle at the time."

"Tell me about the wizard," Eyenon snapped back.

"If I tell you, will you tell me what's happened to Bors and Percival?"

"I'll see. Be warned though knight," Eyenon said, eyes narrowing, "the truth, or I'll create a private hell for you that will make this maze look like a stroll through the Christian's Garden of Eden."

Suspended, perfectly still, perfectly positioned in the center of the cold chamber, the second son of Uther grinned again. "Tell me what Runes he knows, what spells he can cast."

"Are Bors and Percival safe?"

"Yes, yes and yes. Tell me everything, now. Don't miss out a thing."

"I'll tell you of his life at Camelot."

And he did. But while he told of Merlin at the court, he was careful not to give away the extent or true nature of the wizard's power. Instead, he painted a picture of kind deeds and foolish ways, of spells that made plants grow and wounds heal. On his finger, the Dragon Ring warmed and the Bloodline began its magic.

In the far distance ...

In a dusky room, far away in Camelot, Merlin sought the Dragon Ring as he chanted the ancient words and drew the delicate *Shard* Runes. Each one sent a fine trail of silver spiraling in its wake. And under the full moon, Guinevere stood tall and regal as the glittering light fell about her.

"So how did this Merlin wizard help you find Argath?" For the moment at least, the child looked content.

"If I tell you, will you let me see Bors and Percival?"

"Bors, Percival, who cares? Sorry excuses for knights, both of them. But, I *may* let you see them, *if* your answers satisfy me." His voice sharpened. "Now, go on."

"I can only tell you that Merlin. . . ." Gawain faltered. The room suddenly wavered before him as if a thin haze of smoke had drifted across his vision.

In the far distance ...

Merlin and Guinevere descended the winding stairs from his study and crossed the hall to the Chamber of the Round Table. They stood near the same spot where Eyenon floated in the chamber of Gawain's dream world.

Arthur entered from the chapel and nodded to the couple. His face was drawn and his body frail, but his eyes were full of purpose.

Guinevere reached out and laid her hand gently on his wrist. "Arthur, we've come to speak with you about the Grail ... " At her opening words, Merlin faded back into the shadows.

"Enough drivel. Tell me of the Grail," the child of Uther said, cutting Gawain off mid-sentence.

"If I do, will ... "

"NO! No more questions, no more deals. No more, do you hear, Camelot knight? Tell me about the Grail. What magic does it make?" Eyenon jabbed a stubby finger at him. "TELL ME NOW!"

Gawain blinked fighting nausea as the room wavered.

In the far distance ...

Merlin watched Guinevere and Arthur from the deep shadows.

"It is not for you alone to seek the most Holy of Relics, my lord," Guinevere was saying, "The quest belongs to your fellowship. Who finds the Grail is not important. The Lord's gift is for everyone – all Camelot should share in its glory." The words fell like starlit rain as the ancient *Shard* Runes jagged and jostled for cohesion.

"The meaning of the Grail is beyond me," Gawain said as the walls around him expanded then shrank. "I . . . have no understanding of its power. It's part of the Christian faith."

"But you're part of the Christian faith," snapped back Eyenon.

"I was ... I mean, I am," said Gawain running his fingers through his hair. "I was brought up a Christian, a believer. I was baptized at Powes. But Merlin showed me the Druid path and taught me the lore of my ancestors. I ... I have two faiths – but, but it's who I am." He finished weakly, not understanding why he had revealed so much about himself.

"Tut, tut," admonished the floating child.

In the far distance ...

At the same time, in the real Chamber of the Round Table, Merlin stepped from the shadows, breath held as Arthur listened to Guinevere. The king seemed lost in her words now, drowning in them. Merlin let out a sigh. Guinevere gently entwined her fingers through Arthur's.

"Lancelot and Sagremor must go," she said, looking into his faded blue eyes. "They're the logical choice." Her voice was low, seductively soft. "You're needed here, my lord. Your subjects need you, I need you."

The king nodded, intoxicated by the charmed words, in awe of every syllable, every gesture she made. Merlin leaned over his glowing Rune staff, pale face bathed in the soft light.

In the world of the dream chamber, the boy glowered at the knight standing before him, head bowed. "Who cares about your problems? I've got my own, namely you. I want to know more about the Grail. I want to know about its master. I want to know *who it serves?*"

The final words sounded as if they had been spoken from under water and Gawain looked up, hands going to his temples.

In the far distance ...

Arthur gazed longingly at Guinevere. He spoke the same time Eyenon spoke, "I'll send my best knights, my love, I will. I'll send them today, now. You're right; we should share in the Grail's glories. We must know *who it serves.*" His final words harmonized perfectly with those of Eyenon. Merlin started, almost dropping his staff. A ragged black hole the size of a scullery window ripped through the air before him, its edges shimmering in bright silver light.

At the same time, Gawain also saw the ragged tear. All sound faded and both knight and wizard stared at each other through the lesion.

"Merlin?"

"Gawain?"

"What's happening?"

The wizard drummed his fingers on the top of his Rune staff pondering the question. He wavered, blurred slightly then swam back into focus.

"I'm not sure."

Part of Guinevere's long white dress suddenly appeared at the edge of the rift then swirled out of view.

Merlin spoke. *"Since I came to you in Lothian and shared my essence, things have been different between us, my boy. I don't know exactly how, but it seems as though our connections have become somehow clearer, stronger, especially when danger is present. Perhaps that's what this is all about. Where are you?"*

Gawain told him about the Golden Dragon and Eyenon. When he finished, the torn edges of the rift shifted again, leaving long distorted shadows of Guinevere and Eyenon playing on the wall.

Merlin spoke. *"We have little time, I fear. Listen carefully. Use the Bauble on your surroundings, not on Eyenon. He's real, the maze and the others you've seen are his creation. He is shaping your dreams, doing what he can to find out about the Grail and me. I don't know how far he can take this. I only know you must wake up before he gets any stronger."*

Again the ragged edges wavered and Gawain caught scraps of Guinevere's voice and Eyenon's ranting as the room pulsed back and forth.

"I've lost the Bloodline to Bors and Percival. They may be asleep too. Find them and travel back to the coast, away from Eyenon's influence. I'm leaving for the Terran Stone at Carmarthen tomorrow. I'll be able to help from there. If all else fails you must ... "

Without warning, the lesion sealed and the room rippled back into focus. One second Merlin was there, the next Eyenon was floating cross-legged in his place.

". . . chance, or I'll kill your stupid friends."

Gawain fought for equilibrium.

"Do you hear? I'll kill them all."

"Maybe."

"WHAT! What did you say?"

Gawain fingered the Bauble. He picked a spot behind Eyenon and concentrated. Under his breath, he began the invocation.

"What are you doing? STOP!"

Ignoring him, Gawain spoke the Druid words aloud and the far walls burst into whirling grains that spun outwards. Beyond lay wide fields and distant hills.

"Stop it, stop it. I don't like it." Eyenon's voice dropped from a scream to a childish plea. He flapped his hands as if he could shoo Gawain away. "Stop it. I SAID STOP IT!"

But Gawain swept his gaze over the other walls exploding them into tiny fragments.

Then he felt it – wind and the warmth of sun.

CHAPTER 17

He found himself lying on a hillside, surrounded by a hazy morning mist. Head pounding, he struggled to sit up and saw Eyenon fleeing down the hill as fast as his chubby legs could carry him.

The energy loss from using the Bauble left him momentarily dazed, unable to give chase. All he could do was watch the little boy scamper away, arms swinging wildly for balance, half-jumping, half-stumbling over the small rocks and uneven ground. To the left of where he ran, a small clump of trees jutted out from a bend in the river and Gawain could make out two forms lying near the base of an oak tree. He recognized them immediately. Struggling to his feet, he set off on shaky legs.

When he reached the oak, he found Bors and Percival fast asleep. He knelt in the mossy grass and shook them by the shoulders. Bors woke first and his hand went awkwardly to his sword.

"Steady, it's only me."

The big knight shook his head trying to clear the cobwebs.

"Wherever you think you were, it was just a dream. We've been under Eyenon's control," said Gawain.

"What ... how ... do you mean?"

"I think we came within his range at the second bridge. Somehow, the fog was involved. Perhaps it was just that, I don't know." Gawain looked at Percival, who was also shaking off the effects of sleep. "He used it to confuse us. I think it made us lose more than our way; it made us lose touch with this, here, what's real. God, I don't even remember falling asleep."

He left Bors and went to Percival. "Are you all right?"

"I think so. I'm not sure."

"Do you remember crossing the bridge?"

"Vaguely."

"When you were separated from us, it must have given Eyenon a chance to draw on his ability. I think we were tired and he somehow used the fog like a swaddling blanket."

"All I remember is feeling drained, not sleepy, but as you said, really tired," mumbled Percival still trying to focus.

"What else?" said Gawain.

"I can't say exactly, it was as if I was still walking, not actually walking, if you know what I mean." Percival frowned, putting himself into the rare position of struggling for the right words. "For one thing, I wasn't who I was. I know that sounds odd but I was much younger, perhaps eighteen. And I wasn't in the fog anymore. It had cleared. I was at Alsop on tournament day entering my tent, the green and gold one."

"That's probably when you fell to sleep," reasoned Gawain.

"I suppose," he continued. "But it was so real." He looked up, his blue eyes bright now. "The next part's a little embarrassing to tell – even for me." He managed a weak smile. "When I went in, I saw a young maiden lying in bed. She was striking." He turned to Bors but there were no signs of derision. "When she saw me, she pulled back the covers. She had the most beautiful body I've ever seen – the breasts, the hips. As God is my witness, she had the . . ."

Bors yawned.

Percival turned his attention to Gawain. "Who could resist? I undressed and got into bed with her. Then the strangest thing happened. When I was about to kiss her, she put her finger to my lips and asked about the Grail – right there! 'Who does the Grail serve?' she asked, 'Who does it serve?' God, I answered. Why not. But it wasn't enough, she wanted more. She wouldn't give in no matter what I tried, and you know I have the Druid way when it comes to women," he added, clearing his throat.

"Get on with it," said Bors, rolling his eyes.

"Well, at the risk of omitting the more interesting details," Percival continued, "I told her, I knew nothing more about the Grail than what we saw at the Round Table. I must have convinced her because she suddenly gave in and let me have my way. She was magnificent.

"After we'd finished, she rested her head on my shoulder and we lay back on the pillow. Then I realized, I don't know when, exactly, she'd somehow become lighter. Her head seemed to rest easier. I turned ... Ugh!" Percival shuddered closing his eyes. "I can see it now. The woman in bed with me was no longer a beautiful young maiden, she was ... my mother. My mother! Imagine what I felt, there, next to me, naked, my own mother. I was out of that bed like a banshee at the first sign of dawn. I grabbed my cloths and ran, hell bent on getting as far away as possible."

He paused, running his fingers through his thick hair, his blue eyes showing despair. He took a long breath before he continued. "Then I did the stupidest thing. I don't know what made me, but just outside the tent, I turned. Dear God, the thing was sitting up, smiling as if she knew I was going to take that look. Gawain, I swear I've never seen anything more shocking, not Uther's death, not even the day Brandon was caught in the gristmill – nothing compares. My mother had aged; she was eighty if she was a day. And there she was sitting on the edge of the bed, toothless, naked, waving to me with one hand – the other stroking the brow of a young boy of four or five suckling at her breast."

"Eyenon!" declared Gawain. "What happened then?"

"Nothing really. That's it. I fled into the darkness. I just ran and ran, trying to get rid of that picture in my brain – that's when you woke me."

The three of them fell silent.

"We need to get away from here, back to the coast," said Gawain scanning the fields, "I don't think Eyenon's powerful enough to reach that far. We'll go back across the bridge and follow the river. Once we reach the coast, we'll wait for Merlin to contact us; he'll know what to do."

The others nodded.

"Bors, tell us your story while we travel, it'll help keep our minds focused."

Bors shrugged his giant shoulders, puzzling over the events as he tried to recall them. "When ye disappeared off the bridge, I decided to follow," he began in his broad northern accent. "I was nay more than half-way, when it started to snow. But it wasn't any colder. At least it dinna feel any different." He shrugged again.

"By the time I got to the other side, I was knee deep in a drift. I stopped to touch the snow there. It was nay cold either. It was just ... just snow. I walked on for Lord knows how long, and all the time it just kept snowing, big burly flakes. After a while, when I thought I was lost, I saw *Hartland*, my father's castle. I could see the Yule lamps and Christmas candles shining through the trees. It was like when I was a wee bairn." He grinned at that, his face lighting up for a moment.

"What did you do?" said Gawain.

"I hurried on as best I could through the drifts. I remember somehow feeling happy, aye, easy if ye will. When I got to the castle I dinna notice anything unusual at first. Then, when I got to the drawbridge, I saw there were no guards. That's nay happened before, ever. There's always been someone on duty. My father used to say, 'faith in God, trust in the sword.'"

His big moon face creased into a frown and he looked up at the clear blue sky as if for inspiration. "Afterwards, I crossed to the main gates. They were wide open. When I went through, I could hear sounds coming from high up in the barbican. Someone up there was laughing. I canna be sure, but I thought I heard someone singing as well. I was about to go up the steps to the castle when I had this ... this strange feeling. Lord knows why, but I turned and looked about me at the courtyard and back at the drawbridge. There were nay signs anyone had passed there, none."

He paused, out of breath from climbing the steep hill leading to the bridge. "This time I cross first," he said raising an eyebrow at Percival who planted his heel and swept out a graceful hand.

"No argument from me, snowbound knight."

They crossed without mishap. On the other side, where the hill sloped down, they found the horses grazing peacefully.

They lost no time in preparing for the ride and once they were mounted and underway, Gawain urged Bors to resume his tale.

"I dinna ken how much sense this'll make," Bors said turning in his saddle.

"Do your best, my friend, we may discover some clues that will help us find a weakness in Eyenon," Gawain encouraged.

"Well, after I left the courtyard, I went into the castle but there were nay signs of anyone there either. When I walked down the passage leading to the Kite Hall, I heard someone playing a harp – my father loves the harp. By the time I got to the end, I caught the sound of voices. I though it was a gathering, Christmas vespers most like. I pushed open the doors."

289

At this point Bors reined up his horse and glanced from Gawain to Percival, his face grave, his voice dropping. "Now here's the din of it. There was nay a soul inside. I stood there looking around a room lit by a crackling fire, a banquet table piled high with food, even yon burning candles, and there was nay a person in sight. Yet everywhere around me voices were singing, aye, and talking."

"What happened?" prompted Gawain.

"Well, I walked around, trying to find where the sounds were coming from but I couldn't because they seemed to move when I moved. Even the music seemed to change. Then another strange thing happened. When I went to the fire . . ."

"You found it wasn't hot," cut in Gawain.

"Aye, exactly, but how ... "

"I'll tell you later, go on."

Bors patted his horse's sleek neck and urged him forward and Gawain and Percival closed on either side. "Well, I put my hands into the flames and like ye said, felt nothing. When I turned back, I found myself looking at the most fiercesome knight I'd ever laid eyes on. He stood at the end of the banquet table, arms crossed staring at me. By God's precious wounds, he was huge, all of seven feet. I can see him clearly, even now. Dressed in black armor he was. All black, aye, the breast plate, the chain mail skirt, the helmet, even the narrow grill of his visor." Bors gave an involuntary shudder and rubbed the back of his neck.

"Most of all, I can see that longsword of his. It was ebony black from hilt to tip. Ye both know me, I'm the furthest thing from a coward, but I warrant the sight of that knight was enough to strike fear in the heart of any man alive. He never moved, nary a whit, just stood there waiting. So I spoke. I dinna remember exactly what I said. 'Greetings, where do ye hail from, or something like that.'

"He leaned forward resting his weight on the hilt of that huge black sword of his, and in the deepest voice I've ever heard he said, 'I will let you live if you answer one question ...' "

"Who does the Grail serve?" burst out Gawain and Percival together.

"Aye," said Bors looking suddenly pleased with himself. "Just so, I told him what I knew, what we'd all seen when the Grail appeared at the Round Table, but he dinna seem to like my answer, because when I'd finished, he raised the black sword above his head.

'That's not what I wanted to hear,' he said. And without another word, he struck. I thought I was done for. Somehow, though God alone knows how, I managed to duck under his arm and draw my own sword.

'That's a mistake, Camelot fool,' he said in that deep voice. Then he came at me swinging. By all the Saints he was fast, much faster than he should've been for his size. I dodged to the side. But he seemed to be everywhere. The next swing crashed through a nearby chair sending splinters and padding spinning. Then he swung again. This time I heard someone cry out – like on a battlefield, and from nowhere, blood sprayed over the ground in front of me."

A rocky knoll forced the riders around the fringe of a wooded area and Bors paused in his tale as he threaded his way under low sycamore branches. When the others caught up and pulled alongside, he continued.

"All I could think was that it was one of the invisible guests. 'Tut, tut,' the black knight said, as if what he'd just done was nay more than treading on somebody's toes. I backed away to the other side of the table and he stopped and looked across at me.

"He rested on his sword again. 'Now who did I just kill? Ummmm, could it be that uncle of yours, Gascoign?'

he said. I remember that because Gascoign was always kind to me when I was a stripling."

"What did you do?" said Gawain steering him back to his tale.

"Nothing."

Bors rubbed the back of his neck again then looked up at his companions. "What could I do? I waited. Tried to think. Then the big knight started to move round the table. 'You want to know why he died so easily,' he said. 'He couldn't see me – none of them can, but I can see them, each little one of them – even your father.' Those were nigh on his exact words. Ye know, I dinna recall things well, Gawain, but those words ring true."

Gawain and Percival rode on in silence listening as the incredible story unfolded.

"When he said that, aye, the way he said it, I almost leaped over the table and choked him with my bare hands," Bors continued. "But I knew that's what he wanted. My only chance to kill him would be to upend him, get him flat on his back and drive a dirk through his visor. Ye know my wrestling skills – I've never been bested in a tournament yet. So that's what I planned. Doing it was nay easy, though; God in heaven, the sheer size of him." Bors shook his head. "I suppose I'd taken too much time thinking because he swung again. There was a scream and more blood splattered over the ground before me.

"'Another relative I fear,' he said in that savage, happy way of his. Then he raised the sword again.

"'Stop!' I yelled.

"'Then tell me of the Grail. Who does it serve?' was all he said.

"Why always the Grail? When I edged around to his side, I began making up some story about ancient magic. It seemed to work. At least he dinna notice me getting closer. Perhaps it was when I said the Grail belonged to Merlin or when I said it had the power to heal all wounds, I dinna ken, but he got very interested and lowered his sword. That was my chance. I ran at him shoulder down low. If I could hit him in the ribs, he'd go over backwards, then I could finish him off.

"I hit him fair enough, square below his breastplate, and he flew backwards. I almost bowled over top of him. There was nay weight there. At first, I thought the suit of armor was empty because it clattered around on yon floor like a milk churn. But I was wrong. Once it came to rest, the breastplate unhinged and a wee boy crawled out! He was just as ye said, Percival, a dark haired lad, about four or five. I couldn't believe my eyes. He got up, dusted himself off and glared at me.

"'You'll pay for that,' was all he said. His voice had changed; it was high pitched now, like an angry child."

Bors stopped again. He looked ahead at the high grass waving in the gusting wind, seemingly lost in thought.

"What happened next?" said Percival.

"Nothing."

"What do you mean, nothing?

"Exactly that, that's when Gawain woke me."

They rode on in silence, each one trying to make sense of what Bors had said and of their own dreams. Ahead, the fens spread wide for a mile or so, forcing them to skirt to the left and slow their travel. When they were safely around the last of the bulrushes, Gawain began his tale.

By the time he'd finished it was late afternoon and they rested their horses at a nearby stream. They sought wild berries, unpacked the little dried meat they had left and discussed Merlin's part in what was happening. But Gawain was careful to keep back what he knew of the wizard's greater plans. It wouldn't do to have his friends carry such information if Eyenon were to enter their dreams again.

When they finished eating, they resumed the ride and after crossing a steep valley, they caught the distant roar of the sea. By dusk, they were leading the weary horses along a wide shore in the face of clean salt spray.

"We'll camp there," said Gawain pointing up the beach to a sheltered cove. "Each of us will take turns keeping watch. Percival, you and I will sleep first. Wake us in a few hours, Bors. I'll try to contact Merlin then."

The stars were high in the night sky when Bors shook Gawain awake. "Dreams?"

"No ... no, I slept well," Gawain said rubbing his eyes and yawning.

"What about Percival?" said Bors.

"Leave him rest a while. I think we're safe here." Gawain rose and massaged his thighs. "I need to stretch my legs."

He snapped the top hasps of his tunic together and made his way down to the beach. An offshore breeze buffeted him with gusts of fine sea spray as he walked to where the sea had ribbed the sand.

Alone then on a wide shore mottled with knotted kelp and driftwood. Thoughts of a life so full of mystery and endless struggle. He trailed along the sea's edge looking at the distant deeps where threats lay soundless. *Arthur and the Grail? A Cup of Christ in the middle of a Dark Druid plot. Murder and magic. And why do they look to me? I have a sword but no soul. My sin is mortal. Out there, the seas go on forever, like my purgatory.*

Ahead, tall bluffs shone silver in a climbing moon. Over the water, he watched the waves rise and boom.

He looked down along the shoreline and halted in his tracks. Where a crop of rocks jutted into the sea, he caught sight of a hooded figure in a long cloak standing solitary at the water's edge.

"Merlin," he breathed, breaking into a run.

As he approached, the wizard spoke from deep within the folds of a dark hood. "No closer."

He was facing the waves and did not turn. "I was watching you the while. Tell me, my falcon, what do you see when you look out there?"

Gawain pondered the question. "I see a cold and boundless sea that binds our world."

"And what you feel when you look at this endless sea of yours."

Gawain gazed at the swelling waves. "When I look out there, I feel the hopelessness of Camelot," he said quietly. "I see a king who allows adultery, but reads the bible every day. I see knights losing their ideals, and I see faith eroded. And ... and I feel no matter what monsters we kill, we'll never be able to stop what is happening."

"Umm."

"Runes and wizardry and God and my own soul, I don't know who I am any more. I can't seem to find the strength within me. Sometimes ... I doubt myself." Gawain turned to the hooded figure but deep shadows hid the face.

Merlin spoke again. "Listen, my boy, our hopes don't lie with Arthur or with me. We've both tried fighting for our causes – me for the restoration of my faith, Arthur for his church. Each is a part of a whole – a truth built on tolerance, not dominance. We must learn to live with our differences. In you lies the way to this. Draw on the strength of both faiths, my falcon. This you must do if you are to kill Eyenon and recover the Grail." He paused as a wave hissed over the sand.

"How can I kill him if I can't find him?"

"You can."

"How?"

"We'll set a trap. Right now, as we speak, I'm using the power of the Terran Stone at Carmarthen to reach you, to send this, my image."

"But . . ."

"I believe something went wrong when Morganna warded Eyenon's mother. He didn't grow like the others-at least not the way he should have. His body remained small and so did his intellectual development. He's a little boy, petulant and unpredictable. He knows where to go, but not what to do. Perhaps Morganna miscast the dark Rune, I'm not sure."

Gawain bent down, picked up a smooth pebble and threw it high out over the waves. "When I first saw him, I almost felt sorry for him."

"Don't make that mistake again. Through the Stone, I had glimpses of Bors' dream. If Eyenon had that dream a day or two from now, the Black Knight would have been able to do more than just slay the ghosts in that room – he would have run his sword right through Bors. Imagine, Gawain, he'll soon be able to make the snow cold, the fire hot, just as they are in this world."

Gawain paused in the act of throwing another pebble. "But how could I use the Sithean power on him if he wasn't real?"

"He was in part because he wove all the dream fabric, but in Bors' dream, he couldn't lift a sword, only give the illusion of doing so. Soon, however, he'll be able to make the illusion so real the dreamer will actually experience the pain the weapon makes. Simply put, my boy, if he inflicted a mortal wound, you'd believe it was so and you'd die just as surely as if you really were run through."

A large wave boomed further down the beach. Neither spoke as its wake rumbled over a crop of strewn rocks.

"We're all safe for now," said Merlin breaking the silence. "But if we are to remain so, then we must kill him soon, tomorrow night – before he becomes too strong."

"What should I do?"

"Don't sleep tonight. Instead, travel south along the coast until you get to Meadvale. There's an inn there, a small place, *The Vulcan*. Take rooms but stay awake until midnight. I'll attempt to enter your dream in the hour that follows."

Gawain frowned. "How are ... "

"When I enter, you may not know it right away but you'll find me. Eyenon may fabricate the dream, but I'll still be able to move at my own choosing. The trick will be for me to get to him before he attempts to kill you, and believe me, if he has wind of what we're up to, he won't hesitate in doing just that."

Merlin paused. "Are you all right with this?"

"Yes."

His voice softened, reminding Gawain of his father after one of his theological lessons. "You've done well, my knight. You've never failed me; even when you were a young boy, you always found a way. Remember now, draw on the strength of both your faiths." He paused. "And no more doubts?"

"No more doubts."

Merlin fell quiet. The hood dropped forward a little as he studied the damp sand. "You must put the guilt behind you. I see it in you all the time and it pains me. Picture her at her finest and bind that moment with love. Keep it safe and she will be a guiding light always."

A heaving swell rose out of the dark sea, crest curling as it neared. "I miss the simple life, my boy, days before Uther," he said. "Sometimes I wonder if they'll ever come again. Perhaps we've seen the end of innocence."

The crest whitened and the wave charged the shore smashing over worn rocks. A moment passed and the swirling water gurgled back down the beach leaving behind a crop of shining pebbles blinking at the stars.

"Merlin?"

"Yes."

"Promise me you won't flux anymore."

"I promise."

"Truly?"

"Yes."

"If ... " Gawain didn't get to finish. The cloaked figure before him began to lighten. For a moment it wavered, then rose two or three feet off the shore and drifted out over the sea gathering speed as it gained distance. Gawain watched until it disappeared. Another wave slewed up the beach and he turned and headed back to the cove.

Mulling over Merlin's latest news and planning what to do next, he clambered up the last section of beach to where his friends were talking.

"Percival saw Eyenon," Bors called as he approached.

"What!"

Percival looked disheveled. He was sitting on a long piece of driftwood, head hanging. "I don't know ... it was so strange. I'm not sure if I was dreaming. I know I was here. Well ... I was arriving here," he finished feebly.

"What do you mean?" said Gawain, dropping down beside him.

Percival stared ahead blankly, confusion in his eyes. "God, Gawain, it was so real. We were riding here, just as we did earlier. The only reason I know for sure it *wasn't* real was that when I turned to speak to Bors, I saw Eyenon riding with us. Everything else was the same – exactly: the cliffs, the sea, even the smell of the salt spray."

He lowered his head again, rubbing the back of his neck.

"And?" prompted Bors.

"Well, I called out to you and pointed. You turned to where he was but you seemed to look right through him. I called to Gawain too but it was the same thing. It was as if he wasn't there. God above, I don't know what to think.

When Bors woke me, I had the feeling Eyenon had been with us all the whole time-somehow traveling in my mind, maybe. I don't know. It just doesn't make sense."

He looked earnestly at Gawain. "What do you make of it?"

"You may be right. One thing's for certain, he's getting stronger. I think he's reaching out with his power trying to find us," said Gawain putting his hands on his knees and rising.

"None of us is safe until we finish this," said Bors.

"True, but we do have help," said Gawain and told them of Merlin's visit.

After he'd finished, they ate clams and dug mussels out of the shells Bors had gathered. When they were done, they readied the horses and struck out south for Meadvale. They rode along the beach until weak sunlight leaked over the windswept fields. Where the river emptied into the sea, they cut east across the sparse, grassy dunes and the promise of an easier journey.

From what Merlin had told him, Gawain estimated the ride would take them the better part of the day. If they could keep up their present pace, he reasoned, they should arrive in plenty of time to put the wizard's plan into action.

The journey was uneventful until they reached the Afton forest ten miles north of Meadvale. When Bors broke through to a path crossing the main trail, he encountered a bedraggled group of villagers. They were riding in silence, horses packed with household items crammed into leather hold-alls.

As Gawain caught up, he found Bors talking to a rake of a man in a long brown coat with pockets bulging like potato sacks. He was trying to edge his horse around the big knight.

"And then what?" Bors said, blocking his way.

"They was dead. Like I said, half the town. I never had such a fright. No sir, never."

Gawain pulled alongside and spoke softly to the frightened man. "What happened, sir?"

"Like I was tellin' yer friend here, me lord. God's vengeance struck our town. Last night He come a visitin', He did. Found out them that's sinned and showed 'em the error of their ways, yes sir. Came in our dreams He did, and right awful it was. He showed 'em too." The man's eyes bulged in his weathered face.

"What did he show them?"

"Showed 'em their sins, that's what. Showed 'em righteous vengeance," he said suddenly spurring his horse and forcing Bors to give ground. "Showed 'em proper."

They let him go and Gawain turned to one of other villagers, a young woman wearing a cowl, but she lowered her head vanishing in its brown folds and urged her horse around him. The others followed, filing by silently, disappearing under the branches like wisps of fog.

"What do you make of it?" said Percival.

"Merlin's right. He's getting stronger. God's teeth, let's finish this thing – now, tonight," Gawain said wheeling his horse around and spurring south.

By late afternoon, they spotted two small holdings near a river bend. By early evening, they were riding through the village gates of Meadvale.

A deathly silence greeted them when they entered, reminding Gawain of Lothian. Small shops, a smithy and a few thatched houses lined the street, and even though the sky was darkening, there were no lanterns or candles in any of the windows.

The horses' hooves clattered on the cobblestone as they made their way toward a sign swinging from rusty chains: *The Vulcan.* The deserted inn was well timbered but bowed from age. The knights tethered their horses and entered through a creaking front door.

"Is there no one left?" said Bors eyeing the place and sweeping a flagon of wine from the countertop of a stained bar.

Gawain shrugged off his chain mail and threw it over a chair back. He stretched, watching Bors pour out the wine. "Do ye think it's Eyenon's doing?" he said, taking up the brimming goblet.

"If it is, why is it that ..."

"Here. Quick!"

The two knights slammed down their drinks at the same time and rushed into a small room behind the kitchen. They found Percival bending over a body lying on a crumpled bed.

"He probably died in his sleep," said Percival straightening up. "But look at this."

They stared at the stricken man. From the neck up his face was a mask of pain. The mouth gaped open and the eyes bulged like quail eggs. Pink lines webbed the aging skin. Gawain leaned over and ran his finger across the raised veins. It came away smeared with blood.

"God, it's as if he were about to explode," he said, carefully pulling a blanket over the man. "Let's check the other rooms."

They found two more bodies in the same condition in adjoining chambers. Upstairs they discovered the owner's quarters, a spacious room sporting a large stone fireplace. Thankfully, it was vacant.

"We'll stay here tonight. Tomorrow, God willing, we'll bury the poor souls," said Gawain.

They lit a fire and all the candles they could find to dispel the encroaching darkness. When the place seemed less dismal, they set about preparing supper.

Near midnight, with the fire dying, they pulled up a couch for Gawain. Percival took a chair and set it next to the fire. Bors threw open the wood bin and stacked up enough birch logs on the hearth to get them through the night. Tired and exhausted from the long ride, Gawain lay down.

"I don't envy you, my friend," said Percival tugging off his boots and setting them neatly beside the wall. "To fight a phantom with weapons made of air. Not exactly the stuff of knights."

"Aye, I'd sooner have at the damn Saxons," grunted Bors throwing two of the thickest logs on the fire.

Gawain closed his eyes. "One day, when Morganna's long gone and Camelot shines its beacon light, we'll tell our children of these adventures and they'll live on down the ages. They'll become more than the tales of knights, Percival, they'll become the sagas of kings."

"Ever the poet," said Bors beating away sawdust from his chest with his great callused hands. "Now get some rest before ye send *me* to sleep."

Percival and Bors huddled around the flames and waited in the deep, unnatural silence of the deserted town. And Gawain, finding the place where Athlan always waited, reached for her hand and somewhere, he slipped between the reality and the shadow – into Eyenon's world.

CHAPTER 18

This time it wasn't the hill he always walked down in his dreams, where foxgloves bloomed and yellow daffodils stitched the grassy slopes, but a series of small steps leading to an iron door. And it wasn't Athlan's hand he held, but an iron handle. And, for a moment, the only thing he knew, *really knew*, was that he was in danger. But, like someone drugged, he let the dream lead him on. And it did, whisking him into a world that took away all understanding of who or where he was.

Tabla Rasa.

The queasy sensation in his stomach hit as soon as he opened the door. Salt air stung his face. It was *wet* and it was *cold*. He looked around at rolling seas, at the gray sky swollen with rain clouds and at the ruin of a ship he was on. He took in all the details – the splintered deck, the tall masts and shredded sails flapping impotently in the wind and far ahead the prow plunging through heavy swells. He hung onto the railing of the quarterdeck fighting back a wave of nausea as the ship yawed.

Suddenly, huge drops of rain began crashing to the deck, pounding him with the force of hailstones. He gripped the ship's rail with both hands to steady himself. He was alone, save perhaps ... for something. *What?*

Shielding his eyes, he made his way along the rolling deck. He'd never seen a ship this big. It was the length of a jousting run. The three masts, spaced fifty feet apart, towered above him. A series of capstans, hawsers and crates lined the decks, making his journey to the bow perilous.

Near the center mast, he stopped to look over the scuppers at the waves foaming around the hull. The dread he'd had of the sea as a child knotted his stomach. He feared that one day he would vanish into its fathomless depths where the cold water would fill his aching lungs and the fish would feed on him with their needle sharp teeth.

He blinked away the vision and turned back to the rain-lashed deck. A new truth dawned on him: not only was the ship without sails, it was also rudderless. It was foundering in the ocean, tossing like a keg in the growing storm.

Further along, near the bulkheads, he saw the rusty handles of a hatch poking out from a stack of barrels lashed together near the final mast. Timing the ship's roll, he let go of the rail and lurched across the deck. Dangerously close to losing his footing, he made a desperate lunge for the handles. Fighting for balance as water sluiced around his feet, he managed to jerk open the hatch and haul himself inside.

Panting, he descended the first few rungs of a long iron ladder and pulled the cover closed with a reverberating clang. Relief-at least from the rain and roaring wind. He glanced down. The ladder disappeared into the holds of the ship. He grabbed a glowing lantern from a crossbeam and holding it out to the side, peered down again. The apron of light shone into vanishing darkness. He could not see the bottom.

He descended the rungs slowly, fighting the yawing motion of the ship with each step. When he glanced up a few minutes later, there was only a black canopy. He pressed his body against the rungs and rested. At that moment, a voice floated up from the hold.

"Bet you can't guess who I am?"

He looked down over his shoulder. Far below, he saw a circle of light. Grimacing, he renewed his descent.

"You must be tired, mighty knight, what with all that clambering about. But I want you to know, I think you're doing awfully well-wonderful in fact."

Gawain ignored the voice, concentrating instead on the rungs.

"Do you want to know something else? I've missed you. I'm still mad at you mind, for using that wizard's toy against me. All the same though, I've missed you, I really have. I've been waiting for you down here a long time."

The voice grew clearer and the roar of the wild seas and wind above began to fade.

"My, my, the fish in the deep parts of this sea have especially sharp teeth. Some people say they're even *needle* sharp."

Gawain suddenly clung onto the iron ladder. He closed his eyes, trying to shut out the image flashing in his mind – an image much more powerful than it should have been – an image so real he could smell the oily scales and see the flat, lifeless eyes of the fish swimming by.

"Phew! That was a close one. Nasty, wasn't it?"

Gawain peered down at the circle of light. A small boy dressed in sailor's clothes stood at its center staring up at him.

"Who are you? What do you want?"

"I told you," said the child, "I missed you. I want to chat, that's all."

Gawain descended the final rungs and stepped onto the deck. "I know you from somewhere."

"Only if I let you."

"What do you mean?"

"Watch."

The child moved back. His sailor's clothes were far too big and hung off him in great folds and wrinkles. He smiled, raised his hand and snapped his fingers.

"See."

Eyenon!

In an instant, the fog cleared from Gawain's mind and he knew. *Where's Merlin?*

"Thinking about that old wind bag are you, hee, hee," chuckled Eyenon. "Ummmm, I wonder where he is?" He lifted his sleeve and peeked mischievously inside.

"Why are you doing this? What do you want?"

"I want to know about the Grail," Eyenon shot back, dropping his arm, deathly serious now. "I can't see it and I want to. I'm denied knowledge."

"There's nothing I can tell you."

"Then I'm going to enjoy killing you. I'll be sure to be particularly creative." A man's threat in a child's voice. Memories of the last Eyenon encounter swarmed through his mind. *He's so much stronger.*

"I'm also going to enjoy killing your brainless friends as well." Eyenon closed his blue eyes for a moment, and when he opened them, violet tendrils radiated from their centers. "They won't come into my world so I've gone into theirs. Wish you could be there to see the sparks fly."

The tendrils faded and Eyenon grinned. "Your friends are in deep trouble. Boy, oh boy, if only you could see what's going on. Just think, one word from me, and Bors and Percival will be deader than evil old Uther. So tell me, Gawain, Camelot knight, the Grail, can it hurt me?"

Gawain looked at the ridiculous little sailor in front of him. In the information he'd conveyed, he had unwittingly allowed him to see his knowledge of Merlin. He both hated and feared the wizard. There was something in Merlin's past, something in his wide Druid knowledge the child could not control and it burned in him like bile.

The ship suddenly heaved forcing Gawain to grab for the rungs. "Merlin can tell you much more than I can."

"No! No! No! I don't want that. You tell me."

"Call Merlin. He'll come."

"No, he won't."

"Yes, he will."

"NO! HE WON'T, I won't let him."

"I can feel him."

"You can't. You can only feel what I let you feel."

"I can feel Merlin."

"You can't, shit! shit! piece of shit!" he exploded, stamping at each expletive.

"He'll come when he wants," said Gawain calmly.

What happened next truly surprised him. Eyenon smiled, his anger abating as easily as it had begun. Then the violate tendrils began branching through his eyes again. When they reached the edges, they licked like flames. Eyenon blinked.

"Pop goes the weasel. So sorry. Your friends are all dead," he said simply, shrugging his little shoulders. "That's for playing stupid games with me."

Eyenon crossed his arms and stood legs apart. "Now, before I start to ... "

The world before Gawain suddenly wavered, then swan back into view. *Merlin? Something's happened.*

Eyenon jumped. "What was that? What did you just do? I felt something. What did you do? TELL ME!"

Gawain gritted his teeth. He fought with the new understandings that were blooming – real knowledge of a world he knew and dream fabric of a world he had no control over. He sought for something, anything to give him a center, anything to find stability in this nightmare.

"You changed things. How did you do that?" Eyenon yelled, stamping his little feet again. Then his face reddened and pursing his lips, he jabbed an accusing finger at Gawain. "MERLIN! He's here, isn't he?"

Gawain had no idea what was happening. Slivers of reality speared his dream from all angles. He realized the ship wasn't rocking anymore. Then the ladder he was leaning on changed. It grew thinner, even as he looked at it, it became transparent and for a wild moment, he thought the ship was sinking because the hold itself began to ripple and lighten.

"Enough," said Eyenon, eyes blooming with violet tendrils. And, as quickly as they started, the changes stopped. "Your Merlin is nothing, you hear, nothing, just you wait and see." He spun on his heel and with his overly large sailor outfit flapping around him, he waddled off into the darkness of the bulkhead.

Without Eyenon holding it together, Gawain's world yawed and stretched. The wooden planking of the hull bowed outward and then pulled apart as if a giant had breathed into it. He caught a glimpse through the gaps of wood at the swelling waves and a fish made up of all the nightmare parts he'd ever imagined. He shut his eyes against the horror and when he opened them again, the planking was back in place.

The ladder offered a way out. He grabbed a rung started up. Then he paused. There was nowhere to run. What could he accomplish on the main deck? No, if this was to end, he had to finish it here and now. He peered down the dark passageway in direction the child had disappeared.

The ship creaked and groaned as Gawain blundered from side to side working his way into the hold. Boom! Boom! All around him, the heavy seas pounded the hull. Slowly a strange consciousness of a world other than the one he was in began to filter into his mind. It appeared at first as a random series of pinprick punctures, small specks of light piercing the darkness, like tiny pinholes in a thick blanket. *Like the soldiers in Argath's camp!* The snatches of images flared only momentarily, but they were enough to make him aware – aware that wherever Eyenon was, he was somehow losing control.

Gawain pressed on, stumbling deeper into the fabricated nightmare. When he was close to the entrance of the bulkhead, the ship suddenly lurched starboard throwing him crashing against the hull. Cursing under his breath, he rubbed the side of his head where it had struck the edge of a low beam. Further down the passage, near an empty storage area, a flash of lightening tore through shadows and the tiny holes in the planking began to rip and widen. Within seconds, great jagged tears shredded the air above him. Then the wooden hull yawned open and he saw a figure sleeping in a chair. He saw too, dying embers of a fire and a far door, a low ceiling, a framed painting on the wall and he heard sounds – someone calling in a muffled voice. He couldn't make out the words, but the voice was full of despair. Reality kept pouring in.

HE WAS ASLEEP!

Yet somehow, he was looking with conscious eyes, seeing as if he were awake. He ran to the hull and physically tried to push through the gaping hole leading from the ship into the room with the sleeping figure. His hand went first. It encountered no resistance and seemed to pass through into thin air, but when he turned sideways and tried to shoulder his body through, he felt a wave of drowsiness wash over him and the wooden planking knitted back into place locking him out.

The effort left him drained of energy. He shook his head. Try as he might, he couldn't make sense of anything: the dreams, the reality, Eyenon, Merlin, nothing.

He leaned against the hull. *Dear God help me.* The vessel suddenly rose then slewed to the left, pitching him into a wooden brace. He stumbled to the planking, rolled and hit a cask, but this time there was no pain, no feeling of impact. Then the pounding started again.

He lay still on the rough wood and closed his eyes. He waited, willing the ship to steady. Long moments passed and the motions gradually abated. He cautiously opened an eye. What he saw was then not a bulkhead but a domed ceiling. He turned his head to the left. He was lying in some vast cavern. He turned to the right. His heart skipped a beat. Not twenty paces away, Merlin stood leaning over his Rune staff, white hair in wild tangles around his shoulders. He was dressed in his High Druid robe, coal black, dusted with stars and Runic lettering. Across from him stood the boy child, chubby hands on his hips, little chin thrust out, blue eyes glaring. He was saying or shouting something Gawain couldn't make out. The two stood toe to toe in the vast dark room, illuminated by their own life energy, burning like torches.

Gawain rose. He went to take a step forward but a pressure like an invisible hand held him back. Gritting his teeth, he tried again. This time he made a little headway but it was like wading through a vat of treacle. A few deep breaths and five more struggling steps and he found himself at the edge of the arena of light.

Merlin's face was drawn; he seemed to be at the limit of his mystical strength. Opposite him, Eyenon glowered, cheeks flushed, mouthing curses. Even though the distance between Gawain and the others was now a scant few paces, he still couldn't make out the boy's muffled words.

With the next step, the invisible hand restraining him suddenly released its grip and Gawain stumbled into the circle of light and fell on his knees. He went to speak, but before he could say a word, a sudden bolt of pain tore through the side of his neck. His hand flew to the wound. At first, he thought an arrow had struck him, but when he checked his palm, there was no sign of blood. He looked up at Merlin only to see him clutching his own neck, eyes glazing over.

"You'll all die. Every one of you gone, dead. DEAD! DEAD! Do you hear," the child screamed. Gawain recoiled

310

as the words blasted through the air. He shook his head. He was beyond trying to figure out the changes in this world or trying to guess what would happen next.

Merlin sagged then collapsed. Eyenon frowned. "Stop your stupid games, old wizard. Nothing's wrong with you." He glared down pursing his lips, then for the first time, he caught a glimpse of Gawain. He jumped back, genuinely surprised.

"What are you doing here? I didn't make it so."

Gawain rose weakly.

Eyenon jabbed a stubby finger at Merlin. "It's his doing. He did it. He brought you here, didn't he? I don't like that. I really think he's bad. He's a bad, bad man."

"What did you do? Let me help him," Gawain said rubbing his neck.

"Nothing. I'm going to kill him, he's bad, very bad." Eyenon bent over the stricken figure and placed his hand above Merlin's head. "It's really very simple. All I have to do is think him dead. I can stop his heart beating or stop him breathing if I want. I can even make his nose bleed until his stupid old body's empty."

He paused, tapping his chin in a ludicrous pantomime of thinking. "I know, how about if I shut off his brain and we watch him wriggle around like a creepy crawly? Then he can just stop living. That'd be fun, wouldn't it?"

The violet tendrils began snaking through his eyes.

"You do that and you'll never learn about the Grail." Gawain said quickly. "It's far more powerful than even you could imagine."

The boy recoiled and the tendrils faded. "What do you know? Tell me, TELL ME!"

"Merlin has the knowledge. Let me help him and I'll find out all I can." The request was simple, as direct as Gawain could make it.

311

"The old windbag knows?" Eyenon queried, poking Merlin with the toe of his little sailor boot.

"Yes, more than anyone, but I don't know how much time he has left. If you truly want to know about the power of the Grail, then I need to help him. Look what you've done."

"I've done nothing, idiot knight. He did it. It's his fault. He came here to try something on and see what happened."

Merlin lay curled up now, hand at his neck, fingers splayed wide, clutching at an invisible wound.

Eyenon peered down a moment longer then looked directly at Gawain, eyes once again the clear thin blue of winter sky. "You know how easy it is for me to kill him," he said evenly.

"Yes, and I know I can't stop you. But if you do this, all knowledge of the Grail will die with him."

Eyenon jammed his hands on his hips. "Then find me my answers."

He pointed at Merlin and the wizard jerked like a puppet on a string.

"That's only a warning. Now, help him if you want, but get my answers."

The hairs on the back of Gawain's neck crawled at the sight of Merlin's humiliation. He glared at Eyenon barely able to restrain himself. Finally, tearing his eyes away, he knelt at the wizard's side. He cradled his head and smoothed back the wild hair.

The boy child crossed his arms, muttering.

Gawain stripped off his surcoat and eased it under Merlin's head, then he held his wrist and slipped the Dragon Ring over his index finger. As it passed the second knuckle, Gawain felt something. At first, he couldn't place it, then he became aware of a familiar sensation, hunger – but not for food, for kinship. Within seconds, he was aching with desire to see Bors and Percival.

He leaned closer to Merlin and spoke softly. "What am I feeling? Tell me what I must do?"

Behind him a voice snapped, "I'm getting tired. Really getting tired. What's happening?"

"I need more time," said Gawain.

"I should kill you both here and now and be done with it." The cherub face pushed between them. "Ask him. Go on, ask him." Eyenon straightened, thick hair flipping back as he prodded Gawain in the shoulder.

"It won't do any good. I need more time." Gawain kept his voice even, staring directly into the cold blue eyes.

The child grumbled to himself and stepped back.

Gawain felt for Merlin's mind again. He leaned forward and pressed his head gently against the wizard's temple, hoping the intimacy would somehow provide an easier path for his thoughts.

He stayed there for a moment, like a worshipper waiting divine instruction. Then, without warning, a murky image swam out of the depths of his mind. He recognized it even before it fully formed: Percival. Gawain looked up. Before him, the image of his friend materialized at the edge of the lighted arena.

"What's happening, idiot knight?" Eyenon queried.

Gawain ignored him. He closed his eyes again and resting his head against Merlin's temple, he breathed a question to the ghost. *"Can you see us, Percival?"*

"I'm lost. I've never seen such darkness before. It's like death. You don't know what it's like. I ... "

"I can't make sense of what's happening to us either, but I do know that if we don't help Merlin now, this very minute, Eyenon will kill us all."

"What should I do?"

Gawain was about to reply when a second image swam into his mind – Bors, strangely quiet, strangely pale. It, too, materialized in the shadows outside the light of the arena.

313

Gawain felt the body stir beneath him. At first, it was a mere twitch then he felt the moisture of Merlin's breath. He pulled away and the wizard's eyes slowly opened.

"Merlin," he whispered.

The look in those eyes silenced him.

"What's going on?" Eyenon said screwing up his little face.

"Nothing. Nothing yet. I think he may survive if we give him space to breathe," said Gawain standing up and forcing the child back.

"I'm getting funny feelings about this, tingly feelings, I don't like it. He's trying something on." His icy gaze never wavered from Gawain's face. "You, I don't worry about. Him, he's starting to really bother me."

"You have nothing to fear," said Gawain. "He's barely alive."

"I don't care. Find out about the Grail or I swear I'll finish him right this minute." He raised his hand.

"All right, all right."

Gawain bent to Merlin and placed his hand on his brow. *If ever I needed your help, it's now, Merlin. What happened?*

Silence.

"What? What?"

Gawain looked up at Eyenon. He was about to answer when he caught the smoky shadows of Percival and Bors moving to the side. Then a new realization hit him. Eyenon was unaware of them. In this world he ruled, he was totally unaware of their presence. Hope flooded Gawain as the ghosts closed in, not walking, but gliding. Hard pressed to weave any kind of a story under these circumstances, Gawain found himself urging them on; here lay either death for Eyenon or for them.

"Why does Arthur want it?"

The gliding figures entered the arena of light.

"It's magic, isn't it? That's why."

Gawain concentrated. "It's a talisman, to ward the city."

The ghost of Percival circled to the left, Bors to the right.

"Is it Druid? I know it is."

"No, it's more powerful. Arthur will be stronger than any bard or wizard when he has it in his possession."

The child bunched his little fists and pounded his thighs. "He won't have it, I won't let him."

The shadowy figure of Bors halted. *He still can't see them.* Gawain cut the thought words off even as they formed, fearing Eyenon might read them.

"Make the windbag tell you who has it." The voice, growing deathly cold, had lost all of its hysteria. Gawain went to reply, but before he could, he felt a coldness floating up from beneath him. An ethereal Merlin rose slowly, stepping out of his body as if he were stepping out of a suit of armor. The spirit form of the wizard passed through Gawain and then floated behind Eyenon, assuming a sentinel position with the other two.

Three ghosts evenly spaced, now surrounded Eyenon.

"Well, what else, moron knight?"

As Gawain began to answer, a bright red spark flared at the edge of the arena cutting off his words. It came from the shadow of Merlin's outstretched hands. A moment later, the spark blazed in a mantle of crackling light.

"Who has it?"

The spark burned a deeper red.

"WHO HAS IT?"

The Bloodline suddenly burst from the magician's hands in a flaming streak. It thrummed, arcing from one shadow knight to the next, imprisoning Eyenon in the center. The child started. A look of surprise swept across his face and for the first time, Gawain saw fear in those wide blue eyes.

The Bloodline deepened to an arterial crimson.

"What's going on? I ... I don't know what's happening," Eyenon said his voice edgy with panic.

"Nothing."

"Don't lie to me."

The three shadow knights stepped back leaving the blood circle behind. It purpled and solidified. Then it thinned out to a keen knife-edge.

"What is it?" cried Eyenon, a dribble of spit gleaming on his chin as he followed Gawain's eyes. He thrust his hands in front of him, sweeping the air blindly. "What are you looking at? There's something there, isn't there? I can't see it. I CAN'T SEE IT!"

The blood ring began to spin, lazily at first, then it gathered speed and as it did, it began shrinking.

Gawain, still kneeling at Merlin's side, watched the glowing circle pass over his head. There was no sound as it went by, nothing, save a flash made up of all the shades of red Gawain had ever imagined.

Slowly, inexorably, the circle began to close around the child.

"What's that?" Eyenon jumped as his sweeping hand contacted the spinning Bloodline. He pulled it back to his chest, nursing it.

Gawain saw blood – real blood.

"What is it? What's there? Tell me, please." Eyenon held his hands out, palms up. "It hurts."

The shrinking circle touched his arm.

"Gaaaaaawain, help me, pleeeeease." His eyes widened with terror and his voice shook. Gawain instinctively looked for a way to help. He started forward but what happened next held him fast. The red disc scythed through Eyenon's arm. Bone and dangling strips of skin spun from its edges and splattered outwards in ragged chunks.

The terrified child uttered a howl as his arm fell away like a limb sawn from a tree. The next instant the shrinking disc cleaved into his body.

Gawain stood staring, helpless to do anything.

Finally, the screaming stopped. Eyenon's mouth butterflied open as the disc sheered through him. His torso toppled to the ground and for a ghastly few seconds his legs remained standing before they too tumbled forward.

The disc continued to contract, spinning faster until it collapsed into a fiery ball. Then it winked out. In the after light of its brilliance, Gawain saw beyond the dark. He found himself looking into the room where Percival lay asleep next to a crackling fire. At the foot of a couch next to him lay another figure, Bors. Behind him, a splintered door hung off its hinges. Then Gawain saw himself for one dizzying second before he was himself.

CHAPTER 19

Gawain struggled awake. The first thing he saw when his eyes focused was Bors lying in a thickening pool of blood.

He struggled off the couch, shook Percival awake, then dropped to Bors' side. Part of a crescent shaped blade was jutting from a gaping wound in his friend's neck. Gawain gently eased the big knight onto his back, took a pillow from the couch and placed it under his head.

He had scarcely finished when he felt Percival next to him. "What happened?" he asked groggily.

"I don't know. We have to get this out and close the wound."

"What is it, a Saracen blade?"

"Could be. From what I've just seen, nothing would surprise me. I'll look downstairs, perhaps there's something we can use in the kitchen. Wait here with him," said Gawain rising to his feet.

He crossed to the splintered door and was about to pull it open when a gaunt figure wearing peasant's rags blundered through rubbing his eyes. Behind him, Gawain could see others milling around on the balcony, bumping into one another, looking blankly at the weapons they carried. *Argath's camp!* thought Gawain.

Percival drew his sword but Gawain stayed his arm.

"What happened here?" Gawain asked taking of one of the villagers by the shoulders and turning his pale face toward him.

The man shook his head trying to focus. "My, lord. I don't know. The last thing I remember was going to bed."

Gawain eyed the others who seemed equally baffled. "Later then, right now I need to know if there's anyone here with medical skills."

A potbellied villager with a monk's tonsure crowning a wine red face came forward and introduced himself as Anson. "I have training as an herbalist, my lord," he said and without waiting for a reply, shuffled to Bors' side.

While Gawain and Percival watched him work, they tried to discover what had happened. The last thing any of the villagers remembered, it seemed, was falling asleep. None of them had the words to describe the nightmares that followed, or the strange feelings of disembodiment they'd experienced. They argued, talked and tried to make sense of it all. And when Gawain told them a little about the Dark Druids, they backed away, crossing themselves hastily.

Finally, the herbalist finished stitching Bors' wound and sprinkled it with a powder from a pouch slung on his belt. He packed the suppurating area with a poultice of leaves and ordered one of the men to find a clean sheet and tear it into strips. While he busied himself binding the wound, the others, who had no tasks to share, slowly wandered off, arguing, waving arms, still trying to come to terms with what had happened.

The knights spent the next few days in the village repairing the havoc caused by Eyenon. Anson worked tirelessly: tending to the stitches, changing the dressing and feeding Bors mixtures of herbs and seasoned meats.

At the end of the first week, his diligence paid off. Early one morning, Bors opened his eyes and croaked for water. The two knights hurried to his bedside. Gawain nodded his thanks to Anson and holding the big knight's arm, eased him to a sitting position. "How do you feel?"

Bors' eyes were bleary but the redness had gone. "Like the fool that I am," he groaned running his fingers over the wound.

"Here." Gawain passed him a mug of water from the bedside table.

"Are we safe?"

"Yes. Eyenon's dead."

Bors took a long drink and sighed.

"Who did this?" said Gawain.

"Someone, God knows who. A villager, I ken. I was putting logs on yon fire. Both ye and Percival had been asleep for a couple of hours when I heard a noise downstairs. I went to the door and looked out. At first, I dinna see a thing, it was so dark down there. Then I saw someone moving." He reached for the mug again and Percival passed it to him closing his fist around the handle. Bors took a long slow drink then sank back into the pillow. He sighed and continued. "The next thing I knew, the bottom of stairs was full of people but they were nay normal."

"What do you mean?" said Gawain.

"They were sleepwalking."

Gawain glanced at Percival.

"When I called down, there was nay an answer. That's when I saw the weapons, the scythes and clubs, and their eyes. God above, they were sprung wide and staring. I went back into the room and started to bolt the door, but just as I did, a wave of weakness came over me. It came from nowhere; near brought me to my knees."

"The Bloodline," muttered Gawain.

Bors looked at him, puzzled.

"Somehow it broke," said Gawain. "I think when Merlin entered Eyenon's dream. I felt the same thing. The moment we separated, we all experienced it."

"Yes, I did too. In my dream I fell against a shed or barn or something, I can't remember," said Percival scratching his head. "But I know I couldn't get up."

Bors nodded. "Aye, after the Bloodline broke as ye say, I lost all my strength. Try as I might I could nay budge the damn bolt. The sleepwalkers were on the landing by the time I finally got the thing to slide home. Somehow, Lord knows how, I managed to shut the door, but just as I did, one of the sleepwalkers jammed his scythe between the edge and the damn frame. I put my shoulder to the door and heaved. It must have snapped the blade clean because I heard an almighty twang. The end bounced off something, maybe the ceiling then it must have struck me in the neck. That's all I remember. I dinna recall another thing."

He looked up at his friends' intent faces and took another slow drink. "Arthur's Knight, felled by a peasant's scythe," he said dejectedly.

Gawain patted his shoulder smiling. "I think you still have a few dragon-slaying days ahead of you yet, my friend."

The two knights spent the next few weeks helping Bors build up his strength, ready for the long journey back to Camelot. In the evenings, often when the others were asleep, Gawain sought the stars and Orion, drawing on its power to contact Merlin, but it was always the same – the aching emptiness of space. Deep in his heart, the question he needed to ask was waiting: who was the third son, and where in this wide world of growing horror was he?

When Bors had fully recovered, they bid farewell to Anson and the villagers and set out north, following the winding coastline back to Camelot. They traveled slowly, staying sometimes three or four nights in the towns and hamlets they came across, allowing Bors time to rest. The days turned colder and under clear November skies, they finally caught their first glimpse of the towers and spires of Camelot.

By late afternoon, they were riding across the last of the open fields. Braving a cold and blustery wind, they crossed the bridge marking the city's boundary. The first thing that struck them was the scarcity of people. Shuttered windows and deserted shops loomed as they rode through the quiet Druid quarters.

Starting up the King's Road to Caerleon, Percival caught sight of a figure heading toward the city gates. With his face hidden beneath the brim of a tattered brown hat and a bone thin dog in tow, the solitary figure halted reluctantly when the knights rode up to him.

Gawain pushed up his visor and leaned over his pommel. "What's happening here? Where is everyone?"

Dark pools of eyes peered from the shadows of the hat. "Gone. Like as not they've had about all they can take."

"What do you mean?" pressed Gawain.

A thin hand pointed towards Arthur's castle. "Go see fer yerself, knight. See what yer great king's brought about."

The next question was on Gawain's lips when the man gave a tug on the lease pulling the dog to him. "Him that's God fearing," he muttered turning his back on them and shuffling off towards the river.

When they crossed the drawbridge leading to Caerleon, the hollow clumping of the horse's hooves echoed in the emptiness. The great gate to the castle hung open and they passed beneath the massive portico unchallenged. The gardens before them lay unattended and overgrown with knotgrass; even the fountains had stopped running, leaving their wide white basins stained and mossy. They continued in silence, following a path cracked and plugged with dying weeds to the entrance of the castle.

At the top of the steps, they looked at each other apprehensively. Each had the same question on his lips: How could all this have happened in such a short time? But it wasn't until they entered the main hall that the extent of the neglect became truly evident. Only a few candles and oil lamps burned. In the shadows of the empty hallway, Gawain could see the grey shimmer of cobwebs in the rafters.

They walked down the passage, dust swirling around their feet. When they entered the Shield Hall, they were shocked to see two of the high, stained glass windows depicting the Ascension smashed and glittering on the ground.

They wandered into the next hall, the one Arthur used for assizes, only to discover it bereft of furniture. The room beyond led to the Round Table. They crossed through it wordlessly and opened the door to the sacred chamber.

The Round Table stood intact, the seats all in order. Then, for the first time since they entered the castle, they saw signs of life – four tallow candles, each set evenly on the table. In the center stood a single white candle, the flame burning in a perfect heart shape.

"Gawain, Bors, Percival, it's so good to see you."

They hadn't heard Guinevere enter and they started at the sound of her voice. She crossed from the chapel entrance, her graceful movements making her appear to float. She wore a simple white gown that flowed from her neck and trailed behind her as she walked across the cold stone floor.

"Your majesty," said Gawain, bowing.

"My knights, I've missed you all. You'll never know how much. Please, no formality." Her voice sounded weary, heavier than Gawain had ever heard before. She opened her arms wide.

Gawain stepped forward and embraced her. The other knights looked on in astonishment.

"Bors," said Guinevere, holding her arms to him.

There was no avoiding it, he stepped forward sheepishly accepting the extraordinary greeting. Percival followed and afterward stepped aside head lowered.

"We have a lot to talk about: what's happened here, and to you three. Please, sit. Bors here," she patted the seat nearest the first candle. "Gawain, Percival." She gestured to her left.

They took their places and waited. She gathered herself, so much a queen in the golden glow of the candles.

"Where to start." She gave them a wan smile. "A few weeks ago Merlin sent me a message, though much of it you'll need to clear up for me. He told me you had managed to defeat the Dreamwalker. Gawain, perhaps you can help here, Merlin's note made little sense at that point."

Gawain nodded, noticing how pale and drawn her face had become since they'd left. He recounted the events starting from the time they'd entered the village to the time he'd fallen asleep. He told her about the floundering ship, the sea crashing against the hull and the horrors of the hold where Eyenon lurked. When it came to the final battle and the part the Bloodline played, she leaned forward, anxious not to miss a word and for the first time that day Gawain smiled, heartened to see the color back in her cheeks.

The candles had burned down by the time he finished. Steepling her hands, Guinevere leaned forward and began her story.

"In the short months since you've been gone, the king has found little comfort in this great castle of ours. Indeed, he's found little comfort in anything ... save praying in the chapel."

Gawain glanced at the others, surprised at the bitterness in her tone.

"I've tried to get him to see the effects of his absence. I even showed him Rankin's stained glass window, the one of the Ascension. The guild smashed it after we were unable to pay them. But it made no difference. Nothing has, he just spends more time praying." She stopped, staring at the small candle, mouth pursed, fingers tracing the Table's edge. They waited in silence, gloomy shadows leering on the wall behind her.

Gathering herself, she continued. "With the others gone, I've had little influence. The times I've spoken to him, he's only become more difficult, more withdrawn. All he thinks about is bringing the Grail back to Camelot and restoring the city to its former glory. Bringing the soul back to the body of Christ, he says."

She gave them a quick smile. "I told him the city needs the hand of a strong king, not the magic of a Holy relic." She paused then, her eyes growing misty. "I know it's my fault, all this. It started with me, but I've offered to leave, to go to a nunnery, to go into exile if need be, but he won't have it. Sometimes I think he keeps me here just to punish me." She stopped to brush away a stray tear with the palm of her hand. *Her courage only serves to make her beauty more remarkable*, thought Gawain.

"I've sinned before my husband and lord, before God and all I hold dear but I cannot take the blame for what's happening now – not for this. He's neglected his duty as a king. He's forsaken his people. That has been his choice." She reddened and lowered her head.

"My lady," said Gawain. "You've suffered and endured, but you're loved and held dear by everyone. What's past is past." He placed his hand on her shoulder, ignoring the glare he got from Bors.

"Thank you, my knight with the soulful eyes. You're right, now is not the time to grieve or lay blame." She patted his hand and braved a smile.

"You said you have news of Merlin," said Gawain changing the subject.

Guinevere reached into her sleeve and pulled out a tightly rolled scrap of paper. "Yes, this. It came yesterday by way of his raven."

Gawain took the parchment and unrolled it between his thumb and forefinger. He held it near the candle flame and read the tiny writing. Much of it contained advice on defending Camelot, but the part that caught his attention was the tiny scrawl at the end.

> *... I'm traveling again, my Lady. This time north to a Stone that will allow me to commune with Neume's spirit. It's a risk I must take. Place your faith in Gawain. If I'm successful, I'll return before the first snows come to our beloved lands.*
>
> *Your dutiful servant,*
> *Merlin*

When Gawain finished reading, he carefully rolled up the message and handed back it to Guinevere. "The first snows are almost upon us," he said glancing at the thick walls as if he could see through them.

One of the candles winked out and the chamber dimmed.

"Come," said the Guinevere. She stood and led them to where an apron of light spilled under the chapel door. "It's time to see your king."

The knights followed, faces set.

Hundreds of votive candles bathed the small chapel in burning gold. They lined the aisle and angled out from wrought iron holders high on the transepts but most blazed in hallowed glory above the nave where Arthur kneeled in devotion before a simple wooden cross.

"There," said Guinevere, nodding toward him. "He prays for God's guidance like this every day, every hour."

Even though her tone was hushed, the resentment behind it was clear.

"We'll remain here until he's finished," whispered Gawain.

"That could be a very long time. Stay here." Guinevere walked up the aisle, her long dress sweeping out in a hissing arc behind her. When she reached Arthur, she knelt beside him and assumed a posture of prayer. A long moment passed then she spoke to the side of her clasped hands but he seemed to take no notice. She resumed praying then rose slowly and returned to the knights.

"Now we wait," she said.

Arthur's head remained bent. They could hear his Latin phrases spiraling up into the dome above the nave:

"Et in terra pax hominibus bonae voluntatis.

Laudamus te.

Benedicimus te.

Adoramus te.

Glorificamus te."

They stood patiently in the shadows of the burning candles while he continued his devotions. Gawain sensed Bors' restlessness and was about to turn and warn him to keep his place when Arthur rose.

He's changed, Gawain thought immediately. It seemed as if his youth had been drained from his once strong body, leaving behind the husk of an older man. He walked stiffly down the aisle. Gawain could see well before he arrived, how thin his sandy hair had grown and how sallow his features had become. But only when he neared, did the extent of the malaise become evident. Tiny cracks lined his face and the eyes that once shone with passion were now dulled with defeat. *All this in a few short months! God's truth, what happened?*

The three knights bowed as he approached.

"Why are you still here? I've commanded all my knights to go seek the Grail. How can I expect our Savior to listen to my prayers if I cannot do His simple bidding?" The shaky voice filled Gawain's heart with sorrow.

"My Lord," said Gawain slowly straightening, "we've returned from Meadvale with good tidings: Eyenon is dead."

"I care naught for the pagan plot. There will always be evil in man's heart until he's seen the glory of the light and heard for himself the true word." Even the anger in his voice sounded feeble.

Gawain swallowed dryly. He knew Arthur's love of the Christian life was strong, but this! For the first time the welfare of knights and subjects came second.

Arthur suddenly grasped Gawain by the arm, breaking off his thoughts. "I've seen the work of our Lord and I've beheld the Grail in all its Glory. It must be found and brought back here, to Camelot. It's God's will that this place be His city here on earth."

Clasping his hands together, the king thrust his head heavenward. Gawain glanced from Percival to Bors. He saw the same thing on each face – astonishment.

"May He bestow in us the glory of His faith. May He forgive our sins and shed everlasting mercy upon our souls. May He ... "

At a loss, Gawain closed his eyes and slowly put his hands. In the background, he could clearly hear Guinevere's impatient sigh.

The prayer droned on. Minutes passed then Arthur suddenly broke off. "You must join the others immediately," he exclaimed, eyes blazing. "Now, this instant."

"Sire, if all of your knights are sent to seek the Grail, who will enforce your law here at Camelot?" ventured Percival.

"Only God can raise this city to its glory again. The Grail must be found and brought back. The Lord has shown the way. Now, I command you, go. Do not return to me without the Cup."

Gawain opened his mouth to speak but stopped when he felt Guinevere's gentle tug on his sleeve.

"GO NOW!" Arthur's voice, edged with hysteria, echoed thinly around the walls of the chapel. "Fetch me the Cup. Don't fail me in this," he added in a whisper. Then in an old man's gait, he turned and shuffled back between the pews to the nave.

"Come," said Guinevere and they retreated from the chapel and exited through the darkened room of the Round Table.

The knights followed her down the dimly lit hallway and up the wide stairs, no one saying a word. At the door to her chambers, she stopped, fumbling with her key. Twice, three times she tried to fit it in the lock. Gawain stepped forward and she turned, blue eyes swimming with tears, lips trembling. He took the key gently from her hand and opened the door.

A faded red carpet covered the flagstones. Against the far wall, a chest yawned open, clothes bundled on top. To the right, chairs lay scattered around a small table. Nearby, an easel propped up an unfinished painting. The only source of light filtered in through a stained glass window overlooking the northern part of Camelot.

Guinevere crossed to a small fire smoldering in the hearth and taking an armful of logs from an iron holder, threw them on the embers. Ashes exploded in a speckled grey cloud and she stepped back dusting off her dress. She turned to the others who stood mutely watching.

"As you can see, we're short of help. I've sold all my silver, even my favorite arras to pay for fuel and food. Seems there's no one who will work here anymore. There's no money, Arthur's emptied the royal coffers to fund the knights on the Grail quest. We've nothing left."

She turned back to the glow, the struggling flames highlighting her thick red hair and the glistening lines the tears had traced down her cheeks. "I'm so ashamed."

Bors stepped forward. "Tell us how we can help ye, my lady."

She braved a smile. "Dear Bors, always my champion, always there for me. If only Arthur had an ounce of your strength and courage." She turned to the others, frustration creeping back into her voice. "There's little any of us can do now. Every time the subject of money or Camelot comes up, he refuses to talk. Reason is closed to us."

"What of Merlin, my Lady?" said Percival.

"You know as much as I do. Will he return before the first snowfall? Who can say? We all seem to be at odds: Merlin hunting Uther's sons, trying to discover Morganna's plans, Arthur seeking the Grail, hoping to regain glory in the name of Christ." She drew in a long shuddering breath, "And me, trying to hold things together, trying to keep what little we have."

She turned back to the hearth, her eyes brimming with tears. A hush fell over the room and each knight stared uneasily at the sputtering logs.

After a long moment, Gawain broke the silence. "We'll work to restore order while we wait for Merlin, my lady."

"The king has commanded us leave," cut in Percival. "We cannot disobey his direct order. It's against everything we've fought for, everything we believe in. Remember our oaths?"

"But he's sick; you've seen him."

"Gawain's right," said Bors. "We canna let things slide any further. If we leave, who will restore the city? Who will protect Guinevere? If there's none here to enforce the law, there may be nay any Camelot to bring the Grail back to."

They fell silent again glumly watching the flames struggle with the damp logs.

Guinevere's next words cut through the stillness, "If Merlin doesn't return by the first snowfall, I intend on leaving Camelot – forever. I will not stand by and see all I love destroyed."

No one said anything.

"I know what I've done," she continued. "Arthur's never found it in his heart to forgive me, never, even though he's found it easy to forgive those who've broken our walls and desecrated our home, I cannot restore my life as he aims to restore his; I have no Grail to save me."

She leaned her head against the hearth. "I'm afraid we're all lost unless Merlin returns."

"And Lancelot," said Gawain gently, "What's become of him?"

"Gone," she said after a while, her voice empty now. "Gone with Sagremor. He won't return. He said he would sail for France when the Grail is found."

"And you, my lady?" said Gawain.

She looked up, the sadness in her face nearly breaking his heart. "I've always been partial to the cloistered life. Perhaps there I will find the peace I've sought for so long."

The cheerless evening drew on and they sat together huddled around the fire watching long shadows ghost over the hearthstones. Outside, the streets so quiet before, now began to fill with sounds of drunken voices. Somewhere distant they heard a scream followed by laughter, and then unearthly silence. Gradually the revelry grew until Bors could stand it no longer and went to the window. He saw the city as he'd never seen it before, torches bobbing amidst roving bands, and far away a house burning in the cold night.

They talked through the long hours trying to unravel Morganna's plot and the meaning of the Grail, but it always came to the same thing – Merlin's return.

So they waited; waited for the first snow to fall and the wizard to appear. As each day passed, they talked to the merchants and the guildsmen and went to the houses of the poor and at night they took to the streets in their shining armor and quelled the rioters.

The days rolled by and the wintry clouds thickened. Frost came, whitening the cold streets and filigreeing windows, but the snow held off. And at the end of each day they scoured the road leading north, but there was never a sign of Merlin.

Through diligence and diplomacy, Bors, Percival and Gawain finally managed to placate the merchants and traders and convince the innkeepers to close their doors earlier to curtail the drinking. They found the hiding place of a band of errant knights in a holding north of Camelot and let Bors deal with their leader. And there was peace.

On the last day of November, thin clouds spread across a clear blue sky and a hazy ring wreathed the sun. The few servants who had returned to the castle shuttered the windows and stocked up fuel for the fire. Candles were lit and doors battened against the gathering wind. In the Great Hall, Gawain and Guinevere set out supper while Bors and Percival went down to the cellars to fetch wine and oil for the lamps.

Windows rattled and shook as the storm winds gathered. The chill in the vast room ran so deep even the roaring fire couldn't provide relief.

"It's only a matter of hours before the first snow, my lady," said Gawain carrying plates of steaming venison to the table. "If he doesn't come tonight, the roads will soon become impassable."

"And ... "

"We must carry out the king's wishes."

"Then I'll to Brecon, to the cloisters," she said simply.

The windows rattled as Guinevere spoke and the wind howled about the castle's ramparts sending drafts across the stone floor strong enough to rustle the dress around her ankles. A serving girl entered and set a tall wine jug on the table.

"No matter what you and Bors and Percival do, without a king this city is doomed," said Guinevere.

The door chattered with another violent gust and somewhere deep in the castle a window banged loosely against a frame. Guinevere suppressed a shiver.

"I saw Arthur this morning. He was sitting at the Round Table, a single candle lighting the room. I jumped when he moved. I didn't see him at first. He was deep in the shadows. I thought he was at prayer but he was just sitting there staring into space. I was able to talk to him a little. Sometimes it's possible when he's away from the chapel. I told him Merlin would return soon, and to cheer him up I said he might have more news of the Grail. He seized me by the arms and shook me, accusing me of hiding things from him. He demanded I tell him everything I knew. You should have seen his eyes, Gawain. I swear by God's precious breath, they were as red as any demon's."

She leaned her head into his chest. "I'm so frightened. What shall we do? It was all so right once. What have I done? I fear for Camelot, for you, for my very soul. Oh, Gawain, what a terrible mess I've made of it all."

The wind howled again, and when Gawain took her in his arms, he saw the first white flakes swirling out of the sky behind her.

"We go on, because that's what we do," he said quietly. "We fight because what we fight for is right. It's all we have."

Outside, the snow began eddying in chaotic patterns. Guinevere looked up, her blue eyes full fear. "Will he come?"

"He will, because he's the same as us. As long as there's hope, a chance to make a difference, he'll not give up," said Gawain holding her gaze steady.

"I wish I had your faith. Sometimes I think you're made of the same brick and mortar as this castle," said Guinevere.

The snow began to layer the naked trees and they watched the world whiten together. After a moment, she turned to him. "Arthur once told me when the snow falls, God rejoices because it reminds Him of the purity of women. I must be an embarrassment."

"No," Gawain said. "You're the queen and Arthur's wife. No matter how you choose to live your life, those facts will never change. You can go to the cloisters – the facts won't change. You can remain here and fight for Camelot – the facts won't change, you'll always be our queen."

He cupped her shoulders and turned her back to the window, to the growing storm. "The world out there may appear to change, but it hasn't. It's different, yes, but underneath it's still the same. It's like us, Guinevere. We are not given to know what happens in our lives. Look at Argath, Eyenon, the Grail. Who could have predicted those things? It doesn't matter what befalls me, I'm still Gawain. I grow and learn but I am always Gawain underneath. We don't lose who we are. Your love and noble birth are your essence, Guinevere."

He dropped his hands from her shoulders and held her fingertips. "We will survive this," he said softly. "We will live long into our old age and the world will know of these days."

The serving girl returned and set a loaf, a platter of hot meat pies and a tureen of gravy on the table, then left with a curtsy.

In the silence, the wind found its way into the castle, blowing down the passages, beating about the walls. The door rattled again, but this time differently. Both of them turned. The latch snapped up.

CHAPTER 20

The door swung open. Even in the dim reflections and the warm light of the candles, Gawain could see the toll Merlin's fluxing had taken. The wizard leaned over his staff, feebly beating the snow off his shoulders and cloak with his free hand. He shook his head and even though he dislodged the snow there, his hair remained just as white. But what Gawain noticed most was his stoop. He took it all in as Merlin crossed the floor, green eyes shining at the sight of his friend. Despite what he saw, Gawain's heart soared when the wizard smiled. "Merlin, you don't know how glad I am to see you. What's happened? What have you been up to? Where have you ... "

"In the name of the great Henge will you ever learn to slow down? You never cease to amaze me. Questions, questions, questions. Let a man breathe, boy."

He wriggled out of Gawain's arms and shuffled over to Guinevere. He bowed so low he looked for one precarious moment as though he might topple over.

"Your majesty, I'm a little late, I fear."

She took him by the elbow. "Come, my lord, sit by the fire, warm yourself, and when you're done tell us all that's happened."

"I will, my lady, but first I must eat," he said eyeing the food. "Gawain, a little wine to help the digestion perhaps?"

They moved to the table, and just as Merlin set about stacking bread and a generous helping of shepherd's pie onto a trencher, Bors and Percival entered. They clamored around him but he silenced their questions, waving them off with a bony hand as he shuffled over to an armchair near the fire. He sat with an umph and pulled the trencher onto his lap. Seemingly oblivious of everyone in the room, he tore off a piece of bread and dipped it into the steaming gravy. The knights fell back, watching, waiting for him to finish. Finally, after mopping up the last of the pie he stretched and then ruffled the crumbs out of his beard.

"Judging by your faces, I'd better give you a full account of what has befallen me," he said leaning back in the chair and lacing his fingers across his stomach. "When I left for the Terran Stone at Carmarthen, I had only one thing in mind, to increase my mental power and confront Eyenon. But, as is often the case with Stones, there were some surprising side effects in store for me. I have a theory on these you know ... but another time," he muttered absent-mindedly. "Where was I? Ah yes, it wasn't the dizziness or the visions that shocked me when I touched the Stone, it was what I heard – a voice full of urgency. I couldn't tell at first whether it belonged to man or woman." He paused reaching for more wine.

"*Earth, air, water, fire*, it rang in my head. I knew they were the elements that made up the Druid arcumen. But what could they mean? What was it trying to tell me? Then I suddenly made the connection: Argath was a Serpent, creature of the earth. Eyenon was a Dreamwalker – he was of the air. Once I had that, I realized what it meant – the other Dark Princes were also aligned to the arcumen: one to fire, one to water.

"But Athlan," said Gawain before he could stop himself.

"Indeed, my boy. Which did she carry? Until now we had no way of telling," said Merlin tapping his temple. "The voice inside me stopped after a while. It was as if the person behind it sensed I'd made the connection. Then I realized where I'd heard it before – Neume! What made it difficult for me, you see, was that it was her voice in full vigor, not the voice of the old woman I last remembered.

"She had the answers I sought but at what cost? She's been dead these many months. The only way for me to find them would be through the Terran Stone at Harlech," he said turning briefly to Gawain and raising his empty chalice.

"Using the Stone there has resulted in insanity, even death in some cases. You see, that particular Stone was never fully formed. It's rumored to be the last Terran Stone created before the Far Druids vanished – some say there was not enough magic left to shape it properly. Who knows? All we do know is to invoke it results in wholly unpredictable behavior. There was once a Druid priest, Lamis, who invoked it after he'd used a *Shard* Rune. The story goes, he'd lost his brother in a hunting accident. The *Shard* would increase with the Stone's power and enable him to reach beyond, to the other side and find his brother, so he thought."

Merlin ran a finger around the rim of the refilled chalice and stared at the rapt faces from beneath bushy eyebrows. Gawain smiled to himself, knowing how good Merlin was at drawing these moments out. "I suppose you could say his plan worked – in a way. Because he did indeed increase his powers but in doing so, he also increased his capacity to love far beyond what he could ever have imagined. When he crossed to the other side, his love shone like a beacon. All the dead souls waiting there felt it. They flocked around him like moths around a candle – seeking his warmth, his love, a chance to know life again. He had no hope of finding his brother in the growing multitudes. Then they began their feeding."

"What happened?" pressed Percival as Merlin paused to take a drink.

For once the wizard answered a question without frowning. "Somehow he managed to escape, but not until the lost souls had absorbed most of his life force. Eventually, he returned to this world. When he did, though, he found himself unable to feel any emotion: love, anger, even hope – he felt nothing. He was like a shell whose seed had dried up. He simply had no purpose anymore." Merlin shrugged his shoulders. "But the oddest thing was, he lived longer than any man known, well over a hundred years. Some say he was too afraid to die after what he'd seen. But I believe he was too empty to care about death and it just passed him by."

He took another slow sip of his wine.

The company watched him in silence. Outside, the snow piled up on the castle stones, hissing as it feathered against the stained glass. Merlin stretched his back. "Like it or not, I had to try the Stone," he continued. "So, after Eyenon's death, I journeyed north. Once I reached the sacred cave, I cast a spell of longing – not on me, mind, but on the walls. No matter what temptations there were on the other side, you see, I'd always feel the need-the longing to return."

Merlin cocked an eyebrow and the group nodded at his wisdom. He smiled. "When I touched the Stone, cold bit through my skin. Despite my wards, the magic of the Terran found my soul as easily as a hound would find fresh scent. In that instant, I traveled to the other side." Lowering the cup, he dabbed carefully at the corner of his mouth and Gawain reflected: *there's so much more to this man than magic.*

"Darkness fell around me in that forbidding place. Woeful voices floated out of the long shadows, ghostly shapes drifted by like November leaves." He shuddered. "In the distance, I could see silhouettes – hills, or what passed for hills, and valleys, but none like I'd ever seen before. There were no trees, no grass or plants to give comfort. Everything was formless. It was like standing on the Earth before the Sidhe had fashioned it.

"The ghosts, for that's what I'll call them to keep things simple, didn't seem to notice me at first. Maybe it was the spell I'd cast earlier. I don't know.

"As my eyes adjusted to the gloom, I looked around. Behind me, maybe twenty paces up the slope an old wooden fence ran the length of the hillside. It seemed to mark some boundary between worlds because behind it, the sky was different, a dull, pearly gray and the clouds there were moving.

"Ahead, unformed rocks and lumps of what could've been headlands stretched out to a black, waveless ocean. How in the name of the great Henge was I ever going to find Neume in this land of lost souls?

"As I stood there wondering what to do next, I thought of the poor old Druid, Lamis, and what he'd done to get their attention. But I had no overwhelming source of attraction, no great love to entice these poor souls. The only thing I had was my knowledge of Runes. I ran through the ones I thought would be most useful and decided on a *Farquart* Rune. This Rune gives the caster greater empathy, bringing him closer to the person he's talking to, so he's seen as a friend, someone to trust. If a wizard of my ability casts it, it can be daunting. I drew the Rune. Success! One of the ghosts glided toward me.

'What are you?' I asked as it closed.

"There was no answer. It didn't seem to understand.

'I'm looking for someone.'

"This brought a response. It stopped and opened its arms. I didn't understand what it wanted at first, so I stepped towards it. I sensed a faint glimmer of warmth – like a tiny ember glow. I went closer still. Suddenly, the ghost lightened in color, then grew transparent. Moments later, it simply vanished.

"I was about to try a different Rune when I was struck by an unaccountable feeling of loneliness. It started as a mild sensation at first, but it soon grew into a deep longing. That's when I knew."

Merlin placed the chalice beside the chair, leaned forward and wagged his finger. "The ghost had entered me! I could feel its frail soul pulsing within my body!

"Now, I could hear the voices of the other ghosts as well, dry whispers. They were pleading for me to embrace them, to kindle their souls, to stay them from the eternal darkness. As they gathered, I searched for Neume. I called her name in the ancient tongue. At first, there was nothing. I called again, and again. Then, out of the throng, a single Druid voice full of panic reached me.

'You must extinguish the soul within you, Merlin – NOW!' it cried out.

"I found the small spark I'd nourished and used my power to smother it – the glow ebbed and the loneliness disappeared. The other ghosts around me began to glide away- all that is, except one.

'Merlin, only you could manage this,' it said.

The shape hovering before me was so thin I could see through it to the headlands and the flat, dark sea beyond.

'Neume, you must help me,' I whispered, still in fear of where I was.

'I know what you've come for, but first I must enter you and when I'm finished you must extinguish my soul too,' came the reply.

"I moved forward. Her shadow lightened and in a blink of an eye, she entered me. A few moments later, the loneliness grew again and this time I was plummeted into the deepest despair I've ever known. Then she spoke. Her words are still with me now.

'You bear the pain well, Merlin. My time is at an end. What you feel is the sadness of my life – the sum of my regrets. Stand firm and I will tell you what I've learned in this terrible place.' Her voice was weaker now she was within me. Perhaps it was closer to who she truly was in that dreadful place.

'All you've been through, everything, was brought about by Morganna. She began plotting her revenge the day you tricked her mother into lying with Uther. When Arthur was born and you took him away, she swore she'd see you die – you, Uther, Arthur, anyone who had a hand in the deception. She's been consumed by revenge ever since.

'When you left with Igrain's child, Morganna had little knowledge of Runes. What was she then? Nine, perhaps ten? Yet, even at that age, she showed a rare talent for drawing her power from living creatures rather than the elements – a sure mark of a Dark Druid.

'As soon as she was old enough, she ran away from Crickhowell and journeyed north to Radnor. The Dark Druids there were only too glad to take her in when they learned of her talents. By the time she'd reached womanhood, she'd discovered more of the arcane lore than the entire coven, even the mysterious Hecate. But she was not content. The need for revenge festered within her. Long years passed, but despite all she'd accomplished, she was never able to cast any of the Dark Runes at her command without unpredictable results.

'In my time here, I've learned much – often more than I've cared to, but what Morganna did next shocked me out of all measure. One day she found out about the Marred witches. That's when her plan for revenge truly took shape, Even you, Merlin, have little knowledge of this small sect of Dark Druids. There's no time to tell you all I've learned since coming here, but know this: at the core of their beliefs, they are what the Christians call, Devil worshippers.'

"I'd heard of these Druids before but I'll admit my learning was vague at best," said Merlin, drumming his fingers on the arm of the chair. "Something I should have attended to long ago. Anyway, Neume continued, her voice fading to a mere whisper.

'Morganna traveled north and soon joined them. And just as before, she surpassed everyone in learning. It did her no good though; the proper Rune casting still eluded her. She was at a loss, her efforts in vain. Then, one night, under what the Marred witches call a blood moon, the darkest of forces came to her.'

"Neume's voice became difficult for me to hear at this point, it was so faint. But the words she spoke next rang in my head like the clash of long swords.

'On that night, Morganna made a pact with this Christian Devil,' she said. 'For full knowledge of the twenty-four Dark Runes and how to cast them properly, she pledged her undying allegiance in a terrible oath. From that moment on, she was bound to him in life as well as death.

'The first task he had for her must have made her happy, for it was near and dear to her own evil heart. Destroy the Grail and free me from my prison, he told her, and I will rid Camelot of its Christ worshippers.'

"Neume's voice began to tremble at this point and it became more difficult for me to understand her. 'You've no idea of this Dark One's power, Merlin,' she went on. 'But as long as there's a Grail he's unable to use it. He fears that talisman, hates it. It has magic beyond even your own considerable understanding; while the cup exists, he cannot break out of his prison; he's held captive in the wasteland forever.'

"She stopped, and after a long moment, added, 'I feel the lightness of my being. I dread where I must go.'

"I could feel her slipping away." 'There's but one thing more,' she whispered. Now I had to guess at her words, they were so faint. 'The fourth son is known to me.'"

Merlin paused and reached for the jug on the table. He glanced around at the fixed stares and open mouths and casually poured the scarlet wine into the chalice.

"Her voice was little more than a dying sigh," he continued, setting the jug down and sipping the wine. Everyone remained motionless. Guinevere had instinctively slipped her hand into Gawain's. Bors was hunched forward. Percival had crossed his arms as if he were hugging himself.

Merlin rose and crossed to the fire. Outside thick flakes were spinning down with incredible gentleness. The wizard rubbed his hands together in front of the flames and turned to the expectant faces.

"These were her final words as I remember them. 'The fourth son has been among you all along, and his work is far from done.'"

The knights looked at him dumbfounded. Percival fought for words but couldn't seem to find them. Bors gaped. Gawain held his hand up, stemming the rising questions and spoke for all of them.

"Who, Merlin?"

His voice echoed in the bare hall.

"Argath earth, Eyenon air, now the child of water, whose job it was to slip into our midst and undermine our noble cause, to weaken our king and destroy our faith. It was his job to steal the queen's heart and ... "

"Stop it! Stop it!" cried Guinevere jumping up.

"*Lancelot!*" exclaimed Gawain.

"Lancelot du Lac," corrected Merlin, emphasizing each French syllable. "Lancelot of the lake."

The words struck Gawain like a war hammer. And in the silence that followed the only sounds that could be heard were Guinevere's gentle sobs.

Gawain went to comfort her but Merlin stayed him, "No, my falcon. If she is to gain the strength to rule here, she must bear this alone."

The others shifted uneasily.

"Where is he now?" said Bors.

"Arthur sent him after the Grail, along with Sagremor," said Merlin. "Unfortunately, poor Sagremor had no idea he was helping Morganna complete her side of the bargain."

Merlin gestured and Percival brought more wine. Running his finger up the handle of the jug, Merlin continued.

"After I released Neume, I discovered something else. She'd left a small, fleeting message in her passing – a picture, the location of the Grail."

The snow swirled past the window in a sudden flurry seeming to take warmth out of the flames. Somewhere a door clanged shut and bolts were shot home. The great gray walls stood resolute, implacable.

This time Percival stepped forward. "Where, my lord?"

"First you must understand the significance of what I said earlier: Lancelot knows. By now, he may well have killed Sagremor. He'll stop at nothing to obtain the Grail, and once he has it, he'll most certainly destroy it. If he manages that, Morganna will have fulfilled her part of the bargain. Then who knows what evil she will unleash in the name of revenge."

All eyes suddenly turned as the door swung open and Arthur came clanking in. He was clad in tarnished armor – helmet dented, greaves battered, scabbard streaked with rust but on his face he wore a look of triumph. He strode ahead, joints squeaking.

"Come on, come on. We must leave, now. The Lord has spoken. Gawain, Bors, Percival, we have work to do." He looked at Merlin and grimaced as if he had tasted something bitter. "This is no place for wizards. You're on hallowed ground. Be gone. Back to the cave with you."

"Arthur," said Guinevere. "Please."

Gawain caught the faint movement of Merlin's hand. The gesture was subtle but Gawain recognized the beginning stroke of the *Por Fell* Rune.

"I don't care if ... ." The king stopped in mid-sentence as if he'd forgotten what he was about to say. "Bors, I, I need to sit a while."

He sagged where he stood and the big knight caught his arm and eased him into a chair. Before Arthur hit the soft cushion, his head lolled forward and the first sounds of soft snores filtered through his visor.

Guinevere knelt by his side, her hand going to his breastplate. "Arthur?"

"It's all right, my lady," said Merlin, gently easing her away. "He's just sleeping, taking a much needed rest, that's all."

She looked at him, a question rising to her lips but before she could speak, Gawain cut in. "For the sake of our dear Lord, Merlin, will you not tell us where the Grail is?"

"The talisman lies far, far north of here," Merlin answered, "hidden in a castle named *Corbenic*, in the heart of the fens beyond our borders. Those living near call the area the wastelands. The Dark One lies imprisoned there, held captive within its boundaries by the Grail's magic. We must assume Lancelot's close by now. He's had a long start."

"The snow will slow us down considerably," said Percival.

"You and Bors perhaps – Gawain, I can help travel much faster."

"What about Arthur?" said Guinevere.

"He'll be safe here." Merlin went over to the sleeping figure and patted his shoulder gently.

"Gawain, if you're willing, I'll flux you as far north as the *Isolate* tower – a place marking the boundary of the wastelands. *Corbenic* lies somewhere beyond, deep in the barren wilds. After that, I'm afraid I cannot help. All Druid magic seems to lose its power north of the tower. Not even basic Runes work beyond its ancient walls. Also, crossing the wastelands may not be the most dangerous part of your quest. Somewhere along the way, you're sure to meet up with Lancelot and I've a feeling he's no longer the knight we once knew."

Merlin turned to the others. "Bors and Percival, you must follow by horse. I won't have the essence left to flux you after I've sent Gawain. The journey to the tower will be difficult enough. Who knows how long it'll take Gawain to cross the wasteland. You must wait for him at the tower. We'll need all three of you to safeguard the return of the Grail."

"What else can you tell us about this tower?" asked Bors.

The wizard shrugged his frail shoulders looking at a loss. "Nothing I'm afraid. It's virtually unknown to me. I've only been there once, at the end of my mapping. When I tried to open the door, I found it sealed shut. My magic had little effect on the wards guarding it. Mind you, I was in a weakened condition," he added quickly.

The others nodded and Merlin continued. "Maybe there are answers to the Grail mystery inside. I don't know." He turned to Gawain. "Hopefully, you can find out when you get there, my boy."

Merlin took up an ornate poker from the side of the hearth and pushed the logs back. A blaze of sparks shot out. "My lady, you must keep Arthur here and enforce the laws yourself. Hold court as he would. Rule in his name, you know how. The people will listen to you. Have the guilds meet first thing in the morning. After we talk to them, I'll leave for Brecon. I'll be able to contact Gawain from there. Unfortunately, I cannot risk fluxing again, so I must travel the conventional way."

"We'd better wait until the snow stops," said Bors.

Merlin crossed to the casement and stared out at the white trees. "Hopefully this is the last of the bad news. Magic fuels this storm. I have no idea how strong it is but I believe Lancelot's behind it. More than likely, he drew on his water essence to cast it. When I get to the Stone at Brecon, I should be able to re-align the spell. Meanwhile, we must all play our part. We'll begin our quest tomorrow. Now it's time for us to get a good night's rest."

After a fitful sleep, they gathered in the empty banquet hall the next morning. Outside, the snow continued to fall steadily as Merlin prepared the Runes that would send Gawain to the farthest reaches of the realm. Guinevere stood by the fire dressed in a royal blue gown that swept the ground, a circlet bearing a single golden lion nestled in her hair. Her eyes were sadly distant as she watched the knights pack the last of their supplies.

Merlin stooped with a grunt and set a triangle on the bare flagstones. When he was satisfied with the alignment, he carefully balanced one of the thin wires on the apex and waited for it to settle. Once the red tip pointed north, he moved Gawain into position and waved the others back. Gnarled hands and crooked fingers cut the air and the first of a series of Runes took shape. When they formed, he drew a second series, this time with softer strokes, creating wisps of pure magic at the intersecting lines. Clutching his staff, he spoke the words of binding and a rumble of muted thunder shook the room.

When the magic took hold, Gawain had a last glimpse of two faces looking on: Guinevere and Merlin, youth and wisdom, grace and power, and suddenly his doubts disappeared. He knew, even as the world around him collapsed, that they would survive. Love does not die that easily, he thought. There would be no requiem for Camelot.

Away to hunt the last dark prince loosed upon loveless shores.

Bitter cold that could have been the unrelenting snow.

Through streaking light, incandescence burning the way.

Then dark.

And out of the void, materialized the husks of naked trees stripped bare by a far northern winter. Brown hills powdered with snow lined the horizon. To his left a castle keep sheered up from the landscape in a single, massive column of stone. He shivered as biting wind gusted across the barren valley. He was there – here, at the *Isolate* tower. And with his first uneasy steps, his boots crunching through the frosted earth, he felt both fear and wonder.

Built with stones the size of hardened warriors, the tower loomed above him. It reached to an impossible height. Gawain thought he was approaching a cairn built by God to mark the very boundary at the world's end. Nearing the west wall, he searched for signs of life, but the hard gray face of the tower was as forbidding as the land itself.

When he climbed the rough slope leading to the entrance, he realized from where he stood, that he could not see a single window or parapet. He hammered on the door with the hilt of his sword and listened to the hollow booms rumbling within. When they died out, the only sound left was the low thrum of the icy wind blowing across the riveted seams of his helmet.

He grasped the iron ring bolted into the door and turned it. The latch moved a little, then stuck. He unsheathed his sword and jammed it through the ring. Grabbing the haft and the blade, he twisted. The latch moved with a groan and the door creaked ajar. He put his shoulder to the weathered wood and shoved. The door swung in. *Perhaps the great*

Merlin neglected to try this, he mused to himself. *Sometimes might is better than magic, my tricky friend.*

He pushed the door further and the wintry light behind him knifed into the darkness revealing a cavernous interior. Around the walls of the empty chamber, a granite staircase spiraled high up into maw of the tower.

As he walked to the first stair, two startled bats flew up from a great conical brazier set in the wall and he stood watching until the sounds of their leathery wings faded into silence. The step came up to his knees. He tapped the huge stone with his boot. *Who in the name of God built this?*

Bracing himself for what lay ahead, he placed his hand on the rough edge, gave a grunt and clambered up. It was going to be a long day. After he'd struggled up several steps, he peered over the side. He judged himself some twenty feet from the floor. Although the light below cut clearly into the chamber, he found he hadn't yet climbed into darkness. He glanced up, surprised to find the same amount of light above as he had first seen from ground level. Scrambling over the next few steps, he kept his eye on the curve of the spiraling staircase and used the wall for support. As he ascended, the darkness receded.

He continued climbing, armor clanging with each step, sweat beading under the leather rim of his helmet as his breath billowed out in steamy clouds. And always the canopy of pale light pushed ahead, illuminating the harsh stone walls above him. Step by giant step, he wound his way up the never-ending spiral, until the floor below was little more than a white smudge.

Up and up. He climbed ceaselessly, winding around the vast wall, tiring, slowing and once stumbling and almost falling into the yawning abyss. But he gritted his teeth and somehow found the strength to go on. Then, when he began to doubt he'd ever reach the top, the stone column disappeared between two heavily timbered beams.

Aching in every joint of his body, he clambered up the last remaining steps and staggered onto a wooden floor. His jaw dropped. He'd entered a great vaulted chamber.

Sweet Lord!

He stood on shaky legs, stunned by the extraordinary sight that met his gaze. Everything loomed in giant proportions: a table and chairs made for someone eight or nine feet tall, a huge bookcase crammed with tomes stacked on shelves reaching up twenty feet or more, pallets, easels, flasks, bottles, vials and maps, all in vast proportion.

Walls of hard granite, feet thick, formed the perimeter of the circular chamber. He brushed a cobweb aside and made his way across the cluttered floor. His boots sent clouds of dust puffing into the frigid air as he skirted a strongbox the size of a kitchen table. He glanced up. Above him, iron riveted beams crisscrossed a great domed ceiling. Further ahead, at the center of the chamber, he could see dozens of ancient globes suspended from chains of varying length. To his right sat an oil lamp the size of a milking pail on a colossal table.

Who in the name of God lived here?

A weak light filtered through four arched windows cut into the wall, north, south, east and west. He crossed to the nearest one. When he touched the rough casement, he felt a tingling at the nape of his neck and looked up. Above the peak of the arch, he saw a silver glyph carved into the stone, but he recognized no aspect of its Runic design. Turning from the markings, he gripped the ledge and peered over.

The height made him dizzy. Below, a vast gray haze of cloud spread out, obscuring most of the landscape. In the far distance, however, he could see a forest running from the east side of a valley and climbing up the slope of a broken plateau. Further, he could make out a faint curl of smoke – the first sign of life in the forbidding land.

Gawain felt above the world. *How was it possible for anyone, even with Runic power, to build such a place – and for what purpose? A lookout, as Merlin said.* He peered down into the clouds again. Above the arch, the glyph rippled like sunlight on waves, changing, moving fluidly-writing, etching. He felt a moment of disorientation and then the clouds shrank. Unaware he was in the grip of an ancient magic beyond even Merlin's understanding, he saw.

It was like looking down into a crystal ball. Snow fell in that ball, steady flakes swirling, burying the holdings, the guilds, the smithies and the inns under a thick white blanket. He saw figures braving the storm and crossing the street: two merchants, cloaks pulled tight, huddled under eves, a yeoman toting a pitifully small bundle of wood on his back, an old woman with a scarf wrapped around her face. He saw light from candles glowing in windows.

Camelot! He found the tall towers and ramparts of Caerleon. Everything was impossibly bulky with snow. He looked down at the gardens where the fountains, showing only as humps in the drifts piled against them, stood like mute sentries, and it dawned on him he could see, actually see what was happening at that very moment in the beleaguered city.

He gazed passed the hulks of houses and gabled roofs following one of the deserted roads leading out of the city. Even through the veil of snow, he could make out the bulges of the city guilds where the road wound down to the bridge. Out further, on the east bank of the river, he could see where the snow ended and rays of a low sun slanted over the Welsh mountains.

Gawain traced the long sweeping curve of the storm encircling Camelot. It looked like some unearthly waterfall spilling from the heavens. As far as he could see, not a flake strayed across the river or the fields binding it to the west.

Merlin's right. It's a spell. What did he call spells this powerful? Ambient spells, Haard Druid spells?

He tried to recall what the wizard had told him about the small sect that had separated from the Dark Druids and vanished long ago. Something about madness taking hold. *But how does Lancelot know their spells? And Ambient ... What was it he said about them? How did they work?*

He drummed his fingers on the ledge. "Once cast, Ambient spells create a perfect balance between two opposing forces, my boy." *Yes.* He could see Merlin now, hunched over his staff, long finger wagging out his words. "This forms an energy exchange – like hot and cold liquids mixing until they even out in temperature. The magic is sustained as long as the two forces flow."

So what's the source of the energy? He shielded his eyes as he stared into the blur of flakes. *When will he make the boundary?*

How long he stood at the window, he had no idea, but slowly the Runes in the arch dulled. The scene faded, he blinked away the dizziness and turned. Starlight was streaming through the open portals. Dark shadows ribbed the chamber. Hours had passed.

He left the window in a daze, crossing the wooden floor, avoiding stacks of tomes and scattered scrolls. He climbed into a huge worn leather chair in the center of the room and gazed around at the ancient walls and vaulted ceiling. "What magic is this, Merlin? Far Druid, or something yet you haven't told me? So many, many secrets," he breathed.

His grey eyes swept back to the window. *'Dark Druids get their essence from pain and suffering, from the life force of others, my boy.'* His heart raced as he recalled Merlin's words. "Dear God," he exclaimed, clutching the arms of the chair as the awful truth dawned upon him: the snow would only stop falling when the last person in Camelot was dead.

He sat as still as the camber's dusty artifacts, pictures of Camelot and friends filling his mind. If Merlin didn't make the boundary soon, Morganna would walk into an empty city then Caerleon, everything, would be hers for the taking.

He rose and crossed to the south window, thoughts of Athlan stealing their way into his mind as he tried to stop himself asking the question that had haunted him ever since Merlin revealed her fate – what would the child of fire have looked like? What havoc would he have loosed upon the world?

At the window's edge, he braced himself, but what he saw was free of magic: rutted fields and thorny hedgerows standing out in stark relief. In the distance, a jagged mountain range ribbed the horizon, and further off, he caught the glint of a river crossing the land like a battle scar in the bright moonlight.

The view from the next window was much the same, but when he looked out of the fourth window, the one he judged to be north, he saw a landscape that filled him with dread – a vast expanse of broken earth that seemed to stretch to eternity. From this height, it looked as if some malevolent being had pummeled and kicked the land in a sullen rage. There was no recognizable landform, no lakes or moonlit rivers, just endless miles of scarred, barren soil.

Overwhelmed by the appalling death, he backed away, jumping when he bumped against a scroll jutting from a honeycomb rack.

He returned to the chair rubbing his temples. How was he ever going to find his way through such wilderness? Was Lancelot out there waiting? Is this what it would all come to if he failed: Camelot a dying husk, the world a place of morning?

I know, Merlin, find a way. He struggled out of the giant chair and returned to the north window crossing through the streaming starlight. When he leaned over the ledge, the glyph above the arch rippled, glowing with cold fire-not like sunlight on waves this time, but like moonlight on ice. Below him, the intricacy of the wasteland sprang to life.

He *saw* the broken earth and the black rotting land in harsh detail.

He *saw* the limitless vista of petrified stumps and endless moss-covered trunks, the ponds and brackish lakes lying like blackened corpses.

All was disease, all was death, measureless wreckage, boundless ruin.

How can it be so?

He shrank from the intense pictures cramming his mind, but the Far Druid glyph held him in its iron will and amidst the vast destruction below, he saw a silver thread, a fine line shining in the terrible tapestry. A bolt of anxiety shot through him. The glyph above the arch began to write. He caught his breath blinking in disbelief as the landscape took on even greater definition.

The thread became a narrow path that began at the base of the tower and wound its way across the scrubland dales to where the dying began. He followed it for endless miles until his mind could take no more, then he caught a glimpse of something so hauntingly beautiful his hand rose to shield his eyes.

The glyph above him flared, breaking into five Runic letters, each a burning flame in the dark above the arch.

ᚲ ᚲ ᚾ ᚱ ᚠ

And Gawain *saw*.

In the middle of the decay stood a castle as pure and as serene as the sun itself. Its white towers and tall spires, its battlements and golden flags defied the surrounding horror.

In sheer size and design, it dwarfed Caerleon. It was magical, mystical, and Gawain found himself barely able to breathe in the face of such majesty.

Then the glyph faded and the castle winked from view.

Gawain staggered back from the window. The edge of the moon, caught in the corner of the arch, sent a beam knifing over his shoulder into the room.

When he left the casement, he knew; he understood the purpose of the tower. It was a watchtower built centuries ago to guard the precious castle – a heart beating in a dying body. *See the heart that feeds and learn why your magic fails ...* The words from the dream in Neume's cave rang in his mind as he stared at the arcane books and scrolls and the masses of parchments burying tables, and he felt the weight of all the growing impossibilities.

Bone-weary, he pushed aside a desk from a spot near one of the bookshelves. He dragged two cushions off a nearby chair and dropped them on the floor. There would be time enough in the morning to figure out how to get to the castle. For now, he needed rest and sleep to clear his aching head.

He lay on the cushions, staring up into the high dome. He gazed at the massive globes that looked so much like distant planets and wondered how Merlin could ever get through the storm. But he was Merlin and he would find a way with his charms or wards or failing magic. He would forge a path no matter how thick the snow, no matter how difficult things got. But for all his wisdom, Gawain thought sadly, he still couldn't open a simple door. *Has he, as my father said, relied too much on magic?*

Outside, the wind howled, battering the walls of the gigantic tower and jumbled memories filled his mind. So far from friends. Wanting so much to love again. He closed his eyes, hands clasped behind his head, fingers laced in locks of thick hair. *Days of lying in tall grass, her skin soft like rain filled earth. Her smile a calm sea to sail in. Llewellyn may have been her husband but he was never her true love. He was never that. I had a name, Artemisia for a child. But Merlin was right; you were gone through no fault of mine.* And in his stomach, before he fell to sleep, he felt the heaviness of failure and a growing fear of what awaited him in the appalling wastelands.

CHAPTER 21

T he dreams came beneath the stars on top of the curve of the world. And when they did, the glyphs inscribed by the Far Druids to reveal the heart's desire and guard the Grail glowed a ghostly gray. Then slowly, as Gawain's thoughts of Merlin faded, they swam into Runic letters.

Time.

All four glyphs silvered with celestial power. In unison, they reached for his mind.

And in his dream, Gawain traveled. He followed the path he'd seen from the northern window, the magically charged Runes guiding him. He set out on the faint trail somehow knowing it was right, that where it ended, he would find the answers. There was no sound, no wind, no sensation, only the broken earth beneath his feet and a sullen sky above. He journeyed, never tiring, never faltering as he crossed the ruinous land.

He walked at an incredible pace, moving effortlessly over black clods of sterile earth, skirting marshes full of rotting soil. He had no control over the direction he went. His feet took him with a will of their own.

The dream hours passed and he came upon a petrified forest. When he broke through to the other side, he followed the decaying shoreline of a flat, brackish lake. And further, his effortless strides took him to a range of hills punching up from the rank earth like a fighter's knuckles.

On and on.

And when he climbed to the top of a flat plateau, he saw more death.

He crossed a still river and stopped to look into its stagnant water. He saw for the first time, in all the forsaken land, a sign of life – a fish longer than his arm floating up to the surface, its pale white belly coated in slimy water. It turned its head and looked at him beseechingly. But Gawain forged deeper into the wasteland, not wanting to think about the strange human face attached to the pulpy neck or the large flat eyes brimming with black tears.

He lost track of time – even dreamtime. The journey was an endless trek through a carnage of despair and lost faith. He wept as he walked and he felt hope seeping from him like blood from an open wound.

Then, out of the timeless expanse, he saw the bright and glorious *Corbenic*, its pure white turrets and golden flags towering high in a windless sky. His heart leaped and love poured into his empty soul. And for the first time since he started the dreadful quest, he looked over his shoulder. As far as he could see, small indentations marked the rotting earth – his footprints, each one a perfect shape, each one filled with blades of soft green grass. They trailed away, vanishing in the distance like tiny lily pads.

He knew, even before he began walking again, that he would wake long before he ever reached the glorious castle. But that was fine, because he also knew he would find this place again, and next time it would be easier, because all he had to do was follow those small, verdant footprints.

The dream faded as quickly as it came, but before it did, Gawain saw in the bright glow of the castle, a dark figure lurking by the outer walls. There was something familiar in its slow sullen steps. He broke into a run . . . .

The guardian glyphs faded and he awoke, cold sweat soaking his body.

The sun hovered high above the eastern window, flooding the tower chamber and lighting up the tiny dust motes in its beams. Still stiff and sore from the climb the day before, Gawain stretched painfully. There wasn't much time if he were to descend the long staircase and make the holding he'd seen on the plateau.

He went to each of the windows and looked out on low clouds and distant hills; all was still and quiet, the world a normal place.

One day I will return here with you, Merlin. It will be worth it to see your face. But for now the wastelands and the castle Corbenic. Follow footprints laid in a dream full of living, breathing grass. Find the Grail and return to Camelot, where, if you're successful one more time, you will have stopped the raging storm and kept safe the realm of Arthur. Then what I wonder. Then what?

But first things first.

Taking a last look around the ancient chamber, he crossed to the winding stairs. When he began his descent, the dark figure slinking in the shadows of the white walls of Corbenic flashed through his mind – and in the solitary light behind him, the Far Druid glyphs faded into the ancient stone, their warning sung.

Down.

Descending the dizzying staircase was far more dangerous than the climb up. He stumbled often, once barely managing to stop himself from tumbling into the great well of darkness. Sweat soaked through his padded undershirt. He clambered down each giant step, skinning hands against the rough wall when he fought for support. His boots sent echoes flocking through the stillness as they scraped and clattered on the hard stone.

Down a never-ending spiral, dwarfed by the backdrop of the curving wall, his breath pooling into the frigid air.

The light shining through the door at the base of the *Isolate* tower materialized so subtly at first, he scarcely noticed it. To his tired eyes, it appeared as a speck, a distant candle. Then, as he neared, it grew into weak afternoon sunlight that shone into the chamber from the door he'd left open.

More winding steps, then ... the end. Finally, blessedly, the end.

Stumbling off the last stair, he slumped down on the stone floor. Leaning his back against the wall, he crossed his arms over his knees and let out a long sigh. He lowered his head and closed his eyes. He stayed there for a long while, but the stiffness in his legs and the wind gusting through the open door forced him to his feet again.

It was getting late, but the thought of spending another night in the tower left him in no doubt. He would use what light there was and seek the place where he saw smoke rising from the distant plateau. Once he got there, he would be able to stock up on food and get some rest before he set out for the wasteland.

Wincing from a painful cramp in his back, he crossed to the entrance and stepped outside. The bitter wind made his eyes water. Light dry snow whipped through the air. It would be a long journey. The chain mail he wore scarcely served to keep him warm, even the quilted vest and woolen leggings barely warded off the wintry blasts.

Head bowed and shoulders hunched, he made his way across the lonely valley, the tower and the dying world behind him. Snow flurried in cruel gusts. A knight bereft of friends, he trudged on toward the naked trees and the broken plateau where the solitary holdfast lay.

After an hour of weary travel, he came to the first oaks and tall elms of a wooded vale. When he entered, the wind picked up, beating about the trunks and stark limbs. In the failing light, shadows of naked branches loomed around him. The path slowly vanished, leaving only a gradual slope leading to the plateau.

In the distance, a wolf howled and Gawain drew his sword as he made his way between the bare elms. Deeper into the wood, the wind dropped and the snow whispered through the trees. He skirted a fallen trunk and found himself facing a clearing. Shifting shadows and darkness pooled in the open space before him. He could barely see to the other side. Somewhere to his left, he heard a snap. He jerked his head up. A branch swung, sending a thin line of snow sifting down. Tightening his grip on the sword, he stepped into the clearing. At that moment, a deep voice broke the silence.

"Guinevere was really very good in bed, you know. She knew how to appreciate a knight with an appetite for the finer things. If you know what I mean."

Gawain spun around. No one. He peered into the darkness, into the trees edging the clearing. Shadows from the high branches overhead clawed the snowy ground.

"I don't think your king could find it in his pitiful soul to mount the poor woman."

The taunting seemed to have no point of origin. Gawain stepped into the clearing, sword in hand. The dry snow fell steadily, hissing as it brushed almost seductively against his face.

"Lancelot, I know who you are. I killed your father and your sorry brothers; you're the last of your ill-gotten breed." Gawain's voice held firm, despite the teeth-chattering cold. "Now it's your turn."

"Let me assure you, idiot of the Round Table, the chances of you defeating me in a sword fight are next to nothing. Look at you. What a sorry excuse for a knight, your armor couldn't protect you from a woman's embrace. You should be wearing clouts."

At the last word, the wind suddenly picked up beating about Gawain's shoulders and sending him staggering back.

"Ha, ha, ha."

Snow whirled, blinding him and he held his hand up trying to shield his eyes from the stinging crystals.

"Ha, ha, ha."

"Even now you resort to magic," said Gawain, the air ripping away his words. "Just as you did to seduce Guinevere."

The wind suddenly dropped and the falling snow whispered again. The change left his ears ringing. *How in the name of all that's Druid does he do that? And where has his accent gone?*

"You truly are stupid. Do you think for a moment I needed help with that? All I had to do was crook a finger and she came running."

The wind rose again, biting through Gawain's chain mail as he weighed his reply. He held his sword steady searching the darkness. "You're no different than your brothers. You seek protection through Morganna's magic like a child seeking safety between his mother's legs."

Silence.

The temperature suddenly plummeted to a bone-chilling cold, enveloping Gawain, numbing his fingers and freezing his hand to the iron hilt of his sword.

"Remember that Neume bitch? She was right about me. Before I skinned her, she said she felt my presence, felt my cold in her dreams. Ahhh, but what would you know? You tire me, shit-eater." *Argath, Eyenon, the same language. The same inflection. He's changing, just like the others. Dear God, they were all going through a stage, evolving. Did you know this Merlin? Morganna didn't get the Rune casting wrong ...*

A sudden movement to his left broke his train of thought. The air shimmered and Lancelot materialized. He stood at the center of the clearing – dressed in full ebony armor. *Bors, your dream!*

Gawain gripped his sword with both hands. Lancelot smiled, legs apart, long blade gleaming as he slowly drew it from the scabbard. The lank hair hanging over his eyes glistened with melting snow. "I'll flay you after I've killed you and then I'll hang your carcass in a tree for the crows, or maybe the *falcons*, to eat."

He raised his sword sighting down its gleaming length. "Merlin's whelp," he breathed softly, "your days of fetch and carry are over."

He lunged. Gawain barely managed to sidestep the blade. The dark knight sneered then moved in, wristing the tempered sword and cutting at Gawain before he could regain his balance. Metal squealed as the steel bit through the thin breastplate and Gawain fell back clutching his side.

"First blood, I rather think," said Lancelot circling to the left.

Gawain eyed him warily, a warm trickle running between the quilted vest and his skin. Lancelot looked as fresh as if he'd just stepped out of his sleeping chamber. In his present condition, Gawain knew he had no chance. He looked around for something to give him an edge but he saw nothing save the bare, forbidding trees. *If it is to be done, then it will be done bravely.*

"How rude of me, I almost forgot. How's Arthur doing now? Still on his knees, is he? In the chapel, that is." Lancelot chuckled at his own joke. Then he lunged again. But his time Gawain was ready and moved back easily.

"Feeling a little cold, brave knight?"

Gawain didn't answer, choosing instead to circle to the left. The temperature suddenly plummeted and the raw intensity of the wind made him wince.

"Brrrrr! Funny, it doesn't seem to bother me," Lancelot said.

Despite the biting cold, Gawain held his sword steady and closed in. The black knight flashed a grin. Then, to Gawain's surprise, he closed his eyes and bowed his head as if he were before some holy altar. The result was instant. The ebony armor he wore suddenly crusted white and a deep frost raced over the surface in hissing, crackling patterns. It grew wildly, spreading until it covered all the armor and then his entire body. In seconds, a hoary layer of ice, inches thick, encased the dark knight.

Gawain didn't hesitate; he drew the sword back and aiming at Lancelot's neck swung with all his might. A screech rent the clearing as the honed edge hit the ice. A loud crack rang out and the top quarter of the blade snapped off. The jarring impact vibrated along Gawain's arm, spinning the broken sword out of his hands. A white cloud puffed up where it skittered through the snow.

Lancelot remained unscathed, looking like a marble statue in the eerie light. Hand still numbed from the impact, Gawain searched for his dagger. He plunged his deadened fingers under his vest. *Maybe I can drive the tip through the ice, into the bastard's neck.* He found the rough little handle and tore the dagger free of its sheath. Something made him look up. The wide eyes of Lancelot were open, staring at him from behind the blue green ice.

Gawain wavered for a moment. Then, with a snarling thrust, he drove the dagger at the exposed throat. He half expected another jarring impact but it never came. On its way, the blade rimed with frost and before the tip reached Lancelot, it turned into a thick, blunt icicle that clattered uselessly against the knight's protective coating.

Freezing pain shot through Gawain's fingers and he grimaced. He looked down to see frost growing like some white fungus over the hand clutching the dagger. He tried to brush it off but it clung on stubbornly. He gritted his teeth against the pain, grunting when it suddenly speared up his arm. Then a loud crack erupted and great chunks of ice splintered, and began spinning away from the statue in front of him. A moment later, the black knight burst out from a hailstorm of shards.

Gawain forgot the throbbing. Eyes locked on Lancelot, he dropped to his knees and swept his good hand under the snow searching desperately for the broken sword. He bumped the handle and drew it into his palm.

"My, my, my, it was chilly in there," said Lancelot flicking the remaining crystals off his armor like someone brushing away breadcrumbs after a meal. He glanced at Gawain's frozen hand, hard blue eyes glowing in the dusk. "Here, allow me." He bowed his head again. The result was no less dramatic than the first time. The ice shelled away and the pain died down to a dull throb.

Gawain rose to his feet switching the broken sword into his right hand. Even though his fingers still ached with numbness, his grip held firm. "No more magic. Face me like a man," he said, circling the dark figure.

Lancelot's reply was as cold as his sneer. "Make no mistake, knight, I can and will reduce you to the simpering fool you are."

With that, Lancelot stepped back and bowed his head again. Gawain reeled. There was an explosion of pain the like of which he'd never encountered before and he thought, in the instant before he stopped thinking, that he'd truly died. The shimmering cold hit him like a mace; every fiber in his body shook, tightened to breaking point and then froze into crystalline latticework.

Laughter rang out, a sound echoing too loudly in the clearing. He stood there then, the last of Uther's sons, glowing eyes taking on a flat silver sheen as the snow tumbled down silently, covering the branches of the lonely trees and settling with incredible gentleness over the thick block of ice encasing Gawain.

Without so much as a glance back at the living statue, Lancelot turned north and set out, abnormally long strides pounding a path between the snowy trees.

In the solid block of ice, Gawain's vision dimmed and his world shrank into darkness. And in the long hours to come, there would not be so much as a single drop of water to show the ice would ever melt. For in all the frozen silence of those barren hills, the magic held firm, happily drawing on his life as it fueled the second of Lancelot's ambient spells.

The visions came later that night when Orion wheeled high above the silent glade. Through the ice fields of Gawain's mind, shapes and shadows clawed their way into his consciousness as light from the distant stars shone between the branches and bathed the block: Merlin by the armory, grunting in his efforts, his voice muted in the blizzard as he shook his fist. 'You are young in this Morganna; I will teach you the true meaning of revenge.' Then a vision of snow cascading out of a limitless sky in sweeping flurries. And Merlin again, this time near the Druid Quarters, a man humbled, stumbling, robe trailing sadly behind but his voice still full of dogged rage – so much more a knight than wizard. Slowly the starlight faded and inside the blue-white ice, Gawain's life ebbed while the ambient Runes thrummed in perfect harmony.

Early the next morning, a ray of sunshine stabbed through the frosty branches searing the ice block in fiery rainbows, and more visions came. Somewhere far north, past the *Isolate* tower, Lancelot striding over the broken earth, boots pounding the crumbling soil and smashing through the rotting limbs of long dead trees as he made his way toward the white castle.

That night the bitter cold slowed even Gawain's thoughts as death crept closer. The final visions came when the moon broke through a furrow of dark clouds and ran a thin blade of moonlight across the ice block: Merlin near a tree line, in a high mountain pass, riding through sheeting rain, beard dripping, sodden tip of his felt hat drooping sadly over his shoulder.

A cloud drifted across the face of the moon and sudden darkness cut off the image. Minutes passed. When it cleared, silver light bathed the ice again. Now Merlin was ducking into the narrow entrance of a cave. At the rear stood the ancient Terran Stone. The bedraggled wizard hurried through the gloom and dropped to his knees before it.

Then a bank of thick clouds roughed up against the moon and the silver beam disappeared. In a fleeting scene before final darkness swept away the thinning light, Merlin closed his eyes and reached out to the Stone with a trembling hand.

CHAPTER 22

P ower flowed.

The Dragon Ring on Gawain's finger pulsed and cowardly death retreated like night before the warming rays of dawn.

The visions returned: Merlin, teeth chattering, robe dripping, wet hair plastered to the sides of his face. The Druid words came too, with their haunting sounds.

"ᛗᛉᛁᚠᛏᚺ ᚷᚠᚱ ᛋᛉᛁ ᚷᚠᚱ ᚱᚠᛏᚺ ᚷᚠᚱ."

The Dragon ring pulsed stronger as the words bound and their ancient harmonies rang out through time and space.

"ᛋᛉᛁ ᚷᚠᚱ ᚱᚠᛏᚺ ᚷᚠᚱ."

The Dragon Ring warmed. Above Gawain, water pooled in perfect beads. Slowly, almost reluctantly, each tiny drop began to tremble then run down the sides of the frozen prison in spidery trails.

The Runic words again, this time stronger, ringing, singing.

"ᛋᛉᛜ ᚷᚠᚱ ᚱᚠᚦᚺ ᚷᚠᚱ."

Now the trails ran down the block of ice in rivulets.

"ᛋᛉᛜ ᚷᚠᚱ ᚱᚠᚦᚺ ᚷᚠᚱ ᛋᛉᛜ ᚷᚠᚱ ᚱᚠᚦᚺ ᚷᚠᚱ"

With the last phrase, a sharp crack ripped through the clearing and the block exploded sending Gawain stumbling forward where the inertial thrust at Lancelot had taken him.

"Gawain."

Pulse.

"Gawain."

He heard muffled words.

Another pulse of elemental power, another and another-until he spread his bare hands under the snow and pushed himself up onto his knees.

And if Merlin's could have seen him then, he would have wept, because the face rising from the ground had aged ten years. The ambient spell had done its job. The once young knight now looked almost as old as his father the day Merlin had first come to the castle.

As more energy reached him, Gawain struggled to his feet.

"Gawain," He heard the muffled words again, but this time they sounded weaker.

He stood, swaying for a moment. Then he lurched forward, arms out, icy water running from the joints in his rusty armor and streaking the breastplate a dirty brown.

Another blast of energy roared through the ring. He jerked right, turning to where the trees grew sparser and the Tor River split the frozen land. Under graying clouds, he crossed a rutted field, seeing but not understanding, each step stiffening then stuttering awkwardly.

Visions flashed in his mind as he gradually neared the river: past, present and something else, an ancient castle situated near a bend where the water flowed south, grey battlements hunched up against low clouds. Then out of nowhere, he saw a dark cave where a robed figure lay slumped against a glowing stone, drool gathered at the corners of his lips, one hand outstretched, the other dangling at his side.

By the time Gawain reached the tree line, the pulses and visions had weakened, leaving him blundering toward the river. Then it happened. The energy disappeared and the images died all together.

"My falcon," a muffled voice cried in his fractured mind, "My falcon."

Beyond the stark embankment, the icy water churned over humps of massive rocks.

"Gawain, stop. *XFR* ... stop ... *XFR*." Suddenly the strange garble of words and melodic chants ceased.

Silence.

Gawain heard a muffled roar. Wind thrummed across the open fields and bit through his armor.

Cold. Dear God, so cold.

Light – late afternoon haze filtered down through thick clouds.

Before him, an embankment sheered off to a thundering river far below. He halted. His fists spasmmed as pain grated through the joints in his body.

He backed away from the edge turning stiffly, the bones in his neck cracking like dry twigs. The river snaked south across a white landscape dotted with bracken and gorse. *There, that way, somewhere a castle.* Where this knowledge came from, he did not care. All he knew was that he would find help once he reached its walls.

Fighting back bolts of pain, he set out south. As his boots crunched through crusts of icy ground, the castle slowly etched itself in his mind, filling in details with each passing mile – four tall gray turrets, a drawbridge and circular bailey. He trudged on following the winding river through wooded plains and open fields, on throughout the remainder of the day and the long cold night. And how, he puzzled, did he ever escape the ice and find himself on the edge of a soaring cliff?

Dawn broke and with it, thick snow began to fall. The cold seemed somehow harsher now, crueler. Coughing deeply, he forced himself to take each unsteady step, knowing if he stopped to rest, he may never find the strength or will to rise again.

Then, shortly after rays of sunlight glazed the hilltops, he rounded a long, sweeping curve and halted. Before him loomed the castle he had envisioned, its great battlements sheering up against the winter sky.

Teeth chattering, legs like lead, and a rasping cough burning in his chest, he ploughed through the drifts up a narrow pathway to the castle moat.

At the wooden drawbridge, he faltered almost falling, but somehow he found the iron chain strung the length of the bridge and halted, hanging on as another fit of coughing hit him. The snow fell now in heavy, blurring flakes, hampering his vision. He lifted his hand to shield his eyes and in that moment, he knew he would never make it to the sanctuary on the other side.

With the next unsteady step, he fell to his knees and toppled forward, his armor squealing eerily. The world dimmed. But before the darkness claimed him, he saw light flickering through the snow. Someone was coming. *Athlan?*

But that was all.

The scene in the Terran beam vanished as Gawain absorbed the last of the magic and found himself once again standing on the path leading to the Stone. He turned. Although his memory was still fragmented, he could see clearly now. Next to him stood the young woman who was for so long just a ghost. He caught his breath when she looked at him. It was the face of the woman running across the drawbridge!

"Soon now. We're so close," she said, pointing between the towering foliage to the crest of the hill, "See?" But he didn't; his eyes were only for her.

At the top, the Stone blazed. Gawain could feel its vitality pulsing with the rhythm of distant stars.

"Look to your courage, Knight Gawain," Rhiannon said taking him to the far edge. "We're almost there." She let go of his hand and began her descent to the base of the Stone.

Gawain scrambled down behind her, knowing this was the end. That here, where the magic flowed, he would heal and go on to kill Lancelot – find him somewhere in the wastelands and put an end to Morganna's murderous revenge.

The chittering in the moat grew louder when they neared and Gawain watched Rhiannon enter the living swell and wade toward the Stone. Shoveling his feet under the bristling crabs, he followed.

Close to the center, the creatures snapped and waved angry claws – come as they had from the depths of Natal Brack to worship at the Stone, center of efficacy. *Life in the margin of death. A pilgrimage taken each year ... or ... .* He knew-he knew their need for this magic, for the fleeting beauty the light brought to the dark and terrible world of the lake.

When he neared the Terran Stone, every creature in the moat fell silent and the words in his mind then were as much in reverence as to declare his healing whole.

I am Gawain, Knight of the Round Table, Arthur's champion, Merlin's friend. I have survived cruel luck throughout the dogged years of my life. I am the slayer of Argath and Eyenon and of my own true love. I am lost in two faiths, but I believe in the goodness inherent within me.

He stepped up to the monolith, the testimony resounding inside his head. And it came to him then, when he reached out to touch the smooth warm surface, this was not the end.

Dear God!

The Stone exploded and in that instant, all his memories found their rightful places, binding together like the closest weaves of a tapestry.

He rested his arms across his knees and looked down at Rhiannon slumped against the bow seat of the little boat. *Sweet Jesus, I owe you so much.* He glanced over his shoulder – an hour's rowing, maybe more, then the shore. Bending his back to the task, he pulled on the oars. In the distance, the strange attendant crabs were filing into the lake. He concentrated on rowing, knowing instinctively their fury at the Stone's destruction was far from vented.

Half way across the lake, Rhiannon stirred. He pulled in the oars, thankful of the rest and kneeled beside her. He smoothed back her dark hair and spoke softly. But whatever far place she had withdrawn to was beyond his reach. Yet, she was alive. He thanked God for small mercies and took up the oars again.

Once he got her back to the safety of the castle, he could seek Orion and contact Merlin. He'd know what to do. Lord, was it really only days since he was encased in the ice?

His mind turned to Merlin again. What had happened to him since he left?

The snow!

Camelot!

Gawain froze. *Has he managed to end Lancelot's spell? In the name of all the Saints, how long until I reach him? Two or three hours – barring mishap, and that's if it's nighttime when I get back and Orion's up.*

He scanned the twilight for signs of the deadly birds. It seemed far too quiet. He drove the oars back into the lake and began rowing. The only sound came from the rhythmic plop as the blades rose out of the water.

He rowed on. Plop, plop, plop, *scrape!*

He lifted the oar peering at the spot where slow rings pooled. The ripples suddenly widened. A bristly limb broke the surface rising gracefully into the air. The claw at the end opened as wide as a dog's jaws and then snapped shut with bone crunching power. Presentiment swept over Gawain. The motion was the same the other crabs had made on the beach of the Terran Island. He ploughed the oars back into the water and pulled until they bent. At the boat's movement, the claw disappeared into the depths, leaving behind a wake of oily waves.

Almost an hour passed before the shore loomed out of the dimness behind him. No sign of any more creatures; the air was clear, the lake once again calm. Another ten, fifteen minutes, then the small vessel ground up onto the beach. Taking Rhiannon gently in his arms, he stepped onto the bow, balanced on the curved rib for a moment, then jumped.

As he hit the sand, he dropped to his knees. Still cradling Rhiannon, he struggled to his feet. The cliffs were near, no more than a hundred yards away. With his second step up the beach, he heard a splash behind him. He turned.

The water around the boat rippled then churned into froth. A moment later, a crab the size of a battle shield, broke the surface. It reared up and drove its claws into the side of the boat. Splintered chunks of wood flew into the air as the angry pincer chewed and gouged at the planking. Another crab surfaced by its side, fleshy eyes on stalks, pale body rising above the water on eight, no *ten*, spindly legs.

Holding Rhiannon tight to his chest, Gawain ran up the beach, but the sand sucking at his feet, slowed him to a crawl. A dozen paces and the splintering sounds stopped abruptly. He knew without turning the creatures had seen him. His mind churned. The beach spread in a smooth wide crescent to where the cliffs loomed. He stood little chance of covering the distance before they overtook him but there was no other choice. Grunting, legs miring, he slogged desperately through the sand.

CRACK!

He shot a look over his shoulder. What he saw almost caused him to drop Rhiannon. Twenty or more of the shield-sized crabs were struggling out of the water and scrambling up the beach. But that wasn't what riveted him. Standing alone in the lake behind them was a single crab that towered twelve, fifteen feet in height. In one massive, encrusted claw, it held the entire boat. Water cascaded off its carapace and splashed back into Natal Brack as it began shaking the vessel like an angry child shaking a broken toy. Gawain stared in disbelief. The creature curled back its claw and flung the boat bouncing up the beach into the other crabs.

Then it saw him – it looked. Even from where he stood, Gawain could see its saucer eyes focus with a milky vengeance. The creature lifted a giant leg clear of the water and ... Gawain turned. A hundred yards. Further up the beach, the sand might be firmer. If he could make the rocks near the cliff ... .

He ran, feet splaying, sinking to his ankles. He'd barely covered twenty yards when he felt a spray of sand hit the back of his leg.

He dropped to his knee setting Rhiannon on the beach. Drawing his sword, he whirled around. The crab in front of him came up to his waist. When it caught the flash of the blade, it reared back. Hissing like fat on a campfire, it took only a moment to recover, then it came forward, raising its front claws in a challenge, like a boxer ready to fight.

Gawain drew back the sword for the killing stroke but stopped with the blade above his head when he heard a soft chant behind him. Rhiannon spoke the Druid words in a hoarse whisper.

The result was instant. The crab dropped from its battle stance and began snapping randomly at the air.

"Get behind me," she said weakly. "Please, now."

Without taking his eyes off the creature, Gawain lowered the sword.

"I think I can ... Gawain!" she exclaimed as she caught sight of the monster striding out of the lake, water sluicing off its great shell.

He stepped in front of her, sword ready. Once the crab gained the shore, it sped up. It raced across the beach, great gouts of sand spraying from its legs as it thundered toward them.

Rhiannon tugged Gawain back. "Stay still."

She took two unsteady steps in front of him and dug her heel into the sand. She shuffled backwards, scraping a wide circle around where they stood. The monster was less than twenty yards away when she stepped back inside the ring. Pointing to the furrow, she sighted down her arm, tracing its outline and speaking rapidly.

The sand stirred at her commands and began filling the shallow track her heel had left. Within seconds, the channel had smoothed over, leaving only a faint ridge. She closed her eyes and lowering her head, concentrated on the *arrant* ring she had created.

The behemoth stopped barely a yard from the charmed circle. Gawain stared up at the dripping carapace, sword raised.

The milky eyes seemed confused. They swiveled on thick fleshy stalks, looking up and down the beach, turning, sweeping over his head. It couldn't see them, Gawain realized. It was as if it no longer knew what it was doing here. He felt Rhiannon's hand slip into his. She raised a finger to her lips.

They stood perfectly still.

The crab was so close, Gawain could smell the rank odor of its last meal. A long minute passed and it suddenly lifted a bristly leg and took a jerky step forward. Gawain felt the vibration as the claw drove into the sand inches outside the circle.

Rhiannon spoke again. This time the Druid words were barely audible.

The other legs lifted, but in mid stride, they hesitated. The thick joints angled and the ponderous body slewed sideward.

SNAP, SNAP.

Two massive pincers came up in the boxer stance and the shield-sized crabs nearby hurriedly backed away. Gawain glanced at Rhiannon. He was about to whisper for her to get back when the creature suddenly swept out a claw and snatched up one of the retreating crabs.

CRACK.

With nonchalant ease, it scissored the crab in two. Then, opening its cavernous maw, it stuffed one of the wriggling halves into the grinding darkness. Rhiannon shuddered at the shell-splintering sounds as the creature slowly pulverized its meal.

When it had finished, it dropped from the fighting stance and kicked with its back legs. *Phuut! Phuut!* Sand showered in great arcs sending the others cabs scrambling back to the lake. Suddenly looking bored with the whole venture, it turned and made its way down the beach in huge lumbering strides, its body swaying from side to side like an overloaded wagon.

Rhiannon and Gawain watched, protected by the *arrant* circle. The monstrous crab waded out ten, fifteen yards into the lake then finally submerged.

"By the Saints, I've seen some sights, but that." He couldn't tear his eyes from the waves rolling away in slow rings from where the creature had disappeared. Rhiannon's hand slipped from his and she slumped to the sand.

Gawain knelt by her side and lifted her head up. "Rhiannon."

Her face was drawn and her skin seemed somehow thinner. She leaned against his knee and looked up through dull eyes. "I had to use my own life force to fuse the Rune." A frailness had crept into her voice. "I'll recover, a little anyway. At least we're safe."

"You're as brave as any of Arthur's knights," he said brushing her hair back with his fingers.

She held onto his arm and struggled to her feet.

"You need to rest," he said steadying her.

She shook her head. "No. It's not over for them. We've taken away their light. We've condemned them to eternal darkness. Can you imagine what that must be like? No hope, no joy, nothing to live for? We must get out of here now, before the charm wears off."

He took her hand, eyes leaving hers reluctantly and sweeping the surface of the lake. "Can you walk?"

"Yes."

"I can carry you."

"No, I'm all right, honestly."

"We'll rest when we get to the stairs," he said as they left the safety of the *arrant* circle and made for the cliffs.

She led, walking slowly, following the line of cliffs. While they traveled in the twilight shadows of the towering rock face, he told her of his life – of Athlan, Uther, Merlin and the dark knight he was tracking, and she told him of hers, of her village and of Bercilack.

When they reached the stairs cut into the cliff, they rested. She looked back over the sand and the flat brooding lake, her slim hands laced around her shins.

"The wastelands are like this," she said rocking slowly back and forth. "It's full of death. Always has been, for as long as anyone can remember. You'll face more of those things there, perhaps worse."

"If Lancelot gets to the Grail, all is lost, Arthur, you, me, everything we know," said Gawain quietly.

She stopped rocking. Her brown eyes held his and she saw in them the iron strength that had brought him this far. She turned away knowing nothing she could say would stay him.

"I have no choice in this, I ... ," he began as she rose and went to the stairs.

CHAPTER 23

Two hours passed before they reached the cliff top. Only when they walked through the tunnel leading to the castle did they feel safe from the nightmares below. Gawain unclasped the *Tarn* necklace as the gems began to fade and the damp steps swam out of the gloom.

Up then through the glyphed wall and along the dungeon passage. They walked in shadows, the only light coming from a weak afternoon sun filtering between the bars of the overhead grating. Up more worn steps and under a fluted archway where a stone face leered down at them from the masonry, then out into a long hall, dark and cheerless. They walked side-by-side, footsteps hollow in the silence and he thought of Camelot the last time he'd visited – the cold drafty halls, the unlit passages and windows yellowed with tallow smoke.

When they came to the end of the hallway, Rhiannon slid the iron bolt to the side and pulled open a stout door. She stepped back from the threshold of the room she first brought him to when she had rescued him from the blizzard.

"Is there somewhere with a view – a place I can see the stars tonight?" he said glancing up at the high stained glass windows as he entered.

"To contact Merlin?"

"Yes."

She took in his broad shoulders and thick graying hair and she couldn't help thinking of the shattered Terran Stone and what it must be like to have the light taken from your world.

"My chamber has such a view," she said quietly.

A winter cloud drifted overhead and the hall faded to dusk. The floor lengthened with shadows and a deep silence entombed the castle. Gold and silver threads in a tapestry hung on a wall reflected the setting sun as the solitary cloud passed. Her eyes shone with the brown of late autumn. Her small firm breasts rose and fell in a haunting rhythm. Somewhere he could hear ice cracking as the river struggled south.

He turned to go, heart drumming in his ears. "We'll need supplies. If you get the food, I'll track down candles and a taper. Do you have a fire in your room?" he said clearing his throat.

"Yes, but we'll need wood."

"I'll get that too."

She left for the kitchen and he went to gather the provisions, thankful to be alone.

By the time he'd collected what he needed, night had drawn in and light snow tumbled out of the starless sky. He gathered up the armload of wood he'd chopped and joined her. He waited while she closed the lid on a whicker basket stuffed with candles, food and blankets. She straightened, brushing away strands of hair with the back of her hand and they made their way in silence to the steep winding stairs.

At the top, they crossed a wide landing and Rhiannon opened the door to her room. They entered. He dropped the pine logs by the hearth and went to the tall windows. He threw them open and digging his fingers in a drift of snow, leaned over the ledge. The winter fields before him lay white and silent. Stark trees lined the river all the way to the frozen hills. He looked up. The clouds obscuring the sky were not heavy, they'd thin out later then he'd find Orion.

Rhiannon knelt, preparing the fire, dark hair a waterfall over her smooth shoulders, slim arms pale in the wavering candlelight.

"Here." He closed the window and went to her side. "Let me." He snapped a handful of branches and stacked them in the iron holder on the hearth. He watched as she rose and swept the damp wood chips and moss from her dress.

"Why have you stayed on so long?"

She shrugged. "I've thought about leaving many times but my home's a long way off, south of the Cotswolds. For a woman by herself, it's a dangerous journey. Besides, it's been almost five years." She opened the basket and took out a loaf of bread, a flat knife and a small pot of butter. "It's a long time, I don't know what I'd find if I went back now."

"And if you stay?"

"I'll manage."

Her brown eyes swam with candlelight. He wanted to say more, to say this was no place for beauty to fade but he fell silent following the tight circle of her waist and the falling curves of her hips as she walked to the table.

Later, they sat in front of a cheerful fire, chairs facing across the table, thick woolen blankets pulled tight around their shoulders. Enormous shadows leaped up the walls while they tucked into the slices of cheese and drank the honeyed wine she had prepared. The logs crackled and snapped and the flames thawing the ice in the wood began to warm the room. Outside, the snow eased and the clouds thinned into ragged skeins.

"Can he really control the weather?" she asked, thinking about what he'd told her when they left the lake.

"The snow, maybe rain – anything to do with water, Merlin says."

"Ah, always Merlin," she said breaking the bread.

"Yes."

She held out the end of the loaf and he took it, his hand touching hers.

"After, if you survive the wastelands and kill your enemy, you'll return to Camelot?" she said, her eyes holding his.

He nodded, words suddenly gone, throat thick. Behind him, his sword leaned against the hearth. Beside it stood his battered boots, one toppled against the other. His chain mail lay draped over a chest, the crest of Arthur's golden lions torn and faded. Rhiannon took it all in with a glance and her Druid senses told her how hopelessly lost he was. Her heart ached for him. The years would come and go and she would live on here alone, trying to hold things together, using her magic to keep the castle from falling into ruin and her own loneliness at bay. Tomorrow he would leave and her world would draw in with its wintry days and long nights, its icy lakes and streams and endless northern winds.

Light in all their terrible darkness. The words seemed to fill her mind.

She rose, and letting the blanket drop from her shoulders, walked to the bed. She slipped out of her long dress and pulling back the quilt, slid between the sheets. Gawain stood rooted to the spot, heart thundering.

"Will you stand there all night waiting for your stars, Gawain of the Round Table?"

He had not expected this, thinking instead to sleep on a pallet or couch. He dropped the bread on the trencher and crossed awkwardly to the bed.

"I ... "

"Hush, knight." She reached up and took his hand. She ran a finger over his scarred knuckles and across the webbing of his thumb and gazed into his wide grey eyes. "When I was a curious little girl, my grandmother once told me there was too much pain in this world. But every now and then, when the old gods of the Sidhe were plotting and planning their wars, happiness would sneak by and touch us."

She brought his hand to her cheek and he knelt by the bedside letting her guide his palm to her neck and then down over the smooth curve of her shoulder.

"Here," she whispered moving back, "while they're busy with their schemes."

Her body was pale and perfect, skin a smoothness incredible to touch. He pulled her to him, aching with need. *Once Percival said finding the right woman was impossible because the now was never enough for them. But it is, here, high in the keep of this forlorn castle.*

All the sadness going, melting away with her sighs and scent of lilac perfuming her throat. *Above the moon, your laugher forever in the stars. I never stopped loving you, Athlan, not ever, not even now.*

Let go. Surrender the shame. Leave only the mortal sin, which damns me. Dear God, I'm so sorry.

Let go!

He felt her small breasts pushing against him. Wanting to stay there forever – keep at bay the shadows of murder and the iron stare of death. Wondering why he was ever chosen to travel this bleak land to slay monsters and quest for the Grail. *When God and Druid fight for a place in this bewildering world, which one first?* Questions that never cease.

So much warmth after so much cold. Away from the place where demons lie. Her mouth finding him in the gold of the firelight. Crushing kisses full of empty years.

He pushed against her, then in her, taken by forces far more ancient than Merlin had ever dreamed. Halls below bereft of life where only haunting winds now cry. Dungeons with their secrets. Dark, dark water, cold and drear. And here, with a soul shining its beacon light, Gawain closed his eyes and felt her heart beat with his, felt the moisture in her short gasps and the gentle trembling as she buried her fingers in his hair.

Afterwards, they lay together, her long hair splayed across his chest. In front of them, stars powdered the open window.

"I can feel the strength in you when you look at them," she said, her voice thick and dreamy in the snowy stillness.

He leaned on his elbow and traced the curve of her cheek with his fingers. "Somehow they protect me. I don't know how," he said.

"It's the Druid in you, the grounding, a place you can feel the power of the elements. For me it's the earth, when I walk in a field or sit beneath a growing tree. It's only my training that allows me to channel the energy. That's the difference, that's all. You feel the same strength out there, in your Orion. You just don't know how to use it." She kissed his knuckles then opened his hand and pressed his calloused palm to her cheek.

"You can teach me," he said.

"I can help, yes. But Merlin would be a better teacher. My training is limited."

A smile touched his lips. "But learning from you would be a lot more interesting, my lady."

She grinned dropping his hand and searched under the quilt. "The teaching could take a long time, knight. It's truly complex, you know."

She led him deep into her world again under myriad stars, far from loam and smashing teeth. Far from leering gargoyles perched atop bedposts and the ... *Let go.*

She felt his sudden pain and her Druid senses flared but she held back her powers. *No Runes. No magic. Not now. Just this.* She rose to meet him, taking over, her hips thrusting to give more pleasure, her lips kissing away the tears tracing thin lines down his cheeks. "I'm here, I'm with you," she breathed. Her fingers ploughed through his hair, pulling him down to her breast, anything to stop the hurting. He kissed her gently, staying her panic. And moments later, with the salt of his sadness still on her lips, she felt him stiffen, but she didn't know if it was his need she felt or her own quaking fear.

Later, in the ember light of the fire, he looked at her sleeping, finding there a rare peace and in his heart he swore to come back after he'd killed Uther's last son and returned the Grail to Arthur. Because, of all the power in all the elements, what he'd found in the quiet of this castle had finally chased away the horror of the long ago murder and freed him from its grip. Closing his eyes, he laid his head back on the downy pillow and fell into a deep and dreamless sleep.

He awoke to Rhiannon's gentle shaking and the full glory of Orion.

"Your stars," she whispered nestling into the hollow of his shoulder.

"Yes."

They stared out of the window at the blazing heavens and she kissed his neck as he searched the vast constellation. "I want to be a part of your power," she said, but he didn't hear because he had already found his star.

Merlin was waiting.

The tired face, scored with riverbed lines, shimmered into view. The lips that always seemed pursed in thought broke into a wide smile sweeping the years from him.

"You do not die easily, my boy." His words were as clear as the stars pulsing around him.

"What's happened at Camelot, Merlin?"

In the distance, Gawain saw high peaks and a flatness that could be the sea. He was camped out somewhere in the Welsh hills.

"I've dispelled Lancelot's cursed ambient Rune. The snow has stopped falling, that much I've been able to do." He paused. "I don't know how many deaths there have been. Perhaps as much as half the city is gone, mostly the old and infirm, I suspect," he added sadly, "Arthur is alive but I can't tell if Guinevere's been so lucky."

"And Bors, Percival?"

"Also alive, as far as I can see. By now they must be half way to the *Isolate* tower."

"And Lancelot?"

"In the wastelands. I'm afraid no matter what I do, my magic won't penetrate that place," he said, shaking his head ruefully. "But what of you, my boy? Tell me. After I channeled all the power I could, I lost contact. The last thing I remember was trying to get you to Bercilack's castle. There's a Terran Stone hidden there. I thought its power might help you."

"You were right. Somehow, I made it. Whatever you did got me to the river. From there I just went south. It seemed the natural thing."

"Indeed it was, my boy," Merlin said folding his hands over his Rune staff and nodding wisely. "Now, tell me of the castle. What happened there?"

Gawain told him of Rhiannon: how she'd found him at death's door and journeyed with him to the Terran island, how he'd lost his memory and had to battle the crabs and how he got here, where he lay waiting with her for news of the last dark knight.

Merlin listened intently, stopping him only to ask questions about Rhiannon's abilities, especially how she made the *arrant* circle and the sacrifice she'd made in saving him from the giant crab. And when he'd finished his tale, the wizard instructed him to give her the Dragon Ring.

The stars swam back, their brilliance blinding him. He felt for the ring, and tugging it off his finger, offered it to Rhiannon.

"What's this?" she said brushing away the thick curls tumbling into her eyes.

"Merlin's Dragon Ring," he said. "He asked me to give it to you."

"I don't need it, Gawain – just you. Here, hold my hand, find your star."

He did and he traveled through Orion's power with greater ease than ever before.

Merlin was stooped over tending to his fire; behind him, the hoarfrost whitened the fields. The small coppice of larch trees sheltering him stood out in harsh relief against the mountains.

Gawain turned to see Rhiannon enter the firelight. She looked as regal and graceful as Guinevere ever had.

Merlin took up his staff and went to her. "You've done well, child."

She bent to one knee, bowing deeply.

Merlin held out his hand to her and she rose. Gawain went to step forward – but found he couldn't move. He tried to speak but no words came and he realized this time he was there only as a medium. All he could do was observe.

"ᚷᚪᚹᛅᛋᛏ."

"ᛗᚪᚱᚱ."

"ᛋᛁᛚᛏᚠ."

"ᛞᚪᚱᛗᛗᚪᚠᛋ."

The archaic words they spoke sounded different to him. The melodic chords lacked the power and intensity they had when casting spells, now they took on the inflection of questions and statements.

The two continued the singsong conversation, Merlin stopping every now and then to touch her shoulders, sometimes patting her, other times shaking his head ruefully.

An early dawn light rose behind the mountains and still they talked, the Runic words taking on the beauty of some long lost ballad. Gawain listened, half feeling the emotions, half sensing their strange power. After a while, the rhythm lulled him into drowsiness and pictures formed and swam nonsensically in his mind. How much time passed then, he had no idea. He was no longer of their world, of any world.

Finally, they fell silent. They stood looking at each other, the bond between them strengthened by the Runic intimacy. She turned away from his blazing eyes and bowed again, but he lifted her chin. Then he pulled her to him and held her like a father as she leaned into him. He kissed her brow and returned to his place by the campfire. She smiled, watching him reach out to the bright flames. And as she did, the last few stars swam back in a dawn-pale sky.

Then she was next to Gawain in the warm bed. He was sleeping soundly. She sat up and looked at him wondering what she'd ever done to deserve such a rare gift. All those years with Bercilack, all the shame and guilt. Never this, never touches that fired her skin or words rich and thick with passion.

She rested her chin on her knees and gazed down at him wondering how her world could seem so right, so alive in the short time he had come into her life. "Gawain?" she breathed, tasting the poetry of his name. "What's happening to me? This is my twenty forth year and for the first ... "

He stirred, opening his eyes. The breath caught in his throat. Rhiannon looked the same as the first day he'd seen her when she'd rescued him on the bridge – somehow Merlin had given her back the vitality she'd used in charming the crab from the depths of Natal Brack.

"Rhiannon, Merlin has ... "

She touched his lips. "Hush, my knight, I know," she said. Then she kissed him, tracing her fingers from his cheek to his neck, thrilling in the strength she found there.

He took her hand and gently pulled it down to her lap. "Everything will be lost if I don't stop Lancelot," he said.

She drew back slowly. "You won't return."

"I will, but I have no choice in this."

"The wasteland is nothing but death. You don't know what's out there. It's all like Natal Brack. It will claim you like everything else," she said turning away from the world swimming before her.

He cupped her shoulders and turned her to him. "Look at me, Rhiannon." He ran his hands down her arms to her wrists and held them tight. "When this is over, I'll return. Nothing will stop me. Nothing. I will take you with me back to Caerleon. You'll meet Arthur and Guinevere and they will be amazed at your bravery and beauty. There will be no more unshared moments."

Silence.

The wind stirred, thrumming against the iron hinges of the window. With dawn breaking in the east, harsh mountains speared the sky, jagged peaks like broken glass.

Her brimming eyes searched him. "This you promise?"

"Yes, this I promise."

She twined her fingers through his and her Druid senses told her he'd spoken from his heart.

Rubbing tiny circles on the backs of his hands with her thumbs, she said, "Can you track him?"

"I think so."

"I'll help you."

"No, it's too dangerous. Besides, Merlin said there is no essence in the wastelands. Magic won't work there."

"True." She reached for the white quilt, breasts catching the sun as she pulled it around her shoulders. "But I have a way around that."

"And just what way would that be?"

"The *Isolate* tower, the one you were in. Merlin told me if it allowed me to enter then I might be able to help because of our bond, and I know I can," she said.

"How?"

"Because of something I never told Merlin. When I was little, my mother used to tell me stories about the Far Druids – what she knew of them, anyway. She said they came from across the Irish seas and set the Terran Stones in our country many centuries ago. Then they selected a few of us and taught us how to use the Runes. Do you know they were the ones who built Stone Henge? All those Stones are old Terran Stones. I went there once during the solstice with my parents. They told me over time the Stones would absorb enough elemental power they could be used again." She stopped, breaking into a smile. "One day I'll take you there, my knight, and fill you full of their power, as you've filled me with yours."

She leaned forward cupping his face in her hands. "What Merlin doesn't know, is that I'm a descendent of those Far Druids. Perhaps from a night of wild lovemaking high in an old castle," she added slyly.

"I'm the one who is supposed to rescue damsels in distress, not the other way around."

"Ummmm, and when you staggered half dead over my drawbridge, what did this damsel do?"

He considered for a moment. "Used her Druid charms and stole my heart."

"Ah, so you admit it's mine?"

"Truly."

"And your love?"

"Lost."

"Where?"

"Perhaps I should look." He ducked under the covers, pushing her back.

"My own questing knight," she giggled into the soft pillow.

They spent the remainder of the day preparing to travel, Rhiannon rounding up the horses and drying meat for the journey while he secured the castle and procured help from a neighboring crofter to feed the animals.

They ate their last meal in a room lit with all the candles Gawain could find. Across from a great oak table, Fennris and Brighid slept curled up near the hearth, legs twitching. Rhiannon wore a splendid Druid gown hemmed with braided Runes.

Hands touching and laughter. Her hair wild tangles when he brushed it back and kissed the curve of her neck. The *Isolate* tower and the death beyond too far away to spoil the purer magic growing between them.

Later in bed, the hours scented with her as Gawain made love with a passion he never knew he had. And when the stars came up, they lay in each others arms telling childhood stories: Gawain the boy who fought a fevered boar that charged his friend and Rhiannon the little girl who got lost for a whole day in jostling market crowds.

When the candles burned down, they made love again, this time slowly, chasing away fears of the encroaching dawn.

They left under a weak sun and rode in silence along the same embankment Gawain had walked after he escaped from the ice. Where the river snaked east to the woodlands, they cut north across a range of wintry fields. Then, in the late afternoon, they made the climb up to the high plateau now thick with snow. From the top, they caught their first glimpse of the tower standing gray and solitary in the distance.

They descended and rode over snowy fens dotted with sedge and wild grass. Even though the going was easier, they didn't make the tower until dusk.

Neither of them wanted to walk up the final slope to the small wooden door. Instead, they set to building a fire under the stars where they were free of the tower's powerful magic.

The next day they awoke to white skies and the promise of more snow. After a breakfast of maize cakes and pullet strips cooked over an open fire, they broke camp in silence. When all was cleared away and packed, they stood shivering in the cold trying to brave the goodbye. There were no words. Gawain took her in his arms and Rhiannon buried herself deep in the hard mail shirt, not feeling the rings biting into her cheek. And behind them, the implacable stones of the tower went on forever into white skies.

The wind gusted, keeing through the gorse, and they pulled away from each other with a lingering touch of fingers. She went to the door without looking back, tears blurring her way. He waited until she entered the yawning chamber then swung up on his horse and wheeled around toward the wastelands. The last words he'd whispered to her rang in his mind as he rode over the hard ground: '*You are the measure of all things true and beautiful. I will return, and when I do, we will take the Grail to Camelot together.*'

He had traveled little more than a mile when his horse began to show the first signs of nervousness. Passing by bare trees whose scratching branches seem to reach for them, it shied and Gawain patted and stroked its long damp neck. A little further, past a clump of blackened heather, it almost threw him after catching its reflection in a deep still pool.

Finally, Gawain dismounted and unloaded his supplies. He looked into the animal's wide eyes, slipped off its bridle and turned it loose. Watching it bolt back toward the tower, he hoisted his pack on his back, adjusted the leather straps and struck out on foot.

He hadn't walked more than a hundred yards when he crested a ridge overlooking a valley filled with low mist covering what should have been snow-bound fields. Instead, from where he stood, he could see only a broken, blackened earth, crisscrossed by vast trunks long reduced to rotting logs.

It was the same as he'd dreamed earlier, but this time he did not fly over the land with ease: he set off walking, each heavy step taking him further away from the tower and Rhiannon.

The fog swirled about him as he descended, and the dead earth beneath his feet caved and crumbled. He journeyed on, desolation turning into a deep sense of foreboding when he entered the valley – death and always the mist, swirling, dripping, disorientating.

After a while, he stopped and peered into the gloom, seeking any familiar landmark. But there was nothing. *Where are the footprints of my dream?* All was a great flat wilderness that seemed to stretch out forever. If he could somehow locate the dead lake and journey directly ahead from there, he would come across the still river where he'd seen the strange white fish. Then he would be able to find the basin ringed by ghastly hills – the place where *Corbenic* lay.

While Gawain struggled on, fighting the growing sense of hopelessness and despair, Rhiannon climbed the last of the giant steps in the tower. She looked around in awe as she entered the Far Druid chamber. When she crossed the room, the glyphs above the arches began to glow. Recognizing the danger, she spoke softly in the Druid tongue and they dulled, like bees swept with smoke.

Despite her weariness, she didn't stop to rest but went to the northern window overlooking the wastelands.

Leaning over the stony ledge, she forced herself to look down.

The mists below were patchy from this height but she could see, as Gawain had, the vast destruction spread like a festering wound across the land. An ineffable sadness touched her at the sight and she backed away from the casement, frightened the death beyond would somehow lay claim to him as it had to every other living soul within its borders.

And miles distant, Gawain trudged on, crossing the humps of blackened earth, feeling the very strength within him bleed away. But he held fast, thinking of Rhiannon the night Orion had taken them to Merlin, how they had lain in each other's arms after making love, and how, in the snowy stillness, she'd told him what she knew of this terrible land.

"Although our myths tell of a great blight sweeping across the north after the Far Druids disappeared, the Christians have their own tales. The old priest from Ormscliff said the Dark One was responsible," she had told him, her eyes still liquid with passion. "He said he escaped from hell and when he strode the land, lightening streaks flew from his heels, scorching and poisoning everything they touched. When the Christian God learned of this, He became full of anger and bound the terrible creature in great chains then cast him back into the depths of hell. Later, He summoned a man called Joseph who arrived with a Holy Vessel to seal the breach. When God and this Joseph departed, they left the land as it was, burned and dying. The priest said God would not allow it to be healed, he wanted everyone to see the mark of evil."

She had told the tale in a hushed voice. Gawain smiled, taking heart amidst the boundless ruin as he recalled her words. How impossibly wide her eyes had grown when he began his story about the Grail's appearance at Camelot. And later, when he told her of Morganna and the pact, she had grasped him, squeezing his arm, the pieces of the puzzle falling into place so easily for her. "You know what this means," she said, blanching. "He's coming."

He hardly had time to ask what she meant when she hurried on. "Lancelot. Remember, in your dream – sparks flying from his heels, just like the Dark One! It's beginning. He's come to free his father. Sweet Bran, Morganna never got the Rune casting wrong as Merlin thought. The four sons were needed to ensure success. They were *supposed* to be a combined force – the acumen, the four elements. Individually, they had weaknesses: Argath was too much like a serpent, killed too easily by light, Eyenon was too much like a child and killed too easily by trickery, together though, they would have been unstoppable. When the Christian God sent Arthur the message – I believe it was to warn him of the danger. He knew. Don't you see, Gawain? Bring the Grail to Camelot and restore the faith, restore order. If Lancelot destroys it, he succeeds on two fronts: chaos reigns in Camelot and with the seal broken, his father is free to sweep through our land and take Caerleon."

She was out of breath when she finished. Then the color had drained from her face. "Now Lancelot's in the wasteland, he may be getting stronger, growing more powerful, the same way Eyenon's dreams were getting more powerful. You must be careful, my knight."

She had shivered then and he'd put his arms around her. "I think it's all this that's affecting our Runes, making them so difficult to hold," she'd whispered into his chest. "Maybe the Grail is tied into our magic – when the talisman was safe our abilities were steady, now it's in danger, the Runes falter." Then came her final words, each one with him now as they had been when she uttered them, wide eyes unblinking, fingers pressing white puddles into his flesh. "Two faiths,

Gawain, bound together – Christian and Druid. You're the key. You're meant to find the answer to all this."

He sighed. Her intelligence had shone for him that night as brightly as her remarkable beauty.

Fists clenched, he forged on, memories of her untouched by the blighted land, his energy sloughing away. Wanting so badly to stop, to see her face, see her smile, hear her laugh ... .

High in the tower she sought him. She used her Druid senses, but no matter what she did, her magic refused to work. It was as if it, too, had become a part of all the appalling death.

Lancelot spat, sending thick phlegm horse tailing though the air. He scanned the flawless wall in search of an opening, a breach of any kind that would get him into the cursed castle. He blinked. His eyes, once piercing blue chips that could spot a rabbit at twice the length of a jousting run, could now barely make out the battlements rising from the inner courtyard. He shook his head. The damn place seemed to be eating away at his mind as well as his magic. How in the name of all the sluts he was going to take when this was over, could he get the Grail? He ground his heel into the dead earth and spat again, this time sending the phlegm splatting against the wall. Oh, would he get even when he got back to Camelot, would he have some *fun* then.

"God-rotted Christ Cup," he grunted, his voice sounding muffled, as though he were speaking through the grill of a visor. He scowled at the hills and the late afternoon sun and cursed again.

If Gawain could have seen him then, he would not have recognized him. He had a different look since he had entered the wastelands – his *father's* look. His face had flattened, his lips thinning into fleshless lines that framed a mouth bearing rows of sharp teeth. His nose had also changed, collapsing into hollow nostrils and his eyes, which had grown larger, now shone flat and silvery white.

The creature called Lancelot felt its way along the wall again, more carefully this time, tracing a path back to the locked gates. With any God-rotting luck, maybe, just maybe, he could find a way into the damn castle.

The same night the Lancelot creature prowled the walls, Gawain unpacked his supplies, ate some of the dried mutton he'd prepared earlier, and bedded down. He lay on the blackened earth and pulled up the blanket Rhiannon had given him. He smelled the faint scent of her and curled up bunching it under his cheek. Closing his eyes to all the death around him, he fell into a dark and dreamless sleep.

Far away in the chill of the *Isolate* tower, Rhiannon slept by the window overlooking the wastelands. Above her, the glyph glowed a gentle white and when she began to dream, it changed to the silver of distant stars. Within minutes, the Runes above the other windows shaped themselves writing in the stone, their essence centered upon the sleeping figure.

Out of the darkness, she saw Gawain's earlier footprints – little green splashes blazing a trail to *Corbenic*. She swept the land and found him more than a mile north of the trail, huddled asleep under a blanket. He was lost. If he kept going in that direction he would surely die, for even in her dream she could not see the end of the wastelands.

She touched the Dragon Ring and sent a vision to him – *footprints*. The Runes above the windows flared in unison and their ancient magic cut through the wasteland with ridiculous ease.

By the time dawn broke, the thing called Lancelot had tracked the entire outer wall and it was seething. Other than the locked portcullis, there was no door, no postern, not so much as a lookout. It was enough to make the creature howl, and it did. Throwing its head back and opening swollen jaws wide, it wailed in frustration.

Gawain woke with a start and sat up. A chill ran through him and he looked west to where a ring of desolate hills lay shrouded in fog. *What was that?* He knelt and packed up his bedroll. When he was done, he threw it over his shoulder and headed back down to the valley toward the hills and the strange cry that had awoken him.

A mile south of where he'd camped, he entered a petrified forest. A small path cut westward between the blasted trees. And although he didn't know it, his feet now fell with pinpoint precision into each dream footprint.

He walked the better part of the morning under hazy skies. By the early afternoon, a light rain had begun to fall and the blackened ground turned into a thick paste that sucked at his feet as he struggled up the rise to where the Lancelot thing had first seen *Corbenic*.

Below, in the wide circular basin ringed by the brooding hills, stood the castle. Even in the rain, it shone with unearthly majesty. Gawain drank in its beauty – its stately towers, battlements, flags and the sweeping wall. He started. The tower dream flashed into his mind. Near the white wall a figure lurked – a shadowy outline, hunched, pacing back and forth – Lancelot? He peered into the distance, but he knew the answer.

No magic.

Face to face.

He raced down the hill.

CHAPTER 24

The Lancelot thing punched the wall sending part of its hand flying off like bark from an old branch, but it didn't seem to notice. Underneath, where the finger had once been, a half-moon claw glistened wetly, pressing out of the skin like a spring bud.

"Nazarene," it screamed in a strangled voice. "'astard, 'astard." It kicked at the implacable wall. This time nothing broke off, but a pinprick of pain shot through its foot as another new claw jabbed out of the blackened stump that was once its toe.

To the left a grating sound suddenly shattered the silence. The Lancelot thing spun around, its flat silvery eyes narrowing as the portcullis began to rise. When it cranked over the halfway point, the creature peered at the entrance suspiciously then loped forward.

The white path beyond the gate lay deserted. The Lancelot thing grunted. The path arrowed between rows of lush green hedges, ran through an archway, and disappeared in the gardens of the main castle. There was no sign of anyone in the courtyard: no people, no animals, no sounds, not so much as a bird chirp. The stooping creature stepped onto the path. Shielding its large eyes from the glare coming off the walls, it cast a furtive glance behind. It spat again, this time sending the black bile peppering over the crushed white rocks.

" 'rail," it grunted, "I 'ome." It scampered toward the castle, the clawed feet poking out of its boots churning up rocks and tiny stones.

Gawain caught a flash of light as the portcullis opened, and he raced down the hill. It took only moments for him to reach the entrance. Guessing Lancelot was already inside, he sprinted down the white path. He had no time to marvel at the hedges with their carved rows of saints and angels, or to wonder how the lush green grass of the geometric lawns lay so flat and even. He flew headlong through the arch to where a flight of steps swept up to open doors. Panting heavily, he bounded through the portico and into the silent castle.

He found himself in a lavishly furnished banquet hall. Braziers set high on each wall burned brightly. But most of the light came from tall white candles placed on the tables. There were no shadows, no dark areas. From where he stood, he could see a long, elegant balcony overlooking the brightly lit hall. He stepped forward, still breathing deeply, feeling exposed. He sidestepped between rows of benches. Golden platters and goblets glinted in the candlelight as he stole to the far end of the room where two wide staircases swept up to the balcony.

He stopped at the foot of the left staircase, scanning the silent tables. Nothing. He kept his back to the wall and took the steps two at a time. At the top, he cast a last quick look below and headed to the end of the balcony. Tall candles burned in chandeliers lighting the passage beyond. He took a deep breath and ran, wondering as he passed beneath them, why they all burned at the same height and why none had any wax dripping or gathering on their bone white sides.

At the far end of the passage, an open door led to a narrow chamber. He ducked inside to a room lined with old tapestries depicting biblical scenes. There were no candles here, only a single burning oil lamp bracketed on the north wall.

One more door lay recessed in an archway across the room. When he saw it, he felt the hairs on his neck rise. He moved forward warily. From the corner of his eye, he saw a marble statue of a mother cradling a child. Behind it, glass and gilt embossed frames encased magnificent paintings – a king's treasure. He ignored them, focusing instead on a small dark canvas nailed to the back of the door. Above it were written the words *Atre Perilleus*. As he neared, he saw what it was – the crucifixion, Christ at Golgotha. Black bile dripped from Jesus' face and ran down his pale body in thick liquid strings.

"Lancelot," he breathed.

He inched open the door and slipped into the next room. A small aisle led to a nave flanked on either side by rows of polished wooden pews. He'd entered a chapel. He looked up. Transepts and arches blazed with the same tall candles he'd seen in the hall below, but here they flickered, here wax ran in thin lines down their leathery sides.

Shadows played on walls as he slid between rows of pews. Then he saw it. On a simple pedestal in the center of the nave sat a small chalice – a white cup reflecting pinpoints of candlelight with dazzling clarity.

"'wain, shit."

Gawain spun around. The Lancelot thing lumbered out from behind a buttress. Gawain froze. The creature bulged impossibly in what was left of its knight's armor. Tiny iridescent scales plated its arms, flashing like oil on water as it moved. Its chest had swollen to the size of a rain barrel, but the face ... . Gawain sucked in his breath at the sight of those flat silvery eyes.

The thing called Lancelot advanced jabbing the air with a clawed finger. "Ooou die."

"What in God's ... ?"

But before Gawain could finish, the Lancelot thing sprang, moving with blinding speed. Glistening claws raked Gawain's throat, opening four razor thin lines as he reared back. The creature thrust its head forward and spat. Bile sprayed between pointed teeth. Gawain staggered, black phlegm bubbling on his skin.

Trying to blink away the caustic saliva, he groped for his sword. But before his hand found the hilt, the Lancelot thing was on him again, claws out like scythes.

"'wain shit die. 'rail shit die." The mouth distended grotesquely as the creature struggled to rasp the words, giving Gawain a precious few seconds.

He twisted away ripping the sword from its scabbard. Another blast of bile hit him drenching his neck and cheek. He brought one hand up to shield his eyes and swung the sword blindly with the other. Whether it was luck, chance, or some greater guidance, he didn't know, but he felt the blade shudder in his hand as it sliced through the creature's shoulder, carving away flesh and bone in a hail of dark, sizzling blood.

The thing called Lancelot howled. It threw back its head and rent the air with a cry that shook chunks of plaster from chapel transepts. Then it spun around, flat silver eyes strangely placid, showing no trace of anger, but the claws lengthening, shredding the skin away like worn cheesecloth.

Gawain retreated, wiping the bile from his face with the back of his hand. The Lancelot thing came after him, mouth yawning, teeth gleaming. Gawain stumbled backwards, desperately seeking room to swing again. But in his efforts, he tripped over the foot of a pew and fell sprawling into the aisle. The sword clattered to the ground skidding out of reach.

"Oooo die." The words were barely human now. Above him, threads of saliva glistened as they ran over the creature's thin lip. The metamorphosing horror had shed most of its hair. Two scarlet welts pooled on his forehead and Gawain could have sworn in that moment horns were about to rip their way through the waxy scalp. But that's all he saw, because when the thing opened its jaws to tear his throat out, a light of such blinding intensity suffused the room that the whole world turned white, leaving them both stunned in its wake.

The Grail shone.

The Grail radiated.

The Grail *was* light.

Silence.

Stillness.

In the impossible brightness, Gawain saw a ghost moving – a faint figure gliding out of the shimmering distance with airy grace. When it neared, he could make out a cloak billowing, then hair ruffling, as if a wind were blowing through an open window somewhere. His heart almost exploded when he recognized who it was – Rhiannon!

She floated passed him and then angled away, gliding backwards. She opened her arms wide as she moved and objects appeared magically around her – pews, kneeling pads, the embroidered carpet leading to the nave – all materialized out of the ghostly white, like ships looming out of a fog bank. Then she stopped and looked down. At her feet lay his sword – not a flickering image like the other objects, but a silver blade shining brightly even above the haze of white that was his world.

He knew what to do. He went to it. The ghost glided further back, behind the Lancelot thing then turned away. The bewildered creature in front of her blundered in circles, trying to cover its lidless eyes in an attempt to shut out the dazzling Grail light.

Gawain closed in easily avoiding the clawing hands. He drew back the sword in a silent arc and swung. The blade thrummed through the air. Then it sliced through the creature's neck just below the jaw and sent the head spinning from the sloping shoulders. In that instant, the Grail light died and Gawain's true sight returned.

He saw the thing in front of him stagger back drunkenly, a fountain of dark blood erupting from the gaping neck. He sidestepped watching the creature stumble passed him, arms out searching. Two, three, more lurching steps and it blundered across the aisle into a row of pews. Canticle parchments fluttered to the floor as the benches tumbled back. The blood eased to pulsing gouts and flowed down the front and back of its body like dark treacle. The slender nave candles hissed then flickered and the chapel dimmed. Finally, the Lancelot thing slumped onto a nearby pew as if it were thankful it had at last found a place to pray.

Gawain stood still in the ringing silence, sword in hand, the last death in this chronicle over. No more ghosts. No more monsters to chase through unremitting lands, just the Grail, the unassuming cup sitting atop the pedestal in the nave. *And how could such an innocent looking relic contain such monumental power?* he wondered.

He stepped around the body of the Lancelot thing and leaning his sword against one of the fluted columns, made his way up the aisle to where the Cup sat on a small square of royal blue linen. With each step, the burning from the bile on his face and neck lessened and the blistering slowed.

He halted before the Nave. The Cup was plain. It contained no mystical essence, no sign of the intricate design he had seen at Camelot. It was at best a simple, white chalice. Feeling the last vestiges of pain subside, he cradled his hands and took it, and as he did, the burning vanished and his skin healed.

He carefully tucked the Cup under his torn mail shirt and retrieved his blackened sword. Blood from the body of the Lancelot thing was oozing into the aisle and he stepped around the smoldering tendrils.

He left the death and the silence and went out through the room full of art and down the passageway to the balcony. Only when he stepped onto its broad flagstones did he stop and turn. All the candles had gone out, leaving behind a well of darkness.

He ran down the sweeping staircase and into the banquet room. Making his way between the tables, his footsteps sent hollow echoes whispering up to the rafters. Out then into the God-given air, not caring if the candles behind him ever burned again because Rhiannon was waiting and nothing in this castle or this forsaken land would keep him from finding her and this time staying forever.

When he walked through the gardens, he could smell the rich aroma of new grass. Above him, thick white clouds sailed to new horizons and from a patch of blue sky, a golden sun flooded the dying world with rare warmth.

At the portcullis, he heard a far off cry and shading his eyes, he scanned the heavens. A solitary falcon swept by then circled the turrets. After a curious moment, it gracefully swooped down to the battlements and flew away to the south. *So where to now, daring bird – master or mate?*

But he knew the answer. He turned to the hills, his heart light, his steps strong.

YESTERDAY'S FALCON

EPILOGUE

The journey back to the *Isolate* tower was like the long ago journey of his dream. His feet flew with a lightness that devoured the endless miles. And never in all that blackened, dying world did he lose his way, or fear he would be unable to find the tower and Rhiannon. He crossed the broken earth, marveling at his power, not knowing if it came from the Grail he carried, or the love filling his heart.

He strode on, even when the sun set in a cloudless sky and darkness fell, he never tired, never faltered. Only once, when the canopy of stars filled the heavens, did he look up and see Orion, but even then, he never slowed his relentless pace.

When dawn broke the next day and the sun gleamed off the blackened land, he pounded his way through rotting valleys and flat still rivers, boots full of reeking mud. And always his gray eyes remained fixed high on the distant horizon. Then finally, in the warmth of the late afternoon, he climbed a hill and saw the distant turret of the *Isolate* tower and below a glen etched with patches of green.

Home.

His heart sang as he covered the final miles. He crossed a series of rills furrowed deep in the earth and made his way up a knoll bristling with blackened, twisted brier. At the top, a fresh wind blew and in the distance, green trees fringed a snowy vale. Then he saw her waiting on the slopes where he'd freed his horse.

She wore a long woolen cape that shone white in the late sunlight. He called and when she saw him, she ran calling back, almost stumbling in her need to get to him.

Her eyes, her tears, her hair, the scent of her, a river of passion when he swept her up in his arms.

"The Grail ... I have it," he breathed between her crushing kisses. And when she finally broke away from him, he held it in his fist for her to see, but she couldn't because all she could see though her tears were his gray eyes and the iron strength in his soul.

They walked to where she had tethered the horses, her head on his shoulder, her hands locked around his arm. They mounted and rode across the white fields to the castle. On the way, she told him about the tower and her visions and he told her of the battle with Lancelot. Miles of her. A journey to end and start. Laughter and love in a winter world.

"Tonight," he said when they came to the snaking river, "we find Merlin."

She reined her horse and turned to him, eyes twinkling. "In my bed?"

He chuckled, surprised at the rare sound. "In your bed."

And that night, after the lovemaking, they opened the window on the stars and traveled together.

They found Merlin in Arthur's castle, alone in his room amidst his books and scrolls, reading under the light of two smoking candles.

He looked up as Rhiannon went to him and fell on one knee.

"No." He wrestled himself out of his chair waving a trembling hand. "Stand, my child." When she rose, he shuffled over to her and whispered in her ear. She turned to Gawain, eyes running with starlight and spoke a single Druid word. He found he was no longer just the medium of travel – now he could move, participate. He walked forward and Merlin beamed.

"My falcon," he said, voice thick with emotion, arms out wide. "You've done all I've asked, all I've ever asked of you. Now it's time for rest, for peace in your life – lives," he added, glancing at Rhiannon from under white eyebrows. "Set out for Camelot in the morning, both of you."

The candles flickered and Merlin began to fade.

"We are all about to go forward," the shimmering figure said.

"And you, Merlin, what of you and Camelot?"

"The storm has ended; the city is recovering. As for me, I will do what I have always done, my boy – keep safe those I love, protect the realm." The wizard's face broke into a smile, the years gentler on him in the dimming light. "And pass on the wisdom of our faith to the children."

Stars.

A silver night bright with hope and distant suns wheeling across the heavens.

In the cold December room bereft for so long, Rhiannon pressed against him, yearning for his warmth and the love in his pilgrim soul. Her fragrance everywhere as she kissed him. Gawain caressed her shoulders, hands moving, flowing like forest water over the precious curves of her body. And when she whispered yes, her breath warm in his ear, he closed his eyes. She smiled, her face buried in the hollow of his neck, because she knew.

And moments later when Orion burned at its zenith, the tiny seed she'd yearned for was sown – a child to love and hold and take on all the hope and pain of growing.

And Gawain slept. For the first of many nights to come, he fell into a deep and dreamless sleep, sound in the knowledge that he had in this, in all things, prevailed and found the triumph Athlan had prophesied so long ago.

Printed in the United States
111798LV00002B/182/A